ROOTED IN DECEPTION

LAURA CHURCHILL DUKE

AUTHOR OF TWO CROWS SORROW

Cover image: Tamar Marshall, from a photograph by George Lewis
Author photo: KShills Photography
Editor: Andrew Wetmore

ISBN: 978-1-990187-47-6
First edition November, 2022

MOOSE HOUSE
PUBLICATIONS

2475 Perotte Road
Annapolis County, NS
B0S 1A0

moosehousepress.com
info@moosehousepress.com

We live and work in Mi'kma'ki, the ancestral and unceded territory of the Mi'kmaq people. This territory is covered by the "Treaties of Peace and Friendship" which Mi'kmaq and Wolastoqiyik (Maliseet) people first signed with the British Crown in 1725. The treaties did not deal with surrender of lands and resources but in fact recognized Mi'kmaq and Wolastoqiyik (Maliseet) title and established the rules for what was to be an ongoing relationship between nations. We are all Treaty people.

My dear friend Harold Benedict shared many stories about his life working in lumber camps around Windsor in the 1940s. He described the conditions, explained the terminology, and talked about the clothing worn. He answered many phone calls and spent a great deal of time sharing his stories.

One of the stories in the book, about the burning of the work overalls next to the fire, was one of his own, and I knew I had to include it.

Harold passed away in 2021, just shy of his 94th birthday.

I **dedicate** this book to Harold to honour our friendship, and to thank him for all his help.

This is a work of fiction, drawing on very real events. The author has made use of characters who appear in the historical record, and has created or dramatized conversations, interactions, and events. Any resemblance of any character to any real person, with the obvious exception of the historical personages, is coincidental.

Rooted in Deception

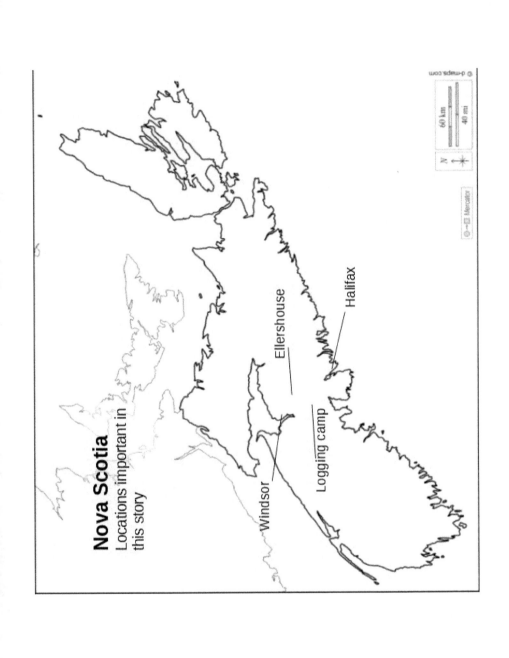

Nova Scotia
Locations important in this story

Windsor

Ellershouse

Logging camp

Halifax

N

60 km
40 mi

Mercator

© d-maps.com

Part 1: Into the Cellar

Liverpool, England steamship landing, 1900
Ungerwood & Ungerwood

1: How to fall asleep

Liverpool, England, December 4, 1905

John Kavanagh was dead.

The new John pulled his wool cap firmly down on his head and turned the collar of his thin coat up around his neck to shelter himself from the stiff, cold breeze blowing off the Mersey River. He scanned the rows of brick buildings along the Albert Docks, looking for the one they had described to him.

The dockyard was crowded with horses pulling carts of cargo toward the ships lying alongside the pier, while other carts headed with supplies toward the markets in Liverpool, or to warehouses along the Mersey.

John tried to dash between the carts, while avoiding the piles of dung on the roads.

He looked up again. All the brick buildings looked the same.

"Pardon me, sir."

A woman with broken English, with a bundle tied on her back and a small child at her side, barrelled into John, causing him to stumble.

He looked into her pretty face; his scowl quickly replaced by a grin. This could be exactly what he needed. "I'm assuming you're heading to the steerage office as well?"

At her nod, he continued, "Here, let me carry this for you."

Taking the bundle from her back, he walked alongside the woman and child, letting her lead the way across the docks, down a large set of stairs, and through a dark tunnel. They finally emerged in a dimly lit room where over fifty people waited for the ticket agent to appear. There were hardly enough seats to accommodate everyone.

John's guide walked straight toward a bearded man, propped up against a big, black trunk. John hid his disappointment and joined the family on the trunk.

She said something to her husband in a language which he could only guess was Russian. From the gestures, he concluded that the husband was trying to find out what had taken them so long. The answer had something to do with the child, who looked sadly at his toe poking through one of his shoes.

"It's past nine. Where is the agent?" a would-be passenger yelled, brandishing his pocket watch.

"We're all going to miss the crossing at this rate!" another said.

From somewhere in the crowd, a woman started crying.

According to John's calculation, another thirty minutes passed before the agent arrived. By this time, the air in the small room had grown stale, and about as half as many more people had crowded into the room.

John took off his overcoat and, using it as a pillow, dozed against the trunk. If he had learned anything in life, it was how to fall asleep in the most uncomfortable of places.

The woman's shoe nudged him awake. She indicated a line was forming at the agent's window.

John stood to join the family in the queue. He patted his pockets, as if looking for something he might have dropped. "Please." He motioned to the family to go ahead of him in the line.

Once their backs were turned and the crowd was slowly swallowing the family, John knelt again in front of the black rusty trunk. He stuck his pocketknife into the flimsy lock and popped the lid.

The secret to success, he knew, was to act as if the thing you were stealing was your own. So with confidence he rummaged through the trunk. He found the father's dark overcoat near the bottom. Holding it up, he figured it might be a bit long for his short five-foot-three frame, but nothing a good needle and thread could not fix.

He stood up and quickly put the coat on, donning his own overcoat over top. At the last minute, he tucked a stale loaf of bread from the trunk under his arm. He refastened the lock as best he could and rejoined the queue, pulling his woollen cap down over his eyes, careful to cover the long white scar just above his right eye. He did not look in the family's direction again.

"Name?"

John hesitated a moment before answering the ticket agent.

"John." This was going to be the start of his new life.

"John what? We have a long line of passengers to process."

He thought for a moment before answering. "John Ryan."

"Just yourself making the crossing?"

"Yes, sir."

The agent quickly scribbled down his information and exchanged the ticket John had purchased earlier for a boarding ticket. The agent forcefully slid it through the hole in the glass and then pointed to a man in uniform, who guided John down to the ship's landing stage for boarding.

John stood silently on the dockside, waiting for the tender to take them out to the SS *Siberian* where it lay at anchor in the harbour. In the distance, he could just make out the red stripe along its bottom and its red stack puffing out black clouds of smoke. She was making steam, meaning she was getting ready to leave.

A cacophony of languages washed over John. He looked around at the hundreds of people now gathered, whom he would be cooped up with for the next two weeks for the journey across the Atlantic.

John had always wanted to leave his life behind, but he had never thought it would be for Canada. The idea had not even occurred to him until his new-found friends in London suggested that life across the ocean would be so much better. Not only were there jobs to be had, but a fellow could start over, which is exactly what he intended to do.

John had wasted no time in finding the steamer's head office in London. He marched in and bought a ticket on the next available liner. He spent the remainder of the money which his friends had pooled together for him on train passage north to Liverpool, where the ship was docked.

What he would do once he reached Canadian soil was another issue. He would figure that out in due course. He would see where the wind blew and make some decisions then.

He had always been good at thinking fast to get himself out of trouble, something he had learned as a young boy back in Ireland.

2: Happy wife, happy life

Atlantic Ocean

Clang! Clang!

John rolled over, pulling his blanket further over his head, the rough horsehair scratching his face.

"Breakfast is served!" The steward walked up and down the rows of bunks with his announcement.

John could not face another morning of salty oatmeal and tea that tasted as if it were made from grass. It may have been more tolerable if he had not polished off the whisky he had nicked the week before.

John pounded the lumpy straw mattress and tried to readjust his overcoat, which was serving as a pillow. He rolled over and got a whiff of his neighbour's foul breath from the next bunk. Flipping the other way, he faced the barricade his right-hand bunk-mate had fashioned from what seemed to be all the poor man's earthly possessions. Although every passenger was assigned to his own bunk, only a thick iron bar separated them. It felt more like one large bed with John crammed in the middle.

"Land today, gentleman!" the steward continued between bell rings. "Stopping today at the port of St. John's, Newfoundland! Only a few more days until Halifax!"

At the news, John's bunk-mate began dismantling his barricade, shoving his belongings into his carpet bag, clearing out his space. "Jesus, Mary and Joseph," he muttered. "It's about time."

The married quarters were elsewhere on the ship, so he did not have to listen to babies crying all night long. The only sounds he had to put up with were the grating snoring of those who had drunk themselves to sleep and the never-ending retching of those who were seasick.

Worse than the sounds was the smell. The cabin was unventilated, save for a single hatch leading to the steerage deck. There were many nights that John had tried to avoid it all by sleeping on the deck above, despite the North Atlantic's winter chill.

By the time breakfast had been served, those passengers disembarking in Newfoundland had made their way to the deck, clearing out a couple of the bunks in John's cabin. When he heard the approaching footsteps of the new passengers coming through the hatch down the steep staircase, he held his breath, hoping for a decent bunk mate. John had still yet to find someone to set him up in Halifax.

"Thomas Forsey, bunk 125 B."

John grinned at the old man in the doorway and patted the empty mattress beside him. Dust particles floated in the air, and John brushed them away with one hand, the other reaching down to take hold of his new bunk mate's case.

"Thank you," Thomas said reaching a hand up to shake.

"The pleasure is all my own." John swung his legs over the side of the bunk and jumped down to greet the man. "Name's John. John Ryan."

"Thomas Forsey. Just come from up home on the Grand Banks. Went up for me old man's funeral by train to Sydney, across by ferry and now going back by steamer to the missus in Halifax. She's been running the boarding house without me for a few weeks now and thought this steamer would get me back soonest. We all know the expression, happy wife, happy life, eh?"

John grinned. Just what he needed to hear.

"Let me give you a tour, and let you know how things work around here."

John put his arm around the older man's shoulder and guided him back up on deck. "A couple of important notes. Don't go past yonder rope on the deck or the crew will get you. The windows to the saloon, for those who can afford first class, are right there, you see. It'll just make you hungry, anyway. If you happen to be chatting to a lady up on deck here—"

"No chance of that, my friend. You haven't met me missus."

"Well, you are devilishly handsome," John said, thumping him on the back. "*If* you do, a crewman comes by and shoos everyone all downstairs by nine. But fear not, because they've learned if they scurry down that set of stairs, they can just reappear on the other side over here."

Thomas guffawed and followed John back down the steep staircase to the table and benches set up in the middle of the bunk room.

"It's almost lunch," John said. "Get your tin plate and spoon they left you at the end of your bunk. I'll show you how it's done."

The men took their seats at the bench and waited until the steward came around and started ladling some sort of substance into each man's dish.

"Better than I thought," Thomas said.

"Any good soup loses its flavour when it looks like it is being ladled from a slop bucket. But what can you expect when you're getting lodging and food for less than one cent a mile."

"I'm going to like you, son," Thomas said. "What brings you across the Atlantic Ocean, then?"

"Great question, my friend. As of late, I had made my way to London, as friends had advised me it would be easy to find work there. But you will never guess what I encountered."

"Pray tell."

"Almost the first thing I beheld when I set foot in that great city was a long procession of men marching four deep, heavily guarded by mounted constables."

"Were they in trouble with the law?"

"Not as you might imagine, but they were indeed in trouble. At the front of the pack, they carried a large black flag with the word 'unemployed' in large white letters. I later found out they were heading toward parliament to protest the lack of jobs. The shopkeepers were closing their shutters for fear of looting."

"Are things really that bad there?"

"They certainly appear to be. So that's when I said to myself, 'Self, things aren't looking so prosperous here,' and I decided that London was not the place for me. I didn't want to be near if trouble broke out. Some of my old friends I was visiting in the area advised me to leave and head to Canada. And, as they say, the rest is history."

"And what do you plan on doing once you get to Halifax?"

"Well, sir," John said, "I'm a tailor by trade." The story rolled off his tongue. "I'm planning on applying to some of those factories downtown to see if they'll take me on with some of the suit tailoring."

"Clayton and Sons is your best bet. Probably the biggest employer in town. You'll find them quite handy to the docks up on Barrington."

"Thanks for the tip. I'll remember that."

"Now, sir, where are you staying when you get to town?"

"I haven't gotten that worked out yet. I can't stray too far. I have a rich uncle down in New York who is planning on wiring me a large sum of money to help me get started. I said I'd be contacting him when I get to shore, with an address."

"Well, until then, consider coming to stay with us. Me and the missus run a boarding house, as I said, and I believe we have an empty room.

The rent's cheap, the location is convenient, and it would be my pleasure to show you around Halifax."

They shook on the deal.

John smiled into his soup. He was set for the next while, anyway. He could talk his way into anything.

3: Five dollars a week

Halifax, Nova Scotia

Thomas opened the front door to his home on Halifax's Smith Street.

John looked up and down the street, taking in his surroundings. To the left, he could see the harbour from where they had come; and to the right, the street seemed to end. This looked to be the fifth in a row of about twelve town houses on a dead-end street.

John rubbed his fingers across the wooden clapboard siding of the townhouse, accustomed to only having seen brick and stone buildings at home. He scanned the area to see if anyone else may have followed them.

"John Ryan, I'd like to introduce you to me missus, Mrs. Jessie Forsey."

"Good evening, ma'am. It's mighty kind of you to allow me to stay with you until I can get myself settled. Coming straight from sea, it will take a while to get my land legs on."

Jessie looked sternly at her husband. She was quite an attractive woman, and John wondered how an old fellow like Thomas could get a fine woman who looked to be at least two decades younger, closer to his own age.

"We have the extra room, and he says he's good for the rent."

"Five dollars a week, Mr. Ryan. For the room and breakfast."

"Yes, ma'am. No trouble at all," John said. He followed Thomas over the threshold, past Mrs. Forsey.

"Where are your bags and trunk, Thomas?" she asked.

"We left them down at the terminal, down at Deep Waters. I'll have them delivered up tomorrow."

"And you, Mr. Ryan?"

"Mine's there as well, ma'am."

John smiled, thinking about the poor immigrant who would be searching for his trunk. John had randomly chosen one from the dock and merely carried it to the storage area, feigning it was his, not wanting to admit he only came with the clothes on his back.

Of course, when it came time to deliver it, the warehouse men would notice the discrepancy in name and take it to its proper owner. At least he had managed to find yet another nice overcoat amongst the belongings in the trunk and added it to his own collection.

"Come now," Thomas said, leading John up the stairs. "I'll show you your room and introduce you to Mr. Fulton, who is also letting a room here."

4: Things we lads get up to

January 5, 1906

"Did you sleep well last night, Mr. Ryan?"

Jessie Forsey was sitting at the kitchen table and had caught a glimpse of John heading down the hallway toward the front door. He retraced his steps and stuck his head in the kitchen door.

"Why do you ask?"

"Here, come sit and have some morning porridge with me." She patted the empty chair next to her.

"Oh, I've had enough porridge in me lifetime!" John laughed to himself, remembering the countless years of only being served porridge. "I've done decades of porridge, you could say."

"What do you mean by that?"

"Not a thing, Mrs. Forsey."

He took a seat at the table and reached for a bowl. As he did his right arm poked through from under his sleeve, revealing a long white scar.

Jessie instinctively reached forward to gently touch it with the tip of her finger. "Oh, Mr. Ryan! That looks like it hurt a lot. Whatever did happen to you?"

"Oh, just typical things we lads get up to," John said, brushing her hand away.

"I guess it's just a match to the ones over both of your eyes. Must have been quite the day! Anyway, I was just asking about how you were sleeping as the neighbours are saying they see you out at the front door at all hours of the night, looking up and down the street. And just earlier this morning, Mr. Fulton said you must have been having a bad dream last night as he heard you call out in your sleep."

"I hesitate to ask what I could possibly have said, for I remember none of my dreams."

"As Mr. Fulton described it, it was something along the lines of 'There he comes. Quick! It's the keeper!' What's a keeper, Mr. Ryan? Doesn't that have something to do with a prison?"

"Sure, I have no idea where that came from, Mrs. Forsey. Perhaps something I picked up on the voyage from Liverpool. There were all sorts of ruffians down there in steerage. Your husband is lucky he didn't en-counter any of those ne'er-do-wells."

"I should hope not." She shifted in her chair, facing him more directly. "Your rent money is due, Mr. Ryan. I'm assuming you have the funds to pay us as promised."

"As you know, my good lady, I am a tailor, and shall be meeting with Clayton and Sons about getting some work from them."

John reached into his overcoat pocket and pulled out a folded envel-ope. "The proof of the pudding is in the eating. Here's the letter I'm send-ing them today."

Jessie took the letter from his hand and began to read:

> Messrs. Clayton and Sons:
> Dear Sirs, Having just arrived from England and being an expert pant maker, I am writing you asking if it is possible to get work from you. I can make them here where I am staying, as I have a good sewing machine and could devote almost fourteen hours a day to the work. I can work on either ready-made or custom work.
> Yours Respectfully,
> J.P. Ryan

"You have a sewing machine, do you?"

"In my trunk. I can't believe that it still hasn't found its way up here. I must check on that today, too."

At that moment, the boarder Mr. Fulton came through the front door, slamming it behind him. The loud bang caused John to jump in his seat.

"Jumpy, aren't you, Mr. Ryan?"

"I'll have my rent to you by the end of the week, Mrs. Forsey," Mr. Fulton said as he poked his head through the kitchen door.

John reached across and took the letter back from Jessie, tucked it in his overcoat pocket, and without a word headed for the front door.

5: But you're a man!

January 9

John stood in front of the grand stone edifice of St. Andrew's United Church. It was the first church he had found on his morning walk a few days earlier. He pulled his overcoat tightly around his neck to try to block the cold Halifax wind.

He made his way to the front door and went in search of Reverend Johnson. Upon spotting him, he called, "Reverend Johnson! Remember me?"

John stepped toward the man, who was seated behind his desk, stretching out his hand to shake it. "I met you a few days ago. I'm the fellow from the birthplace of your ancestors."

"How could I forget you, Mr. Ryan? Irish by birth and tailor by trade, if I remember correctly."

"How right you are, Reverend. I'm still planning on coming to your service this week. I missed it on Sunday, but I shall be attending your fine church."

"How can I be of service today, Mr. Ryan?"

"Well, sir," he began, "seeing I'm fresh off the boat, I am looking for a small loan, just to see me through until my remittance from my uncle in New York comes through. He's a very wealthy millionaire, you see, but has had trouble wiring the money to me here in Halifax, not knowing my address. However, I expect it any time now, so I can easily repay the loan. But, until then, there is a matter of the rent that I owe Mrs. Forsey for boarding me down on Smith Street. So, just a small loan would make a grand difference to this fellow."

"Is that the case, Mr. Ryan?"

"By Jove, I swear on my father's grave, 'tis the truth."

Mr. Johnson looked John up and down, noticing a difference from their meeting a few days before. "Well, Mr. Ryan, you seem to be well supplied with clothes. You have more overcoats than I have!"

"Yes, I have a trunk full of clothes. And about the loan?"

"Maybe you ought to consider going out to earn an

~

Feeling defeated by his visit to St. Andrew's, John deci
once again at the Salvation Army.

"Where's the officer in charge of this place?" he asked upon entering.

"He's upstairs in his private quarters," the young man in the entrance way said.

Pushing past him, John headed toward the staircase in front of him.

"But, sir! You haven't been invited in!"

John had long since passed and ignored the young man's words.

"Good morning, Captain!" John addressed the Salvation Army officer seated behind a large wooden desk. "I'm not sure if you remember me from a few days ago, but I was here, speaking with you before."

"That's right, you were that detective from England. Looking for a man named Dusty, or Duncan, or—"

"Duffy. That's correct, Captain, sir. Michael Duffy."

Without being invited, John sat in the chair opposite the desk. "Well, I just wanted to let you know I found him."

"Oh, that must be a relief." The Captain barely looked up from his papers.

"He was at the Citadel and had enlisted in the Royal Canadian Regiment."

John clasped his hands together in a prayer-like position and rested his index fingers against his lips. He scanned the room, taking in every detail. Then he continued. "Haven't you a collection box somewhere here at the Salvation Army? I really wish to contribute to your work but can't seem to find the box."

This caught the attention of the officer who looked up, shaking his head. "If you wish to make a generous donation, I can take it directly."

~

John stood on Barrington Street, looking at the four-story brick building in front of him. High up, he saw the name *Clayton & Sons* painted across the top, and knew he was in the right place. He cupped his hands over his eyes and pressed his nose to the glass to look in at the showrooms that displayed the latest styles in men's suits. He looked down at his thread-bare overcoat, acquired from the ship, and stared back at the manins inside.

He stood back, took a deep breath, opened the main doors and stepped in. He looked around at the show dummies displaying the latest high-buttoned, small-collared suit jackets for men. He fingered the four-buttons running down the length of the coat, noting how securely they were fastened, and considered the hours that would have gone into creating such a piece.

"May I help you, sir?"

It was a clerk, torn between his directions to be polite to customers and his doubts about John's appearance.

"You can, yes. Can you direct me to the manager?"

"The manager? Do you have an appointment?"

"I am expected."

At the back of the large, open room, John knocked on an open door that read, "William J. Clayton" and waited to be called in. He stood grinning, his hands interlaced behind his back, rocking back and forth until Mr. Clayton looked up at him from over his glasses.

"What can I do for you?"

"I'm John Ryan, sir. I received your letter and your invitation for a meeting regarding my sewing samples."

"But you're a man! As you probably saw in your letter, we clearly thought J.P. Ryan was a woman."

"So sorry to disappoint." John took a seat across the desk from Clayton when the manager motioned him to sit.

"We received the sample you worked on, Mr. Ryan, for the pant samples, and we were very impressed. Mr. McCormick, our head cutter here at Clayton and Sons, says this is the work of a custom tailor."

Clayton rooted through a box of samples behind his desk until he found one with the name "Ryan," pinned to the top.

"I am humbled, sir," John said.

"Mr. McCormick says your work was likely done by hand but is indistinguishable from those done by machine. Your work is even and straight, and the mark of a professional who has been well trained."

"Thank you, your Honour, sir."

"But I see you haven't quite finished the testing piece. With that finished, I can pretty much guarantee that you will find yourself gainfully employed here at Clayton and Sons. We pride ourselves in having over 100 employees here in the factory, and you would be given a nine-hour a day, starting at about $3 a week."

John looked around the room, adding up the hours and the money and offsetting it against the amount of work involved. "Thank you, sir," he said. "And that is why I am here to tell you in person that I regret to say that, as of late, my health has not been good, and I do not have the proper work room yet, owing to the fact that I am still waiting on a remittance from an uncle in New York. In fact, my doctor has advised me, rather, to obtain open air employment, as he thinks this would be better for my health."

"We are indeed sorry to hear this, Mr. Ryan."

"Would you happen to have any work at pressing that I could do instead?"

Mr. Clayton thought for a moment. "Unfortunately, Mr. Ryan, we require expert men at pressing, as much damage can be caused if it is not done properly. I'm afraid that your green hand would not be of any use to us here."

"Yes, of course, I understand," John said.

He stood, and the manager did him the honour of standing to shake his hand. John took little notice of the verbal pleasantries, and soon was standing on Barrington Street again.

With that matter cleared up, John was not quite ready to go back to the boarding house, so he took his time exploring the city. He wandered slowly back along Hollis Street, looking for a warm place that served an Irish stout, a difficult thing to find when the whole province seemed against a good drink these days.

Across the street he spotted the words "The Queen Hotel" etched in glass on a big picture window. He quickly crossed over, dodging the horses and carts going up and down the street.

John opened the door and followed the white checkered floor past the grand marble staircase, running his fingers across the cold stone. Walking through the lobby, he followed the overhead sign toward the hotel lounge, where he found a group of men seated on stools, talking with the bartender behind the counter.

"What can we get you?"

"I'll have your finest stout."

"From the emerald isles, I detect."

The man sitting on the stool next to John swivelled around.

"Right you are." John took his first sip, enjoying the feeling of it going all the way down.

"Only an Irishman could drink that stuff!"

John laughed and took another drink.

"Mild winter we've had here. No snow yet, but I'm sure it's coming."

The bartender wiped the edge of the counter with his apron.

If there was anything one could rely on, John thought, *it was people turning to the weather to make conversation.*

"Let's hope it's not on Thursday," the man next to him said.

"What's so special about Thursday?" John asked, after emptying his pint.

"You might not realize it from looking at this fellow," the bartender said, leaning on the counter, "but he is a world-famous violin player. He and these other two gentlemen are playing as part of a musical concert series down at the Conservatory of Music this Thursday."

"Say it isn't so," John said. He turned to face the man beside him.

"Samuel Altman," he said, sticking his hand out to shake John's. "I'm afraid it's all true."

"There is nothing greater than a symphony," John said.

"You are a man of refined taste, I can tell."

"Back in my motherland, and then later when I lived in England, I would often travel about, trying to take in as many concerts as I could. There is just something that takes you away to another world when you hear the music. I so enjoy the violin, especially played by someone who can attack the notes with crispness and precision. You know when you hear a good performance, heaven hath shed a tear."

"Well, if you have been to concerts in England, then, perhaps you have heard my brother Walter sing there."

"Walter Altman? Why yes, I most certainly have. A finer voice I have never heard."

"Oh, we truly were meant to meet here tonight. Here, then, my new friend."

Samuel reached into his breast pocket and pulled out a small brown envelope. "Two tickets to Thursday's performance. I would be honoured if you would be my guest."

"I am speechless. I wouldn't miss it for the world."

John took the envelope and tucked it into his pocket. "This calls for a celebration. Bartender, a round of drinks on me for my new friends."

"Cheers to that! As those are coming, I'm just going to excuse myself for a moment," Samuel said. He headed toward the lavatory.

John noticed Samuel had left his cap on the counter beside him. With the bartender's back turned and the other men engaged in conversation, John patted the hat and felt something hidden underneath.

He slid the cap toward him, and an ornate sterling silver cigarette case dropped into his hand. John pushed the cap back into its original position, opened the case, and noticed a $5 bill, which he deftly put in his front pants pocket. The cigarette case went into the inner pocket of his overcoat.

After the round of drinks, John stood and passed the $5 bill to the bar-tender. Thanking the gentlemen for a good night, he promised to see them in two days' time, on Thursday.

Peeking out the door, John noticed it had started to rain. *At least 'tis not snow*, he thought.

He looked around the hotel lobby and spied a silver-mounted um-brella in the stand by the door. He tucked it under his arm and headed into the rain for the walk back to the Forseys' boarding house.

6: Don't you fret

January 11

"I murdered an old man one time. He was 75 years of age and I pitied his hoary locks as he knelt and pleaded that I should spare his life, but I had to murder him. I *had* to murder him!"

John slapped his hand down on the breakfast table, looking Mrs. Forsey right in the eye.

She stared back, a look of horror on her face until she burst out laughing. "Oh, Mr. Ryan, you can't be serious! You really didn't murder that old man, did you?"

"Of course not, ma'am. But the Whitecaps certainly did."

"The who? You mean them who go after the blacks?"

"Not necessarily, just a group trying to make sure people uphold the law and behave appropriately. We have community standards, you know."

"Heavens to Betsy. How terrible! In any case, Mr. Ryan, whatever did become of your tailoring job with Clayton & Sons?"

"Well, as it turns out, I've decided to go in a different direction with the tailoring work. My millionaire uncle, in New York, as I've mentioned before, is sending me a hefty remittance so I'm going to start my own business."

"How grand!"

"In fact, I've already been in conversations to engage the building adjoining the branch of Hattie and Mylius there on Hollis Street and am going to go into the tailoring business for myself."

"Down there by the chemists? What a convenient place! Do let me know when you are open."

Hearing a tapping on the kitchen door, John turned around to see the other boarder, Mr. Fulton, poking his head into the room.

"Good morning, Mr. Fulton. Do come join us. We're having a great chat."

"Thank you, Mrs. Forsey, but I am just here to drop off payment for this week's rent." He handed her a crumpled bill across the table.

Jessie laid it on the table, ironed it out with her hand and rubbed her finger along the uniquely curved 'Bank of Montreal' words along the top of the bill. "Thank you, Mr. Fulton," she said before staring directly at John.

"Don't you fret," said John. "You'll have it before the end of the day."

"In that case, I shall go tuck this away upstairs."

Jessie Forsey pushed herself up from the table, and John could hear her creaking up the wooden staircase toward her bedroom, as the boarder made his way to the front door.

John drummed on the table as he sipped his morning tea. His eyes flickered constantly between the front door and the staircase. When Jessie finally reappeared, she was empty-handed.

"That's funny," she said, sitting back down at the table.

"What is?"

"I can't seem to find the key to my box, and I can't get it open. It'll have to wait till later when I can have a proper look."

John nodded. "Well, I must be off. I have some final papers to do up on the business property. I'll just fetch my coat."

John left the room, closing the kitchen door as he headed upstairs. At the top of the stairs, the Forseys' bedroom door was open, and there beside Jessie's wooden box was the $5 bill. John looked around, tiptoed into the room and palmed the money, slipping it onto his pocket. He went to his own room and, coat in hand, went back downstairs.

He poked his head into the kitchen once more. "It's best I give you this now, lest I forget later." He handed Jessie the bill from his pocket.

"Oh, thank you, Mr.—" She stopped mid-sentence, sensing an air of familiarity about the bill. "Is this not—?"

Before she could continue, John reached into his coat pocket and pulled out the brown envelope given to him days before in the Queens Hotel. "And, before I forget, I picked these up for you, as a small gesture of my thanks for having me here, and all you have done for me."

Jessie opened the envelope and smiled at the words Conservatory of Music written across the top of the tickets.

"I hope you don't already have plans for tonight. I thought you and a friend might enjoy a night on the town."

"Land o' Goshen, Mr. Ryan. You shouldn't have."

"Please enjoy on my behalf. The violin player is one of the finest you will ever hear, and he happens to be a very good friend of mine."

John turned and left the room, leaving a grinning Jessie in his wake.

7: It's all gone!

January 12

"Mrs. Forsey! Mrs. Forsey! Come here immediately!"

Jessie rushed to Mr. Fulton's room in her evening gown, which nearly tripped her as she took the stairs two at a time. She had not even had time to take off her overcoat. Thomas met her on the landing.

"What on earth is the matter?" Jessie asked upon seeing her distraught boarder pacing in his room.

"My trunk: it's been burgled! I have just now opened it and discovered several things missing, including some of my lithographic equipment for making prints. But, more pressing, $40 has been stolen!"

"Are you certain?" Thomas asked, coming up to peer into the trunk.

"Of course, I'm certain! It can only be that Ryan fellow. I never trusted him from the get-go."

"Jessie, go check our room to see if anything's missing there, too."

She scurried off, and soon afterwards shrieked, causing Thomas to run down the hall toward her.

"It's gone. It's all gone. That conniving, silver-tongued devil! Everything in my box is gone—my jewellery, $45 at least was here, and those Mexican coins I had been saving."

"The devil!" Fulton shouted over Thomas' shoulder. "Where is he?"

"He's out again," Jessie said.

"The coward!" Fulton spat.

"You have to go to the police, Thomas. He can't get away with this."

"I'll go. But, Mr. Fulton, you're coming with me."

~

Thomas Forsey took Fulton by the elbow and stepped off the electric streetcar near the Halifax police station. They stood looking up at the enormous white building, hoping that, at that time of night, they could find someone to help them—and quickly.

Thomas stepped up to the main desk. "We're here to report a burglary, and someone needs to come quickly to arrest the perpetrator."

"Yes, I see," the young man in uniform said. "If you can please tell me your name, address and the details, we can see to it."

"No, we need to speak to someone in charge, immediately."

"Well, the chief is still out."

Thomas looked at his pocket watch. "We'll wait."

The young man pointed to a wooden bench in the hallway. "I will let Chief Power know you are here when he arrives."

Thomas groaned under his breath.

"What?" Fulton asked.

"Power is now chief. He's a bumbling imbecile."

"Whatever do you mean?"

"The man has botched more cases than I can count."

Chief Nicholas Power - Dartmouth Heritage Museum

"Surely, no!" Fulton was shocked.

"Where would you like me to start? Alphabetically or chronologically? How about the time when the entire city was out at the PT Barnum Circus, and someone robbed the bank of $22,000, and he hunted down two men eating at a restaurant near a train station because he thought they were fleeing the city? Meanwhile, one of the bank employees skipped the country only two days later. It was in all the papers."

Fulton shook his head.

"Or the time he arrested two Irishmen carrying dynamite, claiming they were going to blow up the ship that Prince George was coming on to town. He's going around telling everyone he saved the future king, when the two men were merely miners going to work."

Fulton tried to suppress a chortle.

"And when the ship came in with slaughtered people on it, and—"

"That's enough! I can't take any more."

"That's all when he was a detective," Thomas said. "Now he's been promoted to Chief. Lord help us all."

Thomas kept checking the time, and an hour had passed before a tall man with a full beard and even fuller moustache who beckoned them into his office.

Chief Power sat behind his desk. Thomas raised an eyebrow. If the man had been out, why then was he sitting there looking through a newspaper? He had evidently just finished cutting out an article with a pair of large scissors and was painting an adhesive to the back of it, preparatory to gluing it into a large scrapbook.

Noticing their look of confusion, Chief Power said. "Just keeping a record of my achievements, gentlemen. I have been connected with just about every criminal case of importance and am known for my extraordinary detective skills. These documents will be of great significance in years to come."

He closed the book and looked up at the men before him, who stared back, open-mouthed.

It took a moment for Thomas to realize this was his moment. He recounted the story of the lost money and valuables from Smith Street. "John Ryan, the man who is boarding with us, is undoubtedly the thief," he concluded.

"I have no doubt you are right," Chief Power said, scratching his beard.

"Would it not be possible to get a warrant tonight for Ryan's arrest," Thomas said, "as he might leave the house at any time, especially if he knows we are on to him?"

Chief Power consulted his pocket watch. "Don't worry. We will have him tomorrow and get what money he has left."

Having done all they could, Thomas and Fulton returned home.

~

When the moon was high over the Halifax Harbour, John slipped back into the house on Smith Street, hoping to find everyone in bed asleep. Instead, he heard voices coming from his bedroom. He crept to the landing so he could better hear.

"He is either a burglar or an ex-convict," he could hear Jessie saying.

"He must leave the house," Thomas said.

John shifted his position, trying to see who was in the room, but caused the old staircase to creak.

"Who's there?" Jessie called. She came to look out over the banister, straight into John's face.

"Oh! You're there, are you?" she said.

"Whisht! Whisht! Hush, lady," John said as he joined her at the top of the stairs. "What are you making so much talk about it for?"

By this time, Fulton and Thomas had come out to the hallway. John pushed past them, entered his room, and shut the door behind him.

32

8: A warrant

Rap-Rap-Rap-Rap!

Jessie stood at John's door, pounding loud enough to wake the dead. "Mr. Ryan, it's eight o'clock! Please come out as we need to speak with you immediately."

Silence.

Jessie slowly opened the door and poked her head inside. "He's gone. Where the blazes did he go, and why didn't anyone hear him?"

She threw the door open to reveal a perfectly-made bed. She frantically searched the room for any clue or sign but came up empty-handed, save for a pair of black boots which she waved in the air at her husband, who was now standing in the doorway behind her.

"These boots! These God-forsaken boots are the only sign that this man ever existed here."

The boots were made from black leather, hob-nailed on the bottom, with lots of holes in the soles and heels.

"I'll be," Thomas said. "They look like a convict's boots to me."

"I knew we never should have trusted him, and you're the one who brought him here!"

A loud rap on the front door interrupted the argument. Jessie hurried down the stairs to find a policeman standing before her.

"I'm here this morning with a warrant for the arrest of a Mr. John Ryan."

He held a piece of paper out to Jessie who snatched it from him.

"A little late, aren't you, detective?" Thomas said over her shoulder.

"We've just now put together the paperwork for the warrant."

"Well, he's gone," Jessie said. "He snuck out earlier this morning, and you missed him."

"It's unfortunate that your police force couldn't recognize the importance of this and get themselves together last night when we reported him," Thomas said. "You took no action whatsoever. If you had sent a man down here last night, you would have gotten him without the slightest bit of trouble."

"Everything practical was done to secure the immediate apprehension of the criminal," the policeman said.

"Surely there were other men about in Halifax who could have signed the warrant last night, if you had even bothered to ask. A magistrate, a justice of the peace, anyone! Why do you even need a warrant to make an arrest, anyway? You would have caught him before he flew the coop."

"You really can't think the police department are mind readers and knew he was going to fly the coop, do you? Besides, the charge was merely for theft, so haste was not required."

"Easy for you to say," Jessie said as she huffed back inside the house.

9: Too-small shoes

January 16, Bedford, NS

John sat on the edge of the bed in his hotel room at the Bellevue in Bedford, looking at his worn leather shoes. He ran his fingers along the thin soles. His leather boots would have been so much better for the seven-mile walk from the Forseys' boarding house, along Halifax Harbour, to this out-of-the-way hotel on the outskirts of the city.

He shoved his feet into the too-small shoes he had borrowed from Mr. Fulton's trunk and headed past the front desk.

"Mr. Doyle! Mr. Doyle!" the clerk called out.

John kept walking.

"Mr. Doyle!"

John stopped, finally remembering the name he had used on the register: John Doyle. "Apologies, young lad. I was lost in my own reveries."

"It's just that your bill for the past three nights is due today."

"Well, of course it is." John winked at him. "And that is exactly where I am heading now: out to get your payment. I shan't be but a moment."

John walked out the front door, not once looking back over his shoulder.

10: What can I do you for?

January 26, Ellershouse, N.S.

John walked up to the door of a big two-story house that a local at the station said was the Ellershouse Hotel.

Rap-Rap-Rap-Rap!

He adjusted the collar of his only remaining overcoat, trying to keep out the cold Nova Scotian winter wind. It had been a long day, riding the train west from Halifax for miles through what seemed to be the middle of nowhere. It must have been over 25 miles of pure woodland. Where were the houses? Where were the villages? Never in his life had John seen so much wilderness.

John had decided to disembark at the first sign of any civilization. Surely, being so remote was a good place as any to put down roots, that is, if he could get used to the Canadian winter.

He had never experienced cold like what he was experiencing today. Fortunately, the warmer sunshine of the past few days had melted what little snow had been on the ground; but today, with the temperature below freezing, he was desperate for some ale to warm him.

John knocked again. Louder this time.

A gruff-looking older man came to the door. John could feel the warmth of a fire when the door swung open. But he did not smell the familiar odour of peat. He inhaled the wood smoke deeply, then stamped his feet in place and rubbed his hands together, blowing on them in a failed attempt to warm them up.

"What can I do you for?"

John proffered his hand for a shake. "My name is George Stanley, and I am an agent for the Western Union Telephone Company. I've come to talk to you about your service or, perhaps I should say, lack thereof. And you must be the proprietor of this fine establishment? Mr."—John mumbled something unintelligible, hoping the older man would not pick up on it —"I presume?"

"That's right. Charles Rieck."

John smiled encouragingly.

"Listen, my boy, it's colder than all get out, out here. Come inside by the fire."

John followed Charles past the hotel reception to a seat in front of the fireplace. He was relieved by the warmth.

"Your accent," Charles said. "You don't sound like you are from around these parts."

"You have me pegged! I'm here from London. England, that is. Been here roughly two weeks. And was lucky to land such great employment already. I don't suppose you could pour me a glass of your finest ale, could you, sir? While we sit and chat?"

With an ale in hand, John regaled Charles with the benefits of telephones in rural communities going on the toll system, and how his company could help him. "You would be joining other noteworthy gentlemen in the area, including Mr. Gibson of the Newport Hotel, and Mr. Smiley of St. Croix."

"They have signed up, too? Well, then, perhaps," Charles said. "How much would I owe you then, to put this contract in place?"

"Not a thing now, good sir. You can pay me when the work is done. We are going to have to wait, however, until the winter is through before we can make any installations, and the supplies all need to come down from Halifax."

"Yes, that's probably true."

"While I have you here," John continued. "Would you happen to know of any farms in the area that are up for sale? I've recently come into an inheritance from my uncle and was hoping to settle here in this beautiful area."

"Nothing really comes to mind, for sure, but I did hear..."

"Aye?"

"That old Mr. Harvey, on the Dawson Road up on the Montague Hill, might be wanting to sell. His wife has been working in town, staying down and boarding at the cotton mill in Windsor, and he's left there at the house by himself most of the time. She's only home every other weekend to see him, and he's getting on in age, and the property is all a bit too much for him to handle on his own, I've heard."

"Doesn't he have little ones around to help him out?" John pried.

"He never did have children with his second wife. Now he's married to Ida, the one who works at the cotton mill in town. He's so hard of hearing now, though, I wonder how they carry on any sort of conversation, but maybe it's not about that, if you know what I mean, heh! heh!"

"Sir, you are a fount of knowledge about this place. I bet you can answer the next question, too. I'm looking for a cheap place to lodge until I can get something sorted, and while I finish my rounds for the Western Union Telephone company. Do you have any rooms, per chance?"

"I'm sorry, my friend, there is no room in the inn, as they say. But if you head back down the road, away from town, and turn right at the crossroads, you'll come across the home of David Fisher. You can't miss it. They are taking in boarders all the time. They need all the help they can get, if you ask me. Their place isn't the prettiest or in the best shape, but you can expect a roof over your head and a good solid meal with a decent family."

John stood up to leave, patting his overcoat and pants pockets, in a gesture of looking for money to pay his bill.

"It's on the house," Charles said. "It's been a pleasure doing business with you, Mr. Stanley."

~

Rap-Rap-Rap-Rap!

John stood in front of what he presumed was the Fishers' home on the Dawson Road. The hotel proprietor had been right. It certainly was not the prettiest house he had seen. Rows of wooden shingles were missing, rotten boards in the front porch created large holes, and the entire house needed a lick of paint.

He knocked again, louder. It was cold standing outside in the freezing temperatures, but he was not sure that inside would be much warmer, judging by the broken glass panes in the windows.

"Who's there?" a woman's voice demanded through the closed door.

When she answered the door, John took a step back. He eyed her up and down from the runs in her stockings, to the holes in her threadbare cardigan, to the stray wisps of hair that were falling around her hardened face.

"A stranger, ma'am," he began.

"We can see that," said an older man, appearing over her shoulder.

"My name is George Stanley, and I am here as a representative with the Western Union Telephone Company."

"We don't have one of them contraptions."

"Well, precisely, ma'am. That is why I am here tonight to see if I can interest you in purchasing a toll system when they come to your area."

"We don't have one of them gramophones, like I said."

"It's not necessary to have a telephone now, ma'am. We can help you with that. Already 32 of your neighbours have signed up with us to have it installed when the supplies come from Halifax."

"Why would I need one of them things, anyway? If I need anyone, I can just stand of my front porch and yell," the woman said.

To demonstrate her abilities, the woman moved onto the porch and called, "Jim!" There was nothing wrong with her lungs.

Seeing a young man in his early 20s come around the corner, John changed his direction. "Well, if a telephone doesn't interest you, I'm also going to need to hire some strong young men to help me with the install- ations. Do you know of any who are hard workers, each as strong as an ox?"

The young man climbed the steps to the front porch and gave John a toothy grin. "That would be me. I'm a hard worker, and you don't have to show me too many times what to do. Isn't that true, Ma?"

The woman nodded, putting her arm around her son's shoulders.

"That's good enough for me." John said. "I can pay you two dollars a day."

"That's a lot of money, mister. I don't think I ever seen that much money. I'm in!" He reached his hand out to shake John's.

"Well, that is settled, then. There is another issue, Mrs. Fisher," John said.

"Mary Ann," she interrupted.

"Mrs. Fisher, Mary Ann, I am in need of a place to board, and the good man Mr. Rieck up to the hotel mentioned you were in the habit of having boarders here."

"We're full up. We have Samuel Harvey already living here," David said.

"I would be interested in letting a room for at least one or two months. Long term."

"No room. We've got nowhere for you to sleep."

"Well, what do you charge?"

"It's $2 a week, plus 15 cents for every meal you eat with us," Mary Ann said.

"I'll give you $4 a week. And I'll start with this down payment of $2."

Mary Ann stood open mouthed, looking at him, but then reached for the bill.

"Invite the man inside," she said to her husband. "He's obviously got lots of money. We better be on our best behaviour. Tell Jim and Maurice that they can bunk in with us."

11: Wouldn't that be a coincidence!

January 30

John pulled his cap down tighter over his head and shut the door to the Fishers' house, trying to keep it balanced so its hinges would not squeak. He headed down the rickety steps, almost wishing it was cold enough for snow, rather than the rain that seemed to chill him to the bone. At least that reminded him of home, though.

He trod down the hill a short distance until he came to what he was told was Freeman Harvey's property. He looked around, and took in an orchard, a few farming fields surrounding it, and a barn at the back. In the fields beyond the barn, he could see cows and a pair of oxen. He assumed there were pigs and chickens around the smaller enclosures. *Not a huge place, but manageable. It would do.*

As he walked toward the path to the door, he caught movement behind the window, so he knew the old man had to be home.

He walked up to the door and knocked. Hearing no response, he knocked again, but louder.

Eventually, he heard the shuffling of feet, and the door slowly opened. An old man peered straight at him. "Yes?"

"Mr. Freeman Harvey?"

"Do I know you?"

"Not yet. My name is George Stanley, and I'm here with the Western Union Telephone Company."

"Who? With what?" Freeman rubbed behind his ears, squinted, and leaned toward John. "Come again?"

"I'm with the telephone company."

Freeman shook his head. "Nope. Still can't hear you, boy."

John tried a final time, enunciating each word, practically down the man's eardrum.

"Nope. Not interested."

Not willing to give up, John stuck his foot in the door jamb as Freeman tried to close it on him. "No problem, sir. I've also heard you might be looking to sell up the farm here."

"I've thought about it. You don't look like you've got money enough to buy it, though."

"Not on me today. But I'm coming into some money shortly from my uncle in America." John had quickly adopted a speaking timbre that Free-man could follow.

"I'm not discussing anything without my wife. She lives in town and is only here every second weekend, and just left this past one."

"Fair enough," John said. "But, while I have you here, I am desperately needing to break this $5 bill. You wouldn't happen to have any change, would you? Do a poor, cold man a favour?"

Freeman sighed at the inconvenience. "I've just collected the area's school rates, so you have me at a good time."

Freeman shut the door in John's face as he disappeared into the house.

After what seemed like eternity, Freeman reappeared at the door with change in hand, which he handed through the half-opened doorway.

This time, John caught a glimpse through the house at a newly opened door at the far end by the back door. Judging by its position and barn door structure, John guessed it led to the cellar.

"Thank you, kindly, Mr. Harvey," he said. "I'll be back again to chat once you've had a word with your wife about the deed to the farm."

~

"If you would be so kind as to fetch me a copy of the Good Book, I'd love to sit here by the fire and do some proper devotions," John said to Mary Ann Fisher, who was sitting across from him, knitting a pair of socks.

"We don't have any good books, here," she said. "The boys weren't much for learnin', and me, I never seen the point of spendin' time with readin' and the like, with so many things to do around the house."

"Understandable," John said, changing his tack. "How about the family Bible? You must have one of those? I, unfortunately, had to leave mine be-hind in London."

"Of course, we have one of those. Maurice! Go fetch it for Mr. Stanley."

The Fishers' son, 23 and still living at home, got up, fetched the family Bible off a nearby shelf, and passed it to John.

John blew the dust off the cover and thumbed through the thin pages, stopping at random to make a show of thoroughly studying the pages.

"You a Christian, then?" Mary Ann asked. "God fearin' Anglican like the rest of us?"

"Why yes, ma'am. I was brought up in a devout Christian home, attending church services my whole life."

"That's good. We have a church up yonder in town, used between the Anglicans and the Presbyterians, but we don't want any of them Catholics here. You're not one of those, are you?"

"I shouldn't say!" John thought back to his early days in the Church of England until his family had him confirmed as a Catholic at the age of ten. He did not feel the need to mention that part.

"Would anyone mind if I read a few passages for everyone to hear?" he continued.

"That would be grand," Jim said, coming to sit closer. "I don't read so well, and you've got a fine speaking voice."

John opened at random to the middle of the Bible and began reading from Proverbs.

> Whoever loves discipline loves knowledge,
> but whoever hates correction is stupid.
> Good people obtain favour from the Lord,
> but he condemns those who devise wicked schemes.
> A wife of noble character is her husband's crown,
> but a disgraceful wife is like decay in his bones.

Maybe this is not the best selection after all. He skipped ahead.

> An honest witness tells the truth, but a false witness tells lies.
> Truthful lips endure forever, but a lying tongue lasts
>   only a moment.
> Deceit is in the hearts of those who plot evil, but those who pro-
>   mote peace have joy.
> The Lord detests lying lips, but he delights in people who are
>   trustworthy.

John quickly closed the book. "That's probably enough for tonight."

"What do you think God's punishment will be for not telling the truth? And all that business about a disgraceful wife? What if you are a disgraceful husband?" Jim asked.

"Now, I'm sure that's nothing you need to worry yourself about, Jim," John said. "There's plenty of time for you to be wed. What are you? 25 years? Still a spring chicken!"

"Oh, no," Jim said. "I've got three of them."

"Three what? Years?"

"No. Three wives. All around the county. Trouble is, never got around to officially filling out the paperwork on any of 'em, on account of me not being able to read the forms and what not. I just don't want God to be punishing me for something I can't control."

"Why don't we pray?"

John closed his eyes, and placed his hands on Jim's head, as he had seen others do.

"Dear Heavenly Father, we pray for our brother Jim. May his conscience be clean, and his intentions pure. May he always heed the advice of his elders. We also pray for the Fisher family, that you keep a watchful eye on them. We pray for the Western Union Telephone Company that they have the clarity of mind to send the supplies soon to provide Jim and his brother Maurice with a steady income to help their mother, Mary Ann, who works too hard to look after her family, and to their father, David, who works so hard to provide this beautiful home and to put food on the table."

John sneaked a peek, and seeing the family members beaming, he wrapped it up. "In your name we pray, Amen."

Everyone chorused in with a mighty amen to finish off the prayer.

"Do you really think the Western Union Telephone Company will be sending supplies down soon and that we'll really have a job?" Jim asked.

"If the good man says it's coming, then it's coming," David said.

"That's right, and I can guarantee you a good three years of employment coming with it for you and Maurice."

"Did you hear that, Pa?" Maurice asked, bouncing like a puppy at the thought.

"You are all such a remarkable family, and I owe you so much for taking me in like this," John continued.

"Mr. Stanley—" Mary Ann started.

"No, please, call me George. We are beyond formalities here."

"I've been thinking, uh, George. My family all came over from England. I was thinking that all my cousins there would talk just as pretty as you do," she said.

"From England? Just as myself. Pray tell me, what was their last name? Maybe I knew them."

"Now wouldn't that be a coincidence!" She clapped her hands with glee. "Margaret and William Brown, I'm pretty sure, were my grandparents there in England."

John covered his mouth with surprise. "You will never believe this, Mary Ann. They are cousins of mine. That means we are related. We are family!"

Mary Ann slapped David on the shoulder. "Do you hear that? We're family. I knew I felt a connection with you, Mr...George!"

"You know what I'm going to do? I was thinking that once the Western Union Telephone Company has paid me for my work here, I would build you a new home. I mean, we are family after all."

Mary Ann let out an audible gasp, instinctively covering her hand over her mouth.

"I was going to save this news until later, but there is going to be no need now."

David looked confused.

"When I was speaking with Freeman Harvey the other day, I was telling him about my plan to build you a new home, and he said there was no need. He goes and says that he will sell his house to me for you. He said he'd let me have the house and the whole farm for only $1500."

"Well, I'll be! That beats all, doesn't it love?" David said putting his arm around his wife's shoulders.

"We were certainly blessed the day you knocked upon our door," Mary Ann said.

"We'll have to make room once my sister comes over, though," John said. "You'll really like her, and she'll be a great help around the farm."

"Any relative of yours is one of ours," David said. "But I guess we already said that, since we is cousins, after all."

"One more thing Mrs. Fisher, Mary Ann," John said. "I am sorely in need of some new mitts to keep me warm in this harsh Canadian climate. You wouldn't happen to be willing to sell those fine specimens you are working on there, would you?"

"Oh, Mr. Stanley, you talk some pretty. I don't know what you are saying half the time, but I like it."

John dug through his pockets. "I'd be willing to pay you $1 for those socks and mitts, once you finish them up."

He dug into his back pocket. "Plus, this real-genuine Spanish dollar coin."

"You have yourself a deal," she said as the family gathered around to example the shiny coin, the likes of which they had never seen before.

"This looks like real-genuine pirate treasure," Jim said.

John silently added Mrs. Forsey and her coin collection to his list of prayers of thanksgiving.

12: I have a little business to do

February 2

"David!"

John came around the side of the Fishers' home and found David chopping wood beside the shed.

"I just wanted to let you know that I won't be home tonight. One of the boys can have my bed, so you don't all have to sleep in the one. Can spread out a little bit."

"Where you going to?" David asked, taking a break from his chopping.

"I plan on staying with Freeman Harvey tonight so we can do some business about buying his place. It should be all finished up by the end of tonight, and then I'll be the owner of the farm."

"That's a mighty fine property there. Some would say it's in a busy location, being right at the crossroads, but not me. I like how the brook is right there, and it's pretty handy to everything and has them nice orchards."

John backed away slowly, trying to get out of the conversation until he could turn around and walk down the Dawson Road toward Freeman's place. He travelled halfway before realizing he had forgotten something, and grudgingly returned to the Fishers' homestead. David was in the same place he had just left him.

"That was fast!" David said.

"I haven't been yet. I wish you would lend me your knife for the night."

"What for?"

"I have a little business to do and would like to have your knife."

David reached around, pulled out the knife from its leather sheath, and passed it to John. "She's a bit dull, I'm afraid."

John nodded his thanks and headed again to the house at the crossing. He was at the back door of Freeman Harvey's house, ready to walk in, when he heard voices from inside. He used the sleeve of his overcoat to wipe away the grime on the porch window and looked inside.

45

Freeman was sitting at the table, and looked to be filling out a ledger, adding up sums, aided by 16-year-old Henry Fisher.

Henry's father, Joseph, David Fisher's brother, was standing over Freeman's shoulder, shouting so the old man could hear him. "Do you think you'll still need me to shingle that barn for you come spring?"

"I'm not so sure, Joseph. I'm really thinking about giving this all up and selling out."

"You're thinking of selling the farm? What does Ida have to say about that?" Joseph asked.

"She's living in town, anyway. She won't care. She'd rather I move to town, anyway. I'll let you know if I decide not to sell after all, because that barn will need new shingles."

Seeing his opportunity, John opened the back door and walked into the kitchen to join the other men. Freeman startled when he looked up to see John standing there. He had not heard him come in.

"Mr. Stanley, what are you doing here?" Joseph asked, as if it was his house.

Joseph had met the stranger a few times over the past week, as the man had been lodging with his brother David and his family.

"I'm here to check on my friend, Mr. Harvey, here. Last time we chatted he mentioned he was running low on supplies, so I thought I would bring him something to tide him over."

John opened his overcoat to reveal a brown bottle tucked in the inside pocket. He grinned as he took it out and lay it on the table, accidentally, knocking some of the stacks of money. "What do we have here?" he asked.

"I'm just doing up the rates for the school tax. I collect them around these parts, you know," Freeman said proudly.

"A mighty fine job you are doing, and by my calculations, your numbers all add up," John said as he looked at the books over the old man's shoulder

"Excuse me for a moment," Freeman said. "I've gotta go out back and get us some more wood for the fire. Gets awful cold at night."

"You need a hand, Freeman?" John asked, preempting Joseph.

Not hearing him, Freeman left for the back woodshed.

"I just cannot see why Freeman wants to stay here," John said. "I wouldn't, even for thousands of dollars." He took a seat at the kitchen table across from Henry.

"What do you mean by that?" Joseph asked.

"I mean, the man is so hard of hearing, that someone might just break in and rob and kill him."

"He could just go to bed and shut up everything. No one would interfere with him."

"Just look at the windows, though," John insisted. "They are poor and rotten, and someone might just break in."

"The windows look fine to me," Joseph said.

"Open the hatch there," Freeman said as he returned, "I need to put some wood in the stove."

Joseph got up to raise the hatch and used the poker to straighten it so the hatch would close again. He took out his pocket watch. "It's already eight o'clock. Henry. We need to be getting going. It's already dark, and your ma will worry."

Freeman Harvey's house
Halifax Herald, February 12, 1906

13: Sharper than before

February 3, 7 am

"I've got it! Here it is!"

John entered the Fishers' kitchen, waving a stack of papers in his hand.

David looked up from his mug of tea. "What are you talking about?"

"I got permission of the place this morning, Mr. Harvey's place. These are the deeds."

John reached into his pocket and pulled out a metal ring with two keys dangling from it. "These are the house and barn keys, see?"

"Well, that beats all. Congratulations, George!"

"Like I promised, I want the two of you to move down to the house to live there and take care of the property for me. I got the whole thing for $1500 and will give you $400 a year, and all you require to work the place for me. I'd like you to move down this morning, if at all possible."

"That's mighty kind of you, George. I just can't believe our luck," David said. "Not sure we could be ready by today, but Monday morning for sure."

Both Jim and Mary Ann appeared and came to sit at the kitchen table with David.

"What's going on here?" Mary Ann asked.

"George here got the deeds to Freeman Harvey's house, and we're moving up," David explained as John waved the papers in the air.

"Not today. I can't do it today!" Mary Ann cried.

"No, Monday. I said we'd move on Monday."

"Well," John said, "If you can't move in today, I need you to at least come down today to take charge of the place and look after the cattle and stock, because they have yet to be fed this morning."

"I haven't even had my breakfast yet," David said.

"Finish drinking your cup of tea and come on!"

John paced the kitchen waiting what seemed endlessly for the men to get ready. "Oh, and before I forget, here's your knife back."

David took the knife from John and held it up to the sunlight. "Looks cleaner than when I gave it to you."

"My mother always taught me to return things in better shape than I had borrowed them."

David laughed, and pulled a tin toward him from the centre of the table. He opened the lid and dumped a pile of leaves from the tin onto the table before him. The smell of tobacco filled the kitchen. "One for the road," he said, cutting the leaves to roll his own. "Want one?"

John shook his head, no.

"The knife's sharper than before, too." David tucked it into his belt, rolled his cigarette and stood.

John slid the key to the barn off the ring and passed it to David, then the three men headed down the road to their new home. Jim scurried on ahead, eager to get there.

"Don't be in such a hurry. We will all go down together," John called, slowing the younger man in his tracks.

When they reached the barn, John gave instructions. "I want to sell them right off," he said, gesturing at the animals.

"But you just got the place, George," Jim said.

"Yes, but what am I going to do with this pair of oxen? And those two cows? I need something stronger, more like two horses. Can you do that for me?"

Jim looked at him, confused. "Do what?"

"Sell off these animals and get me two horses. I was thinking we could head into Windsor to see about selling them there."

"Are you sure you want to get rid of the oxen? If we are going to work the land, we are going to need them."

John nodded.

"What're them townies going to do with oxen? Nah, we need to go further up the road to St. Croix."

"See, this is why I need you around. You know people around these parts, more than I do. Will you take me?"

"I reckon I can."

"Then it's settled."

"What's settled? You have a buyer, then?"

"No, you're going to help me sell off the lot of them. No time like the present. Let's go up to the house and talk over a plan."

Jim made a beeline for the back door until John called, "Let's go in around the front."

Seated at the kitchen table, Jim looked around. David, who had followed them in, pulled up a chair. Finally, he asked, "Where is old Mr. Harvey?"

John leaned back in his chair, hands behind his head. "While you were still sleeping this morning, a man came down from Halifax to talk to Freeman about the sales agreement. Freeman then left with him to go to the city to work out the details of the sale. We've been busy!"

"My land! Have you ever. I wouldn't be so good with reading all them papers. Glad he's got someone to help him take care of business."

"I have already paid him $200, and we'll sort out the rest when he gets back."

David nodded. "When will he be back, then?"

"Not til Tuesday. So, shall we off to St. Croix, then?" John asked Jim.

"What for?"

"Just, come on!"

~

With the oxen hooked up to the cart, Jim and John started the journey down the dirt road toward St. Croix.

"How long is this going to take us? Wouldn't it be faster to just walk?" John was starting to get impatient.

"It's about two miles up the road. I reckon about an hour. And if you want to sell the oxen, we gots to bring them with us, George."

John settled back and tried to warm up with a woollen blanket wrapped around his legs. He thought he would never get used to the Canadian climate.

Jim handed him his knitted mittens. "You're lucky we're having such a mild winter this year."

"Jesus, Mary and Joseph! You call this mild?"

"We'd normally have to hook up the sled instead of the wagon, but we ain't had snow in forever."

"Praise be."

Upon entering the village of St. Croix, Jim pointed to a large wooden sign hanging from the side of a building. John could just make out the words, *Sanford & Sons Butcher*.

Jim stopped the wagon in front, jumped down, and looped the leather reins around a post in front of the building. He motioned John to follow him. A bell chimed with the opening door to announce their entrance.

"Good morning."

John scanned the room trying to trace the direction of the voice.

"I'm Jim Fisher—" Jim started.

"I know who you are, lad. What can I help you with?" The older man wiped his hands on his almost-white apron and stepped around to greet them.

John looked around, memories of the shops from his childhood flooding his mind. His eyes took in the meat hanging from the metal hooks in the ceiling, the wooden chopping table at the back, and the sawdust covering the floor. It was all so familiar.

"We're wondering if you would be interested in buying some stock from us," he said. He pointed through the large picture window toward the oxen.

"You're not from around these parts. I'm Alfred Sanford of Sanford and Sons. England?"

"You've a mighty good ear, Mr. Sanford. I've just come from London, in fact. I've purchased Freeman Harvey's place up on the Dawson Road, lock, stock and barrel."

Sanford nodded and stepped toward the window to have a better look at the animals.

"Now, I'm needing to sell these two fine creatures. We also have a cow and a heifer."

"I'm not sure I have any room for any more stock, is the thing," Mr. Sanford said. "What do you value these oxen at?"

"Ninety dollars for the pair of them."

"Why do you want to sell off the stock, anyway?"

"I want to have some repairs done on the place, including the barn, so I can't have the stock there. I have two horses coming from Halifax, and I won't have room for them if I don't clear out the other stock first."

"Oh!" Jim said. "You hadn't mentioned the part about the horses from Halifax. How grand. I'm real good at working with horses."

"I'm busy now, so I'll have to look at the other stock later to make my final decision."

~

"I know somewhere else we can go," Jim said.

"Aye. That was rather disappointing, and not the answer I was hoping for."

John looked down at his shoes, covered in the sawdust he had tracked from the butcher's shop, and knocked his heels together in an attempt to brush it off.

"We'll go see Mr. Spence. He's just a piece up the road."

"Who is he? And, more importantly, is he going to buy my stock? I really need this seen to today."

"He is a good man. He fixes up carriages and farm equipment and the like."

Jim and John found James Spence in his home office.

"Excuse me, Mr. President, sir," Jim said. He approached the distinguished man, with a large black moustache, who was busy at some paperwork. A patch of sun shone through the window and reflected off his nearly-bald head.

"Jim Fisher, my lad, I've told you again and again, you don't need to address me as such."

Jim turned to John. "He's the president for the area here in St. Croix. A real important man."

"Just a councilman, James." He smiled and stretched out to shake John's hand.

"George Stanley, Mr. President," John said with a wink.

"How can I help you, George Stanley?"

"I've got some stock I'm itchin' to sell, and Jim here thinks you might be willing to take them off my hands. I have a pair of oxen, a cow and a heifer and some oats back at the farm. Looking for a mare or two."

"How are you planning on farming if you sell off the cattle, though?" James asked.

"Where I come from, I didn't have any experience with cattle, but I can handle horses."

"Perhaps I can come down later this afternoon to have a proper look," Mr. Spence said.

"That would be just fine. We're at Freeman Harvey's place. I bought him right out of his boots this morning," John chuckled.

"It's true," Jim said. "It's all been settled. I seen the paperwork."

"Well, my land! How much did you pay for it?"

"$1500. I gave him $800 already and I'll owe him the balance on Monday. Besides, I have an uncle in New York City who's died and left my sister and me $1600, and that should be here by the fourteenth of the month."

"Great deal you got there," Mr. Spence said.

"Indeed!" John said. "Harvey is now off in Halifax seeing about the final details. I've got a man, a solicitor, Mr. O'Connolly, working on it. Then, of course, he has to fix things up with his wife."

"Good enough," Mr. Spence said. "I have no way of buying them just now, but I have a horse in the barn I'd be willing to trade with you, if you say you're good with horses. What are you asking for the oxen?"

"A hundred and five dollars for the pair." John glanced at Jim to see if the price difference from mere moments before had registered with him, but Jim continued smiling, blissfully unaware.

"I want a hundred dollars for the horse," Mr. Spence said. "So, we will trade even. I'll be heading your way later this afternoon, so I will come by to have a better look at them, and your other stock also. If they suit me, I'll bargain then. Follow me now to the barn and have a look at my mare and see what you think."

14: Keep the door locked

Noon

It was noon by the time Jim and John hopped off the ox cart in the drive-way back at Freeman Harvey's property. David met them and helped take the animals to the barn.

"Come on in, and I'll make you lunch," John said.

He headed around to the far side of the house toward the front door, but noticed David and Jim taking the direct route to the back door. He beckoned them to follow him around front.

"Why can't we go in the back door? It's right here," Jim complained.

"We can't use that door. Old Mr. Harvey left a lot of his stuff back there in the porch before he left, and it's all piled up. I'm not sure exactly what time he'll be back and exactly what he will still want, so it's safer to just leave it all there."

"I can see that," David said, following John to the front of the house.

"It's kind of a fend-for-yourself meal, I'm afraid, lads," John said rooting through the pantry. He hauled out a loaf of bread that still looked good and put a slab of butter on the table in front of them.

"Brrrr... it's cold today, eh?" David rubbed his hands together to generate some warmth and tested his hands against the wood stove in the corner of the kitchen. "Not much coming out of this one. Want me to go out the back there and get some more wood?"

"I'll go get some wood chips from the shed to get it going," Jim said, walking toward the kitchen door that led to the shed.

"Oh, no, you don't!" John said. "You must use the front door, remember?"

Jim paused for a moment, remembered Freeman's belongings in the back porch, and then changed his direction. "Do we need some logs, too?"

"Don't you worry about the logs," John said. "The wood box is full. I'll warm us up in no time."

When Jim returned, he dumped the chips into the firebox and stirred the ashes to ignite the flames. As he manoeuvred around the stove, Jim

kept running into the clothesline that was strung
clothes, which had been pegged there to dry, swaye.
movement. The more Jim batted them out of the way, the
swung back in his face.

"Careful there." David said. "Remember what happened the last time.
It's a funny story."

"It wasn't funny at the time. I spent the entire fall picking apples for
this farmer, and earned at least ten bucks, and went into the dry goods
store in town, and had me a set of coveralls picked out for working in the
woods. I goes and puts them on, and gets them all wet on the first day,
spilling a bucket from the well. Then, I goes to put them on the rack behind the stove to have them dry."

David picked up the story. "But, what he ain't saying is that part of the
pant leg got caught in the grate without him seeing. He goes to bed, and
in the morning, the coveralls are all burnt to a crisp. Cinders and ashes."

"Didn't even get to have them more'n a day!"

John looked from David to Jim and back again. Then, without a moment's hesitation, he snatched up Harvey's hats, mittens and socks from
the line and stuffed them into the fire. He grabbed a few more bundles of
clothing from behind the stove and tossed them in the fire as well.

Jim stood back, mouth agape.

"Watcha do that for?" David shouted. "You will have too much fire and
burn the whole house down!"

John unpegged Freeman's overcoat and passed it to Jim. "Here," he
said. "For you. For all your help with selling the stock."

"But won't Harvey be needing it?"

"With all the money I've given him, he'll be buying a whole new ward-
robe, he said. And it's far too big for me."

Jim took the overcoat and put it on. He smiled at the feel of it.

"And, while I'm thinking of it," John said, stepping momentarily into
the front parlour, "I want you to give this to Mary Ann. I think she might
like it. It has several nice illustrations."

He handed David a Bible in a leather case that zipped all the way
around.

David opened it, leafed through it, and smiled. "Greatly appreciated.
The pictures sure will help to understand the stories, seeing that none of
us read too good."

"All right, gentlemen," John said. "What's the plan for the afternoon?"
Hearing none, he continued. "You two go out and feed the cattle, and then
we should soon expect a visit from Mr. Spence."

John looked out the window and saw the man himself pulling up the _rive in a horse and buggy. "Speak of the devil, and he shall appear."

"I don't want to be conjuring no devils, Mr. Stanley," David said.

"It's an expression, it just means—never mind. Mr. Spence is here to look at the stock. David, can you please show him into the barn? And remember to go out the front door."

After a few minutes, John joined the three men in the barn. "What are you thinking, Mr. Spence?"

"Fine beasts," Mr. Spence said. "I'll definitely trade you the horse, and I'll take the cow and heifer, too. Have your boy here tie the cows to the back of the wagon. Put the oats in, too. He can drive the beasts back to my place with the oxen."

Jim nodded.

"Then, drive back with the smaller wagon, harness and the grey mare that I showed you this morning. Do you understand?" James looked into Jim's eyes.

Jim nodded again and began hitching up the wagon.

"Here's what I'll pay you," Mr. Spence said, opening his leather billfold. "Eighteen for the cow, as she's proven she can breed well, but only ten for the heifer because we don't know what she's capable of yet. The oats I see were just threshed, but they look pretty thin, so I'll pay you three dollars for those."

"I'm not sure I liked the look of that wagon," John said, thinking back to what he had seen in the barn earlier that morning.

"Fine, well, if you come back up to my place tonight, you can have another look. I have a better wagon you can probably have instead."

John reached out to shake the councilman's hand. "Shall we seal the deal with a drink at Rieck's Hotel up in Ellershouse?"

"I suppose I have time for a small one. I left my wife there in town on my way down here and need to return to pick her up, so I guess that will work well."

~

A short time later, the men stood, ale in hands, at the counter at Reick's Hotel, deciding where to sit.

"Look who the wind just blew in," a man in his mid-twenties said as he approached them.

Mr. Spence shook his hand and embraced him. "George Stanley, I'd like to introduce you to my much younger brother, another George. George

Spence."

John reached out to shake his hand.

"What brings you here today, dear brother?" George asked.

"Mr. Stanley and I just did some business and are here to seal the deal."

"Always something on the go." George slapped his older brother on the back. "Let me introduce you to my good friend Edgar McCarthy, from further up the road at Three Miles Plain. He's a quarry worker and a horse trader."

"Pleased to make your acquaintance," John said.

"You're not from around here," McCarthy said.

"Fresh off the boat from London, I am."

After the round of drinks was done, Mr. Spence stood to take his leave. "Are you good to get back down to the Harvey place, then, Mr. Stanley? I'm heading in the opposite direction."

"Tis no trouble. I can find my own way back."

"Harvey place, you say?" George asked. "McCarthy and I are heading that way, and we can take you down the road with us as far as we are going."

When they were hitched up and ready to go, John asked, "Are you the man who owns the land adjoining Harvey's?"

"Not quite," George said. "I'm across the road and up a bit, but my sheep do tend to stray down there from time to time."

"Just wondering, as I have just purchased the farm from Harvey, and all the contents."

~

Jim arrived back from the Spence household with the mare and wagon at supper time, at the same time George Spence dropped John at the side of the road.

"Shall I tie the horse up in the barn, then?" he shouted down the driveway.

"No, my lad, just tie her up front. We'll go in for tea, and then head back to Mr. Spence's place to switch out the wagon."

"I'm all betwixt and between today. Don't know if I'm coming or going. I've been back and forth on that road so many times, I could drive it in my sleep."

"We aren't finished yet, my lad. Let's go in. I'll boil some water for tea, and fix us something to eat," John said.

"Everything good with Mr. Spence?" David asked as he joined them.

"Which Spence? There are too many of them," John said.

"James, the fancy president one. Why? Who were you with?"

John said, "Everyone around here seems to have the same bloody name! We are going back to James Spence's place after we've had our tea, but I also met George Spence and his friend McCarthy."

"McCarthy. He's a bad man, Mr. Stanley," Jim said seriously.

"He's right," David said. "You need to keep clear of the likes of him. He has a very bad reputation."

"What could possibly be so bad?" John asked.

"You don't want to cross him. He'll beat you up. He's a real fighter," Jim said.

"Even went to court several times," David continued. "The worst was for beating up that mail carrier. What was his name? MacPhee? He and his brother done for him real good."

Jim nodded. "He scares me."

"Duly noted," John said. His glance fell on a mark on right wrist, the head of a long white scar that ran the length of his arm. He smiled to himself and jumped up from the table. "No rest for the weary. Let's get going, Jim. We're heading to the Spence place."

Then John turned to David. "I want you to stay in the house until we get back. Keep the door locked and don't let anyone in under any circumstance. Don't go near Harvey's things in the back porch, either. Do you understand?"

David nodded, and the men left for St. Croix.

~

Yet again, Jim and John arrived by horse and carriage at James Spence's farm. John had travelled these roads so many times over the past few days, he knew every tree and bend in the road. He loved the views.

As beautiful as the surrounding woodlands, streams and nearby mountains were, nothing compared to the grandeur of the night sky. He arched his head from horizon to horizon, taking in the vastness all at once. He had not seen stars like this since he was a boy back in Roscrea, nor had he had a view bigger than a slot through a window in years.

He felt a connection with this wide-open space. Maybe it was because it reminded him of his boyhood, the last time he was truly free.

John jumped down from the carriage and ambled up to James Spence's house. He knocked on the door, then walked in to find the man sitting, once more, at his desk. After a long discussion, James agreed to let John have the wagon with the covered top.

John moved closer to the fireplace, trying to warm his hands in front of the open log fire. "I'll never get used to how cold this country is. Twas never this cold in the winter back in England."

"I have something that you might be interested in buying then," James said. He left the office and returned with a stack of fur coats.

He held each one up, trying to find one that might fit the five-foot-three man. "This one ought to do, and will keep you extra warm in our winters."

John tried the coat on and snuggled into the warmth of it. "As snug as a bug." Then he looked thoughtful. "There is something else I need. While I was in town, there was a most unfortunate accident, and someone took my pocket watch. I really must be more careful."

"Not to worry," James said. He started to rummage through his desk. "I can sell you one of those, too."

15: I killed a hen

February 4

John had drifted off to sleep only hours before, when he heard a loud banging at the back door. He sat upright, trying to orient himself. He looked down at himself, still fully dressed. At least he had remembered to take his boots off.

He looked beside him and saw David's feet in his face, his head at the opposite end of the bed. An old, tattered quilt covered the two of them.

The banging on the back door continued.

John rubbed his eyes and walked out of the bedroom into the kitchen. There, sprawled on the lounge next to the wood stove, was Jim. He was fully dressed as well, boots and all, as he had been in no condition to do much of anything when they arrived back the night before. The lad really had to learn to better hold his liquor. That quick stop at Rieck's should not have left him in such a poor state.

The banging continued.

"I'm coming. Hold your horses!"

John looked around to make sure the other men were still asleep, went through the kitchen door to the porch, and shut it quietly behind him.

"Stop with the almighty racket. You'll wake the dead! Who is there?"

"It's Edgar McCarthy and Maurice Fisher."

"Give me a minute and I'll open the door."

From the other side, McCarthy could hear what sounded like the loud shuffling of furniture, or the dragging of a trunk or a large box. Finally, John opened the door to admit McCarthy and David Fisher's son, Maurice, whom he directed toward the kitchen, where Jim was starting to stir.

"What are you doing here?" John said.

"Well, you see, it's like this," McCarthy said. "I was up to George Spence's place yesterday, as you know, and was heading back home last night around midnight, when the shaft of my wagon snapped. One of my horses is a real kicker, so I was a bit nervous taking her with the shaft in that condition, and there's a little ice on the roads yet."

David appeared in the bedroom door, sucking air between his teeth, acknowledging how dangerous it was to drive like that.

"I thought I'd stop at Frank Murphy's place to fix it. However, being dark and all, I ended up knocking on your door."

McCarthy pointed to Jim and David. "Mrs. Fisher came to the door and invited me in."

David raised his eyebrow and crossed his arms over his chest.

"It was cold out! Don't worry, I had to convince her to let me in."

"I should hope," David muttered "If that was around midnight, and you are just coming here now at, what, seven o'clock? Pray tell me, what you were doing with my wife until now?"

"I'm a married man. Nothing untoward," McCarthy protested. "I stayed in the kitchen the whole time. She does make a mean breakfast, though," he said under his breath.

"What was that?" David asked.

"I had a box of eggs in my wagon, brought them in, and she cooked them up for us as a midnight breakfast."

"She makes great eggs," Jim said.

"Then, when it was light, she said for me to come down here, as her husband was to have the place. She said Harvey wasn't around because he'd gone to Windsor to live with his wife, but that you might be willing to help me."

"I'll come out to help you," John said. "Jim! Maurice! Come along with us."

"We need to get the horses into the barn, too. They've been standing outside all night," McCarthy said.

David shook his head in disbelief at McCarthy's carelessness.

"Ma sent down some bread, butter and molasses," Maurice said, handing a bundle over to his father.

David reached over to receive it, turned his back and started to awaken the fire in the woodstove.

"I'll pay you, Stanley, for your trouble helping me today," McCarthy said.

"Not to worry. Stay the day with us," John said. "Where I come from, you would be considered mean if you asked someone to pay you for a bite to eat."

He picked up the kettle. "We're going to need more water, David. Don't use the water from the well in the yard, though. It's not clean. You need to go down to the river to get it."

David took the tin and walked toward the back door, pivoted as he re-membered he needed to use the front door, and headed to the brook be-hind the barn.

~

By noon, the Harvey house had filled up with an assortment of charac-ters. John looked from person to person as he passed the whisky bottle around the kitchen table. He was not sure how all of Jim's friends had found him there at the Freeman House, but word seemed to travel quickly in the small village.

"Should we start thinking about dinner?" Mary Ann Fisher asked. She had come down earlier that afternoon to help clean up lunch dishes. She put down the dish towel and stood behind her husband, with her hands on his shoulders.

"That would be nice, dear," David said. "I'd like a hearty meal. Some meat and potatoes."

"The cold room is down in the cellar with the potatoes," Mary Ann said. "Jim, be a good boy and go down and get me a bunch."

"No!" John shouted. He stood from the table, scraping the chair so hard across the floor it toppled backward. "No, don't you worry," he said more calmly. "You are my guests here, and I'll go get them for you. Be-sides, the stairs are all rickety into the cellar, and if someone were to fall, I wouldn't have anyone left to work on the farm."

John went through the back door that led to the porch and through the door to the cellar. He opened it wide enough to slip through, and quickly shut it again behind him. A few moments later, he reappeared with several potatoes, using his shirt tails as a basket. He carefully rolled them onto the counter and brushed the dirt from his shirt.

"And the meat? Does Freeman have any of that salted meat left?" Mary Ann asked. "Shall I go check?"

"No," John said. "Let me go see. Harvey's things are all stacked out there for when he returns, and he doesn't want anyone getting into his things. Better if I do it."

John repeated the trek to the porch, looking over his shoulder to en-sure no one was following him.

"You know," he said when he returned with enough salted beef to feed the nine people around his table, "coming through there just now, I real-ized how much of Harvey's things are out there, and with so many people in the house, I'd feel pretty badly if anything were to happen. I'm thinking we need to fasten the door shut to make sure no one goes through there."

He walked around the kitchen, opening and closing drawers, looking for anything that could be used as a fastener. "David," he said when his search proved futile. "See if you can find something that we can use to fasten this porch door to."

David went toward the porch, but John stood blocking the doorway. "I thought I saw a box of old iron bits out there," David explained.

John moved to allow him through but stood watching him.

David dug around the porch, moving boxes in search of a fastener. As he pushed a wooden box to the side, he stopped dead in his tracks. "What's that?"

"What's what?"

"That. It looks like splashes of blood on the floor."

"That? Oh, heavens," John said. "I killed a hen on Friday night for our dinner, and splattered blood all over the floor by accident. Now, would you hurry up and find something to fasten the door with?"

"I think this will do," David said. He held up a wire fastener and a long piece of chain, swinging them like a pendulum.

John picked up a small mallet that was sitting on the windowsill in the porch and called to McCarthy. "Help me drive this into the wall here." He pointed to the wall beside the doorknob.

To a man whose name he had forgotten he said, "In the drawer there behind you is a lock. Get that for me, lad."

John took the chain, wrapped it around the doorknob and connected it back through the wire fastener in the wall. He secured it all with the padlock, then slipped the key into his breast pocket, patting it for good measure, and returned to the table to wait for Mary Ann to finish making their dinner.

~

"How on earth does everyone know this is the place to be today?" John said with a laugh. He held what seemed like his fifth cup of tea for the afternoon.

"It's a small place, George. Not like that big city you are used to," David said.

"I'm going to need to pin everyone's name to your chest. I can't keep everyone straight, and there are far too many Spences to keep track of. Is everyone here in this village a Spence, or related to one?"

"I'm not a Spence, George. My last name is Fisher," Jim said.

"Right, lad." John slapped him on his shoulder.

"Do you have anything stronger to drink, George, my man?" McCarthy asked.

"It's still Sunday. We don't drink on the Sabbath," John said. "Have another cuppa."

McCarthy crossed his hands over his chest. "Just till the sun goes down." He stood to look out the kitchen window. "Not long now." He pointed to the sun, almost at the horizon.

"Heard you traded the oxen for James Spence's horse, and got a covered wagon," McCarthy said. "I have an even better wagon back at home, which you might like. We could do a trade for that."

John tapped the pocket watch he had gotten from James. "It's still Sunday, lad. No doing business on the Sabbath."

McCarthy leaned back on his chair, anxious to change things up. They had been sitting in the kitchen all day, and he was restless.

~

It was well after ten o'clock and the group of men had just returned from a liquor run to the Rieck's Hotel in town.

"What's a big man like you from the Mother Country doing in the likes of Ellershouse?"

McCarthy leaned forward, seizing the brown jug and pouring himself another tumbler of rum.

"He's actually from England," Jim said. "And he's a lot smaller than you, McCarthy."

McCarthy clinked his glass with John's and downed the honey-brown liquid in a single draught. "Let me try that again. George, tell me: why the hell would you want to buy a farm in Ellershouse, in the middle of the boondocks of Nova Scotia?"

"Ellershouse is a lovely place," John said.

When McCarthy rolled his eyes, he continued, "You've got the train station here, a sawmill, a school, some fancy rich man in a mansion on the hill, a house of the Lord, and who can forget the house of liquor?"

"I'll drink to that!" George Spence said.

"We're miles from town, and even further from the city," McCarthy persisted. "What are you going to do around here, besides selling your fancy telephones?"

"Well, to be honest, boys," John said as he opened the third bottle of whisky of the evening, "I've never really had a place to call my own. I feel like I've always had four walls pressing in on me. Know what that feels like?" The way they were freely passing the bottles around the table at this rate, he realized, they'd have to make another trip to the hotel to get them through the rest of the evening.

"Oh, for sure," David agreed. He was the only man who was stone-cold sober, having refused to have a drink all evening.

"I've done my time." John paused and this time poured from the bottle of brandy.

McCarthy cocked an eyebrow, looking intently at him.

"I've done my time wandering around and want to finally settle down." John rocked back in his chair, realizing with surprise how much truth there was in that statement. "I've asked the Fishers to live here and look after the stock for a while, until my sister arrives, and I come back with her."

"And so we will," Jim said.

"After that? I'd like to settle down and have a home of my own here, and maybe even a wife. Or three," John said, looking over at Jim.

Jim glared at John, slicing his finger across his throat in effort to keep him quiet on the matter.

"Three wives? My one wife is trouble enough." McCarthy said. "Who's got time for three?"

"No one. No one does," Jim said. "No one is saying nothing about nobody."

"Well, it's gotten frosty in here all of a sudden," George Spence said. "I'm going to get some more chips for the fire."

He walked toward the kitchen door that led to the porch and the wood pile. He reached his hand out, then remembered it was chained closed.

"Can't go that way," John said. "Use the front door, lad."

"I just don't see why we can't go that way. Makes no sense," George mumbled as he headed for the front door.

"What's so important out there?" McCarthy said.

"Gentleman," John said over the suppositions. "We are nearly bone dry here! What say you we pile in the wagon again and head back up to Rieck's and see what he has left for us?"

"I'm in!" Jim said. He stood quickly but, losing his balance from an excess of drink, thumped back into his chair.

"I'm not going nowhere," David said.

"That is well," John said. "We'll lock the door when we leave, and don't

65

let anyone in until we get back."

He led everyone toward the front door.

16: The front door

February 5, after midnight

When John, Jim, McCarthy and George Spence returned with two more bottles of ale and three flasks of whisky, McCarthy looked down at his watch. He brought the timepiece right to his nose, willing the numbers to come into focus.

"It's after midnight," he finally announced. "Sunday's over with now, so if you have any business to do, get at it!"

He leaned forward on the table and accidentally tipped a tumbler of ale onto George Spence. McCarthy made a motion to drink it off the table, as to not waste any of the precious liquid gold, but John threw an old rag at him to mop it up.

George, who had jumped back in his chair to avoid the splash, said, "That's it! I'm heading out of here."

"Don't go because of a little accident," John said.

"Nah, I gots to get back. Them animals don't feed themselves in the morning. Thanks for a grand evening, boys."

"Don't forget to use—" John started.

"The front door," the other men chorused.

"I got it," George said as he left.

"Where would you like to begin?" John asked.

"I'm beat," David said. "I'm off, too. You gentlemen enjoy yourselves."

"Goodnight ol' chap," John said, patting him on the shoulder. "Next time we'll convince you to have a drink with us."

"I will give you a pony I have, along with a brand new, nickel-mounted harness, plus the second-hand wagon I have out front, and ten dollars, all for that buggy with the top on it you just got from James Spence," McCarthy started.

"I did just get that buggy and haven't had a chance to try it out yet," John said.

"It's a good deal, George. When are you going to get to drive something so fancy around here?"

"Deal," John said with a nod. "I have other things you might be interested in purchasing. I have approximately three bushels of oats, a horse rake and a horse-drawn bob sled."

"I'll take all that for another ten dollars," McCarthy said.

"Anything else in the house of interest to you?" John asked. "Harvey put all he wanted in the back porch there and said everything else came with the house."

"Where is Harvey?" McCarthy asked.

"Gone off to Windsor by now, I bet, to settle up with his wife and give her what she's owed out of the sale. So, anything else you want?"

McCarthy nodded his head over John's shoulder. "I notice that fancy organ in the front room there every time we go in and out the front door. Looks like a nice one."

"I can't play a lick of music," John said. "I have no use for it."

"I have a brown horse you can have in exchange for the organ."

"I've seen that horse," Jim said, trying to find a way to insert himself into the conversation. "It's a nice horse. Go for the trade."

"Great advice, lad," John said. "Another deal, McCarthy. Now, there is another matter of grave importance."

He leaned forward and almost whispered the next words. His hot whisky breath wafted through the air. Jim leaned in closer.

"The hens," he mouthed.

"The hens?" McCarthy cried. "What are you going on about?"

"You need to help me take care of the hens."

"What in the blazes do you mean by 'take care of'?"

"Well," John said, sitting back up and talking as normally as possible under the drunken conditions, "when the Fishers move down tomorrow, they will be bringing their hens with them, and I'm worried there are too many in the pen, and that the two broods will fight. I need to sell them."

McCarthy laughed. "Why didn't you just say so in the first place? How many do you got?"

"Twelve hens and a rooster."

"I'll give you 50 cents a pair. Six dollars for the lot."

"Another good deal, George," Jim said.

"I can't take all them hens with me, though," McCarthy said. "I'm going to need you to help me get them back home. I only have the buggy with the top that I just traded to you, with the one horse."

John stood from the table, drained his cup, and said, "Well then, let's go."

"What? Now?" Jim asked. "It's after one in the morning."

"No time like the present," John said.

"We're going to need two wagons. We'll put the hens in two bags. We'll take one, and you take the other."

"How long is this going to take?" John asked, once they had everything hitched up and were on the road.

"It's only about three miles up the road here," McCarthy said, "so about no more than half an hour each way."

"Make it quick, then, I don't want to be gone too long."

"What are you in such a rush for? Not much happening at this hour of the night."

John drummed his fingers on his leg which was under the wool blanket he had tucked up under his chin to keep warm in the buggy. The drumming not only helped to keep his fingers from freezing but marked his impatience. He grunted responses back to McCarthy, who was attempting to make small talk with him.

John turned his head to the side to take in the view. The moonlight illuminated forest on both sides of the road as far as the eye could see, with hardly a house in sight. They passed a few roads that led to logging camps where men came for the winter season, spending time hauling timber out with horses. They also passed a couple of villages, some churches, warehouses, sawmills and schoolhouses. The journey seemed to take forever.

When they arrived, John knocked the kerosene lantern as he jumped down from the buggy, causing shadows of light to circle on the ground.

McCarthy hitched the horses to the wooden post on his front veranda and took the sack of hens from the back of the buggy, slinging it over his shoulder like a sack of potatoes. He called over his shoulder to Jim, who had just arrived. "Come put your horse in the barn and give it something to eat, then come inside for a few minutes."

"We are heading back," John said.

"What? Stay awhile. I'll go in and get my wife to make us some breakfast. Eggs and toast go well to cure the effects of the drinking, come morning. Trust me. I'm an expert on these things," McCarthy said, tapping the side of his nose.

John paced the driveway. "I really need to get back."

"You can take a few minutes to get something to eat."

McCarthy went up the front steps and could be heard calling for Maggie, loud enough to wake the dead, let alone his four sleeping children.

In the kitchen, John drummed his fingers on the table, waiting for Maggie McCarthy to finish cooking their eggs. She stood at the stove, with a heavy shawl wrapped around her nightdress. Her husband had obviously awoken her from her slumber.

"I've left David Fisher locked up and alone in the house."

"What's the big deal? He's probably asleep. Nothing is going to happen to him."

"I really need to get going and can't wait for you any longer. The sun is rising, and I need to get going." John pushed away from the table, leaving his breakfast half eaten. He pulled on his fur overcoat and headed toward the back door.

"Where are you going? How are you going to get there?"

"I'm going to walk," John called over his shoulder.

"Should I go take him?" Jim asked.

McCarthy just shook his head. "Leave him be. He's got a bee in his bonnet. We'll catch him up once we finish here."

17: Don't touch a thing!

"George! George!" Jim yelled over the jostling noises from the wagon bumping down the road. "That definitely looks like him up ahead."

"See? You are no further ahead. You should have waited for us," McCarthy snapped from the wagon above. "Hop in and we will take you the rest of the way."

John scanned the road up and down, calculating how much further he had to walk. "I don't mind. I don't usually have this much freedom to walk."

McCarthy motioned again for John to get in the wagon. John finally complied, taking Jim's place up front. Jim clambered into the back.

"When we get back, help me load the organ onto the wagon, so we can make another run back to my place," said McCarthy.

"We can't do that yet. These horses haven't been fed yet this morning. What time is it?" Jim asked.

"It's half past eight," McCarthy said. "Go feed the horses in the barn, and then we'll get loaded up."

"Nope," John said. "We don't have time to make another run right now."

He jumped down from the wagon before McCarthy had brought the horse to a full stop. He started pacing the driveway, tapping his forehead, willing himself to think clearly. "Jim, after you feed the horses, come back out with the pony and the grey horse."

John left them to do his bidding, while he went inside the house. He returned a few minutes later to find Jim in the driveway holding the reins of the two horses.

"Let's go!"

"Where are we going now?" Jim asked.

"Up through Ellershouse and then on to Windsor. I want to sell those horses. I need to move them now, because I promised old Mr. Harvey another payment on the property today."

"We don't need to go that far," McCarthy said, taking the reins from

Jim. "Let's go back up and see George Spence. He's way closer, and I know he'll buy the pony and the harness. Besides, we are too late to catch the freight train to take the horses into Windsor."

"You sure George will have the money on him to buy the pony? I need the cash for it right now." John started to pace.

"Just as likely as anyone. Worth a shot."

~

"George! George!" McCarthy called.

George Spence leaned a saw against the barn from where he had been cutting up wood and came to meet the three men in his driveway.

"Can we interest you in this pony? She's a beauty. Mr. Stanley is looking to sell it today," McCarthy said, putting his arm around George's shoulders. "It also comes with this nickel-plated harness."

"You drive a hard bargain," George said. "I wasn't really in the market for another horse, but she is a beauty."

"I'll give you a good price for it," John threw in.

"Fine," George said. "I'll give you fifteen dollars for the pony and the harness."

John paused to consider the offer. "I'll take it."

George went into the house to get the money.

"You know that harness alone is worth at least twenty dollars," McCarthy said when Spence was out of earshot. "It's factory-made, and brand new. You could have gotten a lot more for it,"

"Maybe, but I need the cash now."

"Why are you selling it for so low?"

John glared. "Like I said. I need the cash to pay Freeman Harvey now. It's not yours, so why do you care?"

"Maybe it's not yours either," McCarthy said under his breath.

John walked up to McCarthy until the two were only inches apart, but because of the height difference, John merely stared into his chest. His anger and impatience started to swell. "What was that? Do you have something to say to me?"

"Gentlemen," George said as he returned, causing the two men to quickly step back from each other. "I've had another thought. I'll give you an extra five dollars and take that horse there instead of the pony."

"Sure thing," John said.

Jim unhitched the horse, removed the pony's harness and passed the reins over to George, placing the new harness carefully on the ground.

McCarthy stood glaring; his arms folded across his chest. George did not seem to notice.

Jim hitched the pony to the wagon in place of the horse and motioned for John and McCarthy to climb in to head back to the Harvey house.

McCarthy sat fuming during the short ride, sighing heavily, willing John to ask him what the matter was.

Back at the Harvey house, Jim returned the pony and wagon to the barn, while John headed to the back field to check on the property. McCarthy followed close on his heels.

"What is your problem?" John finally said.

"That's not how trading works. You don't know anything. That horse was worth at least fifty dollars."

"It's not your horse anymore. Who are you to tell me what to trade for? It's not your stuff to sell."

"I'm beginning to wonder if it's your stuff, either," McCarthy said. He took a step closer to John.

"Just what are you saying?" John balled his fists at his side.

"I'm saying you cannot possibly own this stuff. All that stuff that I got from you, there is no way it can be yours, because if it were, you would not be throwing it away for such low prices."

"You mind your own business and I'll take care of mine."

With a quick movement, John reached behind him and seized one of the replacement fence stakes that had been leaning against the barbed wire. He swung the post up toward McCarthy's head.

McCarthy jumped back and dodged just in time to avoid the blow. "You will have to give me more for the horse than the organ, or I will not take it from the house at all. I want more money for my horse."

"You will not be getting anything. How dare you? I own everything in this place!" John threw the fence post to the ground and stormed back to where he had left Jim at the barn.

McCarthy followed him toward the barn, rolling up his sleeves, fully prepared to continue the fight.

"McCarthy! McCarthy!" A neighbour, who happened to be passing by and had heard the commotion, stood beckoning at the side of the road.

McCarthy quickly changed directions and took a deep breath to calm himself before walking toward the old man from the neighbouring community.

John poked his head out from the barn door and watched them deep in conversation. He paced, wearing a path through the dirt.

"And just what did that old man have to say about me?" he demanded when McCarthy returned to the barn.

"He said nothing about you."

"Don't you lie to me. I saw you deep in conversation, and you looking over here and laughing and talking. I know you were talking about me."

"We weren't talking about you!"

"They are all just mad at me, everyone around here, because I'm moving the Fishers in here."

"I don't think the old man cares who moves in here. He's got a place of his own two miles from here."

"I know exactly where he lives."

"You're out of control, Stanley. I'm going back to the house."

"Fine! Tell David or Mary Ann to get back here and lock up the barn."

As he walked toward the house, McCarthy saw yet another neighbour who was unloading a wagon full of household items on the side of the road. "What are you doing?" he called out, approaching the man.

"It's the Fishers' stuff. Today is moving day, and Stanley paid me to bring all their things down from their old house."

McCarthy gave him a hand with a big rocking chair, placing it beside a rickety table. The growing pile on the side of the road looked more like a bonfire pyre than decent furniture.

"The Fishers are moving in here today?"

"That's what they said. Stanley is getting them to look after the place. Better than the old shack they are in now."

"That's true," McCarthy said, as he took hold of the various pots and pans being handed down to him. The handle of one of the pots came off in his hand. McCarthy raised an eyebrow and poked the paper-thin bottom with his finger.

"I think I've got one more load, but it's hardly worth carting any of this stuff down here. Not worth a candle. But who am I to say?"

The man climbed on to the back of the wagon and took hold of a large wooden bureau. One of the drawer handles was missing and the bottom drawer did not fully close.

McCarthy jumped on the wagon to help him. "They're awfully lucky it's not snowing today. That would have made for an unpleasant move."

"Here: let me help you with that." Harold Spence, James' teenage son, ran up the driveway and stood below the wagon, taking the weight of the bureau as the two men passed it down to him.

"Where can I find Jim or George Stanley?" Harold asked once they had added the bureau to the pile.

"Up to the barn, I reckon," McCarthy said. "That's where I seen them last."

"My father wanted me to fetch him, as he wanted me to bring some of the oats he bought back to the house."

"Old James sends you down to do his bidding, does he?" McCarthy jeered.

"He's tied up with council business," Harold said.

"I'm just teasing you, boy. I'll go up to the barn with you."

With the wagon empty, the man snapped the reins and turned onto the road to the Fishers' house for another load.

"Stanley! Stanley!" McCarthy called out, to no response.

McCarthy poked his head into the barn and shouted some more. "Jim! Stanley!"

His voice echoed and caused the pigeons roosting in the rafters to start and flutter about, showering dust and feathers on the men below.

"Where in tarnation could he be? I swear they were both just here. Harold, you climb up and search the hay mow, and I'll look down around the barn here."

"George! Jim! Where'd you take off to?"

McCarthy went in and out of each of the stalls, fearing he'd find signs of a fateful kick from a horse or some sort of accident, but nothing was amiss and there was no sign of anyone.

"Nothing up here!" Harold shouted from above.

McCarthy pushed open the door that led to the lean-to back portion of the barn. "I've found something," he called. "Come here, quick!"

Harold slid down the ladder from the hay mow and followed McCarthy's voice to the back of the barn. "What is it?"

McCarthy pointed to something by the sacks of grain in the corner.

Harold stepped forward cautiously and picked up a large, furry object, which revealed itself to be an overcoat. He held it up by the collar. "This's my father's coat."

"It *was* your father's coat, but Stanley traded him for it, and it was Stanley who left that fur coat hidden here. I don't have a good feeling about this. Keep looking around in here."

McCarthy and Harold began a search through the lean-to, pulling out the sacks of grain and looking under and behind anything they could.

Harold pulled a pitchfork from the wall and began stabbing the loose hay on the floor. Suddenly, he stopped, feeling something buried beneath.

He dropped to his knees, and with his hands dug through the hay, until he unearthed a burlap sack. He looked cautiously up at McCarthy who motioned for him to open it.

Harold slowly untied the rope around the neck of the bag and stuck his hand into the bag. He immediately withdrew it, as if his hand was on fire, and tossed the sack back down to the floor.

"What? What is it?" McCarthy demanded.

Harold just pointed.

McCarthy knelt in the hay and carefully opened the sack. "What in the hell?"

He stuck his hand in the bag and came out with his index finger hooked in the trigger guard of a brand-new pistol.

"There's an older pistol in here, too," he said.

"What the hell is going on?" Harold asked.

"We've got to find Stanley. We need to cover every square inch of this barn again, and if we don't find him here, we need to go down behind the barn and check the woods line."

Harold carefully placed the burlap sack containing the revolvers in the corner and followed McCarthy outside to start the search.

As McCarthy headed toward the house, he noticed John Bates, another neighbour standing in at the edge of the property.

McCarthy startled at the arrival of yet another person. He had not realized that the location of the Harvey homestead on the crossroads meant that anyone going anywhere was bound to pass by.

"McCarthy!" Bates called out. "Where's Harvey? I've come to see if I can take his horse to go out to the lumber camp today."

"Harvey's not here."

"And what's all the furniture doing piled up alongside the road?"

"Come over," McCarthy said. "Let us go to the house. There's too much going on that doesn't make sense, and I'll fill you in as we go."

McCarthy turned to head toward the house, with Harold and Bates close behind.

"So, where is Harvey?" Bates asked again once they were seated around the kitchen table.

"He's gone to Halifax," David Fisher replied. He had just awoken and was starting to light the fire. "Where's Stanley? He'll tell you all about it."

"That's a mighty fine question," McCarthy said. "Where *is* Stanley? I haven't seen him for about an hour. And, in fact, I haven't seen your boy, Jim, either. Where the hell are they?" He drummed his fingers on the table. "Something just isn't adding up."

"What's that over there?" Bates said, pointing to the porch door rigged up with the padlock, chain and metal staple. "What's so important that Harvey has out there?"

"It's not Harvey," McCarthy said. He went to the porch door and rattled and tugged on the chain, but nothing gave way.

"Woah! What are you doing?" David asked. "Stanley told us not to go out there and disturb Harvey's things."

"You're right," McCarthy said. "Stanley told us. Just what is he hiding back there? Fisher, open the door for us. We need to see for ourselves. There might be a dead body down there." He laughed nervously.

"Fine," Bates said. "Open the lock, David."

"I can't. I have no key."

"All right then, break it open."

David hesitated. "I'm not sure, McCarthy. That doesn't sound like a good idea."

"Just go get the axe, the one around back by the woodpile. We'll use it break open the lock."

"Careful now," Bates cautioned.

"We need to get out there, and we need to get down to have a look in the cellar," McCarthy said.

"I think it would be a more prudent to draw open the staple," Bates said.

David fetched the axe from the wood pile and hit the lock with one strong blow. The staple broke cleanly.

McCarthy shook the chain free, letting it fall to the floor. He kicked it to the corner of the room with the toe of his boot. He slowly opened the door. A cold draft rushed through the kitchen from the unheated porch.

"I'll be damned," McCarthy said, hauling the wooden beef barrel away from the cellar door and pushing it back into the corner, where the dust mark showed it normally resided. He then moved a large wooden plank that was jammed up against the door.

"It's like a barricade here," he said. "Fisher, go get a light. We have to go down there."

David retrieved a tin kerosene lantern from the kitchen, lit it from the wood stove, and carried it to the porch. He handed it to McCarthy.

"No, you're coming with me. You take the light and open the door."

David slowly pulled on the cellar door. He breathed in the musty smell of the damp basement and looked down into what seemed like a pit of darkness. His feet would go no further.

"Go on," McCarthy said. "We need to see what's down there, and what's so important to keep under lock and key."

David led the way, taking one cautious step at a time. The floorboards creaked with every movement. "Hello?" he called out to break the silence. His heart pounded so loudly, he was not sure he would be able to hear any response.

McCarthy followed the light, resting his hand on the wall for balance. The stairs were so steep, any misstep would cause him to tumble head-first down into David.

When he reached the dirt floor of the cellar, David swung his lantern around to the right, and back to the left, creating an arc of light as he went.

"What do you see?" McCarthy called from his perch on the second step.

"I can't really see anything, but a pile of potatoes here in the corner. But wait..."

"What is it?"

David took a step closer to the mound of potatoes. "It looks like there is something sticking out of them. I can't quite see."

He squatted down, reached out and grabbed hold of whatever it was that was sticking out from the pile of potatoes. He wiggled it free and lifted it up in the air.

"Oh my God! It's a foot!"

David jumped to his feet, threw the lantern back to McCarthy, who had come up behind him, nearly smashing it in the process. He ran toward the staircase and took the steps two at a time, not stopping until he was outside and was able to gulp in the fresh air.

McCarthy was not far behind him, shouting, "There's a dead man in the cellar!" as he went.

Harold Spence and John Bates, who were still in the kitchen, joined them in the driveway.

"What are you talking about?" John asked.

"In the cellar!" David said, rocking back and forth.

Fred Knowles, who happened to be driving past with his team of horses, heard the shouting, and stopped. "What's going on? What's all the shouting about?" he asked. He jumped down from his wagon and hitched the horses to a post near the driveway.

"There's something buried in a pile of potatoes in the basement," McCarthy explained. "Someone's gotta go back and check."

"It ain't going to be me." David said. "I'm scared as hell."

"I'll go," Bates said. He walked toward the now-opened back door and took the lantern the men had left there.

"I'll help you," Harold said.

"No," McCarthy, said. "You're just a lad. Too young to see that."

"I'll go with him, then," Knowles said.

Bates and Knowles stepped cautiously down the steep basement steps, using their hands on the stone wall beside them to steady their descent. At the foot of the steps was the pile of potatoes, as described.

"Oh, my good Lord." Bates said, kneeling in front of the potatoes. He cautiously reached out to touch what was protruding from the pile.

Bates moved a few potatoes to the side, trying to unearth what was buried below, each movement becoming more frantic the deeper he dug. He tossed potatoes through the air behind him, and they rolled around on the dirt floor.

"There's a hand there, too," Knowles said.

"Lord Almighty!" Bates fell backward from his kneeling position. His hands were dirty, his nail beds were full of chunks of potatoes, and his knuckles were raw from digging through the pile. "There is a whole body here."

Knowles took over and continued to dig, uncovering more of the body. He dug next to the outside wall, where the top of the body would be. Then he recoiled, gasping, "But there's no head! What the hell has happened here?"

He stared at the red fleshy stump of a neck where the head should have been.

Bates gulped, horrified. "Fred," he said urgently. "Don't touch anything. Not a thing. We have to go to Ellershouse to the station to telegraph the coroner."

"That looks an awful like Freeman Harvey," Knowles said, "what we can see of him."

18: Lift that up, Hughie

"Gentlemen," Dr. Reid said to the men gathered around him in the Harvey kitchen. He took off his bowler hat and placed it on the table in front of him. He removed his driving jacket and carefully rolled up his sleeves, preparing to get to work.

For twenty-two years Dr. Reid had served as the area's physician, and later as its coroner. During that time, he had met almost everyone and had attended when most people either entered into the world or left it.

"What happens now?" McCarthy asked. He shuffled around the crowded kitchen, trying to make his way to the front to face Dr. Reid.

"Let's get to that. Thank you everyone for coming out here on short notice, and for such an unpleasant situation," the coroner said.

Dr. Reid was impressed with how quickly everything had come together. Since the telegram had arrived at the Windsor station and he was alerted by telephone to the message, less than four hours ago, the community had worked a miracle. He had sent a message back informing them to call together twelve of the best citizens of the county to constitute a jury at the Harvey property for two o'clock that afternoon.

And here they were.

"Mr. McCarthy, Mr. Bates, Mr. Knowles and Mr. Fisher have filled us in on the details of the discovery of the body, so now it is up to you men to help us determine what has happened here. We need to assess who it is in the cellar, as well as determine if a crime has occurred."

"What do you mean, *if* it has occurred?" McCarthy asked, incredulous. "In case you have forgotten, there is a man in the basement. A man without his head!"

Dr. Reid ignored the comment. "It's not up to us to determine who committed the crime, but merely if a crime has been committed."

He paused and looked at the ashen faces around the room. "I shall begin by swearing each of you in. The law stipulates that each of you must have been living in the county for a least a year, and not hold a criminal record."

"That leaves you out, McCarthy!" someone muttered from the back of the room.

"Watch yourself," he shot back.

"Mr. McCarthy is a witness, as he found the body, and therefore cannot be sworn as a jury member. I have already collected his statement," Dr. Reid said.

"But he's already searched the cellar," someone said. "I thought that's why we're here."

"We also searched the railway tracks," McCarthy explained to the jury. "Right after Knowles and Bates went to the station to call for the doctor, I went out on the side of the road to wait. But then felt I should be doing something, so young Harold Spence and I hitched up the horse and wagon and took off for St. Croix, going through the Plains, along the railway line."

"Did you see anyone?" George Spence asked. He had also been summoned as part of the jury.

"No sign of George Stanley, nor Jim Fisher. We're going out again just as soon as we are finished here. Jim Fisher used to spend some time in a logging camp back in the woods there and would know the land quite well. Harold Spence and I are going to head back there to look for them."

"You are dismissed for that purpose," Dr. Reid said. "Let's move along with what needs to be done here, then."

As soon as he started the procedures, however, someone else spoke up. "Are they the murderers? Why aren't we all out there looking for them, then?"

"Let me remind you, gentlemen, that our purpose here is to view the body and determine who the deceased was, and how, when, and where the deceased came to his death. We are not the police."

The room was silent after the reprimand. Dr. Reid continued. "Let's start with Mr. Francis Stevens of Ellershouse, whom I believe has already been nominated as your foreman."

Stevens pushed his way forward from the back of the room.

Dr. Reid wiped his hands on his trousers to dry the sweat that was accumulating from having so many people in the room. The heat from the woodstove was not helping. If it had not been in the middle of winter and near the freezing point, he could have held the meeting and sworn in the jury members outside. For now, this would have to do.

"Please repeat after me," he said to Stevens. "I, Francis Stevens, do swear that I will duly, faithfully and impartially, and to the best of my knowledge and ability, serve as a jury member in Ellershouse, Hants

County on this day of February 5, 1906."

Dr. Reid repeated the process for each man in the room.

"The jury is now properly constituted," he said. "Shall we begin?"

He realized he was asking this just as much for himself as for the jury members. In over two decades of serving as coroner, this would be Dr. Reid's first time leading a full coroner's inquest. He hoped it would be his last.

He took a deep breath and lifted the lantern from the centre of the table. He looked at his jury. "Shall we head to the cellar, then?" he asked, and led the party toward the porch door.

"There," Dr. Reid said, gesturing toward the pile of potatoes at the bottom of the stairs.

A few gasps were heard throughout the group, mixed in with colourful profanity Dr. Reid had not heard in some time.

"We need to begin by clearing the potatoes away, so we have a workspace."

The men carefully carted the potatoes away, placing them in nearby empty wooden crates.

Dr. Reid knelt by the body and carefully cradled the lacerated neck stump in his hands. They were thankfully saved from any odours, as the cold cellar had preserved the body. But the sight of it caused several men to gag and cover their mouths and noses, willing themselves not to throw up.

"I'm going to do a thorough check of the body to look for any other injuries."

He moved his hands up and down the body, opening buttons, and checking under clothing. "What do you notice here?" he asked, holding up the right arm.

"There's blood on that hand," Harry Miller said.

"Agreed."

When he had finished, having found nothing else of note, the doctor asked, "Does anyone recognize this man's body by his clothing or his proportions?"

"How can you recognize him? There's no head!" John Williams said.

"And just where is the head?" Hugh Brown demanded of no one in particular.

"It's got to be here somewhere." Williams picked up the lantern from the crate where Dr. Reid had placed it. He and Brown set off to explore the cellar.

Starting in the northern corner of the cellar, Williams swung the lantern to and fro. Another group of men, led by Fred Rockwell, searched the southern end.

"Behind here!" Rockwell shouted, moving an old washer tub out of the way. He had spotted a pair of black leather work boots inside a metal box at the foot of the steps. He picked them up and swung them by their laces.

"That explains why he's in his sock feet," Rockwell said.

"No, it doesn't explain anything," Williams said. "Why take off the boots and hide them and cut off the head, and leave everything else here? It just doesn't make any sense."

"There's blood on the heel of one of them," Rockwell said.

With redoubled energy Williams and Brown continued to search the northern end of the cellar.

"What's that?" Williams asked, stopping at a large canning bucket. "Lift that up, Hughie."

Brown followed the beam of light toward the bucket and lifted the lid. "There's something in here." He pulled out a stained burlap potato sack.

Slowly, Brown opened the bag and cautiously peered inside. Closing his eyes, and turning his head in the opposite direction, Brown reached inside, and carefully lifted out the grisly contents.

Brown's hand emerged gripping tufts of snowy-white hair. A pair of eyes came next, followed by a bearded chin and finally a bloody stump.

The men recoiled in horror. Acting upon instinct, Dr. Reid lunged forward to grab the severed head before Brown had the chance to drop the repulsive contents on the floor.

Monson McDonald used his forearm to clear a patch on a workbench. Dr. Reid gently laid the severed head on the worktable. As he let go, the head rolled and rocked around, trying to balance itself. A blood-smeared face, with its white beard and moustache, stared back up at them.

The men recoiled again, repulsed by the sight.

"That's Freeman Harvey," George Spence said, "no doubt about it."

With his index finger, Dr. Reid traced the gash around the neck. The cut was neither clean nor smooth, but instead was ragged and torn, as if it had been sawed at repeatedly.

"That looks like it was hacked off with something dull," McDonald said.

"My thoughts exactly," Dr. Reid said. "Bring the light closer. We need to examine the wounds on his face. I count four of them, see? There, and there."

He rotated the head slightly. "And there, and here also." As he pointed them out, he traced the extent of each wound with his finger.

"They look like knife cuts to me," Brown said.

Two cuts slashed the left cheek. There was one under the chin, partially hidden by the beard hair, and the fourth lay along the right side of the face.

"Now, let's examine the bone here, where the head was removed. What do you notice?"

"I'd say the bone was sawed off," Williams said. "But not well. It's a snaggled mess."

Dr. Reid picked up the head and rotated it in the light. "Indeed. If you look here," he said, pointing to the flesh that hung below the stump, "there are one or two pieces of tissue and skin partly detached from the rest of the body."

McDonald said, "The bone is pretty well clear cut across."

"Yes, and is quite close to one of the bones of the spinal column. That is quite deliberate, and it would have taken some time," Dr. Reid said.

"Couldn't axe blows have done the same thing?" Brown asked.

"No, I don't think so," the doctor said. "I would expect to see some chipping of the bone with an axe. It would have shattered the bone. See here, though? The spine has definitely been cut, not split as by a blow."

He rotated the head again under the light. "What else do we notice?" he asked. Despite the grisly subject matter, he found himself enjoying the reconstruction of the crime—for crime no doubt it was, and of the bloodiest kind.

"There: stop," Williams said. "On the forehead. Looks like a bruise."

A murmur of assent rippled through the group.

Dr. Reid gently felt around the bruise. "There is no sign of a cracked skull underneath."

He placed the head back on the table. "We need to look around for any other signs that may be related to his death."

"I noticed something when we first came down here," McDonald said. "All the blood at the foot of the stairs."

Dr. Reid knelt with the lantern at the bottom of the steps. He asked some of the taller men in the back to move to the side to help the thin sliver of light from the small window get through.

"Yes, you are right," he said. "There is quite a lot of blood here."

"When I was looking for the head, I noticed droplets around in other parts, too," Brown said. "Not as much as is here, but still some."

"And, of course, the blood around the body under the potatoes," McDonald said.

As Dr. Reid swung the light around to each of the areas the men were referring to, juror John Scott, who had been pretty quiet up until this point, shouted, "Wait. What's up there? We totally missed that when we were coming down here."

He pointed to a spot on the staircase, toward the cellar door. "That looks like a hand print, or bloody finger marks smeared along the wall."

"Where?" Brown asked, squinting to see.

"A third of the way down."

"Yes," Dr. Reid said. "Those marks were definitely made with a blood-stained hand."

"Almost like he was clutching at the wall, as if he were falling and try-ing to catch his balance," Scott said.

"Well, then," the doctor said. "You gentlemen have gone above and beyond the call of your oaths as jurymen here, and I think we have found and seen all that we will. We'll leave the body for the undertaker to move upstairs, but now I will need you all to sign your testimonies."

19: Took off like a fury

While the men searched the cellar, Dennis Paul surveyed the forest around him. He made no sound as he stepped through the undergrowth of the thick woods. His moccasins left no trace. Paul cleared his mind and listened for signs of life ahead. On the reserve, he was known as the best tracker and deer hunter; and in his mind, this prey was no different.

When word had arrived at the St. Croix Reserve that the authorities were looking for two likely murderers in the woods, Paul knew they would not be able to hide from him. Blending into nature and hiding in the woods for hours were not skills these fugitives would possess.

Paul crept forward, smelling the air and scanning the sky.

A thin, barely noticeable line of smoke appeared against the dark, accumulating clouds. Silently, Paul followed the smoke. He drew near to a clearing ahead, where two men sat by a poor excuse for a fire.

Paul stealthily moved up behind the younger of the two, placing his hands firmly on his shoulders to prevent him from moving, causing the young man to shriek in surprise.

The second man jumped from his seat, and without looking back, bolted into the woods.

"He took off like a fury," Paul muttered, as he hauled the young man to his feet. He cursed himself, wishing he had brought someone else with him, so they could have captured both men at once. "You are now under arrest," Paul said, "and I'm taking you as my prisoner. You are to come with me."

He hauled the man to his feet and started to push him, steering him toward Newport Station, only a few miles ahead.

"I'm not guilty of Freeman Harvey's murder!" Jim Fisher cried, turning around to face his captor.

"Nobody said you were," Paul said. "But why would you assume I'm here for Freeman Harvey's murderers? Regardless, I'm taking you to the authorities. Move!"

~

In Windsor, Chief Samuel McDonald had received a telephone call informing him of the events in Ellershouse, and the two murderers at large
in the woods. He paced the room, thinking about his next course of action. His towering figure meant that he needed only take a few steps before reaching the end of the room, where he turned to repeat the pattern.

Knowing how thick the woods were around Ellershouse, and that
both rain and the evening were fast approaching, Chief McDonald knew
he had to act fast. He called the Windsor train station and had them get
two men ready to take him, Constable George Singer and Constable
David McLean out to Ellershouse by trolley, as no trains were imminently
departing.

At the station, the two railway men hoisted the trolley from its nearby
shed onto the railway lines and called for the three policemen to climb
on board. Chief McDonald being as big as he was, stood on one end of the
flat bed, while Constables Singer and McLean stood on the other, leaving
just enough room in the middle for the two railway men to pump vigorously up and down on the handle of the trolley.

On a regularly scheduled train, the ten-mile journey would have taken
less than 25 minutes, and would have been far less crowded, not to mention covered and warm. McDonald took out his pocket watch and calculated it would be nearly five o'clock when they arrived in Ellershouse. He
was about to ask the two railway men to pump faster and harder, but
thought better of it, lest they ask him to take a turn.

~

John stood silently, feeling the damp from the earth penetrate his shoes.
No matter what direction he looked, all he could see were trees. The sun
was setting, and whatever light it had provided was masked by thick,
dark clouds rolling in.

There was no doubt. He was lost.

He had had no idea that Nova Scotia's forests were so thick and endless.

After having parted ways with Jim Fisher, all he remembered was following the train track before cutting down a few logging tracks, praying
he was heading in the right direction for Halifax.

In the distance, further into the thick of the trees, John heard men
shouting and then a loud crashing noise as a tree, he presumed, was

felled. He decided to walk towards the noise, hoping to find any sort of road.

John pulled his overcoat tighter across his body, trying to trap in any warmth. The once-clean suit he wore underneath, and the dress shoes, had not been a wise choice for tramping through the woods in the winter. He had, however, been in worse conditions, and could survive this, too.

By the time he arrived at the origin of the commotion, only one man remained. From behind a tree, John studied him carefully.

The young man stretched his back and wiped his brow. Although John himself was freezing, the man had apparently been working up a sweat as he stood there in merely overalls and a flannel shirt.

As if preparing for the end of his shift, the man tucked his thick work gloves inside the pockets of his overalls and laid his cross-cut saw on top of the pile of logs beside him.

"Excuse me," John said, stepping from behind the tree.

Startled, the young man jumped back. "Who are you?"

"I'm just travelling through these parts toward the city but seem to have lost my way."

"I should say so," the man said. "You're dressed pretty smart for the woods."

"You like being out here in the woods?" John asked incredulously.

"It's all I know. Been chopping roads and hauling timber since I was 14 years old. Where are you trying to get to?"

"Halifax."

"Good Lord! Walking? That's going to take at least eight hours. Ten in those shoes, I bet. It's close to 30 miles away."

"Regardless, that is where I am heading."

"You are definitely on the wrong road, then," the man said. "The woods are so thick; you would really need a compass to get you there. Your best bet would be to follow that logging road over there back up and go to the Hartville train station. Then get on a train heading toward Halifax."

"This road here?" Without looking back, John followed the young man's pointed finger back up the logging road, hoping he was doing the right thing.

20: What sells papers

When the trolley carrying Chief McDonald and the others rolled into the Hartville station, one stop shy of their destination of Ellershouse, the station master called out and flagged them to stop.

"Gentlemen," he said before the trolley fully stopped, "we've sent an alert to the entire community to keep an eye out for two men who may be hiding in the woods, along the tracks, or at a logging camp."

"Good work," the chief said.

"There's more! People came forward in droves, wanting to help. So, one of our railway section men organized a group of 40 or 50 people to position themselves along the tracks and roadways. They have the whole section covered and will notify us if they see anything."

"Well done," Chief McDonald said. "Very fast and decisive work. And have we received any word, sir?"

"Indeed, which is why I flagged you down. Two men matching the descriptions of George Stanley and Jim Fisher were spotted along the line here, a little while ago. A tracker from the reserve, Dennis Paul, captured Fisher, and took him up to Newport Station."

"Fine work," the chief said. "We'll head back that way now." He wondered why no one had called out at Newport Station when they went by minutes before.

~

Once a telegram went out that the local police were on the hunt for a murderer, newspaper editor Benjamin Shaw in Halifax got to work. He knew, based on his experience reporting on other murder cases in the province, that stories like these are what sold papers.

He telephoned people at the local station in Ellershouse and discovered that the accused had been masquerading as a sales representative for Western Union. A quick telegram to the company revealed there was no George Stanley on their payroll.

Benjamin handed his nephew and young protégé, Russell Shaw, and Western Union directing manager William McKee, the train fare. He gave them a brief outline of what he had discovered. "Stay in Ellershouse a few days until we have a handle on the case," he said. "Russell, this story is going to make your career." Then he sent the two on their way.

When the train stopped in Ellershouse, Russell looked out the window, squinting up at the station name nailed to the side of the building. They had been going through the woods for so long and he had not seen a building for miles. He rubbed his eyes and confirmed they were indeed at the right station. He nudged his travelling companion to disembark.

With trepidation, Russell stepped off the train, hoping to see some sign of life. The sun was just setting, and the silence of the small village was unsettling.

Russell and McKee received directions to the Harvey homestead from the station master and walked the mile-and-a-half down Ellershouse Road to get to their destination. They peered through the windows but found no one about.

A passerby filled the two men in on the hunt for Jim Fisher, and directed them toward Fisher's home, further up the Dawson Road

"This has got to be the house," Russell said.

They pounded on the door of the run-down shack. Russell looked back over his shoulder at McKee, who nodded for him to try again.

Russell was about to raise his fist again when the door creaked open, and a haggard woman threw open the door. "What you all want? Pounding out here loud enough to wake the dead. I ain't deaf, you know."

Russell, who had just turned 19 and had barely set foot outside the city of Halifax, took an involuntary step back in fear. McKee, the older man by several decades, stepped forward. "Are you the lady of the house?"

"I don't think I've ever been called a lady before," she said, blushing, softening her demeanour.

"Why then, we presume you to be the illustrious Mrs. Fisher."

"I don't know what all them fancy words mean, but I am Mrs. Fisher."

After introducing themselves and explaining they were there from the *Halifax Herald*, the two men asked if they could come in and ask the Fishers some questions. "Have you ever had your name in print in the newspaper, ma'am?" Russell asked.

"I don't reckon so. I don't think I've actually ever read a newspaper. Couldn't read all them words. But I'd be famous if I was in a newspaper, wouldn't I be?"

"Indeed, you would," Russell said with a wink. "Let me go ask my husband. We're just about to have dinner." With that, she slammed the door. They heard her hollering David's name thunderously through the house.

As they waited, they noticed a teenage boy coming around the corner, pushing a wheelbarrow full of household items.

"You're working really hard there, son," McKee said.

The boy stared at the two men, but as he rounded the side of the house, he called back over his shoulder, "I had nothing to do with it!"

Russell and McKee looked at each other, confused. "I didn't accuse him of anything, did you?"

"Maurice!" Mary Ann yelled, as she stepped back onto the veranda. "Go get another load and bring it back before dinner."

"Are you moving house?" McKee asked.

"Well, we were supposed to have done. Freeman Harvey's place was to be ours, or that's what Stanley had told us. We moved all our stuff up there, but now they found the man murdered, I guess that means we're not going to be living there after all. Doesn't seem quite fair. What a mighty fine mess this all turned out to be."

She led them to the kitchen table, which young Maurice had already retrieved. Russell loosened his collar and took his coat off to drape it over his arm. The wood stove was chugging, and the musty smell and lack of ventilation was enough to drive anyone away.

"Care to join us?" she pointed at the chipped plates that each had a scoopful of what Russell presumed was some sort of stew, and a hunk of at least day-old bread.

"We ate before we came but thank you kindly. We'll just sit in the front room until you're finished." Russell looked down at the family's meagre meal. There was nothing like enough to share with visitors.

"Might not be a chair back for you in the front room. Maurice might not have brung them from up to Harvey's yet," Mary Ann said.

After the family had eaten, Russell and McKee joined them around the kitchen table. Russell perched on a crate, while McKee opted to stand at a slight distance.

Mary Ann gave a blow-by-blow account of the previous two weeks' activities, describing in particular George Stanley, from his habits to the company he kept while in town. David nodded along.

"He also gave me something kind of special." Mary Ann left the room and returned with a silver coin in her hand. She held it out as an offering to the two guests.

McKee took it in his hand and examined it closely under the candlelight. "That's a Spanish dollar," he said, squinting to read the inscription. "It is dated 1794."

David leaned forward, encouraging the man to strike a deal.

"I'll give you a quarter for it," McKee said. He dug in his pocket, pulled out a coin and passed it into David's waiting hand. David tucked the quarter into his pocket, smiling as if he had just gotten the better deal.

"So, the police are out looking for your boy, Jim?" Russell asked, getting around to the subject at hand.

"They should be out looking for that McCarthy fellow. He's a hardened criminal around here, and everyone knows he's a bad seed," Mary Ann said. "He's the one up to no good. He's got that look to him, and I don't trust him one little bit."

"You've had run-ins with him, then?" Russell said.

"He was here Saturday night, he was. Came right in and insisted on spending the night here with me. I tried to keep him out, I did, I refused him entry."

David shifted in his chair, the muscles tensing along his jaw.

"Oh, I eventually let him in, after he basically forced me to, and then, the next morning, he up and said that Harvey was dead."

"How did he know that?" Russell said.

"I asked him the same thing. And he said he had it in a dream."

"Police should be going after him!" David repeated.

Russell closed his notebook and asked about accommodations in the area for the night.

"Maurice can take you up to Rieck's hotel. It's the only place you can find a room," David said. "We'd have you here, but half our furniture is still up on the road there by Harvey's place."

~

By this time, the sky was completely dark, with no stars in sight. Rain or snow was coming. John hoped it was rain, as it was too mild for snow. Once again, he found himself lost amongst the trees, wandering aimlessly.

He had followed the logging road for a while, back toward the train tracks, but was spooked upon hearing noises, and thought he would be safer in the dense forest. Now, however, he was cold, hungry, tired, and lost.

Through the trees ahead, John could just make out the faint glimmer of a lamp, a beacon in the night. As he approached, he noticed several make-shift buildings, which he figured must be one of the Spence brothers' logging camps.

The camp was silent. Scanning the area, John could only see one lone man leaning against the rough log house, smoking a cigarette. The man pulled the ear lugs of his cap tighter around his face against the cold.

John took a step closer to have a better look, unaware of a large branch in his path, which snapped under his weight. It split the silent night air.

"Who's there?" the man called.

Hearing no answer, he took a cautious step toward the tree line. "Who goes there?" he called again.

His hunger overtaking him, John stepped forward from the shadows into the outer edge of the lamplight.

"Who are you?" the man, annoyed at the lack of response.

John merely stared back, not saying a word.

"You're a bit far from home. There is nothing around here for miles and miles," the man said more softly as he noticed John's muddy suit and city shoes. "No one can survive a winter in the back woods of Nova Scotia dressed like that."

Sensing he was safe, John stepped further into the light, still saying nothing, not wanting his accent to betray him.

"Come on in and have some supper with the men. Rain's a coming."

~

"We need to regroup," Chief McDonald said to the men gathered back at the Hartville station.

They had just returned from Newport Station, where they had seen Jim Fisher put on the Kentville Express train toward Windsor, accompanied by Constable McLean. The young man had put up no fuss and seemed more scared and confused than anything else.

It was now time to focus on finding George Stanley.

It was cold, dark, and the rain was starting to fall in sheets. The only thing Chief McDonald could count on was that no matter how miserable it was for them hunting the woods for the runaway murderer, it would be even worse for George Stanley, the big-city man from England.

"I want three men to come with me," he said, looking around the crowd. Those dressed in thick winter coats tucked under their overalls and wearing thick woollen caps to ward off the rain stepped forward, ready to help.

"We're going to head along the St. Croix River down to Paunke Lake, toward William Spence's lumber camp. I'm assuming you gentlemen know the way. We've received word there might have been a sighting down that way."

They nodded to the chief.

"Constable Singer, take another group up toward the little dam on the St. Croix River," he continued.

"I've already been up that way, and there was no sign of him there," a man said.

"And you are?"

"Hibbert Chapman. My sister Ida is, was, married to Freeman Harvey, so I have an interest in finding his murderer."

Chapman pulled back the flaps of his raincoat to reveal a rifle slung at his side. "Let's go find him."

Constable Singer scurried to catch up.

~

"If I knew we were going to have so much company today, I would have worn my best suit!" William Spence said to the group of men who were walking up the wooden track toward the camp.

The lead man did not laugh at this attempt at humour but stuck out his hand. "I am Chief McDonald of the Windsor Police."

William Spence stood straighter to address the man more respectfully. "What brings you back to our neck of the woods on a dark and rainy night, sir? This cannot be a courtesy call."

"Did you just imply you had others dropping by today?"

"Why, yes. We had a man here for supper with us. He left not 20 minutes ago."

"Damnation!" McDonald muttered. "What did he look like?"

"Short man dressed like a townie," Spence said, pointing toward the two officers. He quickly realized his mistake. "No offence."

"Did he have an accent?"

"Couldn't rightfully tell. He hardly said two words."

"Which way did he go?"

William Spence pointed further up the logging road toward Hartville and the train line. McDonald and his men followed in that direction, without so much as a goodbye.

21: We have a witness

On the other side of the lake, Constable George Singer and Hibbert Chapman walked along the railway tracks between Hartville and Ellershouse, stopping every few moments to listen for sounds of life in the nearby woods. Chapman stopped dead in his tracks and raised the rifle, peering through the raindrops.

"Breathe easy," Constable Singer said. "He's not in this area. But he couldn't have gone far, as he'd never survive in the woods in these conditions and with his lack of knowledge."

"I really don't think he's down by William Spence's logging camp. He wouldn't have likely known about it. He's probably over toward Robie Spence's camp. I know this area like the back of my hand. Let's turn off here, up Sawdust Road, and head down toward the river and Hartville. There's a crossroads there, and we can sit and wait for a bit, as we could get him coming or going from either direction."

When they came to the crossroads, Chapman took to one knee behind a large tree, his rifle at the ready. The rain beat down on him, and he huddled closer to the tree to try to find some protection from the incessant, near-freezing drops. "What time is it?" he asked Constable Singer.

"Half-past eight, I reckon," he said, confirming his guess by lighting a match and checking his pocket watch. "We'll give it a few more minutes, and then we'll move further down toward the lake."

The sound of a twig snapping in the forest behind them caused them both to whip their heads around. Constable Singer lowered the light from the kerosene lantern to a bare minimum. He placed it on the ground and stealthily took out the revolver he had tucked beneath his trench coat.

Chapman raised the rifle to his shoulder, steadying his gaze down the barrel, waiting for further noises to draw a bead on.

The night was dark, the forest was thick, and the rain kept pelting down. The sound could have been anything from a deer to the wind.

Snap!

Another branch broke in the woods, and the two men caught a

glimpse of a white collar through the trees.

"There: that way!" Constable Singer whispered urgently.

Sensing the movement from the road, the figure bolted through the woods, leaving a thunderous sound of breaking branches as he went.

Chapman sprang from his position and gave chase. Constable Singer increased the light from the lantern, shining it into the woods to help the pursuer.

"Stop where you are!" Chapman shouted. "Put up your hands or we'll shoot."

"Don't shoot! I've stopped." A feeble, almost resigned voice came through the rain.

Constable Singer followed the sound of voices and, as he strode toward them, exchanged his revolver for handcuffs.

When he arrived, Chapman had his rifle pressed to the man's temple.

"Please, don't shoot me," the man pleaded. "I'm not going to harm anyone."

"Enough," the constable said, signalling to Chapman to lower his weapon.

The man sighed and stuck out his hands with his wrists up, as if he had done it many times before. Constable Singer cuffed him. The prisoner kept his eyes to the ground and spoke softly.

"Let's head up toward the sawmill with him," Chapman suggested. "I work there, and there's a telephone. We can call for help."

Constable Singer half-dragged and half-pushed his captive up the road.

"Why am I being taken?" John asked softly.

Constable Singer laughed, but realized the question was serious. "Freeman Harvey has been murdered."

John gasped. "My God, it can't be that that old man has his head cut off!"

Constable Singer and Chapman glanced at each other and continued to move the prisoner, his hands cuffed behind him, along the road.

"George, you spent a lot of time at the Harvey house, I've heard," the constable said. "Had you seen anyone else around the house, or anyone suspicious?"

"Well, now that you mention it, there had been a crazy man around there."

"Do you know what his name was? Was it McCarthy, by chance?"

John abruptly stopped walking, which caused his captors to pile into him.

"Come to think of it, I think that is exactly what his name was. Mc-Carthy!"

The caravan began walking again, and as they rounded a corner, they could see the long, white sawmill up ahead.

John slowed his pace and turned again to Constable Singer. "Am I not under British laws, being a citizen from there?"

"You're in Canada now, George."

"I'm just replaying the events of the weekend in my mind," John said. "David Fisher was in the Harvey house all weekend and never left at all from Saturday morning."

He let his comment hang in the air.

"He would have had plenty of time and opportunity," Constable Singer said to Chapman. "I think it's something we need to consider."

A few minutes later the men entered the mill. Chapman led the way to room with the telephone.

While the constable called in the news, Chapman sat down across from the man he was sure had killed his brother-in-law. He glared at the small man with the odd accent. A hundred questions ran through his mind, and it took all his restraint to not reach across the table and strangle the man himself.

"You!" was all he could say.

The prisoner glanced up, making no effort to escape, let alone make eye contact with his captor.

Chapman could not hold it in any longer, and spat out, "Why did you kill old Harvey?"

"I kill Harvey? Me? No! I've never shed a drop of human blood. I wouldn't kill a hen," John said evenly. "I tell you, I'm completely inno-cent."

"Sure, you are," Chapman muttered. He stood as he heard Constable Singer hang up the phone in the other room.

The constable had caught the tail end of the conversation. "Are you saying you had nothing to do with the murder, then?" he asked as he came into the main room.

"I was just on my way out of the woods when you caught me. I was coming out to tell you what I knew about the murder," John said, gaining more confidence.

"You did know about the murder, then."

"I would say that I am guilty of part of it, but I'm certainly not guilty of it all." John looked Constable Singer in the eyes. "Old man Fisher and his son Jim—they had way more to do with it than I ever had."

"I need to warn you," the constable said, "don't talk too much right now. You'd better not tell me about it till we are back at the station."

"You see," John said, ignoring his caution, "I was talking to Old Man Harvey on Saturday morning and making plans with him, and deciding what we were going to do about the property, because he had agreed to sell it to me."

Constable Singer pulled out his notebook and started taking notes.

"I told Harvey what my plan was, to have the Fisher family move in there and take care of the place for me until my sister came over, and I came back to take proper ownership. But then, Harvey said to me not to have the Fishers go there. He said he did not mind the old man going there, but he certainly did not want the rest of the family, especially the woman, Mary Ann, and the boy, meaning Jim."

Constable Singer kept writing, knowing if he did not say anything, the man would continue to talk.

"Then, after I had that conversation with Harvey, I left him there at the house and went back up to the Fishers'. That was Saturday morning. But David and Jim were not home."

"Weren't they? Where were they?"

"I frankly don't know."

"What happened then?"

"I returned to the Harvey house and heard loud talking in the cellar, so I went and looked down there and yelled to find out who was there. David and Jim Fisher both yelled back that it was them. I knew their voices right off, anyway. I asked them what they were doing, and they replied they were getting potatoes and turnips. It was pretty dark down there, so I asked them if they didn't want me to bring down a light. They answered me right back, rather harshly, I might add, saying no, they did not want me to bring a light down there. So, I left them in the cellar, be-cause they obviously didn't need my help. I went out to feed the hens."

"So, you left them in the cellar? Were you gone long?"

"No, I was out just a short time, and came into the house, and I saw Jim washing blood off his hands in the sink, asking his father for some hot water and soap."

Constable Singer turned to Chapman. "Have your lumber mill people prepare a cart and team of horses for us, please. We're going to drive Mr. Stanley here into Windsor, but we're also going to make a stop along the way to pick up Mr. Fisher. We're going to need to speak to him as well."

~

Constable Singer climbed the rickety steps to the shack's front porch and carefully knocked on the Fishers' door, lest it come off its hinges.

"Open up! Police!" he called through a crack in the window.

Mary Ann Fisher scuttled to the door. Her hair was falling from her bun, and she pulled the two cardigans she was wearing closer to her body to block out the cold from the winter's rain.

"What do you want?" she asked, her lip curled back like a guard dog protecting her property. "Why we so pop'lar tonight?"

"We're looking for a Mr. David Fisher."

"What do you want with him? You've already taken my boy."

"I'm right here," David said, appearing over her shoulder.

"You are under suspicion of the murder of Freeman Harvey and need to come with us to Windsor."

"What are you talking about?" Mary Ann cried.

"We have a witness who says you were alone most of the weekend at the Harvey house, giving you opportunity to have committed the murder."

"Who's your witness?" Mary Ann asked. She stepped around the constable, trying to look into the carriage stopped in front of the house, which was being guarded by one of the drivers. "Who is in there?"

She caught a glimpse of movement and squinted her eyes to have a better look. She took a few steps closer, while trying to stay under the covered porch. "That's George Stanley in there. Is he the one who is accusing my husband?"

"He's one to talk," David said, coming out to join his wife. "He may have been in the habit of staying here at night, but he was all kinds of other places during the day. And his morals are questionable, for all the time he spent reading the Bible in the house."

Constable Singer relaxed his pose, knowing he was about to get an earful.

"Like, how he was here Friday with a bottle of liquor at eight in the morning. Eight, I say!" Mary Ann said.

"Then, that night, he borrowed my jackknife, saying he had a job to do, and didn't come back until Saturday morning," David said.

"That is true, constable," said Mary Ann.

"I am entirely innocent of anything you are accusing me of, especially murder. Edgar McCarthy was the first man who told me about old man Harvey, telling me there was a body in the cellar."

"That damned Edgar McCarthy," Mary Ann spat. "He's bad company.

Very bad news."

"All right, then," the constable said. "I'm sure you all have things to say, and you'll have the chance to say them. But for the meantime, I'm taking you into Windsor now, Mr. Fisher."

"You know that man's a criminal, that McCarthy. Not me!" David protested.

"You wouldn't be taking my husband away if you knew what that man McCarthy told me."

Seeing the constable had turned his attention back to her, Mary Ann continued, "On Saturday night, he gone and told me that he'd had a dream that Old Man Harvey was dead. Doesn't that say something? He knewed what was in the cellar before anyone went down there. He's the one you should be hauling in."

"Thank you, ma'am, we'll be sure to have a word," Constable Singer said. He pulled a pair of heavy steel handcuffs from his trench coat pocket.

The sight of them caused Mary Ann to moan slightly. "Listen! McCarthy also said to me that it was him who was in charge of the Harvey place because Harvey was in the cellar. I know that to be true."

"As I said, ma'am, you will have a chance to tell us everything you know. In the meantime, we need to hear everything your husband knows about this matter, and we need him at the station in Windsor. Good evening, ma'am."

Constable Singer led David, in manacles, to the cart. He bent down and manacled the two prisoners together, then climbed into the cart himself and told the driver it was time to take these men to their fate.

~

When the train pulled into the Windsor station, Chief McDonald used the cuff of his coat to wipe away the condensation that had accumulated on the window. With four bodies in the small compartment, the air had grown stale and had warmed the room considerably.

He looked out the window through the peephole he had created. It was well past ten o'clock, and it was still raining heavily. It had been a rough day and night, and he was exhausted.

He looked at the two men sitting across from him. One in his fifties, with long greying hair, and a vacant look on his face. He wondered how much David Fisher understood of what was happening to him, and to his son, Jim, for that matter, who had been brought in earlier that afternoon.

The other man, maybe not quite 40, looked rough. Although he was small, Chief McDonald saw a feistiness to him, evidenced by the scars above his eyes, along his wrists, and the missing back teeth. He had a resigned look on his face that Chief McDonald recognized in those who had been through the legal system before.

The chief put his hand into the breast pocket of his uniform and felt to make sure the money was still there. Before he had put his two prisoners onto the train, he patted them down, looking for any weapons or incriminating evidence. He had found a white handkerchief on David that appeared to have bloodstains on it. David claimed to know nothing about it. He had also taken a jack knife from David's coat pocket.

But his most interesting find was a lot of cash. David Fisher had a mere 25 cents to his name, while George Stanley carried $53, more than enough to escape and make a life of his own somewhere else.

"Are we ready, boys?" he asked. He stood and nudged Constable Singer to take the lead.

The two prisoners were manacled together again, sandwiched between the officers, who conveyed them to the awaiting carriage that would take them up the two blocks to the courthouse building, and to the jail in its basement.

22: Only half the teeth remained

February 6

William Medford Christie, known as Medford by all in the town of Windsor, where he had practised law for most of his career, stood in front of the Harvey house. Always the perfect gentlemen, Christie was dressed smartly in his suit, which he sheltered from the persistent rain under an expensive umbrella.

Despite the miserable weather, Christie tingled with anticipation. This was a good case, even if the circumstances were barbaric. This is exactly why he had become a barrister, and more recently the county's crown prosecutor. He loved the hunt, and the thrill of putting all the pieces together.

He ran his hand over his slicked-back hair, and then across his face, smoothing down his bushy white moustache. His facial hair had gone completely white, utterly mismatched to his thick mane of dark hair above, making him look much older than his 55 years.

Christie's gaze roved around the property, taking in the meagre barn, the small story-and-a-half home, and the few animals in the back field. He exhaled slowly, thinking. Clearly Harvey had not been well off, but he was not as poor as some of the others in the neighbourhood.

He walked up to the front door and, before entering, tapped his golden ring on the door frame three times for good luck, a ritual he had adopted when he became a member of the Freemason society a few decades earlier. He rarely took the ring off, and to him it was almost as important as the wedding band on his other hand.

Christie walked into the house and met an overpowering aroma of alcohol. Stepping in further, he found the source strewn about the kitchen and parlour. Over a dozen whisky flasks and ale bottles lay around the rooms, signs of a drunken orgy of some sort.

He called out to the people he could hear moving about. A man in his seventies came in from the porch and stuck out his hand.

"Levi Brown, and this here is my son, William." Levi pointed to a teenage boy coming into the kitchen behind him. "Besides being the local undertaker, I also have the great honour of being, or I guess having been, Freeman Harvey's nearest neighbour. We live down there, handy the road to Halifax."

Christie tried the handshake marking his Masonic brotherhood, but got no response, so continued. "Medford Christie. Crown prosecutor for Hants County. I am here to survey the scene, in preparation for the case. What brings you here, Mr. Brown?"

"William and I are here to bring the body up to the kitchen and lay it out on the day bed to get it ready for the funeral. We're going to build the coffin after that—I'm the village carpenter. But I guess we won't need to make it as long, maybe a head shorter!"

Levi laughed at his own joke, but quickly covered his mouth, realizing his offence. "I meant no disrespect, sir," he mumbled, looking at his feet.

"Fill me in on the details, my fine fellow," Christie said, patting him on the shoulder. "Did I hear the surveyor was here last night?"

"Yes, sir. He came up last night when I was here. He drew the maps of the whole property and the house. I brought Ida back from Windsor with me, and he was here drawing when we got here. Ida checked it over and thought he done a good job."

"Ida? Meaning Mrs. Harvey?"

"That's right, I brung her here last night. She was in quite the state of shock, let me tell you."

"Why don't you give me the lay of the land, and then show me what you found in the cellar?"

Levi led the way through the kitchen into the porch, and slowly opened the cellar door. "I noticed this last night when I came down to examine the body. Starting on the back of the porch door here, leading into the kitchen, there is a bit of blood there, and then here on the threshold of the door."

He pointed to the floorboards. Then, picking up the lantern in the porch, he went a third of the way downstairs, before stopping and pointing again. "If you look here, you can see the mark of a man's hand, and it looks like it was made with the right hand. See, four fingers and a thumb."

Christie grunted an agreement.

"From the opening of the cellar door up there, you can see what looks like spots of blood on the steps all the way down."

The two men descended the stairs, and Levi swung his lantern around the dim space. Christie covered his mouth and nose with his handkerchief to mask the cellar's damp, musty odour.

"There is a pool of blood right here at the bottom of the steps."

"Under here?" Christie moved forward and lifted what looked like the cover of a meat dish to reveal a pile of ashes underneath. He glanced up at Levi with a confused look on his face.

"These ashes must have been placed to try to soak up some of the blood and covered so no one would track it through the house. But you get the idea."

Christie followed along as Levi continued the tour of the basement.

"Over here, there is a half bushel basket, and if you look at it closely, you can see the marks of a man's fingers in blood. As if someone was carrying it with bloody fingerprints."

Christie nodded again. The man was thorough. He had to give him that.

"Now, sir, I would advise you examine the potatoes."

Potatoes were scattered everywhere, lying where they had been tossed during the unearthing of the body, as well as those the jury members had stacked in crates. Levi knelt, picked one up, and showed it to Christie.

"There's even blood on a lot of these potatoes."

When Levi swung the lantern around, Christie sucked in air between his teeth. A rough canvas tarpaulin covered the body, so he could only see its faint outline. He said a silent prayer of thanks for that blessing, as he had not quite been as prepared as he had thought he would be.

"The head is there, under that bucket on the bench."

Christie was not sure how Levi could be so cavalier about the whole situation, but assumed that, as the village undertaker, he would have seen more than his fair share of death. Christie was not sure if he had ever seen a dead body before. He talked the talk of being big and brave, but when it came down to it, he did not think he would ever be fully ready, or for the nightmares that would probably haunt him afterwards. He said another word of prayer, thanking the Good Lord, for allowing him to live in a place where heinous murders like this were rare, indeed.

"So, my son William and I are going to remove the body from here, take it up to the kitchen, lay it out, wash it, and prepare it for burial. Might be a good time for you to go check the barn and the fields."

"Are you trying to get me out of the way?" Christie said with a laugh.

"Yup." Levi smiled thinly. "It will simply be easier for William and me to prepare this particular body without an audience, even an audience of one. Once he's prepared and, in his casket, it will be less..." he paused for a moment, searching for the correct word, "less upsetting for those view-ing the remains of Freeman Harvey."

~

"Mr. Christie! Mr. Christie!" William called out to the back fields toward the prosecutor, who was sheltering in the doorway of the barn. "We've found something, Come quickly!"

Christie hurried through the raindrops to join the young man at the back door. "What is it? What have you found?"

"Well, when Pa was just about ready to start washing up the body, he asked me to go and fetch some boards, and when I came back with some I seen in the basement, he said they were too long, and to go and fetch him a saw. So, I poked around in the porch here, and come see what I found."

He led Christie into the kitchen, where a dull and broken old instru-ment lay on the table. Upon first glance, it looked like an ordinary hand saw, but only half the teeth remained.

Christie bent over, taking a pair of spectacles from his breast pocket to examine it more closely. "I'm seeing smear marks across the blade here, like something was wiped away."

"But look at the handle," Levi said, pointing to a red stain. "It looks fresh."

"That definitely looks like blood. We're going to have to send it to my office and have it more thoroughly examined though, to be sure. Where did you find it?"

"I seen it over there, behind the porch door, in the corner," William said.

"Why wasn't it discovered during the inquest yesterday?"

"I don't know, sir, but, you see, if you open the door from the kitchen into the porch, and then open the cellar door, it kind of makes a hidey-hole or a corner back there that could be missed. I just happened to have closed the doors behind me and seen it there."

William took Christie to the porch to show him the pool of blood on the floor where he found the saw, tucked behind the meat barrel in the corner. "Do you know if this is Harvey's saw, or if the murderer would have brought it in?"

"No, it's definitely Harvey's," Levi said. "I seen him use it to trim apple trees before."

Christie rested his index fingers on his lips, sighed, taking it all in. He tried to piece together the facts.

"I'm just about to warsh the body," Levi said. He paused, thinking, "I suppose, Mr. Christie, as prosecutor, if you are up for it, you can come and examine it."

Christie followed the two men into the kitchen and veered toward the pile of clothes on the table.

"Yup," Levi said, anticipating his question. "Those are Harvey's clothes I just took off him. Joseph Fisher was here the day the body was discovered and said them were the same clothes Mr. Harvey was wearing on Friday night when he was here visiting."

Christie took note. Then, pulling the spectacles from his breast pocket, he leaned forward to have a closer look. "Undoubtedly, these are blood stains on his clothes."

"I believe you are correct, Mr. Christie," Levi said.

Levi then turned toward Freeman Harvey's body, which was laid out on a few long planks on the kitchen day bed, covered in a white bed sheet. "I'm going to pull back the cloth so we can examine the neck stump."

Christie nodded, thankful to Levi for being so considerate with his warning. He clenched his jaw, closed his eyes, and braced himself when Levi folded back the blanket, revealing the body from the neck to the waist. He took a deep breath and slowly opened his eyes, trying to look at the situation from a purely professional point of view.

"If you look closely here at the neck stump," Levi said, "the bones are cut through, and are not separated at the joints."

Christie nodded, seeing the jagged bone fragments.

"The only thing I found on the body was this small red spot on the left arm. I couldn't find anything anywhere else."

"That's important," Christie agreed.

Levi replaced the sheet over the body. He then drew back a different corner, beneath which he had placed the severed head of Freeman Harvey. He motioned to Christie to draw closer. "There's a cut here on the face below the temple, see there? And here's a cut an inch-and-a-half long running back of the cheek—both here on the right side of the face."

He rotated the head on the board. "And look here now, sir. There's another cut here on the left, and if you look just below the ear here, there is a hole. I could actually plunge my finger in it, it's that big."

Levi had his finger poised and ready to demonstrate, but Christie shook his head, indicating that he believed him.

Levi then tipped the head back, revealing a vertical cut, three or four inches long, running from the chin down the neck. Where this cut stopped, the head had been severed.

"I've seen enough, thank you, Mr. Brown," Christie said as Levi recovered Harvey's head with the sheet. Christie flopped down on a chair, rested his elbows on the kitchen table, and cradled his head in his hands. How did any of this make any sense? Why would someone defile a body like this? It was the ultimate act of disrespect.

If George Stanley was their murderer, then what was the motive? The pieces of the puzzle were floating around in his head, and he was trying to make sense of everything he had been told and witnessed.

Did Stanley pretend to buy Freeman Harvey's farm and stock, and lead the Fishers to believe he was placing them in charge? Was he trying to sell the contents of the house for cash? Apparently, he had an extremely large sum on him at his arrest. Did he need Harvey out of the way? Or was it that bad seed, McCarthy, who was seen at the place over the weekend and apparently had knowledge of the murder before it came to light?

Whoever was guilty seemed to have lured Harvey toward the cellar door, maybe struck him in the head with a heavy piece of wood to weaken him, and then slashed his neck.

However, everything Christie had heard about Harvey told him that, although he was advanced in years and stone deaf, he was nevertheless sturdy and plucky. Surely, he would have not given up without a fight. Christie's thoughts turned to those marks on Harvey's face: were they a sign of an intense struggle for his life?

Whether there had been one assailant or two, Harvey must have been forced down the stairs, where he grasped at the walls until he was beaten down, leaving blood stains to mark the awful descent.

At the bottom, when was he overpowered? Immediately? Was he unconscious when his body arrived in the cellar, if he was not yet dead? The pool of blood at the foot of the stairs showed where the head was probably severed, and where the old man had drawn his last breath.

Christie shook his own head to clear it. There were more questions than answers. He stood up, deciding at last, on his course of action. He would need to get back to town and speak with the constables and see what they had gleamed from the Fishers and Stanley before Thursday's inquest.

"Thank you for that most..." lost for words, Christie paused, "enlightening experience." He gathered up his belongings, took the saw, which Levi had carefully wrapped in newspaper, and headed to his carriage to continue the investigation back in Windsor.

23: Cain was our first

February 7

James Spence sat in a crowded pew at the Saint Louise Union Church in Ellershouse. The church was packed. Normally, he would hate being in such a confined space, but today he did not mind it. The woodstove off to the side of the sanctuary could only do so much to combat the well-be-low-freezing temperatures outside.

He had tried to get to the church early to secure a good seat, but it seemed that everyone else had had the same idea. As each new person arrived, he had had to slide toward the centre of the pew, and now he was trapped.

He glanced around the sanctuary, from the stained-glass windows on each side, to the vaulted timber arches that went up and across the ceiling. Looking up at them, he was reminded of the ribs of a boat or a whale.

James craned his neck around to see if the stories he had heard were true. The church had been built by Mr. Ellershausen, for whom the village was named. The man had made a fortune in the lumber business after immigrating from Germany.

On the left-hand side at the front of the church, there was a private door, to be used exclusively by the Ellershausen family. Stories abounded about the family striding through the door and sweeping majestically across the front of the church to their special pew at the last moment.

But that was years ago, before the family had gone bankrupt, sold everything, and left town.

James settled back into the pew and thought about the man he was here today to remember. *Poor Freeman Harvey. What exactly had happened to him less than a week ago?*

Part of him still felt bitter, for all he had personally lost. He had had to return all the goods and chattel he had purchased off George Stanley to the Harvey family. He understood, but he was still out a great deal of money.

James stood with the rest of the congregation as the Reverend climbed the stairs to the small altar at the front of the sanctuary.

"Cain was our first murderer. From Genesis 4 we hear these words: If you do not do well, sin is crouching at the door; and its desire is for you, but you must master it. Cain told Abel his brother. And it came about when they were in the field, that Cain rose up against Abel, his brother, and killed him."

The Reverend continued his sermon about the evils and crime of murder before ending with a prayer. "Blessed are the dead who die in the Lord. Blessed indeed, says the Spirit 'that they may rest from their labours, for their deeds follow them.'"

When the Reverend had pronounced the benediction, James, with the rest of the congregation, followed Freeman Harvey's earthly remains outside. They walked solemnly toward the cemetery across the street, for the final act of interment, and their chance to say their condolences to the family.

Laura Churchill Duke

Part 2: The Trials

Crown Prosecutor Medford Christie
courtesy of Welsford Lodge No. 26, Windsor, NS

24: A midnight tea

February 8

It was early on Thursday morning, and Chief McDonald was still shaking off the cobwebs. He had already been up for hours. He had been at the Windsor jailhouse with Constable Singer to meet the jailer before the sun rose.

It was not only McDonald who was sleepy. Smith had to get the prisoners ready for the day's events. He rattled his keys against the cell bars to awaken the three men inside.

When David and John were ushered to their cell, they were surprised to find Jim, who had been captured earlier, asleep on the wooden bench. With the bodies of three men inside for several days, the air was stale, and the smell of body odour was rank.

"Rise and shine, gentlemen!" Chief McDonald cried, gesturing for David, Jim and John to stand. He manacled each man to the next and led them down the hallway.

Three men of the law escorted the prisoners up the stairs to the road, toward the carriage waiting to take them to catch the early train to Ellershouse. Their chains rattled as they shuffled along in silent synchronicity.

Once the prisoners were on board the train, sitting in their own compartment, their shoulders relaxed as they watched the scenes pass by through the window.

When they arrived in Ellershouse, Chief McDonald could hear noise from the platform. With the early morning sun now fully in the sky, he had a better view.

He saw crowds of people on the platform and the nearby road. They were shouting and hollering up at the train, hurling curses at the accused murderers they knew were on board.

Chief McDonald took a deep breath. Constable Singer slid open the train's compartment door and led the accused along the narrow hallway and down the stairs toward the hungry lions who waited.

"Murderer! Murderer!" the shouts and accusations were loud and clear.

"Send that Irish Paddy back where he belongs!"

John kept his head low, looking only at David's feet in front of him to guide his way.

"Let's lynch him! Push him in front of the train!" others shouted.

John glanced up at the angry faces before him, villagers he now recognized and knew after only a few short weeks in the community. Some people in town had recognized his accent and started spreading tales that he was not from England, as he had claimed, but from Ireland.

It was just the excuse people needed to bring forth the anti-Irish sentiment that had long simmered beneath the surface.

Constable Singer cleared a path with his baton and tried to walk swiftly into the station, the men trailing behind him.

"I'm a Freemason," cut one voice above the rest, "and for just ten cents I would hang all them Irish papists from here to New York."

John flinched but kept following, as his shackles gave him no choice.

Since the 1820s, as the number of Irish landing on North American shores increased by the millions, so did the hatred toward them. Not only were the Irish threatening to take away jobs; many, if not most, were dreaded Catholics in a largely-Protestant land.

Many still believed the Irish were poor, uneducated beggars who would place a strain on the system, commit crimes, and fill Canadian prisons.

The fact that John was indeed an Irish Catholic and an accused murderer further fuelled their fire.

Once through the angry mob, the group of men arrived safely at the Ellershouse hall. What should have been less than a five-minute walk had taken three times as long. They were grateful to Crown Prosecutor Medford Christie, who had cleared a path through the crowd toward the hall and then led them up the few steps to the front door and inside the building.

Christie then turned to address the men. "I'm going to give you the overview of what will be happening today," he said, staring intently at David, Jim and John.

The room was long, open, and narrow. At the far end of it, facing the main entrance, was an elevated platform with a long table. Christie pointed to where Coroner Reid would sit as he presided over the inquest that morning. To the left was a chair for the testifying witness. There was a second table on the floor in front of the platform, facing Dr. Reid, for the attorneys. Rows and rows of chairs were set up behind this, where shortly the crowds now out front would sit to witness the proceedings.

Off to the side, in the wings of the elevated stage, sat twelve chairs for the jury members. who had examined the body with Dr. Reid on Monday.

"Now, gentlemen, do you have any questions?" Christie asked.

The men stared wide-eyed ahead but shook their heads, fear rising in every inch of their bodies.

"I understand that you have declined to take the stand this morning," Christie said.

"That's right, sir," John said, his head downcast.

"That is your right. I shall not press you further."

John's gaze lifted and locked with Christie's. "I am completely innocent, you know. This trouble was all brought upon me, and the authorities have been unnecessarily harsh."

"We will let the jury decide that. Do you have any further questions, Mr. Stanley?"

"That's not my name," he said almost inaudibly.

"What? What did you say?" Christie put his hands down on the table and leaned closer to John.

"George Stanley isn't my real name."

"Figures!" Exasperated, Christie threw up his hands in despair. "Then what, pray tell, is your real name?"

John thought for a moment. It had been so long since he had uttered the words to anyone. Maybe since childhood. Giving that up would be like giving up the only piece of him he truly had left.

"Well?"

"William." A picture of his older brother floated to his mind. Where was William these days, and had he managed to stay out of trouble, unlike himself?

"William what?" Chief McDonald prodded.

"William Kavanagh."

"Lord have mercy on us!" Christie said.

He tapped his ring three times on the table for strength, and then shouted, "Let the crowds in and let us proceed. It's near enough to 8 o'clock."

~

"I now call this inquest to order," Dr. Reid said from the table at the front of the room. As he stood to make his opening remarks, a hush fell over the assembled onlookers.

115

Villagers from the nearby towns had crowded in, sometimes two per seat, trying to catch a glimpse of the three men, including two of their neighbours, accused of murdering Freeman Harvey.

Few had turned out to support Ida Harvey, who was sitting in the front row, dressed in her mourning black, with her head bowed. Ida was new to the community, having married Freeman Harvey only three years earlier. As she lived in Windsor, close to the cotton mill where she worked, and only came home on alternate weekends, she had had little chance to make friends in the village. Levi Brown sat with her, not only as her closest neighbour, but as her closest friend.

Despite it being well below the freezing mark outside, the room was starting to heat up with all the bodies pressed together in the small space. Outside, a skiff of snow was falling, the first snow since the turn of the new year.

Russell Shaw brushed the snow off his hat, careful to not let the melting drops fall on his reporter's notepad. He shifted his weight on the hard wooden chair, aware of the loud creaking noise it made each time he moved. This would be the first major court case he was to sit through, although he was told many times it was an inquest. Not a court case.

Russell scanned the room, wondering what had brought so many people out on this cold morning. Surely, all these people were not here to pay their respects to Harvey. It was more likely a morbid curiosity.

Eventually, he locked eyes with Dr. Reid at the front of the room. The man looked nervous, as if, like Russell, the doctor was feeling his way in a new position.

As Dr. Reid opened the inquest, Russell stretched his fingers and started recording the session in shorthand.

"On Monday, February six, in the year nineteen hundred and six of our Lord, the body of Freeman Harvey of Dawson Road, Ellershouse, was found decapitated in the basement of his own home. After which, a jury was quickly assembled, who searched the house and examined the body. At that time, we gathered much information, and today, we will continue by taking further evidence."

It will be an interesting morning, Russell thought as he heard many in the crowd react to hearing the gruesome details for the first time.

"Three men were arrested in connection with the murder of Freeman Harvey," Dr. Reid continued. "We have before us David Fisher, Jim Fisher, and—"

A few boos rose as villagers condemned and shamed their neighbours, men they had known all their lives.

"—And Mr. George Stanley. However, we have recently discovered his real name is in fact, William Kavanagh."

A murmur ripped through the crowd.

"I always knew there was something suspicious about him."

"The Irish are not to be trusted."

"He has the look of a hardened criminal. I knew it all along."

"I never trusted him. Not from the moment I first seen him."

"I would like to remind everyone that we are not here to determine either the guilt or innocence of these men. This is an inquest, and not a trial. We are here instead to determine if there is evidence that foul play was indeed committed, and if there is enough evidence to proceed with the charges," Dr. Reid said.

"He could have hardly cut his own head off now, could he?" a voice shouted from the back. A few of the men chortled.

Dr. Reid nodded at the Crown prosecutor, signalling he could start the procedure.

"Good morning ladies and gentlemen," he said turning to face the crowd. "My name is Medford Christie, King's Counsel, and I have come in from Windsor this morning to examine the witnesses."

Christie pulled at the lapels of his black robe and rocked from heel to toe, looking at the crowd. He tugged at the lapels a few more times, trying to circulate the air around the three-piece suit he wore beneath the gown. He remembered how his mother and grandmother had told stories about swaying while wearing their hoop skirts, to keep the air moving to cool them down. He tried that now but realized he had not said anything in a few seconds, concentrating too much on his own comfort.

"Ahem." He cleared his throat and called his first witness, Edgar McCarthy, to the stand.

McCarthy swaggered to the front of the room, knowing all eyes were upon him and that he had a reputation to uphold. He sat in the witness chair, leaned back, crossed his ankles, and folded his arms across his chest.

He introduced himself as a 30-year-old labourer of Three Mile Plains who had known Freeman Harvey for the past five years. He told the story of how he had only met George Stanley this past Sunday morning at the Harvey place, when he had stopped in to see about getting his wagon fixed.

Russell closed his eyes. It was unbelievable how much had happened in just four days.

The reporter took copious notes, trying to capture McCarthy's telling of the weekend's details from the coming and goings of the neighbours, to the fastening of the cellar door, to the trips to Ellershouse for alcohol. He included every detail: how Stanley refused to let them use the back door, saying to only use the front, and how McCarthy had assumed the man had bought the place from Harvey.

He ended with describing how they found the body in the cellar.

"I ran back and rallied the rest of the men to see what was going on. By the look of the potatoes, I thought someone was killed and buried under them, but I didn't stay long. Bates went in and pulled the potatoes away. All we could see was the red flesh where the head of a man should be, and then Jack Bates said, 'That's Freeman Harvey!'"

Russell shuddered at the thought. He could not even imagine such a sight.

From how McCarthy was describing George Stanley's behaviour that weekend, it seemed that there would be some doubt as to who really owned Freeman Harvey's possessions.

"Stanley and I had just had an argument, when a neighbour came along," McCarthy continued. "I asked him if I oughta take all the stuff Stanley was selling. The man advised me to take nothing, as he thought there might be trouble. I then asked him if he would make inquiries around the village or up to town about Freeman Harvey. Something just wasn't settin' right with me. Stanley was standing right there watching us talk but was too far to hear nothing. I went back toward the house, and that was the last I seen of George Stanley."

When it came time to ask about McCarthy's whereabouts at the time of the murder, he said he had been with George Spence the whole time.

Russell could hear the whispered comments in the room. Some said McCarthy couldn't have been involved in the murder, while others called out for his arrest. McCarthy had left for thirty minutes, presumably to go up to Ellershouse to get more beer, but it still would have given him ample time to commit a murder.

"Did you get home?"

"No, I broke the shaft on my wagon," McCarthy said. He explained how he ended up at the Fishers' house and gave a box of eggs to Mrs. Fisher who cooked them for them.

"So, it was a midnight tea," Christie said.

"I guess you could call it that."

A few people in the crowd chuckled, while a few women shook their heads in judgment of the thought of cooking a strange man breakfast at midnight, with her husband and sons gone from the house.

Sensing the feeling in the room, McCarthy qualified his statement. "We just sat there and talked by the stove till morning. I was sober."

The next part of McCarthy's testimony only ended up casting more suspicion on the man himself, Russell thought. He never asked where Harvey was, claiming it was because he was sure that the old man had gone to Windsor to live with his wife.

"Did you dream Harvey was dead, as another witness claimed you did?" Christie asked.

Christie caught Mary Ann Fisher's eye, sitting behind the barrier directly behind her son and husband. She glared right back at him, not blinking. Christie felt a cold shiver run down his spine and quickly turned away.

"No, sir. How could that be possible when I was not asleep? I was up all Saturday night with Mrs. Fisher, and then all night with George and David and the rest of the men."

"And did you start trading on Sunday?" Christie said.

"No, I never trade on a Sunday!"

The crowd nodded their approval. At least he seemed to follow one Biblical teaching, if nothing else.

McCarthy talked about the various trades, and money passing hands between himself and George Stanley, and ended with an explanation of them taking the hens to his house at four o'clock on Monday morning.

"Is that about the time hen-houses are generally robbed?" Christie eyed him suspiciously, knowing the man's reputation in the community.

McCarthy leaned forward defensively in his chair, placing his forearms on his legs as he spoke slowly and clearly. "I did not rob those hens." He leaned back and continued. "I bought them at fifty cents a pair and the rooster for a quarter."

"Do you remember meeting a man on the way home and saying to him that there was a dead man in the cellar?"

"No! I met no one, so far as I know, and I said nothing to nobody about any suspicion."

"Would you be surprised if I produced a witness to say that you had done this?" Christie leaned in and stared McCarthy down to ascertain if he was lying.

"Well, yes, I would be. Though, before we drew the lock, I said that there might be a dead man in the cellar."

Christie then turned toward the twelve jurymen sitting in two rows of chairs to the side. "Does anyone have any questions for the witness?"

One juror in the back row put up his hand, and when acknowledged, stood to ask his question. "Is it true, that before he left, Stanley threatened to brain you?"

"Yup! Just before he left, he grabbed a stake and threatened to hit me in the head with it."

"And one more question, please," the juror continued. "Who suggested that you search the cellar?"

"It wasn't me. It was Bates."

After a pause, the doctor said, "As there are no further questions, you may return to your seat."

McCarthy wasted no time getting up. This time there was a lot less swagger to his step.

Next to the witness stand was Councilman James Spence, who recounted the trading that happened between him and the accused, and that he had heard a rumour of Freeman Harvey wanting to sell his property.

"I was told a lawyer named Courtney in Halifax was looking after Harvey's business interests."

Christie tapped his fingers to his lips and strode back and forth before the crowd. "I know a Courtney in Halifax, but he is not a lawyer. You took it all for gospel?"

"Yes." James lowered his head in shame. "Smarter men than I have been taken in."

James Spence's son, Harold, was the next to take the stand. He shared the story of finding his father's fur coat, and a bag with two revolvers in it, beneath some hay in the back of the barn. Then Levi Brown, Freeman Harvey's neighbour, described finding the bloody saw behind the locked door at the top of the cellar stairway.

Christie returned to his table and pulled a rusty saw from a box. "Is this the saw you found?"

There was an audible gasp in the room as the community saw the rusty, bloodstained tool.

"Yes, it's the same one, but it had a lot more blood on it then than it does now," Levi said.

"And you believe that this saw was used to decapitate the head of Freeman Harvey?"

Levi had to take his time answering, as the loud groans coming from the room would have drowned him out. The women buried their heads in their husbands' shoulders, only sneaking quick peeks so they could at least say they had seen the awful weapon.

"Yes," Levi said when the room quietened again.

"And what were the conditions that led you to believe this?"

"I examined the head thoroughly to prepare it for burial, and it definitely had the appearance of being cut with a saw, the bones being cut through and not separate at the joints. The head was cut with a knife on both sides, and the face was cut with something like a small-bladed knife. The wound on the throat, just under the chin, was larger than the other cuts. The only wound on the body was across the left arm."

Some spectators shifted uncomfortably in their seats. Others leaned forward, taking in every word, in hopes that someone at home would ask them to repeat it.

Following a short recess, partly so the crowd could digest what it had heard, and settle down once again, Dr. Reid called Jim Fisher to be examined. Knowing he was next on the docket, few strayed from their seats during the break, fearing they may permanently lose their places.

To get Jim to the witness chair, as he, David and John were still manacled together, the three men had to walk together from their table to the witness chair. Each step created a rattling noise that echoed in the small room. Men in the front stood to get a better look at the spectacle, causing those at the back to stand on chairs, just to get this once-in-a-lifetime chance to see accused murderers.

Once Chief McDonald had separated the prisoners, David and John returned to the table, while Jim was sworn in.

Jim answered basic questions about how he had met Stanley, was offered a job by him and ultimately asked to move into the Harvey house to look after it.

"What do you know about Freeman Harvey selling his place?"

"Old Mr. Harvey had been talking about selling off the place, and then my father came and said that George had bought the whole place and had even seen him pay for it. Then George said that a man had come from Halifax, and that that man and Harvey had gone away to see about the house business."

"Where was George Stanley on Friday night?"

"He often stayed at our house, but on Friday night he was not there with us."

"And then," Christie said, "you were drinking at Freeman Harvey's house all Sunday night until Monday morning?"

"No, sir. There was no drinking Sunday night. We began that on Monday at 12 o'clock midnight. We got into the liquor as soon as the clock struck twelve."

All the talk of liquor was making many in the crowd uncomfortable. The Temperance Alliance was still strong in Hants County, and some of the members silently noted how much work they still had to do for the cause in the areas outside Windsor.

"And can you please share with the jury the conversation you heard Mr. Edgar McCarthy having with a neighbour on Monday morning when you were returning from dropping off the hens?"

"As we were coming back, McCarthy shouted over to this man, saying 'Freeman Harvey's dead in the cellar with his head cut off!'"

In the gallery, McCarthy tried to stand to shout an argument, but a rough hand beside him pulled him back down. All eyes turned to him, confirming the reputation that he had worked so hard to earn.

"Quiet! Quiet!" Dr. Reid shouted above the rattle of the angry crowd. "Proceed, Mr. Crown Attorney."

"And how did you come to leave with Mr. Kavanagh on Monday morning?"

"Who?" Jim asked, looking around.

"Mr. Stanley."

"Oh, right. Well, on Monday morning, he up and said to me that he wanted me to clear out with him to some big city and that he'd give me $25 to go with him. But I never did get the money."

"When did you find out that Freeman Harvey was dead?"

"The first I knew about the dead body in the cellar was when McCarthy told me that there was a man in the cellar with his head cut off. When I went off with Stanley, I did not know Harvey was dead except what McCarthy told me. Stanley never mentioned it."

"That's an outrage!" McCarthy shouted from his seat. Christie turned to look at him, giving him a long, dark stare that silenced the man.

Jim looked down at Stanley and continued. "That morning, too, Edgar McCarthy told me that he was going to send policemen after us for the murder of Freeman Harvey and me for my woman-kind business."

"What is this woman-kind business you refer to?"

"On account of me having three wives."

At that, several people snickered, while others gasped at the audacity. Russell looked around at the crowd. He suspected that most people had never heard of so many loose morals in one sitting—from the drinking, to lying and fighting, and now polygamy and murder. They should try coming to Halifax!

"Is that when you decided to leave with him?"

"Yes, I was really scared about being arrested. Stanley and I first hid in the barn for a bit. I was in the hay mow and Stanley was on the floor of the barn. I was feeling kind of sickly then. Not sure if it was all I had to drink, or not sleeping much, or feeling scared about what might happen. But that's when I heard McCarthy say he was going to have Stanley arrested for the murder of Freeman Harvey. So, we left the barn together and then crossed the brook."

"When did you find out that Mr. Harvey was indeed dead?"

"I didn't know nothing until we got to Newport Station. Stanley sent me into Gibson's to get a flask of whisky. He gave me the money to buy it, but I didn't end up getting it because I was talking to the folks there and got distracted by what they were telling me."

"What happened after that?"

"Well, Stanley said we'd better head into the woods, so we did. I then told him what I was told up to Gibson's about how Freeman Harvey was dead and buried in the cellar."

"And what did Stanley say?"

"He said it weren't true. That it was a lie."

"Then what happened, Mr. Fisher?"

"Well, by this point, it was starting to get dark and cold, like it was going to rain, and so I said we should go back home. But Stanley said we couldn't go home because they'd all blame me for killing Old Mr. Harvey, and then they would blame him."

"Did Mr. Kav—Stanley, say anything else to you?"

"He said that he was just as much to blame as me, but I didn't know what he meant."

"Do you think Stanley is as much to blame as you?" Christie leaned over and looked right into Jim's eyes. He could see beads of sweat rolling down his temples.

"Yes. More. He led me."

Christie pursed his lips, nodded, and looked over to Dr. Reid, who also gave a slight nod. It was what they had suspected all along.

When Jim sat back down, Chief McDonald re-shackled him and released David Fisher, who then made his way up the stairs onto the platform and into the witness seat. He kept his head low, avoiding eye contact with anyone.

David recounted meeting George Stanley two weeks earlier when he, a perfect stranger, knocked upon his door looking for lodging. On the Friday night in question, David said that Stanley had told him he was planning on staying at Rieck's hotel for the night, left, but soon came back to borrow his jackknife.

"And when was it returned?" Christie asked.

"Saturday morning, he brung it back. And I've had it ever since."

123

"Did you examine the knife when he brought it back? Did you see any blood on it?"

"Nope."

Russell continued transcribing as David Fisher talked about finding blood on the porch floor. Apparently, Stanley had told him they had killed a hen the night before, and the blood was from cutting the head off the hen. *Seems like a reasonable explanation*, he thought.

"When you were arrested, the constables found a white handkerchief in your pocket that appeared to have bloodstains on it. Where did that come from?" Christie leaned in to ask David.

"I couldn't tell you where that came from. I only had one handkerchief in my pocket, and that was an old blue one. This is the coat I was wearing when I got arrested. I didn't know nothing about a white handkerchief."

Christie nodded. "Going back to the knife, Mr. Fisher—"

"I never carry a white handkerchief, and I was wearing this old coat when they took me to Windsor," David repeated.

"Thank you, sir. The knife. Was there a difference in the condition of the knife when you loaned it to Mr. Stanley and when you got it back?"

"Speaking of the blue handkerchief, I have seemed to have lost it, and would like to get it back. I never had no white one."

"We will do our best to locate your blue handkerchief."

To move the proceedings to the next question, Dr. Reid said, "Perhaps if a white handkerchief had been found in Mr. Fisher's pocket, it was put there by someone else. Let us drop the matter of the handkerchief."

Thankful for the assistance, Christie again asked about the knife. His patience, which he normally had an abundance of, was being pushed to its limits.

"When I gave it to Stanley, it was dull. When he gave it back, it was very sharp, like a razor. I didn't use it to cut anything because it had blood on it."

Christie turned his back to the crowd, trying to keep his composure with the witness. He turned around again, directing David to return to his seat.

Russell shook his head. *Didn't he just say he found no blood on the knife? Why is now saying there is blood?* The man was just as confused as Russell felt.

He checked his pocket watch. It was nearly eleven o'clock, and they had been at this for almost three hours, sometimes going in circles. He hoped the jury was not as confused as he was with some of the witness statements.

Finally, George Spence was called to the stand, and only had one question to answer, regarding his whereabouts on the Friday evening. The answer came easily. He'd been with McCarthy all evening, except for a few minutes when McCarthy went into Ellershouse to get them some whisky.

"Ladies and gentlemen," Christie said, walking to the front of the platform to address the crowd, "that is the end of our examination this morning. I am now going to ask you to vacate the premises, so the jury can deliberate."

There was an audible groan from those hoping to witness more of the story unfold, or to hear the final verdict.

As the crowd filed back outside to the well-below-freezing temperatures, Chief McDonald and the other constables led the three accused men to an outbuilding away from the crowd, but where they could still be watched. With the men still shackled together, and a riled-up crowd nearby, there would not be much chance of escape.

Around the building, spectators peered through the windows, trying to get a glimpse of the deliberations happening inside. They looked carefully at the jurors, searching for any hint of the verdict.

After a few moments, Dr. Reid could be seen writing something in his ledger. Then he summoned the three prisoners back into the room. Bystanders tried to make their way in, too, but the constables barred their way.

"The jury has come to their decision," Dr. Reid said to the three men on the floor below him. "The jury has concluded that Freeman Harvey came to his death by murder at the hand of the man called George Stanley last Friday night. David and Jim Fisher, you are both hereby released from custody. The preliminary trial of the man known as George Stanley will commence on February 12, in the Windsor courthouse."

A constable unshackled David and Jim and directed them back outside where Mary Ann sat waiting.

"We're released!" they shouted.

A crowd gathered around them to hear the verdict. Enjoying their moment in the spotlight, the father and son shared their stories again with anyone who would listen.

Inside, John bowed his head, and tried to remain standing as his knees almost gave away. He showed no emotion on his face and said not a word as Chief McDonald and Jailer Smith led him back to the train station, protecting him from the people who had gathered on the side of the road to catch a glimpse of a real-live murderer, and to hurl insults, like snowballs, at the prisoner.

25: A seat near the front

February 12, Windsor

Russell Shaw elbowed his way through the crowd. Being younger and smaller than most, he could easily slip through gaps, snaking his way to the main doors of the Windsor courthouse. With temperatures well below zero, he was happy to be in the middle of the throng, stealing the extra body heat where he could.

When he was at the front, he halted at the base of the cement steps where two police constables stood guard until instructed to open the doors.

Russell craned his neck to look to the top of the four-story brick building before him. Technically, he could only see the two main floors and then dormers at the very peak, where he guessed was an attic. From the front, he could see a few small windows of the basement.

He had received directions from the proprietor of the Victoria Hotel, where he had stayed the night before. When he presented himself at the front desk and explained his reason for being in town, the man had stuck out his hand and had given it a hearty shake.

"This case has brought quite a bit of attention to our small town, which I must admit has been good for our business," he confessed to Russell.

Without giving him a chance to respond, the man continued, "The name is Doran. Thomas Doran. You need anything, you just let me know, and I will show you the best hospitality in town. You can probably tell from my accent that I'm not from these parts, but I have made it my business to find out the best places for you to visit to make the most of your time in Windsor."

"Thank you, Mr. Doran," Russell said. "I do hear a lilt in your accent. The motherland?"

"I came here from Ireland, so I did. And you would think, because of that, I'd have a bit of compassion and feeling for our man Mr. Stanley, or

Kavanagh, a good Irish name, coming from the same homeland. But I cannot find it within in me to find anything in common with a man who commits a murder."

"Speaking of which, where can I find this prisoner? Can you direct me toward the jail?"

Drawing on the back of an envelope, Doran created a map leading from the hotel to the courthouse, only two blocks away. He explained how the jail was in the basement of the courthouse, and because the building was set into the slope of a hill, around the back, the lower windows were fully exposed, and on warm days in the summer, you could often walk by and see the prisoners putting their faces up to the window, sticking their arms out, trying to get a whiff or feel of the fresh air.

"Sometimes," he had said, "they call out to those walking by the streets, until Jailer Smith hears them, and puts a stop to it—for that day. Although that will not be happening in this weather."

Russell eyed the big wooden door, willing it to open, but it stood firm in its closed position. Although he had hardly slept a wink the night before, the adrenaline coursing through his body kept him awake. His uncle-cum-boss had been proud of the work he had been doing, praising him for his art of journalism. Papers were flying off the shelves, and Russell was not about to disappoint his uncle, now. He was bound and determined to get a seat near the front, where he could catch all the action and see every bead of sweat and every drop of spittle.

The Windsor courthouse really was quite magnificent and could equal anything he had seen in Halifax. The hotelier had told him this was actually the second courthouse on the site, the first having burned down in 1897 during the Great Fire of Windsor, when practically everything in town had burnt.

One of the best stories Doran had shared with him was that of Florence Shand's wedding dress. Apparently, Miss Shand was to get married right before the great fire occurred, and, instead of leaving her wedding dress with the dressmaker, her father had the foresight to take the dress with him so the sawdust from the neighbouring furniture factory would not ruin it. He got permission to hang the gown in the courthouse's safe until the wedding day. When the entire town burnt to the ground, including the courthouse, the safe survived, and after it cooled and people could open it, they found that the wedding dress had remained perfectly protected inside.

There is something lucky about this building, Russell thought. He could feel it around him.

The bells of several churches chimed the nine o'clock hour, pulling him back from his reverie. He readied himself, standing tall, elbows out in position, foot poised in the air.

When the door was flung open and the constables moved aside, Russell took the stairs two at a time to the courtroom on the second floor. He plopped down on a bench at the front, closest to the defendant's box, took out his pencils, and placed his notebook on his lap.

Once settled, he looked around the courtroom, which had filled to overflowing in minutes. People pushed into to the vacant spaces around the room, and he could hear voices coming from the stairwell. It seemed that many had come from all points of the countryside, well beyond the town limits, to take in the momentous event.

In the final minutes, Ida Harvey, dressed in a long black dress, black gloves and a small, veiled hat, walked solemnly to the front of the room, to a seat that had been reserved particularly for her. As she walked by, people murmured and pointed to the poor widow.

It was close to ten o'clock before the door from the outer chambers opened and Justice Farquhar, Esq. glided in, followed by two barristers who took their seats at the facing tables. A few moments later, the jailer came through the door, with the handcuffed prisoner close behind.

Russell shifted in his seat to get a better look, but could not fully see the man's face, as he kept his eyes to the floor. Smith led him to the box beside the magistrate.

Russell saw how pale and nervous the man looked. For someone who had committed one of the foulest and most deliberate murders in the history of the province, he, at the moment, certainly didn't look the part.

The journalist had been writing reams about Stanley, but this man did not equate with the mad criminal he had imagined. *He is so small.*

Farquhar, looked around at the heaving crowd. He hoped there would be no riots or emergencies that morning under his watch. There would be no easy escape, judging by the number of people in the room. This was, by far, the largest crowd he had seen in his courtroom over his decades as justice of the peace.

"Good morning, ladies and gentlemen." Farquhar's thick Scottish accent floated through the air, causing the crowd to sit up and listen. People were not accustomed to hearing this lilt, so they had to pay closer attention so as not to miss anything.

"The information and complaint of William Medford Christie of Windsor, in the said county of Hants, one of his Majesty's Counsel learned in the law, and prosecuting officer in and for the said county of Hants, taken this ninth day of February, in the year of our Lord, one thousand nine hundred and six, before the undersigned James Farquhar, Esquire, one of His Majesty's Justices of the Peace, in and for the county of Hants, who saith that George Stanley, otherwise called William Kavanagh, at Ellershouse in the said county of Hants, on or about the second day of February in the year one thousand, nine hundred and six, murdered Freeman Harvey."

Justice Farquhar put down the document he had been reading and looked up to make sure he still had everyone's attention. He then continued. "Who do we have before me today?"

Christie stood and addressed the court. "I am here to represent the interests of the Crown."

At the adjacent table, the young barrister stood. "I am Hadley Tremain on behalf of the prisoner. I must inform you that I have been brought into this case most unexpectedly."

What Tremain had wanted to say was that, since he was the most junior member of their firm, the file had been tossed upon his desk only days before. Knowing it was a futile case, no one else in the office wanted it, and being the newest employee, he was thrust into the middle of one of the county's biggest murder trials.

"There is a good deal of evidence to be gathered, and I need time to accomplish this. I ask, for an adjournment," Tremain said.

In the prisoner's box at the front, John nodded his head slowly in agreement, still refusing to meet the eyes of the crowd in front of him.

Christie stood to comment. "We the prosecution agree to the adjournment."

The judge nodded. "Then we shall make it so."

"Thank you, your Honour," Tremain said with relief.

The crowd grumbled in the background. They were not happy to have travelled great distances and fought for seats in the gallery, only to be told that nothing would occur that day, and that they would have to repeat the process the on another day.

Justice Farquhar listed the names of the witnesses, who were seated amongst the crowd, asking them to approach the bench, then instructing them to return the following Tuesday at ten o'clock in the morning.

26: Adamantly protesting

February 15

"Have you seen this headline? The scoundrel!"

Chief McDonald tossed that day's edition of the *Halifax Herald* onto the desk of Crown Attorney Christie, in his office on Gerrish Street in downtown Windsor.

Christie raised an inquisitive eyebrow as he flipped through the pages of the newspaper until his eyes fell upon a headline. He raised the paper in front of his face, and in his most professional voice, read aloud, "Alleged murderer proposed marriage to a Halifax lady."

He groaned and put the newspaper back down on his desk.

"Where does this reporter come up with this, and where is his integrity?" Chief McDonald asked, without expecting an answer. He knew headlines like this sold newspapers.

"Ever since that Forsey woman, his landlord in Halifax, recognized him from the account of the murder in the newspaper, more and more keeps coming out of the woodwork, and the headlines keep getting more sensational," Christie, said, shaking his head. "Hard to know what to believe any more."

"I'll give that reporter credit, though. He would make an awfully good detective. All that dirt he managed to dig up about our man's activities in those first weeks in January. It does make for an interesting read," Chief McDonald said.

"I can tell you that Mr. Stanley is none too happy about these headlines, either," Christie said. "I just came from a visit with Jailer Smith, who filled me in. Smith has been supplying our friend with the newspapers, perhaps a bad idea, for now he is on a writing frenzy, appealing for justice based on what he reads."

"Is he now?" McDonald asked, taking the seat opposite Christie's desk.

"He said the *Herald* printed a story in which he was accused of being a member of an Irish secret society, which had for its object the killing of old men. The paper accused him of murdering an old man under exceptionally cruel circumstances, and claimed he was an escapee."

"Yes, I remember that edition."

"Let me find it."

Christie opened his drawer and pulled out a stack of clippings he had collected over the past few days. He scanned through them until he found the one of interest. "Here it is. Last Friday's, and I quote, 'It has been ascertained by the *Herald* that the man's name is not George Stanley, and he's probably an escaped convict from a prison in Ireland. He made the acquaintance of Mr. Forsey, and being a man of very slippery tongue, he secured lodging at Forsey's boarding house. The moment Mrs. Forsey saw him, she suspected him of being an escaped convict. He could look no one straight in the eye and there was the criminal appearance all over him.' That about sums it up."

"And he probably took none too kindly to that."

"Indeed, he did not," Christie said. "He says that these claims are coming out just when evidence is being collected against him, and is prejudicing the minds of the whole community. He says it will be impossible to receive fair and impartial justice from men who primarily form their opinions from reading the newspaper. He feels he is already regarded as a monster."

"The headlines are indeed a bit outlandish," McDonald admitted.

"I've never seen a reporter jump to more conclusions to make a good story and sell papers," Christie said. "There are plenty more just like those."

"Oh pray, do share." Chief McDonald took out a pair of spectacles from his breast pocket and leaned in closer for a better look as Christie flipped through more clippings.

"After writing that George Stanley, John Ryan, or William Kavanagh, or whatever his name might be, had the look of a notorious, repulsive convict-—"

"Well, he does have that hardened look to him, would you not agree?"

"Hindsight, my friend. You of all people should understand that."

"I do, but one look at him, and counting all the scars covering his body, you can easily tell he's been in his fair share of scraps. But continue about our repulsive convict..."

"'The few belongings he had showed unmistakable evidence of being prison articles, in fact, there is now at the Forsey house a pair of prison boots that he left there. There can be no question that this man is a notorious criminal,'" Christie read.

"Prison boots, eh?"

"There's more. He goes on to write that 'there is a possibility of this man being the one who set fire to St. Luke's Cathedral.'"

"In Halifax? But didn't that fire happen nearer to the beginning of December? He couldn't have possibly been the culprit, as his ship didn't arrive in Halifax until December 20."

"Yes, yes, indeed. The reporter does go on to say that, but the point was already made. And, as for the boots, it's not until the next day that he writes, 'it was first thought they were convict boots, but they are hobnailed with ponderous soles and heels but are obviously ammunition boots and are stamped with the firm name of T. Mabane & Sons, Leeds, 1901.'"

"And now, the claim is that he proposed to a woman in Halifax! It's hard to know what to believe with this man and seems that the reporter here is just capitalizing on that just to sell a few papers. The damage has already been printed."

"And according to Smith, Stanley is still adamantly protesting he is innocent," Christie said.

"The courts will decide that."

"George Stanley may be right, after all. He may be convicted even before we set foot in the courtroom. There goes my profession!" Christie said with a laugh, leaning back. "We will need to try to have a word with that reporter, though."

27: Be careful what you say

February 16

"You have a new shirt!"

Christie looked the prisoner up and down and wondered who had been supplying him with new clothes. He was met with a silent stare.

"Where did you get the new shirt?" he tried again.

John glared back at Chief McDonald and the crown attorney. "I know what you want. You want to know if I murdered Harvey."

"No one asked you who murdered Harvey, but if you know who murdered him, you had better tell us all about it," McDonald said.

"You will need to be careful what you say, however," Christie added. "Whatever you say might be used in evidence against you."

"I know all about that." John crossed his arms and continued to stare at the two officials before him.

"So, do you know who murdered Mr. Harvey?" McDonald asked.

"Edgar McCarthy did it. He is both a murderer and a robber."

"And how do you know this?" McDonald asked.

"He stayed at Harvey's house all Friday night. We were up drinking all the way until the next morning. At one point, McCarthy sent me up to Rieck's hotel for liquor."

"And then what happened?" Christie said.

"I went up to the hotel and I left Harvey and McCarthy in the house. I was gone quite a while getting up there and back. When I got back, Harvey had gone, and Edgar McCarthy was there alone. I asked McCarthy where Harvey was, and McCarthy told me that Harvey had gone to Windsor. "

"We don't even really know who you are. What is your name?" McDonald leaned down to look the prisoner in the eye.

"Where are you from?" Christie asked.

"Roscrea, in Ireland. I am an Irishman."

"Smith, you can return him to his cell."

28: It's a really nice knife

February 20

Eight days later, the preliminary court trial was back in session.

Long before the hour of opening, crowds were wending their way to the Windsor courthouse, and by ten o'clock there was an even larger attendance than in the previous week. Men and women alike had braved the cold winter morning temperatures to wait outside in hopes of a seat, or even a glimpse of the murderer. The audience in the courtroom extended outside the rail, crowding up to the edge of the desks of the learned counsels.

Justice Farquhar welcomed everyone to court and began the morning by swearing in Miss Lucy Curry as the court stenographer. The young woman sat up straight, knowing the importance of her work. She stretched her fingers and arms beside her, then resumed her position to record the day's proceedings.

"Before we begin, your Honour, I would like to make a request," Tremain, for the defence, said. "I ask that the witnesses be removed from the courtroom and not be allowed to listen to each other's evidence."

Tremain held Justice Farquhar's gaze. Asking witnesses to leave the room was a relatively new procedure and was bound to cause disagreement from those who would have to wait sequestered, possibly for days on end, in another room in the courthouse.

"Agreed. Sheriff, please see the witnesses to the adjoining room."

Over 25 men, and Mary Ann Fisher, filed out of the room. Many turned to glare at both Tremain and Justice Farquhar for spoiling their entertainment. There was a subdued but intense battle over who would get the seats thus vacated.

Joseph Fisher was the first witness called to the stand. He testified that he had called at Harvey's house on Friday evening, before the supposed time of the murder. He said he saw and talked with Harvey, who, mentioned he was thinking of selling his property.

"While I was there, George Stanley came in, and started engaging in conversation with Harvey, and I left shortly thereafter, leaving the accused along with Mr. Harvey," Joseph said. "I never saw Mr. Harvey again." He paused, thinking about what he had just said, and added, "alive."

Christie let that final word float in the air before he resumed questioning. "When were you next at Mr. Harvey's house?"

"It was the day of the inquest with Dr. Reid. Maybe on the Monday?"

In his cross examination, Tremain grilled Joseph about the timeline over the weekend, but the man remained steadfast to his story and was not to be shaken from it.

After an hour, Justice Farquhar dismissed Joseph. He left the witness box and returned to a seat in the gallery that his wife had managed to keep free by placing her carpet bag beside her on the bench. He squeezed in while the court called his brother, David Fisher to the stand.

A few moments later, the sheriff led David through the side door and into the courtroom. Upon entering, David stood dazed, like a deer frozen to the spot. The sheriff nudged him along toward the witness box, where he awkwardly took a seat.

Christie approached the witness, and after he was sworn in, began asking him questions, trying to get him to share the same story he had told ten days earlier at the inquest in Ellershouse.

Halfway through the examination of his own witness, Christie returned to his desk in search of a drink of water. He was tired and needed a break. David Fisher was a painful witness to question. Every query was met with either a long-drawn out answer or a memory failure. It was more than tedious.

He took a deep breath, tapped his ring on the desk three times to gain his focus, then started his questioning again. "Can you tell us about the negotiating that the accused did with Mr. Spence?"

"Who?"

"The accused, who you call Mr. Stanley."

"Ah, yes. He traded a horse for a wagon with Mr. James Spence, but I didn't think it was a very good wagon. I mean, it was an okay wagon, and probably better than any wagon that I ever had, or maybe ever would have. But I knew that Mr. Spence probably had a better wagon than that, just knowing how fancy he was and how he's in the carriage business, so I thought that Stanley could have done a bit better than that, and that the horse he traded was mighty fine. So, I said for him to ask for a better wagon."

"So, Mr. Spence and George Stanley traded a horse for a wagon. When did this conversation take place?"

"Mmmm…" David paused and scratched his head. "I just can't remember exactly when."

"And there was a great deal of drinking that happened in Freeman Harvey's house on Sunday night, is that correct?"

"I don't do any drinking. That's not what I do, but the other boys like their liquor. I think they like the brown jugs from up to Rieck's hotel the best, and you can get some of the bottles there for 25 cents."

"Thank you, Mr. Fisher," Christie said, cutting David off before he got into full flow about the range of items available at Rieck's hotel.

Christie asked a few more questions that received equally drawn-out answers. He gritted his teeth, trying to remain patient. "Then, on Monday morning, what transpired?"

David looked blankly at him, and Christie reworded the question. "What happened when you were moving your furniture to the Harvey house? Did you have a conversation with someone?"

"I had conversations with lots of people."

"Did you have a conversation on Monday morning with Edgar McCarthy about moving your furniture?"

"I don't rightly recall."

"In an earlier statement, Mr. Fisher, you mentioned that Mr. McCarthy said he didn't want you bringing your furniture there."

"Yes. I had that conversation with him."

"And what did you talk about, or what did he say to you?"

"He said, 'I'm going to stop that furniture coming in. Mr. Harvey is in the cellar with his head cut off.' That's what he done and said to me."

A few people could be heard shouting that they had the wrong man on trial.

Russell, who was leaning against the outside wall of the courtroom, was trying to balance on one foot while using his bent knee as a table on which to take notes. He cursed himself for not having arrived earlier that morning to get a seat in the gallery.

As he heard David Fisher's statement, his head snapped up to attention. This was big news. David Fisher just said that McCarthy had previous knowledge of the murder—before the body was even discovered. How was this possible? Was McCarthy really involved in the murder and, as the crowd was shouting around him, had they arrested the wrong man? Or, in those few days in the jail cell together, when David and Jim Fisher spent time with Stanley, had he planted some seeds of an alternative explanation in their pliable minds?

Christie continued his questioning. "Did you have another conversation with Edgar McCarthy on the Monday morning?"

"I had lots of conversations with him."

Christie turned his back to the crowd, and took a deep breath, trying to maintain his professional composure, a task that was becoming increasingly difficult in the face of this man's answers. He had questioned lots of ne'er-do-wells in his time, men who were evasive, or downright liars. He prided himself on his ability to winkle out the lies in a man's testimony. But faced with simple obtuseness, he was totally at a loss.

He turned back to David and asked him the same question, for the fourth time. "Did you have a conversation with Mr. McCarthy in the early hours of Monday morning about Freeman Harvey?"

"Yes."

"What was the conversation?"

"There was one point when the rest of the men went with Stanley up to Ellershouse village for more liquor. McCarthy did not go with them but went outside for a bit. Then, he comes back in, and I heard him plain as day say, 'By God, I saw Freeman Harvey going across the field! If it was not him, it was his ghost with his head off!'"

The courtroom erupted. Justice Farquhar banged his gavel, calling repeatedly for order.

When things calmed, Christie resumed his questioning. "Who was with you when Mr. McCarthy made this comment?"

"I'm pretty sure Stanley, my son Jim and one of the Spence boys were there, but I'm not sure. They could have been, or they may not have been."

"But you just said the men all went up to the hotel for more drinks. How could Stanley and the others have heard McCarthy make these comments?"

"Well, maybe it was after they came back when it happened. I can't quite recall."

"All right, then. What did you do or say when Mr. McCarthy made these comments?"

"I went outside to look for him myself but saw nothing. When I came back in, Stanley offered me a cap of gin, which I refused, because I don't drink the stuff."

"You did not tell this story at the inquest, Mr. Fisher."

"I didn't remember it until now."

"Thank you. Your witness, Mr. Tremain." Christie sat down, relieved to be done with this man.

Upon cross examination, David told the court again how Stanley had borrowed the knife from him on Friday, the day of the murder.

"How can you be sure that the knife that Mr. Christie showed to the court is in fact your knife?"

"I swear it is my knife. I would know it in one hundred. It's a really nice knife, with brass jaws and a crooked blade. I use it for many things, but I especially use it to cut my tobacco."

"Where were the rest of your family members on Friday night, the supposed night of the murder? How can you be sure where your sons were?" Tremain asked.

"I knowed for a fact that they were home, because they were asleep alongside of me."

This got a chuckle from the townsfolk in the courtroom, unused to the country ways.

Once the crowd quieted, Tremain finished his questioning. He looked over to Christie and nodded, signalling he was finished.

A loud gurgle came from David's stomach. "I reckon it is dinner time," he said with a laugh.

Christie pulled out his pocket watch and confirmed that it was indeed noon and realized David Fisher had already been on the stand for over two hours. "Justice Farquhar," Christie said, "I think we had best take a break for dinner and resume the rest of this examination afterwards. I have a feeling that it is going to take some considerable time to continue this line of inquiry."

After the lunch break, Christie felt refreshed and ready to tackle the Fisher examination once again. With contradictory statements and comments that went nowhere, he was not sure the case was any clearer. He tapped his ring three times, took a deep breath, and approached David Fisher.

By the time the afternoon session concluded, David had been on the stand for another two hours.

When he returned to his seat, Christie had never been so happy to see the back of a witness. He closed his eyes and took a deep breath to regain his composure.

Three more witnesses were called to the stand that afternoon, but their evidence shed no further light on the case.

29: Raise your left hand

February 21

It was the second morning of the preliminary trial, in which the jury was tasked with determining if there was enough evidence to move forward with a full trial against George Stanley.

There were at least eight witnesses to get through during the day's proceedings. Medford Christie flipped through the notes in his file, running through the questions in his mind that he had mapped out for each witness. Surely, they could not be as difficult as David Fisher.

His finger went down the list of names. First was David's wife, Mary Ann, followed by their son, Jim. He tapped his ring three times and said a little prayer for patience.

It was warmer today, fitting for the unnaturally mild winter they had been having, which may have accounted for so many people turning up to the trial. Who was he kidding? Christie knew trials like this were big draws. Little happened in these small, rural towns, so when it did, no one wanted to be the one to miss out, or miss their piece of the story to pass around.

As the sheriff led the prisoner in for the day, the crowd hurled jeers and insults across the room.

"Send the papist back home!"

"He's a tramp!"

"Murderer!"

"We should never have let his kind into the country!"

John kept his head low as he made his way to the prisoner's dock.

With the prisoner seated and his papers in order at his desk, Christie reached across to shake hands with Tremain at the defence table and nodded to Justice Farquhar that he was finally ready to begin.

Mary Ann Fisher took the stand, wearing the familiar cardigan with holes in the elbow, pulled tightly around her body. Her hair was pulled back in the same bun, only there were no stray strands hanging loose. She sat in the witness box, glaring, daring someone to ask her a question.

After telling her story about meeting George Stanley, the topic of the handkerchief came up again, and how a blood-stained one had been found in her husband's pocket when he was arrested.

"When Mr. Stanley purchased socks and mittens from you, did he also purchase a handkerchief?"

"Yes, sir, he did, sir. I had boughten two handkerchiefs from a peddler. I sold one of them to Stanley for five cents. The other I gave to my son, Jim."

Not to let the story take on more meaning, Tremain stood to cross-examine Mary Ann.

"Can you be sure, Mrs. Fisher, that the handkerchief we've been seeing in court today was indeed the one you sold to Mr. Stanley?"

"I believe it is," she said defiantly.

"Are there any defining characteristics on the handkerchief that you can identify it by being the exact one you purchased and later sold?"

"No, I 'spose not."

As there were no further questions, Mary Ann returned to her seat.

Jim Fisher followed his mother on the witness stand. His testimony lasted several hours, starting from the moment he met George Stanley until when he ran away into the woods with him and was arrested.

Christie returned to the matter of the mysterious handkerchief that had been found on David Fisher upon arrest. Christie tried to have Jim help him establish that the handkerchief could have belonged to George Stanley. "Did you ever see this so-called gentleman, Mr. Stanley, with a handkerchief?"

"Yes, when we were out in the woods, he blew his nose on a handkerchief and he put it in his left-hand pocket."

To demonstrate, Jim held his left hand in the air and pretended to place something in an imaginary pocket, across his chest.

Christie paused for a moment, replaying that gesture in his mind. "Mr. Fisher, could you please raise your left hand."

Jim grinned at the easy question and raised his right hand high in the air.

Christie turned quickly from the witness, pursed his lips and rested his fist against his mouth, trying to stifle a laugh. Meanwhile, the crowd erupted into laughter as Jim looked around wondering what joke he had missed.

With his composure regained, Christie continued with his questioning. "Was it a white handkerchief?"

"It was pretty dirty, especially after I seen him blow his nose on it."

The rest of the day proceeded with six more witnesses, all giving the same story they had at the Ellershouse inquest.

Throughout the day, the prisoner sat in the witness box, making no sound and barely looking up, to the dismay of the crowd. They had heard about other cases in the area where prisoners made scenes, argued along, and were half the entertainment. George Stanley was actually a boring part of the entire process. The Fishers had been far more entertaining.

By the end of the long day, Justice Farquhar banged his gavel and adjourned the court, saying they would continue Saturday morning.

30: It is false, sir!

February 24

On Saturday morning the courtroom was filled with the same crowd, back for the next piece of the story. One witness spoke of having seen the accused in the woods on the day in question. Then hotelier Charles Rieck was questioned about selling him alcohol.

"How often was George Stanley at your place?" Christie asked.

"I can't rightfully say."

Rieck knew he was on dangerous ground, and he tried to answer carefully. The Temperance Union was very active in the area, and if they heard how much activity was happening at his hotel, he could be shut down, or have the authorities after him.

Upon cross examination, Tremain tried again. He began with a direct question. "Do you sell liquor, Mr. Rieck?"

Rieck lowered his head and mumbled a quick yes in response. It was a worse sin to lie in court.

A few tuts and intakes of breath went through the crowd.

Rieck eventually admitted he had sold liquor to George Stanley. He just could not remember exactly what day it had been.

Finally, it was the moment that the crowd had been waiting for when Edgar McCarthy, one of the principal witnesses, was called to the stand. Those who had not seen him at the Ellershouse inquest had long waited to catch sight of this former criminal, known throughout the county for his reputation of fighting and ending up in jail.

McCarthy went into detail, describing the weekend in February from seven o'clock Friday evening, when he drove over to George Spence's with three horses, intending to make a trade. There he remained until the following afternoon. except for about half an hour when he went to Rieck's to buy liquor.

He had told his story so many times, he knew it backwards and forwards, and relayed what he had to say in a straightforward manner. He ended with finding the body of Freeman Harvey in a pile of potatoes in the cellar, and the subsequent search for George Stanley.

Tremain's cross examination of McCarthy lasted for three hours and held the closest attention of the court. The self-appointed jury within the crowd tried to determine just how guilty McCarthy was, and how much he himself had to do with the murder.

Throughout it all, McCarthy remained unshaken.

Christie returned to the stand with one final question. "If the prisoner says you were at Harvey's house on the night of the murder, what do you say?"

"It is false, sir."

After a dinner break, William Brown was called and sworn in. He testified about finding the saw covered in blood. Tremain's cross examination failed to elicit any further information, so the next witness, George Spence was called to the stand. Spence testified that McCarthy had spent all Friday night with him, thus providing an alibi for the notorious man.

At the conclusion of another long day, Justice Farquhar called for adjournment, scheduling the jury to return the following Saturday for the verdict.

The crowd of men and women stood to leave, disappointed that no conclusion was reached, and they would have to return yet another day, vying again for the best seats in the courtroom gallery.

John hung his head, not making eye contact with anyone, as Sheriff O'Brien led him out of the courtroom, and down the flights of stairs to his cell in the basement.

31: A true bill

March 3

It had been dark for a while by the time Christie came through the front door of his home after a long day at court. He shed his overcoat and boots and left them in the porch so as not to bring the cold in with them.

He called out to his family as he entered the living room, where a roaring fire awaited him. He rubbed his hands together vigorously. Snow had finally fallen a few days earlier and the freezing temperatures from the prior few days had done nothing to melt it away. He had to bundle up and trudge through the snowy streets to the courthouse earlier that morning for their final day of the trial, and he just could not shake the cold from his bones.

Christie turned up the lantern and pulled his armchair closer to the fire. He could hear no sound from his family, so he sat back and closed his eyes with the day's events running through his mind. Today had been a relatively easy day with no witnesses to examine and nothing of consequence transpiring to shed any more light on the case.

He shook his head, thinking. That George Stanley, or William Kavanagh, was an odd little man. He just could not get a reading on him or figure out what was going through his mind. Throughout the trial, the man had just sat there, showing no emotion, not looking up, and not uttering a word. In terms of courtroom drama, this had been a failure. Surely, it was a disappointment for the masses that turned out to witness the trial, especially after hearing about recent trials in neighbouring counties. But it certainly made his job in the courtroom easier.

The foreman had stood confidently in the courtroom, declaring in a loud voice that the jury had indeed found a true bill against George Stanley for the murder of Freeman Harvey. They had all agreed they had found enough evidence to proceed with a trial for murder.

Stanley's response had been so simple. Christie could still hear the Irish lilt when the prisoner stood to say, "No, sur," when Justice Farquhar had asked him if he had wanted the evidence read.

Christie had sighed in relief, not wanting to go back through it all again.

But the man was firm and clear. No, he did not want it re-read. And when asked if he had anything else to say, he remained perfectly silent. So unusual, compared to other defendants Christie had known.

With nothing left to say, Justice Farquhar had committed George Stanley for trial in the Supreme court at the end of May. This would give Christie another two and a half months to prepare for the next trial, and to sharpen his examination questions.

32: A prolific writer

March 9

Chief McDonald sat at his desk at the police station. The desk looked small in comparison to the man of great stature sitting behind it. He thumbed through a stack of envelopes that Jailer Smith had just brought him.

He looked up when he heard a tapping at the door. Medford Christie stood leaning against the door frame.

"I've come for my weekly update, Chief."

Christie entered the room in response to Chief McDonald's gesture instructing him to pull up a chair. "You've just missed Smith. He brought up a stack of mail from the courthouse, and I'm just about to go through it to see if there's anything of consequence."

"What news of our prisoner?"

"Apparently, he's not happy."

Christie chuckled. "Would you be? I mean, Smith is a more than fair and generous keeper, but I wouldn't be so happy in jail either. Although maybe he should have thought of that before committing murder."

"True, true. No, he has been complaining that, as a British subject, he should be treated as such. He objects to the chains that bind his legs, and claims that under British law, no chains are to be used with any criminal unless he has dangerously assaulted someone in the prison after his arrest."

"Is that true?"

"I have no idea. But it's moot, for we are in Canada, and we act under Canadian law and customs. The chains remain."

Christie nodded his agreement.

"He also objects to being deprived of any open-air exercise, and says he has a list of other complaints."

"Sounds like a man who is used to the prison system, or maybe has had it easy elsewhere."

Chief McDonald picked up the stack of envelopes again and shuffled through them. "Our Mr. Kavanagh seems to be a prolific writer."

"Those were all written by him? To whom are they addressed?"

"We have one to Archbishop O'Brien in Halifax, one to the editor of the *Freeman's Journal* in Dublin, one to The Howard Association of London —"

"He's appealing for help from the prison reformers, is he? Little hope there!"

"There's more, and it looks like correspondence to other places in Halifax, London and Dublin, including the Charitable Irish Society in both Halifax and Dublin."

"Have you read through them yet?"

"No, I was just about to. Come in closer."

Chief McDonald fanned the envelopes out across the desk and picked one at random. He opened his desk drawer to retrieve his silver letter opener, and carefully cut through the sealed envelope. He unfolded the letter, flattening it on the desk, then took out his reading spectacles from the breast pocket of his jacket.

He cleared his throat and started to read.

> Sir, in the interests of justice and humanity I have presumed to address you from a penal prison, and under circumstances of embarrassment which I will hope ensure to me a little consideration at your hands.

Christie leaned forward to carefully look at the letter. "The man is certainly well educated. The penmanship is beautiful, and his spelling and grammar are impeccable. Really, not what I would expect to see from someone who committed such a foul murder."

"Just goes to show there are all sorts."

The two men spent the next hour poring over the letters, stopping to read or highlight parts that stood out.

"This one is to the Charitable Irish Society in Halifax. Listen to this..." Christie held up the letter and began to read.

> My present situation is a critical one. I am at the mercy of people, some of whom do not seem to know what they are saying, much less understand the nature of an oath. I am accused of murder of which I am absolutely innocent, a perfect stranger to all parties, a network of contradictory and false evidence has been sworn against me by a family of well-known imbeciles whose only re-

commendation is that they are *facile princeps* in the reprehens-
ible art of lying. These people are known by the name of Fisher.

"To say that the evidence given by this family was contradictory and lying
in the extreme is a mild way of putting it. It's a good thing the Fishers
can't read this!"

"Isn't it interesting how much he is proclaiming his innocence now,
when not uttering a word during the trial," McDonald said.

He picked up the final letter on the table to open when a second one,
stuck to the back, fell away. "Well, I'll be! There's another letter here, and
this one is addressed to you."

Christie cocked his head in confusion. Why would the prisoner be
writing him a letter? Why not request to see him at the jail? He cautiously reached out and took the letter between his thumb and index finger, slipping the letter from its envelope.

Christie raised his eyebrows in surprise as he read the letter, prompt-
ing Chief McDonald to ask him to share the contents.

Christie began reading.

> I should feel very thankful to you if you would refrain from mak-
> ing use of personal remarks in reference to me. I know you are
> completely prejudiced against me so much so, that it will be ne-
> cessary for me to apply to the government to have you removed
> as prosecuting council in my case. You openly called me a mur-
> derer and a tramp and used many other beautiful epithets which
> you have applied toward me.

Chief McDonald chortled in surprise. "There are some pretty hefty accusations there."

Christie finished the letter and put it back down on the table in front
of him. He thought back over the trial and could not remember an in-
stance where he had used any of the words, although he knew those in
the crowd had said far worse.

"I shall endeavour to do better." He bowed his head and tapped his
ring on the table three times. Years as a prosecutor had made him thick-
skinned, but still the accusations cut through him, even if they did come
from a murderer—or an alleged one.

"You have merely done your job, and he is what he is. He's dug his own
grave. Do not let him get under your skin."

"What are you planning on doing with all these letters?" Christie asked, changing the subject.

"We're not sure yet. We've never had this much mail requested to be sent from a prisoner."

The chief restacked the letters and placed them in the top drawer of his desk. He looked up when he heard a knock at the door.

A constable appeared at the door with a manila envelope in hand. "Excuse the interruption, Chief," he stammered. "But I thought you might like to see this. It's just arrived in the mail and has Dublin on the postmark."

Chief McDonald smiled as he reached out to take the envelope. He rubbed his hands together gleefully before he slit it open.

"You seem to know already what this envelope contains," Christie said.

"Well, not the exact contents, but I know the subject matter."

"Pray tell."

"Our man George Stanley, or Mr. Kavanagh, made mention of being involved in the prison system in Ireland, so I sent the mug shot over to the Mayboro Prison in Dublin to see if they recognized him and if they could track down a prison record."

Chief McDonald pulled out two long pages of detailed records. The first page contained a set of fingerprints and hand prints that were no more than half the size of his own. "That's him, all right."

McDonald took the second page and turned it around for Christie to see the mug shots with the likeness of George Stanley on them.

Christie leaned in to read the name of the top of the document. "John Ryan, John Kelly, William George Frazer, William Mansuell, John Kavanagh."

"He has a lengthy prison record starting at the age of 17. Says here, October 31, 1883, he was sent to prison for stealing a watch and chain. Somewhere in Newry. Is that Ireland?"

Christie shrugged, noncommittally. Chief McDonald continued. "Get comfortable. This is going to take some time to piece together."

"Just who is this man?"

~

In his cell back in the jailhouse, John lay on his lumpy mattress, thankful he was not on one of the Irish board beds, literally made from pieces of wood. With the trial looming, and his fate uncertain, images of his childhood flashed through his mind. He started putting the pieces together, trying to figure out how he had ended up where he was that day.

Laura Churchill Duke

Part 3: The Treadmill

Prison mug shots of the man with many names.
West Hants Historical Society

33: Butter Witch

May 1, 1875, Roscrea, Ireland

"John Kavanagh, you little scut! Get yourself down here now!"

Margaret Kavanagh stood bent over the peat fire, the earthy smoke billowing around her. She scowled, looking at the empty skillet. "Where's the rest of the brown bread?"

Her anger rose with the heat of the fire. She spun around too quickly, and nearly caught her neck on the clothesline strung across the tiny kitchen.

"John, you little...!" she called again, knowing there could only be one culprit.

She heard his footsteps on the stairs, coming down from the upper bedrooms, and he appeared in the doorway. "I'm not sure what you are talking about, Mam." He smiled innocently up at his mother. Over his almost ten years, he had perfected the look.

"You most certainly do know what I'm talking about. That last piece of bread was to be my lunch."

"But, Mam! It had to have been the butter-witch fairy! It is May Day, and since you forgot to hang the yellow flowers on the door last night, she probably sneaked in and stole the bread."

Margaret failed to hold her angry face. Looking down at her son, she cracked a smile. She patted him on the head. "You little villain! You and your tales are going to get you in trouble some day. It's lucky you're such a fine thing, or I would have sold you to the tinkers long ago."

"Where's Dad? When's he home?"

"He's off delivering messages for the tannery. You know that."

"With Grandad?"

"Yes, with me dad. Now, skedaddle before I change my mind."

Patting him on the behind, she sent her son out to the street to play with his brother William and the other neighbourhood children. She could already hear them on the road, trundling hoops, hooting and hollering.

Margaret stood in front of the window and pulled back the curtains that had seen better days. She looked up and down Ballyhall at the hordes of children playing. She smiled, her mind wandering back to the days of her childhood in Fancroft, only a few miles to the north of Roscrea. Some things never changed.

She loved her life in this small town, mostly because here she was surrounded by history. From where she stood, she could easily see John's Tower, with new buildings built up around it as if it were no concern to have a thirteenth-century castle in the middle of town.

Roscrea had its fair share of old buildings. It was a historic marketplace that grew up around an ancient monastery. Some said it was one of the oldest towns in Ireland. She was not sure if it was true, but she liked the sound of it.

She loved meandering through the old streets, seeing the castle, the monastery, the tower, all well over six hundred years old. It was a reminder that her life was just a fleeting spark in the history of the world, and that these foundations would remain far longer than she would.

Feeling the baby kick inside her brought Margaret sharply back to the present. She let go of the curtain and rubbed her swollen belly.

She decided to take advantage of the few moments of silence with the boys outside, and her husband at work, to put her feet up and rest her pregnant body. Then she would think about dinner. As she sank into a chair, she shook her head and smiled again, despite herself. *Butter witch indeed!*

34: You have my word

December 10, 1875

"Get your grubby hands away from the jar, lad!"

Mrs. McMahon stood behind the counter of her grocery store and glared down at John, whose face was pressed up against the row of glass jars.

"I'm just looking." His stomach growled as his eyes flitted between the barley sugar, pineapple cubes and strawberry bon bons.

"Looks like you're fixing to do more than just look. What's your name, boy?"

"It's John K—"

John stopped mid-sentence, knowing how angry Ma would be if she were to find out he got in trouble again.

"Well? 'John' what?" She looked down at him, taking a notepad from her apron pocket to record the incriminating evidence.

"John Ryan," he said, feigning obedience but using one of the most common surnames in town. It was the only thing he could come up with fast enough that she would not question.

But she did, at least at first. "You don't look like the Ryan boys. You look more like Thomas Kavanagh's lad. God rest him."

John cringed at hearing his father's name on her lips and he bit the inside of his cheek to prevent himself from tearing up. His da had not been dead and buried a month, and his pain was still raw and close to the surface. "No, ma'am, but I have heard that before, ma'am."

He smiled up at the woman, hoping she would believe him. He pressed his luck. "If you are needing any help at the shop, ma'am, I could come by in the evenings to do the sweeping. You wouldn't need to pay me, just a couple of them barley sugars would do."

Mrs. McMahon's expression softened, and she returned the notepad to her pocket. "I see I've misjudged you, John Ryan. Be back today at half-past four. On the dot, mind you."

"Yes, ma'am. I will indeed, ma'am. You have my word."

"Good lad." She unscrewed the lid, measured a few barley sugar sweets into a small white newspaper cone and extended it across the counter to an eagerly awaiting hand. "You can have today's payment early."

John took the packet, smiled again, and promised his return. With a wave, he left the shop, but not before he instinctively looked past the partition dividing the shop from the public house at the back.

There had been a few times when Ma had sent him out to grocers around town to check if Pa was there in the back, having a pint with his work mates. It was his habit to throw a glance at the drinkers, but now he was just searching ghosts.

Out on the street, he ripped voraciously into the sweets, forcing the entire contents into his mouth at once, crunching them between his teeth.

Well, that was easy. He chuckled to himself, tossed the empty cone to the curb, and immediately forgot his promise.

35: Safe to be a Catholic again

January 1876

"Straighten up, John. Stop slouching! You want to make a good impression."

His mother leaned over him, spat on her handkerchief, and wiped his face. He squirmed. "It's your first day at St. Cronan's and you need to present yourself well."

William, three years older and a young man of almost 15 years, stood still, doing his mother's bidding, highlighting John's squirming. In the background, their baby sister, Maria, not quite a month old, cried for attention, further trying their mother's patience.

John glared sourly at his sister. He was not happy about the addition to the family. He wasn't happy about a lot of things. There had been too many changes as of late.

First, his father had died unexpectedly only a few months ago, before he even had a chance to meet Maria. Then they had to move around the corner from their townhouse in Ballyhall to this inferior home on Rosemount.

He had asked his mother why they had to move, and she explained something about the rent they had to pay to Mr. Maxwell. He asked why they could not just go and live out on the land his father had out in Castleholding, not quite a half-mile away, where he kept a thriving vegetable garden and would have plenty to eat.

"Because there is no house there. You know that, John."

She always has an answer for everything.

And to add to the upset, he had to change schools to attend St. Cronan's Boys School. His mother said they would get a fine education there, but what did he care about that?

He had often walked by the big, two-story stone schoolhouse when he lived on Ballyhall. He never dreamed he would ever go there. John always thought the long building looked rather intimidating, with the stone wall surrounding it and its stark windows. He could not imagine having to spend day in, day out there.

"Mam," William piped up. "I reckon I'm too old to be going to school now and could be bringing in some money for the family."

Margaret sighed. "We've been over this a hundred times. You will do much better for yourself if you have some more learning about you. We'll talk about it again come summer. Maybe you can get some farm work to help us then. We'll be just fine until then. Your father, God have mercy on him," she paused to cross herself, "wouldn't have wanted it any other way."

John noticed that his mother was crossing herself far more often these days, and not just because his father had passed on. Soon after Maria was born, Mam had taken the two boys down to the church and had them converted to Catholicism. She had said something about them always being Catholic, but that their family had apparently given up the religion, or at least appeared to do so on paper. But now it was safe to be a Catholic again. He tried asking her why, but she just told him he was asking too many questions.

Nothing was the same, and John just tried to keep up as he followed along to meet St. Cronan's headmaster.

36: The Black Mills

October 1876

John stood panting with his back against the front door of his house. The metal doorknob ground between his shoulder blades, making an impression in his bony back. It did not matter, though. It was nothing compared to the pain he felt from the walloping he had just received from his mother.

He pressed himself harder against the door, trying to hide from the neighbours, for as soon as they heard what had happened, they would take his mother's side and probably give him a good walloping, too. Word got around quickly in the small town, and nosy neighbours felt it was their job to help bring up a poor, fatherless boy.

Slowly he leaned forward, looking up and down Rosemount. There was not a soul about, so he took a step into the street, rubbing his smarting backside.

He glanced again up the street, sure now that no one had heard the shouting and was coming to find out what the fuss was all about. His shoulders relaxed, and he let out a big breath, leaning more casually against the wall, until the pain in his rear stung him and he leapt forward like a scalded cat.

It had not been his fault; it had been William's. William had spent the morning goading him, making comments about how small he was, how there was not any hope of him growing any more, and that he would never amount to anything. He could feel the anger well up inside of him, tightening in his stomach like a knot.

On impulse, he had reached for the nearest thing he could find, which happened to be the metal pail on the kitchen floor, full of water that his mother had just fetched from the communal pump. He had snatched the pail and tossed the whole thing angrily towards his brother who was standing in front of the fireplace. The bucket sailed through the air, sloshing water behind it.

William ducked at the last moment. The pail crashed into the mantelpiece, catching the edge of the cut glass bowl which was prominently displayed there and sent it to the floor.

William had stared open-mouthed, frozen to the spot, watching his mother's most precious item—the only thing she had left from her mother—smash into a million bright shards on the wooden floorboards.

John lunged to catch the bucket, but not quickly enough. It landed heavily on the hearth and spilled the last of its contents onto the turf fire. A final plume of smoke rose into the air before the fire sizzled out.

"You're in for it now!" William said in horror, surveying the mess.

Their mother came hurtling down the stairs, two at a time, from where she had been attending to little Maria. "Jesus, Mary and Joseph!" she shouted. "What has happened?" She took a step into the kitchen, then stopped dead, looking at the mixture of broken glass, ashes and water with the empty bucket in the middle of it all.

Her face quickly twisted into anger. The scream that tore from her heart released all the frustration, stress, and pain that her current situation had brought upon her. She fell to her knees amongst the mess. Tears streamed down her face.

"I—I—I," John stammered.

His mother looked up. He could see her distress and the tears rolling down her face.

"It was all William's fault! He was over there saying the nastiest things you can imagine. Then, the devil was there on me shoulder, making me do it. Father O'Shea said you should never bear false witness, and that was exactly what he was doing! I had to make him stop, for I didn't want William to go to hell, Mam. The devil caused me to throw that water at him. It's all William's fault!" The words tumbled out of his mouth.

"Me own mother's beautiful cut-glass bowl. Of all the things that could have broken, that had to be it!"

She got up from the floor, her clothes sodden, and glared from one son to the next. "And the fire! That's gone out and cold now. We will now all be cursed for letting the fire die. You've both brought bad luck upon the house."

"But it was William's fault!"

William stared down at his younger brother. This time the look of the devil truly was in his eyes. "Bollocks!" he spat.

"Language!" Margaret roared. "I've had enough of the both of ye. I don't care whose fault it was, ye're both going to pay for this."

With reflexes only a mother in anger could possess, she grabbed hold of John's collar with one hand and William's with the other. She dragged them both to the doorway, where leaning against the wall was William's hurley. To pick it up, she had to release one of the boys, and she decided on William. He was much bigger than her now, but John she could manage.

Upon release, William made for the front door and ran onto the street.

John tried to plead his case once more. "But, Mam, it really was all William's fault."

"Don't be putting the blame for your problems on someone else."

Margaret swung the hurley high in the air and cracked down on John's backside.

Seizing his opportunity, John followed in his brother's footsteps and ran through the open doorway, slamming the door shut behind him. He stopped to catch his breath and check for any nosy neighbours. This is what brought him to where he stood now, rubbing his backside and looking up and down Rosemount.

He looked off into the distance to see if he could see John's Tower at the park, the way he could from their last home. He had imagined himself a great king living there, keeping his prisoners in the tower. He missed those days. Dad had still been alive, it had been before Maria was born, and they still had money coming in from Dad's job delivering messages for the tannery.

Now, every day was spent wondering where the next meal was going to come from and trying to make ends meet so they did not end up in the poor house.

"Whatcha doing, John?"

John jumped, surprised as he had not heard his friend George Frazer come up behind him.

"Away with the faeries?"

"Nah. Just finished me chores and was stepping out for a breather before I came to find the sorry likes of you."

"Up for some fun?" George hooked his arm through John's.

As the boys walked around the corner towards Church Street, George explained his plan. "Once we get to the tower, I dare you to climb up to the second window, and with your penknife, carve your initials into the sill, right next to the sailing ship."

Down Church Street, across from the old St. Cronan's monastery, stood a stone tower, built in the twelfth century, probably by the monks.

"Which window?"

"Come on, John. You ask it like you've not lived here all your life."

"I know about the carving, you eejit. I just can't remember which window it's on."

"Like you've never climbed up there."

John stared at him blankly.

"What! You haven't? Well then, I double dare you now! How did you make it this far?"

John shrugged and watched George point to a window a good twenty feet above the ground. It had a distinctive triangular head at the top, different from the rounded windows elsewhere in the tower. Back when the monks used the tower, this special window had been for displaying relics and treasures from the monastery. Carved into the inside jamb was a single-mast ship.

Over time the stones had loosened, and the mortar crumbled, leaving a rough surface that, with strong toes and fingers, one possibly could scale.

"I'll stand watch over there by the Black Mills. If you hear me whistle, jump down, and call off the mission."

At this, George turned and sauntered toward the old mill, known by the locals as the Black Mills since it had suffered fire damage.

John looked over his shoulder at his friend and then back to the tower. He dug his toes into the brick, causing more mortar to come loose. His fingers scrabbled for a secure hold, and he began hoisting himself up the wall.

His heart pounded faster, which had the unfortunate side effect of making his hands sweaty. Only a few feet from the ground, John began to slip, and would have completely fallen off had it not been for someone grabbing him by the shirt tails and yanking him back.

For the second time that day, for the second time that hour, John knew he was in trouble.

He looked quickly towards the Black Mills for any sign of his friend. Seeing none, he tried to squirm around to see held him in his grip.

"I thought I told you boys to stop trying to climb the tower. You're not only destroying it, but one of you is going to get yereselves killed!"

John nodded up at the groundskeeper. He opened his mouth to give an explanation.

"I don't want to hear any of your excuses. I told you the next time I caught one of you trying to scale the tower wall, I'd skin ya! Now, what's your name, boy?"

"George Frazer," John said, throwing his friend to the angry wolf.

"You wait here, George! I'm going to get me birch to give you a lashing. Then I'll take you home so your dad can give you several more."

"Yes, sir. I'll stay right here."

The moment the groundskeeper disappeared around the corner, John ran for his life to St. Cronan's churchyard, jumped the stone wall, and dove behind a tall gravestone. He could hear the groundskeeper calling George's name loudly.

"I've your name, boy, and will find where you live! I'll get you and when I do, I'll cut you in half like St. Cronan's cross! You mark my words!"

John leaned back and started to laugh, muffling the sound with a hand over his mouth. He finally felt safe. He had always considered this churchyard a safe place to hide.

He patted the tombstone and turned around to thank Elizabeth Cleary for shielding him once again from trouble. John felt for certain Elizabeth would have had a son, and would have wanted him saved, which is why he always headed right for her tombstone. These days he was there a lot, or so it seemed.

John heard someone snickering and looked up to see George pressed flat up against the corner of the ruins of the old Romanesque doorway, which now was the entrance of the present church. He slowly stood up, peered around Elizabeth's tombstone and saw the groundskeeper had left the vicinity. Then he bolted towards George and squatted with him in the corner.

"Where were you?" he demanded. "You were supposed to keep a lookout for me."

"You used my name!"

"It was the first thing I could think of. It was your idea."

"Well, I realized I couldn't really whistle, and you wouldn't have heard it over the saws. Besides, it was gas watching you get caught."

"Well, it wasn't gas for me."

"You got way higher than I ever would."

"What?" John cried. "You mean you haven't done it before? You told me you'd done it before."

"No way, boy. I ain't no climbing monkey!"

As a gesture of reconciliation, George pulled a crumpled envelope from his pocket, and opening it, passed it to John.

"Barley sugar, my favourite," John said. He crunched down on the sweet candy, forgetting the troubles of the day.

37: God-given talents

September 1881

"Where are you going out so late?" John's mother called to his back.

He turned at the last minute to face her. Because he had not inherited his father's height, he stared her directly in the eyes. "Out."

"What do you mean, 'out'? The headmaster said you haven't been at school, and I'm worried that you might be falling in with the wrong crowd, John."

"I'm 16 years old. I'm not a child. I'm going out."

"John, I do not have the time or energy to worry about you, or to try to set you straight. Maria isn't well, and all this fighting and arguing is making things worse."

"Then stop worrying. William is gone. You don't worry about him."

"No, but you're here, and are such a bright boy with a bright future. I don't want you wasting your God-given talents."

"I'm not wasting anything. I'm working with the book binder."

"That's not what I'm concerned about. Where are you going now?"

"I told you, out."

"I think you are going down to the pub. I've been hearing rumours about you spending time with that man who tends bar there. Nasty fellow."

"He is not. His stories are brilliant!"

"The life of a criminal is not brilliant. And how do you know he's telling the truth about being one of Ned Kelly's ex-henchmen?"

"The way he describes him, fighting the police, standing up for justice —it's like I'm right there with him in Australia."

"An outlaw is no sort of life. He's a bad influence on you, John. Stay away. If not for my sake, then for the sake of Maria's health. And stop getting into fights. Don't think I don't notice when you come home with scrapes and bruises. The last thing I want you to become a common criminal like Ned Kelly. We all know how he ended up—at the gallows."

"Yes, Mam," John said.

He closed the door before she could draw breath to say more and headed to McMahon's to see if O'Brogue was there. Most of the town might be frightened of the bartender, but John certainly was not.

38: What does he know?

October 31, 1883, Newry, Ireland

John's knees knocked together as he walked toward the white sandstone building. It was an imposing two-story structure, with a large cupola that drew the eye upwards.

On the muddy road out front, John waded through the crowds of people to find the main entrance, while trying to avoid dirtying his only pair of trousers. He had had several brushes with the law before but had always managed to get off with a stern warning. This would be his first time actually appearing in court. He had no idea what to expect.

For the past few years, he had been drifting further north, finding himself over 125 miles from home, trying to survive on his own. He had gotten by on what he called "borrowing things" and selling them to others, such as this fancy watch and chain that he was now accused of stealing. He had thought himself fairly good at it until he had felt the iron clamp of the constable's hand on his shoulder, catching him in the act.

Now, he stood before the Newry courthouse, about to appear before the Justice of the Peace. He was not even a real judge, or at least that is what one of the other boys on the street told him. He was just some filthy-rich landowner, doing this for his own amusement, getting to exhibit his power over the rest of them, he had said.

He made his way inside the building, and he presented himself to the officials, who instructed him to sit on a bench in the gallery until his name was called.

There was hardly a square inch of space available in the crowded room, but he managed to wedge himself between two men. It was one of the few times he was thankful for being so small.

Despite it being autumn, the room was hot, and the air stale. He could barely make out what was being said at the front of the room and hoped he did not miss it when they called him forward.

"He's guilty, that one," said the corpulent man to his right, leaning across to speak to John's other neighbour. The man's vile breath, smelling of ale, wafted toward him, and John coughed and leaned back to get out of the line of fire.

The rail-thin man to his left leaned forward in response. "He's lucky they gave up transporting convicts to Australia ten years ago."

The thin man's arm was bandaged, and something oozed from beneath it. John tried to lean back further.

Both men chortled as the clerk, having recorded the judgment in the previous case, stood up and shouted, "Seamus O'Flanagan against Jack FitzGerald!"

Judging by the clerk's volume, John no longer worried he would miss his turn.

The two summoned men made their way to the front and a hush fell over room. They took their seats in front of the Justice of the Peace, and a buzz of excitement began within the crowds, surmising what the next case might be about.

John leaned forward, elbows on knees, hoping to gain some insight and learn from those who went before. From what he could hear over the crowd, the complainant, who was wrapped in bandages and used his wife as a crutch, claimed that the other man had beaten him in a drunken fit.

"State your complaint," the Justice of the Peace said.

"I'm fairly ruined by this villain," the bandaged man said through a vicious cough. Even John could tell it was a dramatic performance for the court's sake. "He didn't leave as much blood in my body as would feed a hungry mosquito!"

The courtroom erupted into laughter.

"My wife will have to tell you the rest, for I am not able to say more." The bandaged man threw himself down on the chair at the front of the room while his wife continued the tale.

When she seemed to be done, the Justice turned to the other man. "What have you to say in answer to the charge? Why did you beat the complainant?"

After a long, drawn-out explanation, in which John could only hear half of his reasoning, the Justice of the Peace finally declared his verdict.

"Mr. FitzGerald, you were clearly drunk, and therefore, I am going to fine you five shillings. Please pay your fine before you leave."

The accused man bowed and said, "It's already been paid, your Honour."

The magistrate looked confused.

"I paid 20 shillings when I came in."

The clerk licked his index finger and turned back a few pages in in ledger. "You just owe 15 shillings. There was five shillings for striking the grocer, five more for pulling the preacher off the altar, and this gentleman here makes fifteen shillings. Do you want the change?"

"Nah," the man said. "I'd rather leave it in the coffers. I might be short the next time."

With that, he turned on his heel to leave the room, John was wide-mouthed and stunned by what he had just witnessed.

"John Ryan!" the clerk bellowed.

It took John a moment to realize they were calling him forward, as he had forgotten which name he had given. He stood. His two seat mates wished him luck. He walked, head held high, to the front of the room.

When it was all over, John kicked the chair leg three times. Three months in prison!

Who does that magistrate think I am? Saying I have no class and no calling but crime, preying upon society as other men work at their vocations. Saying I would never amount to anything more than a petty criminal. What does he know? Stealing a watch and chain today, and who knows what, tomorrow. Bollocks! I will prove him wrong!

39: Prisoners' Code

November 18, 1885, Enniskillen, Ireland

It was late at night when the police wagon brought John through the front gates set in the towering stone walls of the Enniskillen jail. High on the hill behind, he could just make out the silhouette of a monument and wondered if one of the rooms in the stone building before him would have a view of it.

He doubted it. Judging by the tiny slots in the wall, he knew he would not get to see much.

He took a deep breath of the fresh air, knowing it might be some time before he got to breathe so freely. Although winter was settling in, and there was a chill in the air, he did not mind. He ran his hands up and down his arms and legs, feeling the fine texture of the fabric, knowing it would be a long time before he felt real clothes again.

John knew the drill. As soon as he entered the jail, he would have to empty his pockets into a numbered sack before stepping into one of the cubicles to undress, wash, and then be examined by the doctor.

He always hated this part, when the doctor stood with his little note-book, marking down each of his marks and scars, from the scar over his right eye, to the one on the front of his right thigh, and then the ones on the left breast and buttock that few saw. All souvenirs from encounters with the wrong crowd.

Today he felt particularly exposed as the doctor took the tip of his fountain pen and prodded the lesions on his neck.

"Hmmm...," the doctor said, as he continued to prod the lumps grow-ing beneath the skin on John's shoulders and right forearm. "Does that hurt?"

He scribbled notes in his logbook, and without waiting for an answer, said, "Scrofula. You been having a fever?"

"Yes, sir," John mumbled.

"These ones here are developing some lesions. It appears they will soon open up and scar, like the other ones across the body."

169

John knew the doctor was not talking to him, but was treating him as a specimen to be examined. Another line in his logbook. He had been through this many times before, and it never got easier.

When that was finished, John was issued the standard prison uniform of a white jacket, pants, and pillbox hat, all stamped with arrows, so that, if one were to attempt to escape, they'd be instantly recognized.

Then came the boots he was supposed to wear for labour duties. Although they were small for his feet, they weighed at least fourteen pounds. When John first put them on, he felt as if he were fastened to the floor. The nails in the soles of these boots, as well as on the shoes he was given, were also hammered with arrow shapes. This meant that whatever ground you trod, you left traces that a prisoner had been there.

Now in his own cell, John tried to stand on his tiptoes to look out the long, thin window near the ceiling. As he had feared, he could not see the monument he had noticed on the skyline on the way in. He could see nothing save for a small slice of skyline.

He lay on his bed, trying to get comfortable, but knew it was no hope of it. He had heard what the uppity town people called it: hard bed, hard board, hard labour. If he had been imprisoned a few decades earlier, he would not have had such a hard bed, but would have had a hammock. *What is wrong with giving a man a decent night's sleep?*

Those same people thought that by giving prisoners hard beds, deliberately serving the same boring food day in and day out, and giving them menial tasks, the prisoners would reflect upon their actions and become better men who would avoid a life of crime. But John really did not see how that helped deter crime. It just made him aim to be more careful in the future.

As he tossed and turned, the day's events kept running through John's head, and he could hear the magistrate's words clearly.

"Mr. Frazer! Mr. Frazer! Are you paying attention?"

John looked up at the magistrate, forgetting the name he had used upon his arrest. He had hoped that by adopting part of his old friend's name, the authorities would not find out he was a repeat offender, and therefore might be more lenient with his sentencing.

No such luck.

"Or should we say, Mr. John Ryan?"

John hung his head, saying nothing.

"You have been moving around a fair bit, and trouble seems to find you immediately, or you it."

John nodded, keeping his eyes to the ground. Different magistrate, different court, but all the same in the end.

"According to the record here, Mr. Ryan, you served three months in Newry, and you were not out of prison a month when you are convicted in Dundalk for stealing an overcoat. The clerk shows me that you served six months hard labour there on the coast. If you went there in January of last year"—The magistrate stopped to count on his fingers—"That means you were released in July, and then, three months later, you were convicted in the Queens Session in Armagh."

The magistrate leaned forward and took off his spectacles to better read the ledger. "You were imprisoned for 12 months, a full calendar year, for stealing boots. Now, here you are in the courtroom of Enniskillen, miles from Armagh where you last served, on four charges, no less, of obtaining money under false pretenses. It seems here, your name is not the only false thing about you, Mr. Frazer, or Mr. Ryan."

The magistrate cleared his throat and continued. "What do you have to say for yourself?"

Without giving him time to speak, and because an answer was not required, the magistrate continued. "You are becoming a habitual criminal, Mr. Ryan. We hope to make your punishment match your crimes and provide you with some time here in our fine facilities to think about what you have done, so that we do not have to see you back in court again. It is at times like this that I wish that we were still able to transport our criminals to Australia, for I would send you there and Ireland would be done with you. Do you understand?"

John nodded, but still said nothing.

"You are hereby sentenced to seven years of penal servitude, in lieu of what would have been transportation to Australia. This is a very serious crime. We hope your time in silence and hard labour will make you see the severity of your actions and will send you on a godlier path. We hope that your experience will put the fear of God in you to never offend again. Case dismissed."

John had balked when he heard seven years. He had been expecting six months, or a year at the most. *What will this do to my mam?*

She was struggling already as a widow, contemplating sending his ten-year-old sister, Maria, out to work as a servant just to help make ends meet. Maria struggled enough with her own issues, not able to handle the pressures of life. Or so his mother said in the odd letter he received from time to time.

In his cell, John massaged his jaw and quietly hummed to himself. Tomorrow was his first day under the silent and separate system, that would apparently last the whole first year of his imprisonment. He had done it before and somehow managed, but never for this long of a stretch.

Being kept in total silence, not being allowed to talk to anyone for a whole year, was enough to drive a man mad, but John was determined to come out the other end. He was naturally quiet, anyway, so it would not bother him as much as some of the others.

It was not like he was going to get to know, or even see the others in the prison, for he knew the moment he stepped outside his cell, a hood would be placed over his head. He could feel the itchy cloth grate against the scrofula marks on his neck, rubbing them raw.

It would be hard to breathe, and even harder to see, and he would stumble in his heavy boots as he was dragged along by the warden. Also, the inmates would be kept apart from each other. This was a part of their punishment and came from a fear that crime could be passed on from one person to another, as if it were some sort of disease like the pustules on his neck.

There was no reprieve, even at chapel. They even had to wear the hood when forced to go to the services. The warden said it prevented them from being identified or from recognizing anyone else, but John knew it was just to make them feel less human. And it worked.

In chapel they would have to sit in their own cubicle so the only person they could see was the chaplain, who always had a message about how their misdeeds would have them burn in hell, should they choose not to repent. John had heard it so many times, he could probably deliver the message himself. If he were allowed to speak, that is.

The separation, he remembered, was only for part of the sentence, but the silence would endure.

The wardens claimed prisoners had plenty of opportunities to talk, saying they could talk to the warden themselves, or the other prisoners about the tasks they were completing, but John knew better than to test this out. In the other prisons, he had seen men merely whisper a word to each other, and then be called before the governor of the prison to be punished. Usually whipping. He had received that a few times.

John did not see the point of keeping everyone silent all the time, not that he could or would share his opinion with anyone. The wardens had to try to enforce it all the time, which just made the prisoners even angrier, and it seemed that someone was being punished every minute of the day. *Foolish rules. What do those rich folks in power know about what it was like to live here?*

Most of the guards were not clever enough to figure out that the prisoners always found a way to communicate with each other, through a cough, a wave, or singing a message when they should have been heartily singing the words to a hymn.

Then, when holding onto the rope during the open-air exercise time, they found ways to communicate in the courtyard. They followed a leader, holding a knot in a taut rope, fifteen feet apart, walking laps around the courtyard. Although they were separated, each inmate still found a way to speak silently and read lips when they passed each other. He hoped the men in this prison knew the same methods as at his previous accommodations. They usually did. It was the prisoners' code, which everyone seemed to know and understand.

With the thought of seven years going through his head, John finally drifted off to sleep.

40: Godliness with contentment

1898, Bradford, England

Early remission. No sweeter words had ever been spoken, apart perhaps from "not guilty."

John was finally getting out early for good behaviour. The governor had read him the document himself.

"Convict Ryan, while here in penal servitude, is always well conducted, and is always regarded as a man of quiet disposition."

He smiled, replaying the words in his head.

His thoughts returned to Ireland, to Tipperary, and especially to his sister, Maria. She had worked for a few years as a servant, but madness had overtaken her, and she had been committed to the Clonmel Asylum, or so said his mother in her last letter. He would like to see her again, and maybe try to talk some sense back into her. *But after so many years, would she even recognize me?* It had been over fifteen years.

What John did know was that he was not planning on staying in England a moment longer. He resented being called a Papist Paddy every time he opened his mouth to speak.

He had left Ireland by boat, setting off toward Yorkshire, to try to start over, after his seven years in Enniskillen. He even tried adopting his grandfather's name, William Mansuell, so his past would not catch up with him, but somehow they always managed to find his record. So, when he went before the magistrate in Bradford, accused of stealing watches worth £500, or so they claimed, they had thrown him back in prison for another seven years.

And here he was, just shy of those seven years, about to get early remission, but he still had another five years of police supervision to go. He would have to check in with the police every so often and stick with certain conditions.

Surely, I can do that. It cannot be worse than the hard labour I endured over the past fourteen years.

Although he could barely call it hard labour. More like, mind-numbingly tedious and pointless work, that was enough to drive some of the men so mad they would take their own lives just to avoid it.

Tomorrow would be the last day he would hear the morning bell awakening him at twenty-past six in the morning. It was his last night on the hard plank beds where he had never managed a good night's sleep.

He was looking forward to breaking his daily monotonous routine. Every morning they would be let out of their cells by half-past six. It was often a welcome relief, because the cells were so intensely cold, it was good to get up to put on their uniforms and get moving to generate some extra warmth.

Before breakfast, when the cell was open, he would have to slop out the chamber pot, tidy his cell by rolling away his mattress, fold his sheets and ensure that his essentials like his chamber pot, plate and mug were properly cleaned and polished until the governor could see his face shine in them. He was not allowed out until they sparkled. Over the years, John had perfected the routine, and was sure he could do it blindfolded.

After chapel services, he started work. Over the past fourteen years, he had performed just about every job there was within the prisons. From head to toe, his body showed the marks and signs of years of toil. His arm muscles had grown strong thanks to turning the crank all day as punishment. He had turned a handle, attached to a large wooden box, over 15,000 times a day, for many a day. He knew because he had counted. It was the only thing he could do to keep himself from going mad.

On the days he was assigned to the crank, he tried to be extra compliant, for it was the wardens who had the power to tighten or loosen the crank, making it harder or easier to turn.

He looked down at his hands. They were rough and raw from the days of working with oakum. Some days, he would have to cut rope, salvaged from ships, into two-foot lengths and then strike it with a heavy mallet to remove the tar, which was hard and crusty, and which coated the rope. On other days, he would spend hours unravelling the twine, turning it into new fibres. By the end of such a day, his hands were black from the tar, and bleeding from the oakum threads.

Sitting in a room with row after row of other prisoners hunched over the rope, not being able to talk to anyone, was also hard on the mind. Wardens insisted on silence.

If he did take a break to stretch his neck to look up, he was greeted with Biblical verses painted on the walls before them. 'Godliness with contentment is great gain'. They never missed an opportunity to attempt to save the inmates' souls.

Sewing mailbags was probably his favourite task, if he had to pick one. He had become quite proficient with a needle and thread. Although he often pricked his fingers with the needles, and the dim light strained his eyes, he quite enjoyed the rhythmic task. If he ever got out, perhaps he would seek employment with a tailor.

The treadmill, though, was the worst. He had heard from other prisoners, much older than himself, that there was a time when walking the tread wheel actually produced flour to make money for the prison, but that had long been abandoned. Now, the men were forced to march for fifteen quarter-hour sessions, climbing up to 18,000 feet every day, going up 24 steps, set eight inches apart, for no reason. Just as a form of punishment. A bell rang every time the wheel went around 30 times, signalling the end of that shift.

Although John's leg muscles had become strong, his back constantly ached and his feet were always sore and swollen. He had heard stories of men who had died using the treadmill, but they still made prisoners keep climbing.

All to save our souls and make us repent, turn to God, and give up a life of crime.

But today will be the last day of that, John thought. *Tomorrow will be the start of freedom.*

41: Released on license

November 22, 1905, Clonmel, Ireland

Twenty-two years. *Twenty-two.*

At the age of forty, this meant, John calculated, he had spent more than half of his life in prison, with only a month, or even weeks, between sentencings.

He had nothing to return to and no money. After having been released six years earlier in Yorkshire, he had made his way back to Ireland, back to Tipperary to track down his family.

There was no sign of his brother William or his mother, whom he could only presume were dead. He had gone to the Clonmel Asylum, only to learn that his sister had died the year before. Died of something to do with her lungs, phthisis, or some other medical-sounding condition.

Had I not been put back in jail, I might have had a chance to see her.

But he was caught stealing a coat and trousers and, because he was still on police supervision, he had to finish out the two years of that sentence, plus another seven years for the new theft. The magistrate wanted him to be thankful that he only got seven years, telling him he could have received seven for each offence.

John kicked the bed leg in anger. So much time wasted.

But now, he was getting out of there. He was being released on license to the London Metropolitan Police, as that is where he told them he would be heading: England. London.

Why not?

Some of the other men in prison had told him there were lots of opportunities there, and even gave him some addresses of people to meet there. He hoped he would have better luck in London than he had those thirteen years ago in Yorkshire.

The governor had repeatedly gone over the rules. He nodded his understanding and consent at each one. Be of good behaviour and not commit any offences. Keep in touch and visit with the supervising officer. Reside permanently at an address approved by the supervising officer, and do not undertake work unless approved. Do not travel outside the United Kingdom.

Sure, I can try to handle that. I only have to follow these rules for another year.

Part 4: The Finale

Mr. Justice Townshend
Archives de la Ville de Montréal

42: More than half his life

Friday, March 9, 1906, Windsor, NS

"Judging by the criminal record," Chief McDonald said, "this man was in prison for twenty-two years, starting at the age of seventeen in 1883'" He peered more closely at the records.

"Good heavens," Christie said. "That's more than half his life. No wonder the man's a hardened criminal. It's the only life he knew."

"If I'm doing the numbers properly," the Chief said as he counted on his fingers, "Kavanagh had less than four years, spread out, that he wasn't in prison."

"I just don't know what to say."

"I'd say he picked up a few lessons when he was doing time."

"And knows just where the bodies are buried."

43: A man of quiet disposition

May 21

"Please, I beg of you. If you have any ounce of mercy in you!"

John pleaded to the men standing before him in his cell. He did everything but fall to his knees at their feet. "I am innocent. I am inno-cent of all you have accused me of. I'm a man far from home, with no friends, and no one on my side."

"You should have thought of that beforehand, Mr. Stanley," Chief Mc-Donald said, unmoved by the prisoner's pleas. In his many years of ser-vice, he had heard the same stories countless times.

"I would just like you to write to Ireland. Write to the Mayboro prison and ask them for a character reference for me, or for them to even send someone over to testify on my behalf."

"They aren't likely to send someone all the way from Ireland, Mr. Stan-ley," Christie said. "Besides, that would take weeks, or even a month, and your murder trial is in just over a week."

"But they will tell you how I have always been well conducted and re-garded as a man of quiet disposition. These officials have known me most of my life, and they will tell you that I could not hurt a fly."

"That is for our jury to decide upon," Christie said.

"I have never contemplated injury to another person. It might not be in their power to say I have been an honest man, nor lived an honest life, but I can assure you they will tell you that I am not a fighter, nor a quar-reller. I may have had to get money by questionable means, but I am a man of peaceful character."

"We understand that," Jailer Smith said.

"If you look at my prison record, you will notice I have never hurt an-other soul. This leap to murder is preposterous."

"We will take what you say under advisement," Chief McDonald said.

"I've written a few letters to the officials at Maryboro Prison, for you to forward along."

He turned, took a stack of letters from his desk and passed them over to McDonald. "If an officer were to come from Ireland, he could also bring letters of character from others in the prison."

"Yes, so you've said," Christie said.

"I am an absolute stranger to all those around about me. I am at the mercy of all! And am without the proper means to pay the expenses of a defence solicitor."

"We hear you," McDonald said.

"I know I have been a dishonest man a great part of my life, but I have never at any time contemplated personal violence to any man. And now I sit here in this tiny cell, my health is poorly, and I am utterly alone. My only offence in Hants County has been to change my name."

"Perhaps you should have thought about that before," McDonald said again. He signalled for the three officials to leave, cutting off any further conversation.

44: We do

May 29

It was an unusually cold day for so late in the spring. The rain was lashing down, causing those coming into town to huddle together under the canopies of their buggies and carriages.

Spectators came to Windsor from across the county and beyond to attend the trial, and so the street leading to the courthouse was lined with muddy carriages. The roads in the countryside were not as well maintained as the ones in town, so swerving to avoid puddles and ruts was a constant activity. Recent heavy rains caused unavoidable mud, forcing many drivers to jump out to try to loosen the wheels. Some of the better prepared travellers had shovels or long poles aboard and used them to dislodge the wheels, while others resorted to pushing from the rear, pressing their backs into the carriage, while their Sunday-best shoes sank into the muck.

More crowds huddled beneath their umbrellas as they disembarked from the train, making their way up the two blocks of King Street to the courthouse.

Trial day brought together every sort—townspeople and countryfolk, who normally would not travel in the same circles. Women, dressed in their finest pastel silks, paraded through, complaining to their husbands about their new hats being ruined by the rain. Gentlemen strolled up the street with their walking sticks, sporting their finest morning coats and top hats. The other half came in their Sunday best cotton frocks or, in some cases, in work coveralls.

Those interested in hearing testimonies in a murder trial were not separated by class. The throng crowded together in front of the courthouse steps, hoping not to be turned away by the limited seating. When the doors finally opened, both men and women elbowed their way in, vying for the best seats to get a glimpse of the man accused of the gruesome murder.

At ten o'clock sharp, the doors at the front of the courtroom opened, and the Honourable Mr. Justice Townshend emerged. The room went silent. He carried a file of papers in one hand and a small metal ear trumpet in the other.

Justice Townshend looked around the crowded room and could smell the dampness from the rain. *Different town, but the same people*, he thought.

As a circuit judge, he travelled often throughout the province hearing Supreme Court cases, and each time it was the same. People showed up in hopes of hearing a tidbit of salacious news to earn them storytelling rights back in their community.

Following Justice Townshend was Crown Prosecutor Christie and the Attorney General, the Honourable Mr. Arthur Drysdale. Both men, roughly the same age, sported similar distinguished moustaches. They quickly took their seats at one of the desks in front of the judge's bench.

Next was Hadley Tremain, accompanied by John O'Mullin, who had come in from Halifax to aide with the defence. They took their seats at the other desk.

When everyone was in place, Justice Townshend called the room to order.

The first order of business was to swear in twelve men from Hants County to serve as the grand jury.

"Gentlemen of the jury," Townshend began, "you have an important task here today, and that is to review the evidence—all 117 pages of it—that has been collected in the case of the King versus George Stanley. You will be asked to carefully weigh the evidence and determine whether or not there is enough to proceed with a true bill against Mr. Stanley, charging him with the murder of Freeman Harvey."

A few men in the crowded room stood to see if they could catch a glimpse of the accused murderer, but seeing he was not yet in the courtroom, sat back down in disappointment.

"I understand Mr. Graham will be your foreman today, and I will expect you to deliver your verdict when you have reached a decision."

Graham stood to take the papers handed to him by the sheriff. A young man who farmed in the countryside over 30 miles from town, Graham felt well out of his depth. He looked around at the others summoned, most of whom, like him, were farmers or quarrymen. He wondered what they all knew about the justice system or about murder trials.

Graham led the eleven men to the anteroom to start the discussions, his head held high, and his determination higher. After the men filed out,

Townshend straightened his papers in front of him and called for the next case on the docket.

By mid-morning Christie was already exhausted. He was involved in virtually every case, representing either the plaintiff or defendant, depending on the charge. Those in the courtroom gallery felt as if they were watching a tennis match, their eyes following Christie back and forth, from one side to the other of the courtroom. It was an exciting morning, with so much happening that many tried to impress the details of all the cases upon their minds to relay back home, or to those who had not been admitted to the courtroom for lack of space.

Christie watched as the sheriff answered a knock on the door at the front of the room, through which the jury had departed. The sheriff stuck his head through the door, appeared to have a conversation with someone, and shut the door again without anyone entering.

"The jury has come to its decision," he announced.

Christie took out his pocket watch, rubbed his eyes, and looked again. The jury had only been out for thirty minutes, and they were already back with a decision.

Justice Townshend did not appear to notice the interaction, nor did he hear the sheriff's announcement.

Christie, who had seen the commotion at the jury door, and was used to Justice Townshend's poor hearing, began waving at the older gentleman, trying to get his attention. His gestures started small, but as they went unnoticed, they became larger.

Justice Townshend stopped abruptly mid-sentence. "Mr. Christie, are you shooing away an insect, or trying to fly yourself?"

The crowd laughed, Townshend looked up and smiled. He then took notice of the sheriff in the corner, and motioned for him to open the door to allow the jury members back in.

Graham led the eleven other men back into the courtroom, where they lined up in front of the judge.

"Mr. Graham, what say you in the matter of the King versus George Stanley? Do you find there is enough evidence to bring a True Bill against the defendant?"

"Guilty, your Honour. We do."

The crowd gasped and continued to search the room for any sign of the murderer.

"Thank you for your time, gentlemen. The sheriff will see you out."

Justice Townshend picked up the pocket watch beside him on the desk and, noticing it was close to noon, called Christie, Attorney General Drysdale, Tremain and O'Mullin to his bench.

Those in the first few rows leaned forward, trying to hear the conversation. With Justice Townshend's diminishing hearing it was not difficult, as he was unable to gauge his whispering.

"Gentlemen, we have accomplished much here this morning, and reached the end of the regular docket with great alacrity. We are still scheduled to be in court for the rest of today and tomorrow, so, as I had previously alerted you all, there would be a chance, should a true bill be brought against Mr. Stanley, that we would proceed with the murder trial. I assume you are all ready to proceed."

He looked around at the four gentlemen, who nodded.

"We will take a dinner break now and shall resume at one o'clock with the trial of the King versus George Stanley." This he said to the crowd in the room. There were a few cheers, and much discussion. The message was passed through the open doors to those waiting in the hallway and down to the gallery below, and those huddled outside under their umbrellas, still hoping to gain entrance.

As a few seats cleared with the temporary adjournment, Russell Shaw, who had been waiting in the perimeter of the room, fought his way through the crowd and pounced on a vacated seat. He pulled out his notebook, along with a sandwich, and sat back, legs stretched out, securing his place for the afternoon's spectacle. He was about to watch history being made and did not want to miss out.

45: Who was the stranger?

William Stephens clutched his letter of summons tightly in his fist. If he were selected to be on the jury, who knew how long it would take, and how long he would have to be away from the mill?

He had been surprised to see the official mark on the envelope when the letter arrived in the mail. He carefully opened it and read the contents.

> *Province of Nova Scotia*
> *County of Hants*
> *By the grace of God, of the United Kingdom of Great Britain and Ireland, King Edward VII, Defender of the faith.*
> *To William F. Stephens, of our county of Hants.*
> *We command you that you cause to come before our justices of the Supreme Court, at the courthouse in Windsor on Tuesday, the 29th day of May 1906, at ten o'clock in the forenoon, the 12 jurors whose names are contained in the panel hereunto annexed, and there to attend the said Supreme Court as petit jurors.*

Stephens had to read the letter three times, and even took it to his wife, Millie, to read it over, to try to make sense of all the legal talk. Though it was seemingly written in English, it contained so many legal terms that it might as well be in some exotic language They finally deduced that he had been called for jury duty; but for what, he had had to find out on the day.

He flipped to the second page and found lists of other men, other would-be jurors. He scanned the list to see if he recognized any of the names.

Walter Davison, Woodville, farmer.
Edmund Dimock, Windsor, clerk.
Alfred Tomlinson, Walton, labourer...

And the list went on. None of the names were overly familiar to Stephens, although he recognized some of the family names, and the communities were not far from his own.

He looked around the courtroom now, seeing if he could match a face to a name on his list. *Who is William Starratt? Who is William Campbell? Who is William White? Why are there so many Williams, and why had my own mother not been more imaginative?*

He nervously looked up and down the rows of men, and at Justice Townshend at the front of the room. When he glanced to the side and caught a glimpse at the room full of people, his face reddened. He hated being on display at the front of the room. He quickly glanced back down at the letter in his hand.

On the bottom of the page, beneath the summons, there was mention of the names being drawn in open court, a week or so prior. Stephens looked around at the white-plastered room and wondered if it had been within these walls.

One of his neighbours, who had been on the jury for the Tennycape murder four years ago, had explained to him how the juror names were selected. It was a long, laborious process, but he supposed not much different than keeping the meticulous records at the mill.

Apparently, the county held a list of taxpayers in a logbook of those who had a property value of at least $500. Before the trial, the clerk had to write the names of every potential juror from his book onto a ticket and then place the folded ticket in a small wooden box.

In an open court with witnesses, the court clerk then drew 12 tickets and recorded the names in his book, and then sent out letters to each so chosen, informing him to report for jury duty.

Stephens had thought about simply not showing up, letting them work something else out and find someone new. His neighbour, however, had warned him that failure to appear in court could result in a fine of $2 a day; whereas if he were to go, he would be financially rewarded.

If he were working in the woods, he would earn at least $2 a day, and here he was only promised $1. But he did not really have a choice, so here he sat, hoping the men back at the mill did not burn the place to the ground while he was gone.

Stephens thought more about his neighbour, and everything he had learned from the Tennycape trial. The man still had nightmares after hearing about the 16-year-old lad being bludgeoned to death by a fellow peddler.

It was more than he had hoped to ever know about a brutal murder.

He was not sure if he could handle the gruesome details of this case, although he had seen his fair share of bloody accidents at the mill.

"Gentlemen of the jury," Justice Townshend called out, bringing Stephens back to the present moment. He folded the letter and placed it in the inside pocket of his suit coat.

"We will now call you forth and swear each of you in, following which, you will select your foreman for the jury panel."

Stephens stood and followed the other men, keeping his head low, and praying he would not be selected to take the lead.

~

It was close to half-past one when everyone had finished taking their oaths. Justice Townshend asked if there were any witnesses seated in the gallery.

A few people stood and were ushered out the door at the front of the courtroom, allowing a few more people from around the edges to squeeze onto the already-crowded benches.

Then it was time to bring in the prisoner.

A hush fell over the room, and those in the back sat up tall, hoping to catch a glimpse of the man who would be led through the door at the front. Some were forced to stand, causing those already standing at the back to hiss their complaints.

The door opened and the accused shuffled across the front of the room, his leg and wrist chains rattling with each step.

Stephens looked up, still reeling with shock from having been selected as foreman. Although he was in a prime location to see everything, there was not much need. The prisoner, who was much smaller than Stephens had imagined, did not look up to meet the gaze of anyone as he entered the room.

Stephens tilted his head to see if he could see the man's face, but there was no sign of expression, no body language to denote any emotion or thought. It was going to be an interesting few days.

After regaining order in the court and reducing the noise level so he could hear, Justice Townshend arraigned the prisoner on the charges. "George Stanley Kavanagh," he said in a voice that commanded the room, "you are hereby charged with the murder of Freeman Harvey, committed on February 2, 1906, in Ellershouse, in the County of Hants. How do you plead?"

The room went dead silent.

"Not guilty, your Honour."

The crowd booed and cried, while some tossed newspapers to the front of the room to show their anger and displeasure.

Unaffected by the storm erupting around him, John sat at the seat behind the desk, waiting for the sheriff to come and unlock the chains on his outstretched arms.

When the crowd settled, Justice Townshend nodded to the attorneys at their tables, signalling the start of the trial.

Attorney General Drysdale stood and brushed an imaginary layer of dust from his shoulders. He cleared his throat and ran his hand over his face from his dark bushy eyebrows to his even bushier, snow-white hair. He paused and turned to the jury, smiling at each man as he looked them in the eyes.

For the next half hour, he outlined the tale of how an old man, living by himself in the countryside, was accosted by a foreigner, brutally murdered, and buried in his own basement under a pile of potatoes. By the time he had finished, those in the gallery were on the edges of their seats, gasping at the details of the gruesome ordeal. They may have read partial accounts in the newspapers, but this was the first time they had heard it described in its entirety.

As the first witness was called to the stand, Russell Shaw reached for a fresh notebook, ready to capture every word of every testimony to send back by wire to the main newspaper office in Halifax. He eyed the first witness up and down, trying to figure out who he was and how he might fit into this murder puzzle. The man was not much older than himself, straight-cut with a vest, bow tie and tiny spectacles. Russell guessed the spectacles were an attempt to make him look older and wiser than he probably was.

"Your name for the record, please," the Attorney General said.

"John A. McCallum. That's M-C, not M-A-C," he said, looking down at the stenographer.

The man likes details, Russell thought.

"You live in Windsor and are a crown surveyor."

"I am."

"You made a survey of the premises formerly occupied by the late Freeman Harvey."

"I did."

Precise and a man of few words, Russell thought. *At least he is easy to transcribe.*

Drysdale unrolled a large sheet of paper and tacked it to a board at the front of the room, angling the board so not only could the jury and witness, but also the judge and crowd in the gallery, could see it. Heads turned and necks strained trying to get a glimpse of the map before them. Russell was once again thankful for his seat with a fine view.

"This plan correctly shows Freeman Harvey's house as it sits near the junction of the roads between that which goes to Halifax, and that which goes to Ellershouse. And it shows the Harvey house in relation to its neighbours."

"Yes, it does."

Drysdale picked up a collection of photographs from his table and handed them to the witness, asking if they represented the front and back of the Harvey house.

Russell felt somewhat annoyed that he could not see the photos from his position, but did catch a glimpse of them as they were handed over to the jury for further examination. Fortunately, he had been to the house back in February, so could picture it perfectly, and even had printed a copy of one of the pictures in the *Herald*.

When the next witness walked up in his three-piece suit, bowler hat in hand, Russell could not help but think he looked awfully familiar.

"Wesley Livingston," Drysdale said, "you are a photographer."

The Attorney General had a habit of expecting people to answer state-ments. Russell did not hear anything that ended in a question mark. The man had a presence and command of the room that could only be equalled by Crown Prosecutor Christie or Justice Townshend. They were all cut from the same distinguished cloth.

Russell racked his brain to figure where he had seen the man before. He had only been in Windsor a handful of days. He was there for a day in February upon discovery of the murder, then again in March for the pre-liminary trial. It was on this second visit when Thomas Doran, Victoria Hotel's proprietor, had filled him in on the workings of the town, and he had explored the area.

That's it! Russell smiled to himself. He never forgot a face or a name. It was the man from the Windsor Kandy Kitchen store downtown.

Upon the hotel proprietor's recommendation, Russell had found the confectionery shop and was drawn in by the luscious display in the win-dow. Inside, his eyes were treated to a feast of rows and rows of pulled molasses candy, sponge toffee, butterscotch lumps, ribbon candy, chocol-ate-dipped coconut balls and the other delicacies, the likes of which he had never seen before. He had stood there, drooling, until one of the clerks had approached him with a sample.

The sponge toffee melted in his mouth; the air bubbles tickled his tongue.

The goods were all made in Livingston's kitchen at the back of the store, the clerk had told him as he reached for another sample. He spun around, only to see a tall counter that served ice cream. He had no idea where to start. It was sensory overload for his taste buds.

As he stood there drooling, Mr. Livingston had come down the stairs, into the main store. Russell knew it was this same man, as the clerk had called him by name. He had ordered one of the clerks to leave the counter to come help him upstairs in the Royal Café restaurant, as the high-society folks were having their weekly meeting and were asking for more hot tea.

And, here he was today, in the courthouse in Windsor, saying that not only was he the proprietor of that spectacular candy store, but also a photographer who recorded local scenery and events—and, Russell presumed, murder scenes. There would have been few people with a camera in town.

Livingston agreed that he had been the one to take the photographs of the Harvey house, the ones previously shown to McCallum and the jury.

Drysdale walked up to the display board and flipped the map over. The board rocked back into position. He stepped to one side. The crowd began murmuring and pointing as they stared at the photographs of Harvey's cellar.

Drysdale pointed to the first picture. "This picture shows the steps leading down into the cellar."

"Yes."

"There is a pile of potatoes here, and some in wooden crates and on the floor."

"Yes, this shows the potato pile near the foot of the steps where the body was found. Beside the pile, you can see a bucket and that is where the head was found."

The woman beside Russell buried her head in her husband's shoulder, but kept peeking and looking away again. He could understand the feeling. It was hard to look, but it was harder to look away.

O'Mullin the defence attorney, stood to cross examine the witness. "In order to get the picture, did you place the bucket and the potatoes in the position shown?"

"Yes."

"You fixed the potatoes and the bucket?" he asked incredulously.

"Not the potatoes, but I did the bucket. But that *is* the bucket the head was found in."

"Again, you rearranged the picture."

"Yes." Livingston hung his head as he admitted tampering with the scene.

Russell felt sorry for the man. What did he know about taking murder scene photographs? He was simply a candy man who had a camera.

Next, an old gentleman with a snowy-white beard walked, with the aid of a cane, to take the stand. Russell was surprised that his voice boomed loudly throughout the courtroom.

"I am the Rev. Matthew Henry, the Presbyterian minister in St. Croix."

Russell nodded, remembering hearing he was the one who had led the service for Freeman Harvey. No wonder he had such a powerful speaking voice and could capture the attention of the room.

"Do you remember visiting Freeman Harvey in February?" Christie asked, taking his turn to address the witnesses.

"I do. It was on a Friday. The first Friday, I believe."

"What time in the day did you visit him?"

"It was in the afternoon, between three and four o'clock. I saw him at his own home."

"Was any other person present? And what took place?"

"I knocked at the door, and it was opened by a stranger."

"Who was the stranger?"

"I judge that it was the prisoner in the dock. I went in with him to the kitchen, where Harvey was. He was sitting at a table with some papers strewn about. I don't know what they were, but I presume that they were papers in connection with his school rates."

All eyes turned to the prisoner, who kept his eyes squarely on the floor, refusing to look up.

"Irish papist!"

"Send the Mick home!"

"Damned Fenian!"

The more insults that were hurled, the more intently the prisoner refused to move.

From where he was sitting, Russell could see the muscles in Stanley's neck tensing, his fists clutching and his shoulders slowly rising and falling as he tried to calm his breathing. Russell intently watched the man of a hundred names. He became more interested in Stanley's reactions than hearing from the old man about his visit with Harvey.

William Kavanagh, or George Stanley, or whatever he was called, perplexed him. Russell could not quite put his finger on what it was about him. The man sat there silently, refusing to react. Russell tried to look into his face to try to get a glimpse of who the man actually was. He noted the numerous scars above both eyes, and those that peeked out from under his shirt cuffs. It proved the man was a fighter and a survivor. Maybe he did have a chance after all.

When Russell's story about the murder in Ellershouse had appeared on the front page of the Halifax *Herald*, Jessie Forsey had marched herself into the office, looking for someone with whom to share her story of how the prisoner had boarded with her. Russell's uncle had sent her his way, since he had been the one covering the story. She shared sordid stories of the accused man stealing from her and her guests, running off in the night, and charming her husband into having him board with them. The man she described hardly looked like the one before him.

From there, Russell had followed leads, meeting many people throughout the city whom the man's deceptions had touched. From all accounts, he could charm anyone into a job, a loan, a coat, or telephone installation. *The man could sell sawdust to a lumber mill.*

The man was a notorious talker. A conniving, convincing, confidence man. Yet, here he was, sitting in the dock, not saying a word. Not trying to talk his way out of anything, and not trying to convince anyone of anything. *What is happening? Is he resigned to his fate? Will he confess to the heinous murder?*

Russell shook his head, realizing he was missing part of the reverend's testimony. *If I had to listen to that loud, but soothing, voice every Sunday, I am sure I would have the best daydreams.*

"What conversation did you have with the prisoner?"

"I inquired where he was from. He said, if I remember rightly, that he was from London. He had been in the country awhile, I don't remember how long, but not a great while. I asked him if he was going to stay in the country, and how he liked it, and I understood that he was going to stay and that he was looking for a farm. He mentioned a farm up Newport way, but he did not know whether he would buy it."

O'Mullin stood, rubbing his hands together, taking his turn at cross examination. "When you left the Harvey house, who was there?"

"George Stanley, Freeman Harvey, Joseph Fisher and his son, Henry."

Russell nodded, retracing the family tree in his mind, remembering that Joseph was David Fisher's brother.

"Was that the last time you saw the prisoner?"

"No, I saw him the next morning in St. Croix near the post office. I was going for the mail, which had come in at ten o'clock, and I met him there.

He was with Jim Fisher. He told me he had bought a farm."

"Did he tell you which farm?" O'Mullin asked.

"He said it was Freeman Harvey's. He also said he expected some relative to come by and by. That is all."

Justice Townshend rubbed his eyes and then pressed a hand against his aching hip. He was tired from sitting in the hard, wooden chair, so he struck the gavel and called for a recess break.

Without waiting for a response, he stood, making his way toward the door at the front that led to the judge's chambers.

Christie and the Attorney General looked at each other and nodded, it was time to leave. They tucked their papers under their arms and followed suit. Sheriff O'Brien approached the prisoner, locked on the manacles, and led him away amidst jeers and insults.

As he reached the door, Sheriff O'Brien ducked just in time as another rolled-up newspaper came hurtling through the air, striking the door frame. The sheriff spun around to discover the culprit, but saw only a sea of innocent-looking people.

46: On to something

With everyone back in place, Justice Townshend, now sitting on a cushion, brought the courtroom to order. The Crown called Joseph Fisher forward to testify.

Joseph, a man in his late 40s, was David Fisher's younger brother. A labourer by trade, Joseph explained how he now lived in St. Croix, but previously had lived near Freeman Harvey, and had known the man for five years.

"When was the last time you saw Mr. Harvey alive?" Drysdale asked, standing at his table.

"The Friday evening. I went to his house, and my boy Henry was with me. We went there about seven o'clock. Mr. Harvey was alone, and he was sitting at the kitchen table working at his school rates. You see, he was the collector of the school taxes for the district and had to go door-to-door collecting them, recording the payments in his ledger book, before submitting them to the county."

"Did you see the prisoner who is sitting in the dock, before that?"

Joseph leaned forward, looking across the judge toward the dock at the man being referred to, as if he had forgotten what he looked like and why he was there. Joseph would have to rely on memory, as the prisoner refused to look up.

"I seen him passing by about a fortnight before that. And I seen him there that night I was at Harvey's. He showed up right after Henry and I had gotten there."

"How did the prisoner get in?"

"He just walked right in through the back door without knocking, like he done and owned the place."

"Did you have a conversation with Mr. Stanley there and then?"

"He told me he wouldn't stay in that house like Harvey was doing for thousands of dollars, and when I asked why, he said the old man was so hard of hearing that someone might break in and kill and rob him. I said that he could just go to bed and shut all the windows, and no one would interfere with him. But Mr. Stanley then up and said that the windows were all rotten and someone could easily break in. I told him I thought the windows were fine. That's the only conversation we had."

"What time did you leave?"

"We left around eight o'clock that evening—me and the boy did. Harvey stayed inside with Mr. Stanley."

"When were you next at the Harvey house?"

"I didn't go back there again until Monday, after they had discovered Harvey's body in the cellar. I went down there into the cellar once the coroner had left. Several people from the village came by all afternoon to have a look. I seen the head. The body was lying in a pile of potatoes and the head was separate."

"Describe the condition of the head."

"It was all covered in blood and dirt. I couldn't really tell anything about it, other than I knew it to be the head of Freeman Harvey."

There were a few gasps in the crowd, and despite the fact it was not overly hot in the crowded room, women fanned themselves more vigorously, signalling their discomfort with every motion.

"Tell us what he was wearing."

"When I left him on Friday evening, he had boots on and those clothes, just like he had come from working in the barn. When I went down into the cellar afterwards and seen the body, the boots were off, but the clothes were just the same."

After a few more lines of questioning, O'Mullin stood to begin cross examination even before Drysdale had completely sat down. "What conversations did you have with Freeman Harvey when you were there that Friday night?"

"I went down to ask him if he needed any shingling done."

"And, what else?"

"I just asked him about shingling the barn, and he told me he was thinking about selling out, and if he did not sell out, he would let me know further on. That was all that was said, and I heard nothing further from him."

"Are you a friend of McCarthy's?"

"Just by sight."

"Do you know what kind of man he is?"

"No."

"I thought you lived in this neighbourhood."

"No, I live four miles away, now."

"But I suppose you know a great deal about the neighbours who live within those four miles of you, though."

"I don't have much dealing with any of them."

Getting nowhere with the witness, O'Mullin changed his course of questioning.

"After the inquest, who did you go down into the cellar with? And what did the scene look like?"

"I could not tell you who went down the cellar with me. There were so many there going up and down. I could not tell you how the potatoes were, but I did see the head on the table. I'm not sure who showed it to me. Someone asked me to go look in the cellar, but I forget who."

"What did the head look like?"

"Like a man's head."

"So, you don't know who asked you to go down there, but do you know why you went down there?"

"I had to go examine the clothes to swear what he had on. I had to be called on."

"Who had to call on you?"

"I could not tell you."

Frustrated with getting nowhere, O'Mullin sighed. "As a matter of fact you don't know very much about it"

"No."

O'Mullin threw his hands in the air and returned to his seat, happy at least that he had proven Joseph Fisher an unreliable witness.

Sheriff O'Brien shuffled Joseph Fisher off the stand and directed him toward the door at the front of the courtroom, reappearing a few minutes later with a boy about 15 or 16 years old.

Russell looked at the boy's scrawny arms poking out of what he could only assume was the child's Sunday-best shirt. The pants were too short, and he had visible holes in his shoes. He was so scrawny, Russell wondered how long it had been since this boy had had new clothes, never mind a full meal.

He also looked scared to death, with his eyes darting around the room, trying to make eye contact with anyone, until he saw the prisoner. For a fleeting moment, Russell noticed that George Stanley looked up, catching the boy's eyes, and there was a faint smile, and an acknowledge-ment of recognition that passed over both their faces. Then, in the next heartbeat, the boy looked away, his face reddening, as if he had re-membered he was no longer to be friendly with the man.

"Henry Fisher, son of our last witness, Joseph Fisher," Attorney Gen-eral Drysdale announced as the boy took the seat in the witness box.

After establishing who Henry was, and the connection to the event, Drysdale said, "When you left that Friday night, there was nobody else in the house with Harvey and Stanley."

"Correct. Mr. Stanley left him there when Father and I went away with Harvey in the kitchen. We left about eight o'clock. I did not see anyone else there except Harvey and Stanley."

When it was O'Mullin's turn to cross examine, he stood so he could look the young boy directly in the eyes, bearing down on him like a schoolmaster searching for the eyes of truth. "You and your father were having a conversation with Harvey."

"Father was."

"There was no difficulty about having a conversation with him."

"No."

"Just an ordinary conversation between your father, Harvey and Stanley."

"Yes."

"So, you were not out of the kitchen?"

"No."

"So, Mrs. Harvey could have been in the house for all you knew."

"Yes."

"McCarthy might have been in the front room?"

"He might have been. I know him!"

The thought of Edgar McCarthy hiding in the front room set the courtroom buzzing, with people whispering and nudging each other. Theories were whispered back and forth, while a few voices from the back shouted for the arrest of McCarthy.

Justice Townshend had to strike his gavel three times before the room fell silent. He nodded at O'Mullin to continue.

"Mr. Spence might have been in the front room."

"Yes."

A meek voice from the front called out, "Hey, now!" Eyes followed the sound to Maud, George Spence's young wife, who sat with her arms folded across her chest, evidently angry at the accusation.

From the bench, Justice Townshend made the motion to hurry O'Mullin along, lest he do a roll call of the entire village.

"Who did you talk this over with since it happened?"

"Nobody that I remember at all. Not even Father."

"You never mentioned the murder to a soul since the day it happened until now?" O'Mullin put his hand on his hip in disbelief, took off his spectacles and leaned forward into the boy's eyes.

"No."

"You haven't talked it over with your father?"

"Not a word. I live with him. I have not heard anyone else in the house talking about it. It has never been mentioned in the house since that time. I am quite clear."

"Is your mother alive? Did you talk to her about it?"

"Not much. Just about Stanley being there that night. She did not talk over with me what Father said about it."

Sitting in the pew, Russell slapped his forehead. He had had just about enough of O'Mullin's questioning technique. Move along! Anyone in the village could have been in Harvey's front room, but it did not mean he had to list them all. And no! The boy said he had not talked to anyone about the murder. Why not ask him about his grandmother? His neighbour? His teacher? Listing more people was not going to change that answer.

If only Russell could have a chance to interview the witnesses, he was sure he could come up with some better questions, and then have a chance to write a great story about the case for the paper. *What was it like to be conned by this little Irishman? What was it like being face-to-face with a real murderer?*

His mind wandered as he imagined the headlines. The absurdity of the next line of questioning refocused his attention.

"How do you fix the date of this conversation, the time it took place?" O'Mullin asked, walking toward Henry.

"Friday."

"How do you know it was Friday?"

"Because it was the day after Thursday."

A few people in the crowd chuckled nervously, not sure if the boy was being a smart aleck.

"How do you know?" O'Mullin pressed.

"It would be what I heard."

"You know from what you heard?"

"I always heard Friday was after Thursday."

"Who was it who told you that Friday was after Thursday?"

"Mother told me."

The giggles that were stifled before could no longer be contained and laughter filled the courtroom.

Russell pursed his lips, wondering how this poor, uneducated lad had made it thus far, and he wondered what his future would hold.

"Who told you about what night it was?"

"I always heard it was a Friday night. I heard it from Mother."

O'Mullin felt like he was wading through molasses, continuing his line of inquiry. "You heard from your mother it was Friday night this oc-curred?"

"Yes."

"You don't know this. You only know what your mother told you?"

"Yes."

Knowing he would not get any further and had already proved the mental capacity of the witness, O'Mullin sat back down, mumbling, "That's all."

Once Henry Fisher had left the witness box, it was filled by Dr. James Reid, who was, this time, questioned by Crown Prosecutor Christie.

The country doctor sat proudly, explaining how he had not only been a physician for 22 years, but also acted as the coroner for Hants County. He described in detail how he was telephoned to come to Ellershouse to examine the body of what was then presumed to be Freeman Harvey. He discussed how he empanelled a jury and how they examined the body in the cellar.

"Where was the body, and what condition was it in?"

Dr. Reid closed his eyes, envisioning the scene. He had recounted the story so many times, it almost played out like a performance in his mind. "The body was found in the cellar, partially covered by a pile of potatoes. The feet were just sticking through the pile, and when we uncovered it, we realized the head was missing. Later, during the examination, someone found the head in another part of the cellar, in an ordinary potato sack, in a bucket."

"Can you describe the appearance of the body and the wounds on the head?"

"There were, I think, four wounds on the face, incised wounds made with a sharp instrument, probably a knife. Two I think were on the left side, one under the chin, and one on the right side. They were in the cheek and under the chin."

Although he had sat through several trials now and had written sev-eral articles for the *Herald* about it, hearing the gruesome description never failed to send chills down Russell's spine. *What would possess a man to commit murder in the first place, and then try to hide it, poorly, he might add, in a pile of potatoes?*

Had he tried to dismember the body and found it harder than he at first thought, and decided to let nature take its course by allowing it to rot? Had he planned on returning to deal with the body later but ran out of time before suspicion was cast upon him and he took off as a fugitive?

Russell looked up at the prisoner, who still sat motionless, wondering what was going through his mind. *If only he would talk, share his side of the story, or provide me with an opportunity for an interview.* So far, the secret was buried deep within the stoic Irishman.

"Give us some idea of the size of the wound under the chin."

"It would be at least an inch and a half, as though the knife had entered and cut a little sideways. Larger than the blade; but the depth of it, I could not say."

"Could such wounds have been made with a knife like the one found here in court?"

Christie reached into a box under his desk and pulled out what Russell assumed the jackknife David Fisher had loaned to the prisoner. Russell turned his head to catch the reactions of those in the gallery, who were transfixed on the weapon that Christie was swinging like a pendulum at the front of the room, as if trying to hypnotize them all.

"Yes, such a size wound could be made with a blade like that," Dr. Reid said, nodding with each swing of the knife.

"How would you say the head was severed from the body?"

"I examined the bone where it had been severed. I would say it had been sawn off. The bone had definitely been sawn. It was not a nice job; it was a poor job of cutting. It was considerably haggard. One or two pieces of skin or tissue were partly detached from the rest of the body. But I am sure it had been sawn because the end of the bone was an even surface and it was very near to one of the vertebrae, one of the bones of the spinal column. It could not have been cut with any other instrument but a saw."

"If it had been cut by an axe, how would the bone have appeared?"

"There would have been some chipping and the outside of the bone would have shown some depressions."

"In other words, the bone would have been shattered."

"Yes."

"Did you notice any other marks on the head other than the cuts?"

"There was a bruise on the forehead."

"Did you see anything in the nature of blood about?"

"Yes, the greatest amount of blood was at the foot of the stairs. There was also blood around in different parts of the cellar, small quantities of blood. There was a small amount where the body was found and there was blood up on the stairway. There were smudges made with the hand."

"What was the nature of these marks?"

"They were made with a blood-stained hand."

With this description, there was a groan through the crowd as they imagined the scene. Dr. Reid helped fill in the pictures in their mind.

"Going down the cellar, the blood-stained hand was on which side?"

"The right. It appeared to have been made as if the fingers were clutching the wall. The marks were about eight inches long, as if he were falling down the cellar steps."

"Was there any blood on Harvey's right hand?"

"Yes, there was some blood on one of his hands."

"When you examined the body again before the funeral, did you notice anything else that could have been the cause of death?"

"There was nothing else to suggest cause of death outside of cutting the head off. The wound under the chin was certainly the most extensive of the lot. I cannot say, however, that that would have been fatal. I can't say for certain that the wounds were the cause of death."

With the grisly image planted securely in the minds of the jurors, Prosecutor Christie sat back down. He tidied the papers on his desk, and finally looked over at O'Mullin and nodded.

As O'Mullin prepared, Russell leaned back on the bench and stretched his fingers, shaking them to bring the blood back after so many hours of frantically writing shorthand as he tried to capture every word of every testimony.

Cause of death, undetermined, he thought. Russell surmised what Dr. Reid was really thinking. He had done his research on the country doctor before coming and knew that he was a staunch believer in temperance, and lectured on the point at every opportunity, across the community. According to other reporters' stories, the good country doctor liked to pepper his speeches with as many statistics as he could, which probably, instead of making him sound wiser, simply confused the listeners.

Russell had heard what hotelier Thomas Doran had said was the doctor's favourite fact. Apparently, 90 per cent of the cases in the hospitals are directly or indirectly because of the evil effects of intemperance, and if we just had complete prohibition, we might even put the hospitals out of business.

Sitting up on the stand, did Dr. Reid believe this whole murderous affair was the result of the evils of drink? Surely, he could not. But then again, Russell had heard the other testimonies, about the drunken scene over the weekend Harvey was murdered. *Maybe Dr. Reid is on to something, after all.*

47: He seemed a little excited

O'Mullin cleared his throat and began his cross examination. Before the trial it had been decided that O'Mullin would do the cross, as his colleague Tremain was good friends with Dr. Reid; they both sat on the Windsor town council.

"Was there anyone who gave evidence before you today, or anyone else who asked you if they had better not retain a lawyer? Either before or after giving his evidence?"

"Objection, your honour!" Attorney General Drysdale jumped to his feet. "This is not the time to deal with the credibility of a witness."

The judge took a few moments to silently review what he had just heard, or thought he heard, and answered carefully. "I suggest that it would be better to examine this witness first and then recall the previous witnesses to contradict him, if necessary."

Drysdale smiled, sitting back down.

Undeterred, O'Mullin continued. "During your time at the Harvey house, did any person try to fit his hand to these particular marks on the wall?"

"I did not notice anyone doing this."

"It did not occur to you that it would be well to do something to check these blood stains?"

"I did not think it to be necessary, because I did not see blood at the head of the stairway."

"Did you examine the head of the stairway?"

"Not particularly."

"This wound on the forehead, did it not leave a dent in the forehead or in the skull?"

"No, it was just a bruise."

"That would not be any more likely than the cuts to cause death?"

"It would not likely cause death."

His time in the witness box being finished, Dr. Reid stepped down. Sheriff O'Brien ushered in David Fisher as the next witness.

Russell leaned back and smiled. He could not wait for this testimony, for it had always proven so entertaining during the last few trials. He wondered what the man would say this time.

When he was ushered into the courtroom, David stopped and looked around, like a deer in a trance. He stood open-mouthed, staring at the crowded room, until Sheriff O'Brien nudged him onward. It took him a few minutes to get comfortable in his seat, and just when the Attorney General thought the man was settled and ready to begin, he would stand and shift position again.

As entertaining as it was, Russell could not help but feel sorry for the man, who obviously was not used to being in town, let alone in front of such a large crowd of people.

To warm him up, Drysdale began with a few simple questions which resulted in the details that David Fisher was 55 years old, had lived in the area for over 25 years, and now resided on the Dawson Road.

"How did you come to meet the prisoner?"

"Well, he done showed up at my house on the nineteenth of January. He came to my house. He came there in the evening about seven o'clock. He said he wanted to get a night's lodging. And, when he came to the door, I says 'Who's there?' and he said, 'a stranger.' So I let him in, and he stayed the night. You see, I hadn't been working all winter. You know, I haven't been well, but we needed the money, because I wasn't working. I'd rented some land, and my sons and I were working it, but the extra money for a boarder would be nice, although we had me, Mary Ann, Jim, Maurice, and up till then, Samuel Harvey boarding with us. He's the dead man's brother, you know."

"What did Mr. Kavanagh say to you about Freeman Harvey's place?"

"Who? I don't know me any Mr. Kavanagh."

"You know him as George Stanley. The prisoner."

"Why didn't you say that?"

"Correction," Drysdale said, "what did Mr. Stanley say to you about Freeman Harvey's property?"

"Well on that Friday night, the first of February, he told me he was going down to Harvey's house to do business about buying his place. He said the business would be done that night. He said he was going to buy the place and he was going to do it that night."

David Fisher then repeated the story of how George Stanley had borrowed his knife, saying he needed to do a bit of business that night. When Drysdale showed the knife again to the courtroom, David confirmed it was his.

When asked when he got his knife back, David said it was not until the following morning. "He come in Saturday morning, and handed it back to me, saying he were finished with it. That's when I seen it was sharper than when I gave it to him. That's also when Stanley came in with a roll of papers, that he said were the deeds to the Harvey place. He also showed me a ring of keys for the house and the barn."

David testified how he was asked to move in and care for the place, to look after the stock.

"Did he make a statement about where Harvey was?"

"I asked him, and he said the old man had gone to Halifax to get another deed. He said he'd paid him $200. Now that's a lot of money. I don't think I ever seen that much money! He said he had £7000 back in London and sent a cablegram to have it wired here, and that his sister had another £11,000 at her command. In the meanwhile, he took out $200 from the bank in Windsor, thanks to help from Mr. Rieck. Plus, he said he had some money he earned from the telephone company."

"What happened after he paid the money, then?"

"He went to Windsor to settle with his wife."

"Stanley went to Windsor to settle with his wife?"

David said, "Stanley is married? I'd like to meet her. He never did mention her."

There were a few snickers in the crowd, but David did not seem to notice. "As I was saying, Harvey went to Windsor to settle the house deal with his wife. That's what Stanley said, anyways. Stanley said the old man wouldn't be back till Thursday."

Then David started talking about some of Stanley's strange behaviour that afternoon. "There were two or three clotheslines right over the stove and a corner full of old clothes like socks and mittens, caps and the like. And all of sudden, Stanley gone and shoved them all into the wood stove and burned them up. I shouted W'oh, as if I were getting one of them work horses to stop, but he didn't listen, just kept on shoving them into the fire. I told him he'd have too much of a fire and burn the whole house down, but he didn't seem to mind. It was all second-hand stuff."

David told about trading stories with the Spences, and moved on to Saturday night, when his son Jim and Stanley left for the evening. "Stanley said to me, 'I want you to stay in the house till I get back. Keep the door locked and don't let nobody in till I get back.' Nobody came by, so that wasn't a problem, but they didn't get back till pretty near handy one o'clock in the morning. I waited up for them."

"Had they been taking something?" asked Drysdale mimicking drinking from a bottle.

"My son was pretty well along by this time. Stanley was pretty straight. He did not show the effects so much."

Russell whipped his head around to catch the reactions in the crowd. He noted they were mixed. Being such a strong temperance community, as predicted, half were making mother-hen tutting noises, while others stifled chortles behind a hand.

"When they got home, did you stay up drinking?"

"There was nothing there to drink in the house this time. They did not bring anything home with them. I did not go to bed, although Stanley wanted me to. I said, 'No, I won't,' and he said, 'You better.' He wanted me to take some stuff he gave me after he came home. It made me sick and I did not go to bed for him until about three o'clock."

"So, he did bring home something to drink."

"No, he did not bring anything with him."

"So, where did you get this mixture you drank, then?"

"He brought it to me in a cup from the table. He poured it out of a bottle and put some hot water and sugar in it. I just tasted it but did not drink it. After a while, I was in the room and he said, 'You go to bed,' and I said, 'I won't.' I was standing by the side of the bed and he chucked me in and covered me over clothes and all. After that, we both went to bed."

Russell chortled, but quickly noticed he was the only one imagining the scene, and quickly disguised his laugh with a cough. "Your son was on the day bed and you and Stanley were in the bed?"

"Yes, we were in the bedroom off the kitchen, and were awakened by a loud rapping on the door early in the morning, which turned out to be Edgar McCarthy."

From there, David talked at length about having breakfast with Mc-Carthy and having to fetch water from the brook with a can.

"Was there not a well in the yard?" Drysdale asked.

"Yes, but Stanley told me not to use it. Not to get water out of the well. He said it wasn't clean. So, I had to go down to the river down behind the house to get the water."

David reviewed the house full of visitors they had that Sunday afternoon, with people coming and going, while making mention of the back door.

"Was the back door being used that day by anybody?" Drysdale asked.

"No. Everything, like the wood and chips, were all brought in by the front door."

"Was not the chip yard handy to the back door?"

"Yeah, it was right by the back door. Going through the porch door would have been the handiest way to get there. But Stanley had said not to use the back door, to bring them around to the front. We did that a half dozen times."

"And why weren't you to use the back door?"

"Mr. Stanley said not to come in and out that way because there was a lot of stuff in the porch belonging to Mr. Harvey, and when he came back, he would want it and it was shut up to prevent people handling it. Then on Sunday afternoon, I hasten to say around two o'clock, the door was fastened shut. Stanley ordered it for it to be shut. He said something like, 'I'm going to fasten that door going into the yard and stop people from going in there.' That's what he said."

"And were you away from the house at all from Saturday afternoon until the body was discovered on Monday?"

"Nope."

"Was there more drinking happening on Sunday night?"

"There was not much going on. A few of them left me at the house and they went to Ellershouse and came back with three flasks of whisky, two bottles of ale and a flask of brandy. Not much drinking going on."

"Well, I never. That's not a lot of drinking? I dare say!" This was a loud whisper coming from behind Russell, from a woman leaning over to her husband. If she thought that was a lot, Russell knew she would be in for a rude awakening when she heard the rest of the story. He had heard it enough times in the other trials to know just what was coming.

"Did anyone else go out before the evening was over?" Drysdale asked, raising his voice over the murmuring crowd.

"McCarthy did about ten o'clock. He went to the door and then came back in. When he did, he said, 'My God. Freeman Harvey is alive! He just came across the field with his head off and came up the road. If it ain't him, it's his ghost!'"

Some of the men in the room yelled out their own accusations and questions.

"How would McCarthy know that if he didn't kill Harvey himself?"

"They've arrested the wrong man!"

"That Edgar McCarthy is a bad seed. He's got shifty eyes!"

Justice Townshend banged on his gavel a few times, trying to get the shouting to stop. "Not in this courtroom!" he said sternly. Once the room settled, he nodded to Drysdale to continue.

"What did you do then?"

"I went out to see for myself, of course. I went up and down the road a bit but seen nothing."

"Was the whisky all gone by the time they saw the ghosts?"

"Yes."

As Russell had predicted, when David described how the men went to town for a second round of alcohol, the woman behind him was equally, if not more, horrified at the debauchery. He could feel her doing the mental math, adding up another three flasks of whisky and two more bottles of ale.

"What time did the party break up on Sunday night?"

"I reckon around three o'clock on Monday morning. Stanley said to me, 'You'd better go to bed,' and I said, 'I won't.' He then said he was going away for a little while. I was standing beside the bed in the room off the kitchen. He pushed me in the bed. Clothes and all I went in."

"Was that the same as the night before?"

"Yes, I was tired."

Russell scrunched his brow in confusion. *Does the man actually have any idea of anything he was saying? The whole weekend seems like one jumbled ball of yarn.* Combined with all the drinking and lack of sleep, it was nearly impossible to untangle.

David finally reached the part in the weekend when, on Monday morning, he was ordered to break the staple on the porch door, and with McCarthy, took the light and went into the cellar, and saw some splashes of blood on the porch floor.

"Was that the first time you saw these splashes of blood?"

"No, I seen it before then. I seen it there on Sunday when I was out in the porch looking for a staple for the door. I seen some splattered on Stanley's pants, too. I asked Stanley about the blood on the floor and pants then, too, and he said he had killed a hen on Friday night and had splattered blood all over the floor. I seen that blood again when I went to go down in the cellar on Monday. I had to move a beef barrel away from in front of the door, but then I just gave a mighty heave-ho, and the door opened."

"When you went down into the cellar, what did you find?"

"Well, at first, I was scared because the stairs went straight down, and I feared I would go down headfirst."

David described finding the pile of potatoes at the bottom of the stairs, saying he could not tell if they were in a pile on the floor or in a bin. Then, after finding a foot sticking out of the pile, he said he ran back up the stairs and outside, in a state of shock.

Russell nodded. It probably was a shock. He was not sure how he would have reacted in the same situation. He would like to think he would have bravely gone into the basement that first time, but when it came right down to it, he was not sure he would have. *This is enough for a lifetime of nightmares.*

Drysdale brought the conversation back around to Stanley purchasing the property from Harvey. "I want to call your attention to a conversation that you referred to with Stanley about him buying the property from Harvey. At any time did the prisoner tell you he was paying or how he was to pay it?"

"Yeah, I heard him talk about it. He wanted me to go down and see the place. That was the Tuesday before the Friday. He was talking about buying it as far back as Tuesday. I went down with him on Tuesday to Harvey's because he wanted to buy it. Harvey came out of the house and went into the barn. They talked as they went into the barn, and I heard Stanley say, 'What are you going to take for your farm?' He said, '$1000 for the farm and $500 for the stock and crop.' That's what Harvey said."

Russell sat up a bit straighter. *This is new information. Could Harvey really have been about to sell his farm to this convict from Ireland after all?*

"Then I heard Stanley say, 'I will give it to you. I can't have the money before three days. I have sent over to England for £7,000 and it won't be here before Friday. On Friday, I will pay you $200.' That's all I heard. Then they parted with that. The $200 was to be paid on Friday and the rest in instalments. I'm not sure if he actually paid the $200."

"But you testified earlier you had seen the transaction take place."

"Did I?"

After several hours of answering questions, Drysdale finally sat down, taking a long drink of water.

David stood to leave the witness box, believing he was finished until Justice Townshend motioned him to sit back down. David let out a huge sigh, mirroring the exhaustion that everyone in the courtroom was feeling after an already long day, that was about to get longer.

After a few moments' pause, O'Mullin stood at the defence table, notes in hand, and began his cross examination. He jumped right into the alleged murder weapon.

"This knife," he said as he picked it up from the evidence table, "it's pretty common. Where did you get it?"

"I got it on New Year's night in a trade. The man I got it from said he paid 75 cents for it."

"And a few strokes on a stone would sharpen it?"

"Yes."

"Did you have some conversation with Stanley about the condition of the knife when you loaned it to him?"

"I said, 'it's dull,' and he said, 'I can sharpen it to do what I want.' So, I loaned it to him."

"And when it was returned, you spoke of your knife being pretty sharp, like someone had whetted it a bit."

"Yes."

"But, not in the sense of a razor?"

"No."

"You mean just an edge was put on it?"

"Yes."

"You did not see any difference in the appearance from the time you loaned it until when you got it back?"

"I said to him at the time, 'It is a good deal sharper than when you got it.' I referred to the big blade. I did not open the small blade."

"When you opened it to cut tobacco, how did it look?"

"Clean and bright. Just like it had been stropped up a bit."

"You are accustomed to using edged tools?"

"Yes."

"It would pretty much lose its edge if used upon anything."

"Yes. When you use it for a day or two, it would lose its edge."

"How would you describe Mr. Stanley?"

"He is a very quiet and civil man."

"Harvey was a strong and active man?"

"Yes."

"More so than Stanley would be?"

"Yes, I should think so. He was a bigger man."

"The first time you heard of the death of Harvey, was that on Sunday night when McCarthy said he saw Harvey or his ghost without a head crossing the field?"

"Yes."

"The next time was when you were unloading your furniture on Monday morning?"

"Yes, McCarthy came up from the barn and said, 'My God! Freeman Harvey is in the cellar with his head off. What are you putting your furniture in for?' The cellar was locked then. This is before the cellar was opened."

"Did McCarthy say anything else to you at this time when he told you to stop unloading your furniture? Something about being in charge?"

"That's right. He said, 'You take your stuff all out. I am in charge here. I have charge of everything in the house. Everything in the house is mine!' That's what he done said to me."

"So, things turned out just as McCarthy had said before the cellar door was opened, with Harvey in the cellar with his head cut off."

"Yes."

Russell scratched his head. Again, this was new testimony from the previous trials. Where did these sudden memories come from? Could they have been planted there by Stanley himself when the men had been arrested and kept in the same prison cell? Or did McCarthy really know what was going to happen, and therefore was involved?

"You could go in any part of the house when you were there with Stanley?"

"Yes, up to the time it was nailed up."

"Was anything said about beef being stolen from the barrel in the porch?"

"Yes, Stanley said that was the reason he was locking it up."

"The shortest way to the barn would have been by the back door?"

"Yes."

"There was no clasp by which this porch door could be fastened on the outside?"

"No."

"On the inside, there had been a stick fastened to the floor?"

"Yes."

"That had been there before Stanley had come there?"

"I could not tell you. There was a bolt going through and fastened to the jamb of the door with a hook."

"The door of the cellar was not fastened securely?"

"I did not take notice."

"Did Stanley ever tell you not to go in the cellar?"

"No."

"Back to the blood in the porch. What else was with the blood? Were there not feathers?"

"I seen feathers in a tin kettle. I have killed chickens before. These were common white feathers. There were some feathers in the blood and some in the kitchen."

"As though someone had killed a chicken there."

"Yes."

Russell, who had been sitting on the edge of the seat, realized he had been inching forward, taking in every moment of the new testimony. It seemed Mr. Fisher had not been sharing the whole story in earlier trials.

Throughout the cross-examination, Drysdale and Christie had been madly taking notes and passing them back and forth, so when O'Mullin had finished, Drysdale quickly jumped to his feet, reminding David that he was not quite finished.

"When was it that McCarthy said that he was in charge and that everything was his?" Drysdale asked.

"That was on Monday at about eleven o'clock."

"After Stanley had disappeared." Drysdale was back to his non-question questioning technique.

"Yes. My stuff was all brung down. He was in the house when he said he was in charge."

"Objection, your Honour," O'Mullin said.

"You have made two expressions that are new," Drysdale said, changing his line of questioning. "You say that McCarthy asked you why you were taking your furniture down and that Harvey was in the cellar with his head cut off."

"Yes. He also said all the stuff was his," David said.

"I want to know, in connection with that, was he talking about the organ or any of the stuff he had bought?"

"He said he had bought all that was in the house and that it was all his. That was just before the door was opened. He said, 'That stuff is mine. I bought it. I'm in charge!' and then he ordered the door to be opened."

"You say McCarthy referred to the man's head off before the door was opened?"

"Yes, he did."

Justice Townshend interrupted the proceedings with a question of his own. "Mr. Fisher, did you not think that was a very strange thing?"

"I did at the time."

Justice Townshend leaned back in his chair and motioned for Drysdale to continue.

"When you heard this, did you make any remark? Did you say anything to him about it?"

"No, I did not because my stuff was all there at the house and I did not know what to do with it."

Russell tried to shake the cobwebs in his head, trying to make sense of what he had just heard.

"Did you ever, Mr. Fisher, have a conversation with the defendant while you were in the jail cell together, after you were arrested, about what really happened to Freeman Harvey?" Drysdale said.

"He did a bit. He said, 'So help me God, there's nobody knows anything about the murder but two men.' Then he said on the Friday night, after he and Harvey had done up the business about the house, McCarthy came in around half-past one. And that the murder took place around then and ended between three or four in the morning."

"What exactly did Stanley say happened?"

"Well, McCarthy ran out into the porch and took the rusty old axe and hit Harvey with it. He fell and McCarthy tumbled him down into the cellar. Mr. Harvey was a strong, able, tough little man. Then McCarthy took my jackknife which Stanley had borrowed, and cut his throat, the jugular vein and the windpipe. He cut the flesh all away, but the knife would not cut the bone. So McCarthy took an old saw and cut off his head."

"And what was the prisoner's role in all of this?"

"Stanley said he just held the light, but McCarthy done all the work. He said he took an old pan that he found in the cellar what had ashes in it and put it over the blood on the steps. He then came upstairs and drove two nails into the cellar door to close it up tight. Then McCarthy went away. That was the only conversation we had."

The story lingered in the air for a moment as Russell tried to make sense of what he had just heard. Was this what actually had happened, but Stanley inserted McCarthy into the equation? Or had McCarthy really been there?

Russell had no idea what to make of David Fisher. The man was ignorant and weak-minded, and it would seem he drew upon his imagination for the greater part of his testimony. If he were a juryman, he would consider Fisher an unreliable witness who constantly contradicted himself.

He did not have time to soak it all in before the next witness was called to the stand. He wondered how the jury was meant to keep it all straight, and he certainly did not envy them.

Fred Knowles, a farmer from Avondale, twelve miles up the road from Ellershouse, was next to testify. He explained in detail how he happened to be in Ellershouse on the morning of Monday, February 5, visiting the quarries in the area, just 400 yards from the Harvey property. Passing by the house on Dawson Road, he saw men in the barn, including McCarthy and a stranger.

"Do you see that stranger here?" Christie asked, taking his turn at examination. He made a grand sweeping motion around the room.

As if the answer was not obvious enough, Russell thought. He guessed he still had to ask the question. At least he actually asked a question, unlike his fellow counsel.

"I would say the prisoner is that man. He resembles him very much."

"Did you stay at the Harvey house at that time?"

"No, I just drove by to the quarries and was there for about three quarters of an hour. I don't think they even saw me that first time. Then I passed the property again as I was returning home."

"What did you see?"

"In driving up, I noticed several men standing around the gate, and a pile of furniture. As I got up to the house, I heard people talking loudly, and I stopped my horse. I had no sooner stopped than a man came running to the door. It was McCarthy."

"What happened then?"

"Well, he called out, McCarthy did. I got out of the wagon."

"Was Stanley there?"

"No."

"Then, what happened?"

"We went into the cellar to check what David Fisher and McCarthy had seen. I went down with a man named Bates. I had the light. When we got down there, we discovered the body of a man covered in potatoes. It was a body of a man, but the head was cut off."

"What did you do then?"

"Well, we left the body where it was, and we drove to Ellershouse to notify the coroner."

Knowles mentioned finding blood on the inside of the door leading to the cellar, on the wall going down the steps, and in a pool at the bottom of the steps. Upon retelling the story, Knowles instinctively put his fingernails to his nose and took a deep breath as if he could still smell the chunk of potatoes beneath his fingernails from unearthing Harvey's body.

Next up was John Bates, the lumberman from Ellershouse who also had happened by the Harvey place, on his way to St. Croix, around ten o'clock on that Monday morning. He stopped and McCarthy invited him into the house.

It was then, inside the house, Bates said, that McCarthy ordered David Fisher to open the porch door and that Fisher and McCarthy went down to check the cellar.

Like Knowles before him, Bates described what he saw in the basement, before and after the coroner came.

In his cross examination of Bates, O'Mullin focused in again on Edgar McCarthy. "When you met the gentlemen at the barn, did McCarthy say anything about wanting to search the cellar?"

"I think he said there was something wrong in the cellar."

"Do you know if the cellar was open or not at that time?"

"It was locked when I first went to the house."

"When the lock was broken, did McCarthy seem excited?"

"He seemed a little excited."

"Did he look like a man who had been drinking?"

"I would not like to say. I did not see him drinking."

"Do you think he had had a drink?"

"He might have."

"Did he act like a man who thought a murder had been committed?"

"I most think he did. He definitely thought something was wrong in the cellar."

Russell looked around, trying to find McCarthy's wife in the crowd. He finally spotted a woman sobbing near the back of the room, with an older woman draped around her providing comfort. She looked like a tiny, meek woman, not quite 30 years old. The poor thing probably had had no idea what she was in for when she married Edgar McCarthy.

The woman behind him must have had the same thought, for she too, was staring back at the woman. Then she leaned over again to her husband. "Poor Maggie back there. She probably wasn't expecting her husband to be made out to be the villain in this story. Although what else would you expect but trouble when you marry the likes of Edgar McCarthy? She probably has no time to notice, what with a babe being born every year since they married. Four children, one right after the other and I wouldn't be surprised if she were pregnant again now."

"Hush now, woman," her husband hissed. "Stop your clanging tongue. Gossip is a sin, you know. I'm trying to listen."

Russell smiled to himself. *I love a good tale. I wonder if he can work that into a story.*

Wasting no time, Christie jumped to his feet to re-examine his witness. "Mr. Bates, what reason did Mr. McCarthy give for wanting the house searched?"

"Because the door was locked, and that Stanley did not want anyone in there. I suppose that was the reason."

After the short interrogation, Arthur Sanford, the butcher from St. Croix, was called to the stand. He talked briefly about how Jim Fisher and Stanley showed up at his shop wanting to sell stock.

"There was further conversation with Stanley as he was trying to sell you a pair of oxen, a cow and a heifer," Drysdale said, insinuating a question.

"Yes, he said he had just come from England and that he had bought the Freeman Harvey place, stock and everything. When I asked him why he wanted to sell the stock he said he wanted to repair the barn and he did not want the stock in there at the time. He said he had two horses coming from Halifax and that he had not room for them and that he needed to sell the cattle at once."

O'Mullin and Tremain had nothing to offer in cross examination.

When James Spence entered the courtroom and approached the witness box, a hush fell over the room. James was a member of the legislative assembly for Nova Scotia, representing the St. Croix area, and was well known and respected in the area. When James spoke, people took notice.

James went over how the first time he met the prisoner was on the Saturday before the body was discovered, when Stanley had arrived at his house with Jim Fisher, wanting to sell some stock. James said that Stanley told him he had purchased the Harvey property, the bulk of the whole thing, and that Harvey was away getting it all settled with a lawyer in Halifax.

O'Mullin was not as kind on his cross-examination. "Besides acting as a legislator, what do you, Mr. Spence?"

"I sell farming implements and have been at it quite some time. They call it trading."

"And do you feel you gave Mr. Stanley a fair price for his stock?"

"When I met Stanley, I felt he had asked more for the stock than what it was worth."

"You made the best bargain that you could?"

James paused a moment, as if pondering the best way to answer the question. He settled upon, "I don't know."

"You thought he was an easy English mark, and you made the best bargain that you could, didn't you, Mr. Spence?"

"I don't know that I did that exactly."

"You beat Stanley down from the prices he asked."

"I gave him all I thought the stock was worth."

Then, O'Mullin moved in once again on McCarthy. "Have you interested yourself in McCarthy's welfare?"

"I don't know."

Russell wondered how much the counsellor *did* know, and if he was trying to save face in front of his constituents.

"Did you not try recently to get him out of trouble in the MacPhee case?"

"That was not recent."

"You did that though. You were bondsman for him."

"Yes."

Russell was confused by the reference. *Who is MacPhee and why did he need bail?* He turned to the woman behind him, who had been so helpful providing details in the past. He looked at her inquisitively shrugging his shoulders, as if to say, who?

She scooched forward to the edge of her seat and leaned right up so her lips were practically in his ear. If she had not been old enough to be his mother, Russell was sure he would have found the encounter completely erotic.

"McCarthy and his brother nearly beat the mailman, MacPhee, to death several years back. Mr. Spence helped get him out of trouble."

Before she could say more, the woman's husband pulled her by the elbow, bringing her back into position beside him. "You are making a spectacle of yourself, woman!"

Russell shrugged by means of apology and turned around to continue listening. *The characters in the courtroom are just as interesting as the ones in the stand.*

48: I could not swear

Just as Russell was deciding the case must be finished for the day, another witness was called to the stand. He looked at his watch, and realized it was almost time for supper. *No wonder I'm so hungry and tired.*

It had been a long day, but Justice Townshend was about to make it
even longer.

George Spence approached the stand. Without having to check with
the woman behind him, Russell knew that George was James' much
younger brother. The latter looked to be about fifty years old, while
George could not yet be thirty. James had the polished look of a politician, while George was still young, and more used to a life of farming and
managing his woodlots.

George talked about meeting Stanley a good fortnight before the
murder, when he saw the man going through his yard as a shortcut to the
Fishers' home. Then, again on a Saturday in Rieck's hotel, when he and
McCarthy were having a drink.

Russell looked around at the crowd, trying to gauge reactions, to the
significance of this statement, but it seemed that the notion had floated
above their heads. Russell knew because of his uncle's interest in the
Temperance Union, but surely, local people would have known and remembered the history.

The Spences' father, Nathaniel, represented Hants County in the Nova
Scotia House of Assembly for almost ten years. During his time in office,
all saloon licenses were banned, meaning you could not go in and be
served a drink of alcohol. Nathaniel's contemporaries felt that the ban-
ning of liquor licenses served only to promote the sale of uninspected
and impure liquor, and that men would have to buy greater quantities, as
they would not be able to purchase a single glass.

Nathaniel Spence, disagreed, and made a big speech in the legislature.
He had said there were many men in the city who would be willing to
step into an establishment and have a glass with a neighbour who would
not have the courage to buy a bottle and take it home and set it before

their wives and families. He argued that many a man would go home without having had the glass at all, and the benefit would be greater than the injury.

Now, here was Nathaniel Spence's own son sitting in a hotel in a small town, having a drink with a soon-to-be murderer. Russell wondered what good ol' Nathaniel would have thought of that. He made a mental note to track down the old man one day and ask him.

Even though the vast majority of Nova Scotians were in favour of temperance, officials had a hard time enforcing it, so many just ignored the would-be laws. *The lack of enforcement shows that the many who are eager to ban the sale of liquor are not equally willing to help enforce the legislation*, Russell thought. What was the point of that? Or at least that is what his uncle said.

When Drysdale had finished with George, O'Mullin took his turn. "Where were you on the Friday night?"

"I was at home."

"What were you doing?"

"I was not doing much of anything. I was talking horse trade with Mc-Carthy most of the night."

"Did you know McCarthy pretty well?"

"No, it was the first time he was to my place that I was home," George explained.

"He was soliciting to make a trade?"

"Yes, he came about eight o'clock and didn't leave until the next night after ten o'clock in the evening."

"Did he not go out of your house at all during that time?"

"He went outside around three o'clock to put the horse in."

"This was in the month of February and the horse was standing outside all this time?"

Not only did McCarthy have a bad reputation with people, but he was also a beast to animals. Russell sucked in air between his teeth.

O'Mullin was not finished with him yet. "Was not McCarthy out from a quarter past eight until nine o'clock?"

"Yes."

"You don't know where he was then?"

"No, I could not swear."

"Are you accustomed to staying up all night to trade a pony that you don't think is worth much? If not, why did you in this case?"

"The man was there. McCarthy."

"Did he have anything to drink?"

"Yes, he had a flask of brandy, a bottle of brandy and a bottle of gin."

"You drank what, Mr. Spence?"

"Only one flask. We had a drink out of the bottle of brandy. He put one of the bottles in the straw in the wagon and the mare reached around and smashed it."

Russell laughed out loud, and his guffaw echoed throughout the courtroom. It seemed he was the only one who found it amusing and had the image of a horse trying to have a drink of brandy. *What's the expression? You can lead a horse to water but can't make it drink? This horse did not seem to have a problem!*

"Why did you go to the wagon?" O'Mullin said.

"McCarthy was going to Rawdon. That was Sunday morning."

"Did McCarthy tell you he was suspicious of the lock?"

"No, he didn't say anything about being suspicious. He just said that Stanley had put a lock on the cellar door, and I went and looked at it."

"Why did you do so? There must have been a reason."

"I don't know." George shrugged his shoulders.

"You don't know why you went to look at it?"

"No, I just went and looked."

"Had you and McCarthy not talked about it?"

"No."

"You had no talk about that lock at all?"

"No."

"You are quite clear about that?"

"Yes."

"Who told you there was a lock."

"McCarthy." George was becoming tired of the barrage of questions.

"Are you positive he never told you about it before?"

"Yes."

"You and McCarthy got intimate in a short time."

"No."

"Do you often do that with people?"

"No."

"You have taken an interest in this case outside your duty as a witness, haven't you?"

"No, I have not talked the matter over with McCarthy. I did not do so with anyone who was talking with McCarthy."

"Have you told anyone to be quiet and careful what they say about the case."

"No, sir."

It was the most expression George Spence had shown all afternoon.

Prosecutor Christie, upon re-examination, came back to the fact that McCarthy was out for an hour Friday evening, and asked George where the man had been going.

"He went driving off eastwards. He went in the opposite direction to the Harvey house and was away about half an hour. When he came back, he brought some liquor with him. He had gone in the direction of Ellershouse where the hotel was, so I assumed he went there to get the liquor. He did not go out again after that and was with me all the rest of Friday evening."

Justice Townshend banged his gavel on the bench and, much to Russell's delight, adjourned the court proceedings until half past nine the next morning.

Sheriff O'Brien appeared before the prisoner, clamped on the iron handcuffs and led him through the door leading back to the jail downstairs. Once those in the gallery stood to leave, Russell no longer had a view of the man, as he was so small. But what he could see was a meek, small man who made no comment, had no expression, and did not argue with the sheriff. It was hard to imagine how such a man could be capable of such a murder.

As he filed out, Russell listened to the comments of those around him. There seemed to be two common themes: first, that David Fisher's testimony had left them more confused than when he began; and second, that maybe McCarthy should also be in the box as a co-conspirator to murder.

49: My favourite

Later that evening, John was sitting at the makeshift desk in his cell, amidst a pile of letters he was furiously writing, when he heard a tap at the cell door.

He turned to see Jailer Smith rattling the large ring of keys, trying to find the right one to open his cell. He found it, and there was click followed by a loud creak as the door was unlocked and swung open.

"Thank you, Uncle," said a pretty young blond woman standing at the doorway. "You may leave us."

The jailer sighed as he closed the door and locked her in with the convicted felon. Deep inside he knew God loved all sinners and that he must leave judgment to the higher power, but he still felt uneasy leaving his niece inside.

She had insisted, however, knowing she was doing the work of the Lord in visiting this poor Irish man, away from home with no friends and family.

"Miss Smith! How lovely to see you!" John grinned and turned around his chair.

"Mr. Stanley. Please call me Winnifred." She looked at the floor and curtseyed slightly, but realizing her blunder, her cheeks turned cherry red.

Breaking the awkward silence that followed, John moved to sit on the edge of the bed and offered the chair to his guest.

"I brought you something, today." From inside a cotton sack, she pulled out two men's dress shirts, neatly pressed and folded. "These should fit as well."

Then, she reached into her overcoat pocket and pulled out a small, damp paper bag. "I'm afraid it got a bit wet as I walked through the rain to get here."

"You shouldn't have!" He took the bag, looking her directly in the eyes, which she had managed to avoid thus far. He smiled, causing her to redden once again.

John held the bag in both hands, noticing the blue inked stamp, Kandy Kitchen, across the front. The wet paper tore easily in his hands and several pieces of toffee, now stuck together, tumbled into his lap. He wasted no time breaking them apart and popping one into his mouth.

"Heavenly." John closed his eyes, imagining the sweet shops of his youth. "They didn't happen to have any barley sugar sweets, did they? They're my favourite."

Winnifred laughed at the sound of the grown man trying to speak through the sticky toffee in his mouth. "No, but I'll be sure to check for our next visit."

John smiled, tossing the rest of the toffee in his mouth.

"How are you doing, Mr. Stanley, George? I'm certain it was a difficult day. As I mentioned, my uncle forbade me from going to court, saying it was no place for a young lady. I do know the courthouse was full of women, though. I watched them walk up from the train station, wishing I could slip amongst them."

"Your uncle is right, lass. It would fill your mind with the worst sort of drivel."

Winnifred rested her elbow on the desk behind her, disturbing a stack of papers John had carefully stacked there.

"I'm so sorry, Mr. Stanley!" She spun around to straighten the mess, and some of the words on the pages caught her attention. "Letters for overseas! And lots of them. Are you corresponding with your family?"

She stopped abruptly. "I'm sorry, again. It's none of my business."

"No, not my family. They are all dead." Realizing she was about to apologize again, John cut her off. "I'm writing to some officials who knew me in my previous life, asking for character letters for my trial. Being here, and knowing no one, I have no one to come to my defence, to help proclaim my innocence."

Winnifred pursed her lips and lowered her head.

"I'm also lodging complaints against the *Halifax Herald*. Have you been reading the headlines about me over the past few months?"

"I'm afraid I cannot say I have, Mr. Stanley. My uncle also doesn't believe in women reading the newspaper. He says it would be damaging to my young mind."

"I must agree with your uncle once again," John said. "It's full of matters that are absolutely false and calculated to prejudice the minds of men against me. I am certain this is what happened in the preliminary trial which claimed there was enough proof to go ahead with this trial."

"Surely it can't be as bad as you say."

"Let's see." John raised a finger as he listed each infraction. "They represented me as a hired assassin and member of a secret society in Ireland with the object of the killing of old men, they accused me of burning down a church in Halifax, and the list goes on."

Winnifred laughed. "Surely no one would believe this to be true."

"It most certainly is false, and all these details do not exist outside the fertile imagination of the newspaper correspondent. They are one and all absolutely false and have no foundation in fact."

"This is a tragedy, indeed when immigrants such as yourself can be treated as such."

"I left the British Isles as an emigrant last December and can account for my movements for many years prior to coming here. I was never part of such a secret society."

"Of course not."

"But I am afraid the damage by the newspaper has already been done, and people's minds have already been made up against me. There is no hope for a fair trial now. Which is why I am also endeavouring, with some of these letters, to raise funds to defray the costs of my defence."

Hearing her uncle returning down the jailhouse corridor, Winnifred jumped to her feet to leave. She dug her hand once again into her overcoat pocket and pulled out a crumpled bank note. She passed it to John.

"Here, please take this. It's all I have, but I want to help you as best as I can."

John hesitated in taking it, but finally did so at her insistence.
"I shall pray for you, Mr. Stanley."

50: He stayed until he went away

May 30

For the third day in a row, the rain lashed down on the streets of Windsor. Russell stood at the doorway of the Victoria Hotel, watching people
arrive on the early trains, coming from Halifax, but also from Kentville
and the Annapolis Valley. If he had any chance of getting a good seat in
the courtroom, he had better risk getting wet now and run through the
downpour up the street to the courthouse.

"You trying to work up the courage?" Thomas Doran, the proprietor,
asked as he came up behind him. "It's raining cats and dogs out there this
morning."

Russell turned inquisitively back at the man standing over his
shoulder.

"What? You never heard tell of that expression before?" When Russell
shook his head he added, "You young fella from the city! Raining cats and
dogs. That expression was coined right here in this town by our very
own Thomas Chandler Haliburton, God rest his soul."

"I've heard the name."

"Judge, politician, author. Wasn't much the man couldn't do. His old
place is the Sam Slick Hotel up on the hill, but we're mighty pleased you
chose to stay at our fine establishment, Mr. Shaw."

Russell smiled and reached his umbrella out of the stand by the door.
If he did not leave now, he would be trapped by another of Doran's tales.

"Sam Slick was the name of the character in Haliburton's tale. It was
he who said the bit about raining cats and dogs. He also was the first to
talk about playing hurling on the ice on the pond up behind the estate.
Birthplace of hockey right here in our little town."

"Hockey I can get behind, just not the rain."

As Russell opened the door, the wind caught it, pulling it from his
hand and banging against the outside wall. He popped the umbrella and
used it like a shield as he walked into the rain and up the two blocks toward the courthouse, careful not to step on the cats and dogs.

~

"I now call the court to order," Justice Townshend announced. "Mr. Christie, you may call your first witness."

It had taken a few minutes to organize court proceedings that morning. The gallery was crowded, with men and women seated, standing around the perimeter of the room, in the corridor and down the stairs to the main floor. Sheriff O'Brien first had to go through the list of witnesses to ensure none of them were sitting in the gallery and all were sufficiently sequestered. He found the Fishers seated in a back row.

"You need to come with me."

"We didn't do anything wrong. We in trouble again?" David asked so loudly that Russell, who had managed to secure a seat near the front thanks to his pointy elbows and small frame, turned around to watch the commotion.

Russell watched as the sheriff attempted to explain how witnesses could not be in the courtroom and had to follow him. Finally, they acquiesced, and the day's proceedings could begin.

Jim Fisher, it transpired, was the very first witness of the day. As the sheriff led him back into the courtroom, Russell could hear him protest, "But I thought you said I couldn't be in here."

O'Brien pushed him along and seated him in the witness box.

Jim looked around at his surroundings and gave a toothy grin to Justice Townshend. Then, upon noticing the prisoner, he leaned forward and waved at him. As if unsure how to react, John shrugged and looked back down at his feet.

Christie gathered his papers, straightened them on his desk, and started by having Jim Fisher explain his relationship with the prisoner.

"In February of last winter, I was living with Walter Baker, farming. I did not see George Stanley at any time until he came where I was working. My brother came with him. That must have been the Tuesday after Freeman Harvey's death."

"I am asking you in reference to Freeman Harvey's death," Christie said. "Was it before or after Harvey's death?"

"It was after."

"When you were staying with Walter Baker, would you sometimes go home?"

"Yes."

"What did you do there?"

"I stayed home. Stanley said he wanted to hire me."

Now that Jim had caught on, he began retelling the story of the early days with Stanley in full force. "I went to the Ellershouse station and stayed there until after the trains had gone, around half-past six in the evening. Stanley was there with me, and we went back to the corner together. I went home and he went left toward the Harvey place. I didn't see him again until the next morning."

From there, Jim talked about how Stanley had purchased the property and had invited the Fishers to stay there. Saturday involved driving around the area making trades, and Sunday McCarthy showed up, as did Jim's mother, to make them tea.

"We had dinner. My mother cooked it. We had potatoes. I don't know where they came from, except that my mother had said to let her go for them, and Stanley had said, no, he wanted to go for them himself. He went out the back way into the porch, but I don't know where he went for them. But he came back with potatoes and my mother cooked them for our dinner."

Russell shuddered. *Were those some of the same potatoes Freeman Harvey was buried under?*

Jim finally came to Monday morning in his story. "Around nine o'clock on Monday morning, I went into the barn. Stanley was in the barn, too. McCarthy was up toward the house. He had said he was going to have me and Stanley arrested because we took $75 from him."

"Anything else?"

"Yeah, and he also said he was going to take me up because I had three wives. He said he was going up to Windsor to have us both arrested."

A few gasps went through the strict Baptist crowd. Russell thought, *It is surprising he managed to get even one!*

"What did Stanley say to this?"

"He said for us to go away."

"Did he say where?"

"To some big city."

"What were you going to do there?"

"Put telephones in houses."

"What about these telephones? Had they been mentioned before?"

"Yes, he said he had all his tools at the Newport Station to put telephones in houses. He said his business was putting telephones in houses."

"What happened then?" Christie asked, taking a step toward the witness.

"We started away. We went back of the barn into the woods and up and around by the railway. We crossed the brook and followed it up and crossed it to the other side toward Newport. We kept to the woods, then followed the tracks to Newport Station. At the station, Stanley told me to go to Gibson's store and get something to eat. When I was there, a couple of people told me that Harvey was dead and was in the cellar with his head cut off. I told them they was wrong, and that Harvey was in Halifax. I came back and told Stanley and he said it was a lie. Harvey had defin-itely gone to Halifax to see to some business."

"What did you do then?"

"We went back into the woods. I lost Stanley and then I was arrested by Dennis Paul, who brought me to Windsor."

When it was finally defence attorney O'Mullin's turn, he rubbed his hands together eagerly and began his line of questioning. "During all this time, was there nothing that you could see about Stanley to indicate that he wanted to prevent you from going anywhere you liked?"

"No."

"Both you and your father were free in the house?"

"Yes."

"On Sunday morning McCarthy came in. Could you say if he had been drinking?"

"Yes, he came in around seven o'clock in the morning and stayed all day. I could not tell if he had been drinking or not."

"Now, Sunday evening, do you remember McCarthy going out and making some reference about Harvey?"

"Yes, he did."

"What was it?"

"He said that Harvey was coming up across the field with his head cut off."

"You are sure still he had not been drinking?"

"To my belief he was sober."

"Did McCarthy stay away all Sunday night?"

"No, he stayed until he went away."

Russell shook his head trying to make sense of Jim's last statement. He guessed it made sense, but Jim had been doing so well, until statements like this came out of his mouth.

"He left around two o'clock in the morning. That is when we went to McCarthy's house. Stanley and I went there, too. We went to take the hens. McCarthy didn't say anything about having money at his house."

"On your way back from McCarthy's, after Stanley had left early and started walking back on his own, did you stop at Miller's blacksmith shop?"

"Yes. We asked Miller if he'd seen a man with a fur overcoat and he said, yes. McCarthy said that we were after him and that we were going to put him in jail."

"What for?"

"He said that Stanley had put Harvey in the cellar with his head off."

Another surprise reaction went through the gallery. How had McCarthy known about the murder at that time if he had not done it himself? Those who already thought McCarthy was guilty, yelled out for his arrest.

Russell sat back, scratching his head, trying to make sense of all the pieces, and this senseless testimony.

"When did McCarthy threaten to have you arrested and what for?"

"That was Monday morning. He said nothing about arresting me for Harvey's murder, but for stealing $75 from him."

"I suppose that is what he meant when he said you had gotten ahead of him in the trade."

"Yes, that's what he meant."

"Are you afraid of McCarthy?"

"Sometimes I am. Sometimes I'm not."

Russell nodded his head. That was a fair assessment. He figured he would probably be frightened of the man, too, even without knowing anything about him. McCarthy had that kind of look about him.

"There are times when you can take care of yourself?"

"Yes."

"When did you hide in the hay?"

"Monday morning. I hid because I did not want to talk to McCarthy. I knew that if I talked to him, I might hit him. I felt hurt about what he said. About the three women."

"Did Stanley say anything to you about women?"

"Yeah, he said that when he had left the old country, he had had two women there as well."

"At any time from Friday to Monday when you went away with him, did you hear Stanley make any reference to the fact that Harvey had been killed?"

"No, he did not."

"Did you hear anyone outside of McCarthy make reference to it?"

"They told me at Newport Station."

"That was afterwards, though."

"Yes."

"Did you see anything in the porch at the Harvey house? Did you see any blood?"

"No, I saw nothing, but I did see some feathers. They were by the stove. Stanley had said he had killed a hen."

"Did Stanley seem, at any time, like he was hiding something about the place?"

"No."

"Had you heard him say anything about buying the property before he went there?"

"He had been talking around about buying a place."

Finished, O'Mullin sat down and Christie stood to re-examine his witness.

"I want to go back to the conversation you say you had with Miller the blacksmith early on Monday morning. When you were examined at the preliminary trial, you said nothing then about Harvey having his head cut off."

Christie flipped through his notes, scanning with his index finger until he found the appropriate section and read aloud. "What you said then was that he had killed Freeman Harvey and put him in the cellar. Is that right?"

"Yes."

"Well, why then did you just add that part?"

"Well, he said that, too."

"You are adding the other now?"

"No."

"But you said before, and your exact words were, 'he killed Freeman Harvey and put him in the cellar.' That's what you said then."

"I said that when we came along and asked Miller whether he had seen Stanley go past with a fur overcoat on and when he said yes, McCarthy said, 'we are after him to put him in jail because he put Freeman Harvey in the cellar with his head cut off.' Then—"

"Objection, your Honour," O'Mullin said. "I object to this cross examination of the witness."

"Sustained. Mr. Christie, you cannot examine him again on this," Justice Townshend said, putting an end to Jim Fisher's final moments on the witness stand.

Jim looked around, confused, as Sheriff O'Brien escorted him out of the room once again. He waved again to the prisoner, who rewarded him with a slight grimace.

51: Yes, he was quite excited

Russell was not sure what had happened during the past hour. *At first, Jim Fisher seemed to have been trying to protect Stanley by implicating McCarthy. Now, at the tail end of this story, he seems to be protecting McCarthy and implicating Stanley.* Russell was not sure how the jury was going to handle any testimony from the Fishers.

And just when he thought it could not get worse, Mary Ann Fisher, the family matriarch, was called to the stand.

When she sat down, she wrapped her cardigan tightly around her body, the coloured fabric of her blouse poking through the thin elbows of the sweater. When settled, she stared up at Christie through beady eyes, as if daring him to ask her a question.

She recounted how Stanley came looking for a place to board, mentioning he was looking for a farm to buy and that he expected his sister to arrive. She explained how he came in the Saturday morning with large papers, like deeds, along with keys, saying they were to the Freeman Harvey place.

"Where had he been the night before? Did he stay at your place?"

"No, he stayed up to Freeman Harvey's place. And, when he come back, he said he wanted us to move up to that place and look after it for him."

"When did you move down?"

"On Monday morning I packed up my stuff and moved down. There were two loads. William Murphy took them. I did not pay him to do so, but Stanley did. After I packed up, I went down with the last load, and when I got there, my husband was there with Edgar McCarthy."

"Were you there when they discovered the body?"

"No, I wasn't anywhere near about the house. I was back at my house. I got frightened so went back to my place."

"What was it that frightened you?"

"When Ed McCarthy done and said that he had charge of the place, and that Freeman Harvey was in the cellar. When he said that, I was right out of there."

Again, those who were certain of McCarthy's role in the murderous affair booed and made a ruckus in the courtroom, demanding full justice for Freeman Harvey. Russell shook his head as he listened, duly writing everything in his notebook.

O'Mullin stood and took a step toward Mrs. Fisher but saw her draw back her lips in a snarl like a junkyard dog, and he instinctively took a step back. He began his questioning from behind the safety of his table.

"How would you describe Mr. Stanley?"

"A quiet man."

"Did he ever talk before you and your husband and sons about going to the Harvey farm and wanting to purchase it?"

"Yes, he said he was going to buy it."

"Did you and your husband go with Stanley and examine the property with Harvey?"

"No."

"You stated in your other examination that you looked it over with Stanley and Harvey the Tuesday before."

"No."

"Don't you recollect that?"

"No."

Russell did not recollect anything about that either, even though he had sat through every trial and testimony since this all began. He flipped back through the notes, resorting to pulling out older books from his satchel, but he could not find mention of it anywhere. But there was a trait that ran in the family. Russell wouldn't have been surprised if Mary Ann changed her story from trial to trial.

"What did McCarthy say to you on Monday?"

"He told me that Freeman was in the cellar. He said, 'Put your hand on my forehead. Freeman is in the cellar.' That's what he said."

"Had the cellar been open at that time?"

"No, sir."

"When you were in the house, did Stanley try to prevent you from going anywhere in the house?"

"No."

"You could have gone anywhere you wanted?"

"Well, I could not get into the porch. Outside of that, I could go anywhere. I didn't notice if the porch was fastened or anything, though."

"In the preliminary examination, this is what you said." O'Mullin read aloud from the court transcript. "You said, 'As far as I know, the door was open, and I could have gone. Nothing was said to prevent me from going at all.' That would be correct?"

"Yes, that is the porch door. I didn't go at all."

Definitely a family trait, Russell thought.

"What time did McCarthy get to your place on Saturday night?"

"He got there at midnight. I am clear about it being twelve o'clock, because I have a clock and I looked at it. He did not put his horse up but left him outside all night long. He had been drinking, and he was pretty full of it when he showed up at my house."

"Did he seem excited when he arrived?"

"Yes, he was quite excited."

O'Mullin looked over at Christie, who shook his head to indicate that Mary Ann Fisher was finished on the stands.

A shiver went down Russell's spine as the woman got off the stand and marched out of the courtroom, throwing an icy glare over her shoulder.

Then Edgar McCarthy was marched in and seated in the witness box. The courtroom spectators met his arrival with hisses and howls.

"He should be on trial here today!"

"He looks as evil as he is."

"The devil in disguise!"

McCarthy stopped halfway to the stand, crossed his arms, and looked out at the crowd, daring them to throw another comment his way.

Justice Townshend struck his gavel several times and said, "Not in my courtroom! You shall behave with more decorum here."

It took a few minutes, but the crowd eventually quieted. McCarthy took his seat and Christie stood up to start his examination.

McCarthy described his first meeting the prisoner on the Saturday afternoon at Rieck's Hotel, when he was introduced to him as Mr. Stanley. Eventually, he came to the part in the story about the porch.

"Do you know anything about a lock being on any of the doors?"

"Yes. After dinner on Saturday, Stanley told David Fisher to get a lock and to put it on the porch door. David looked around and found a wire staple and put it on the door. He had said that meat was stolen from the barrel in the porch, and he was going to put a lock on the door on account of that."

The conversation proceeded with many details about trading.

"Did Stanley say where he got all this stuff?"

"He said he had bought it all from Freeman Harvey—the place and everything in it. Stanley said Harvey had gone to Windsor to settle things with his wife and pay her a share of it, or something like that."

"What happened when you got to your house early on Monday morning, when you delivered the hens to your house?"

"I stayed about an hour, but Stanley did not stay that long. He seemed to be uneasy, and he would not stop. He said that he had locked David Fisher in the house when he left, having locked the front door. I asked him if he had not a key and he said no, he had taken the key. He would not wait but started to walk on back to the Harvey place. After a few minutes, after I did some chores, Jim Fisher and I headed back, and we overtook him at St. Croix."

"One of the witnesses stated that you said to Harry Miller on the way back that Freeman Harvey was dead in the cellar with his head cut off. What do you say about that?"

"I did not say this."

McCarthy then mentioned trading with George Spence the following morning when Stanley let a pony worth $25, a horse worth $50 and a new harness at $20, all go for $20 total.

"What happened after you witnessed this deal?"

"I turned to him and said, 'You cannot own this stuff. The stuff I got from you cannot be your own, or you wouldn't be throwing it away like this.' Then he grabbed a nearby stake and tried to hit me with it, but I dodged the blow and escaped it."

Looking at the tough guy, McCarthy, against the small Irish man, Russell knew where he would have put his money in a fight.

"Then I said to him, 'You will have to give me more for the horse than the organ, or I won't move it from the house at all. You have to give me money for my horse.' That's the horse of mine I'd traded to George Stanley, and who gave it away so cheaply to Spence. Stanley didn't say much else other than he owned everything in the place."

Soon after that, McCarthy said, Jim Fisher and Stanley disappeared. Although he found the fur coat in the hay mow and a sack with two revolvers in it, he failed to find Stanley.

Next McCarthy talked about getting an axe to break the lock on the porch door and examining the cellar. "We saw the shape of a man rolled up in the potatoes. I thought I saw the foot sticking up through. David pulled away a few of the potatoes and discovered it was definitely the body of a man."

"What did you do after the discovery?" Christie asked as he paced back and forth in front of the witness.

"Harold Spence and I hooked up the wagon and drove up to St. Croix through the Plains, following the railways."

"You were searching, then?"

"Yes, we were looking for Jim Fisher and Stanley. We searched until about five o'clock that evening. We came across Chief McDonald and some officers but did not find Stanley."

"It was said that on Sunday night you went out of the house and came back in saying you saw either Freeman Harvey or his ghost with his head cut off coming across the field, or words to that effect. What do you say to that?"

"I did not say that. I've never seen a ghost in my whole life."

"It is also said that when you went from the house to the barn before the door was opened you said that Freeman Harvey was in the cellar with his head cut off. What do you say about that statement?"

"I never said that, either."

"Was anything said at that time about Harvey and the cellar door before it was opened?"

"Not that I can recollect. We just talked about the curiosity of the lock being there, but nothing about Harvey."

"Where were you the Friday night before the murder?"

"I was home, and then I went to George Spence's, arriving there at eight o'clock in the evening, staying there until Saturday night."

Russell had a fleeting thought about McCarthy's wife. *I hope to have that much freedom to come and go as he pleased when I finally get married.* Leaving a wife with four small babies at home in the middle of nowhere was not anything that even would cross his young-bachelor mind.

"At any time when you were at Spence's, did you leave?"

"Yes, between eight and nine o'clock I went to Rieck's in Ellershouse for liquor. But I went nowhere else."

O'Mullin stood to cross examine. "You have been giving evidence a good many times before?"

"Yes." He grunted the response.

"Are there other times, Mr. McCarthy, that you have been arrested or put in jail?"

"Yes, I was up twice for assault, and on trial for stealing. I have been in jail for such things. When I am sober, I try to do as good as I can. I have done things I am ashamed of. I have left my horses outside all night, which isn't good. I wouldn't do that if I were sober. But I've never been arrested for threatening some old maids up in Brooklyn, or anyone else in this county. I did not harm anyone or break anything very much. I paid all costs."

"On several occasions you have been in court giving evidence? And not long ago you were tried here before Judge Meagher."

"That was some three years ago." McCarthy crossed his arms, glaring at the lawyer, who was at least double his age, trying to intimidate him.

"Was it not for you and your brother beating the mail carrier, MacPhee?"

"Yes."

Russell made a note at the top of his page. He wanted to look up that court case and find out just what MacPhee had done to incur the wrath of Edgar McCarthy. *I certainly do not ever want to be on the man's bad side.*

"How many other times have you been in court?"

"Well, that one case there you mentioned, and the others, probably for fighting or something."

"You are quite a fighter then?"

"I never said I was." He spat the words back through gritted teeth.

"You will take your own part."

"I don't know."

Russell could see McCarthy's temper rising and that O'Mullin had him exactly where he wanted him. "Sometimes you will go beyond that, like in the case of MacPhee you went beyond taking your own part."

"I did not do anything to MacPhee."

"But did the court not find you guilty?"

"I was a little mixed up with him, I guess. Yes, sir."

"When this man Stanley took the fence post and made at you with it, you did nothing?"

"Nothing. I just spoke to him. I just told him I didn't think he owned the stuff by the way he was putting it away. I did not attempt to defend myself. I took it quietly."

Russell found that hard to believe. *Maybe he did not think fighting Stanley would have been enough of a challenge. Maybe the man was working on too little sleep and too much alcohol from the weekend.*

After a few more questions about McCarthy's whereabouts during the weekend and what time he did what and was where, O'Mullin finally asked what was on his mind. "I suppose you thought out pretty well what you were going to say today."

"No sir, I did not think it over very much."

"Never gave it a moment's thought?"

"I suppose I thought I was going to be on the stand this morning. I suppose that's all I thought about."

"Did you ever have a conversation with Dr. Reid whether you should be represented by a lawyer?"

"I did talk to Dr. Reid once, but that was for a different trial. There had been an inquest and I wanted his advice."

"You have had some experience."

"I have had a little. I have been on the stand several times."

"When you were on the stand before, you never thought it was necessary to have a lawyer?"

"I was never on as a witness before."

Russell chuckled to himself. *There's a first time for everything.*

"What was the actual conversation you had with Miller that morning?"

"When we drove by, he asked me what man it was that was walking by. I told him it was a man called Stanley who had bought the Freeman Harvey place. He said to me, 'What do you think? Do you think he bought it?' I said I didn't know but that is what he told me. He said, 'Do you think he's alright, or how does he act?' I said that he acted funny up to my place that morning and would hardly sit down and was uneasy to get back. Then he said again, 'Do you really think he bought the place? I don't. Where do you think Freeman Harvey is?' That's when I said that he might be dead, and Stanley might have thrown him in the river."

"Well," said O'Mullin flipping back through his notes, "this is what you swore to before: 'I said he might be dead in the river, or he might be dead in the cellar.' That's what you said before."

"Yes, I said it then."

"But you did not say anything about the cellar now."

"I said he might be dead in the river."

"Well then, why didn't you say the rest of the conversation?"

"Maybe I would have told you if you had let me." With that, McCarthy re-crossed his arms, his flexed bicep muscles easily visible through the sleeves of his thin shirt. He stared at the lawyer, not blinking, until O'Mullin broke the stare by clearing his throat and consulting his notes again.

Regaining his composure, O'Mullin continued his line of questioning for about a half hour, until, exhausted, he finally released the witness. As McCarthy walked across the front of the room to make his exit, he did so at his own speed, sauntering slowly, making sure he caught the eye of as many people in the courtroom as possible.

When McCarthy finally left, Russell felt his shoulders relax. He realized how much tension had been in the room with McCarthy's mere presence. *I hope the next witness will not be as stressful.*

52: The bone was clean cut

Christie then called several witnesses to repeat testimonies from previous trials. Eventually he got to a new witness.

Henry Chapman, Freeman Harvey's wife's brother, who worked at the sawmill in Hartville recounted the tale of helping the constable capture and arrest Stanley on one of the roads in the woods at half-past eight on the Monday in question, in the pouring rain.

On his cross, O'Mullin asked, "Did he say anything when you arrested him?"

"No."

"Did he offer any resistance?"

"No, he said he was a poor, nervous man. I was expecting to meet a great big man, but he was so small."

"You had presented a gun at him?"

"I had it in my hand."

"Did you put it to his ear?"

"Yes. When Officer Singer wanted to put the handcuffs on him, he was not resisting."

"Did the prisoner walk right up to you?"

"Yes, he walked right up between us. I was so surprised he gave in so easily."

Next up was James Hutchinson, a farmer in St. Croix, who said he first met the prisoner in late January when he came to his house wanting to hire a couple of men to put up telephone boxes. Hutchinson said he was not available for work, even though Stanley said there were at least two or three thousand to put up around the province.

"He ended up staying for tea with us. Throughout the meal he talked to us about London and his life there, saying how he had been born there, but just moved here before Christmas. He said his trunk was still in Halifax."

"Did anything of consequence happen during the meal?" Christie asked.

"While we were eating there was a rap on the front door. He jumped up, frightened, and snatched his cap and made for out. He ran to the door and asked who it was. I followed him outside and said that it was a neighbour. He then said to me, 'Oh, that's alright then, I'm just afraid of the dark.' I then said to him that if he was afraid of the dark, I would go with him."

"Where did you go?"

"I went with him toward Freeman Harvey's place. We stopped in front of the Harvey place, and he turned and said to me, 'This old fellow has a nice place,' and I said it was nice in summer."

"What did he say to you next?"

"He said, 'I want to get a place. This old fellow is always in darkness when I come along.' I said that perhaps he had turned in, but he replied that it wasn't that late. He then said to me that the old fellow had money. But I said I'd guess that he didn't have much money at all."

"What made him think that Freeman Harvey had money?"

"He said, 'He has a lot of money because he changed a five and a ten-dollar bill for me a few days ago and told me to come back if I had any more bills to change.' Then, he kept on, 'I think he keeps it hidden in the cellar, for he was so long getting the change for me.' But I said I didn't know anything about that."

Hutchinson scratched his head, recalling the rest of the conversation. "Stanley then said it hurt his head to holler at Harvey because he was so deaf. From there, he went on to talk about the Fishers, and called them all soft fools. At that point, I just bade him goodnight and turned around and walked away."

Russell shook his head. *That does not look good for Stanley*. It was the first time he had heard this story, despite the several trials he had sat through.

Levi Brown, Freeman Harvey's nearest neighbour, was called next. Brown talked about having first met Stanley on the Saturday of the weekend in question, when he happened by the Harvey place and had a conversation with the prisoner.

"What was your conversation at that time?" Christie asked.

"I was standing there speaking with David Fisher when this stranger approached and asked me where I was going and what my business was."

"What did you tell him?"

"I said, 'I'm not going very far, if it's anything to you. I've come to find Mr. Harvey.' By this point, I'd already told him my name, but he asked for it again, so I said, 'I'm Levi Brown, and I'm not ashamed of it.' He didn't know what to say then."

"What did he say, though?"

"He said, 'Well, Mr. Levi Brown, I bought this place. I own everything. These cattle are all mine!' and he gestured to all the outbuildings and surrounding fields. Then David Fisher pipes up and says it were all true, that Mr. Harvey had gone to Windsor to get papers fixed up, and that he'd even seen Mr. Stanley give $300 to Harvey to give to his wife to sign the papers.' That's the first I knew of the deal."

"Did he tell you about any plans for the property?"

"Yes, he said the buildings were all rotten and that he was going to have them repaired and was going to slate the barn roof this summer. Not sure where he was thinking of getting slate shingles in this country. He ain't in England anymore! Then I just left and let them carry on with their business."

Christie's line of questioning then moved to the blood Levi had seen in the porch, the impression of a bloody hand on the side of the stairwell, and finally blood on the potatoes themselves.

"The body was lying in the potatoes when I first saw it and the head was off. The head was over on the table in the cellar."

Russell pursed his lips. The man sounded so cavalier in his description, but he guessed, being the village's undertaker, he was used to dealing with death and bodies in a matter-of-fact way. *But surely having a man buried in a pile of potatoes and his head on a workbench was cause for a bit of emotion.*

Levi reviewed the marks on the body found when he was preparing it for burial. Again, he gave these details completely void of any emotion. His descriptions were virtually the same as those Dr. Reid had given the day before.

"The bone was clean cut. The fleshy part was cut pretty roughly with some instrument that did not cut sharp. After the bone was sawed off, there was a piece of skin cut down leaving a flap. It was cut clean, like it had been cut with a fine saw."

"A saw like this one?" Christie reached into the box under his desk and with a grand motion produced a saw which he held above his head for all to see. The handle was stained dark red in places.

"Yes, that is the saw that my son found when we were preparing the body. At that time, there were marks of blood on the handle—fresh blood, that is. There is less blood on there now than there was at that time."

"Where is your son now? Why is he not testifying to finding the saw himself?"

"He's down in Portland, Maine. That's the last account I had of him, anyway. But he presented before Justice Farquhar earlier about what he found."

"And you believe this saw belonged to Freeman Harvey?"

"Yes, I seen him with it before. He was using it to trim apple trees. But I can't say that I ever saw it hanging up in the house."

Christie placed the saw on his table. The sound of rattling metal reverberated throughout the courtroom.

He went over to the evidence table and again picked up the knife belonging to David Fisher. "Look at this knife in court." Christie held the knife up again for all to see. "What do you say about these cuts in the head? Could they have been made with an instrument like this?"

"I would think so. There was a little hole under the left ear. The big blade of that knife could have made it."

Finished with his arsenal of weapons, Christie took a seat, giving the floor to O'Mullin.

"When did you first go into the cellar?"

"On Monday night. They hadn't finished with the inquest until then."

"You have no medical training, and you are not a medical man."

"No."

"You are not an expert on blood stains?"

"No."

"Did you put any mark on that saw when you had it, and have you had it since you found it?"

"No, I rolled it up in newspaper and sent it to Windsor. I did not put any marks on anything."

"Can you swear that the blood on this saw is human blood?"

"No."

"You have no experience in knife wounds, nor any scientific knowledge of knife wounds?"

"Not very much."

"So, no scientific knowledge."

"No."

O'Mullin let those words linger in the air, creating an awkward silence in the room.

Justice Townshend leaned forward in his seat as if wondering if he missed something with his poor hearing. Hearing nothing, he motioned for the witness to leave the stand. As Levi left the stand and the sheriff searched for the next witness, Russell could swear he heard Justice

Townshend mentioning this was the last witness of the trial.

Ida Harvey shuffled through the door. Russell remembered she was Freeman Harvey's widow, as evidenced by the black dress she wore.

Ida, in her mid-forties, dressed all in black out of respect for the death of her second husband. She explained how they had been married for almost three years, and how she lived with Freeman at the house with her thirteen-year-old daughter. She confirmed that her husband was more than a decade older and would have been sixty-six in July. He was indeed quite deaf.

Ida explained how she went to Windsor last December with her daughter to work in the cotton factory, boarding with someone in town. Every fortnight, she would go back to the house, staying from Saturday night until Monday morning. While there, she washed and cleaned up the house and did the cooking; otherwise, her husband lived alone. The last time she had stayed at the house was the weekend prior to the murder.

Ida testified that she had twelve hens and a rooster when she left that Monday morning.

Wait a minute, Russell thought. *Hold the presses!* He tapped his forehead, trying to remember the details. When McCarthy took the hens up to his place, there were definitely twelve hens and a rooster. Although Christie did not explicitly say it, Russell could make the connection.

He drew a diagram, like a mathematical equation in his notebook. If Ida left twelve hens and a rooster, and McCarthy took twelve hens and a rooster, that means there were no hens or rooster for Stanley to kill. *Just where did the feathers in the porch come from?*

Once again, Christie picked up the saw and held it up before the court. He asked Ida if she recognized it.

"Yes, that is the saw that Mr. Harvey generally used when doing any little odd jobs around the place. It was kept behind the porch door leading from the little hall into the porch. It was hanging on a little nail or peg, or something."

"To the best of your knowledge, was it ever used for cutting meat while you were there?"

"No, not while I was there."

"Do you know anything about the meat barrel being in the porch?"

"Yes, I packed the meat myself in the fall. Levi Brown cut up that meat, though, and did not use that saw for it. He used his own."

"Do you know anything about the feathers being in the porch?"

Good on ya, Mr. Christie, Russell thought. He had the same thought. *Maybe I should have been a lawyer instead of a newspaper reporter.*

"Yes, I dressed a couple of chickens before I came back to Windsor."

"Where did you put the feathers?"

"In a little tin bucket that stood in the corner of the porch. I left them there when I went away to Windsor. It always stayed in the same place until I came back after the body was found, and it was in a different place. I moved it back myself to the porch. It was in exactly the same condition as I had left it. Not a spit of difference."

"And what of the hens?"

"I did not see the hens again until McCarthy brought them back. He brought back eleven hens and the rooster. He said one had died on the road, but he paid for it."

O'Mullin took his turn questioning the widow. "Mr. Harvey was a pretty strong man?"

"Yes."

"A wiry man?"

"Yes."

When O'Mullin finished his few questions, Christie stood to say the crown rested its case. No more witnesses would be called.

After twenty-one witnesses, they were finally finished presenting their case. Russell wondered why the Forseys from the Halifax boarding house had not been called as witnesses. Perhaps the Crown had thought they had enough already.

Justice Townshend turned to O'Mullin and Tremain at the defence table and told them they could call their first witness.

O'Mullin stood and cleared his throat. "Your Honour, the defence does not intend to call any witnesses."

There was a gasp around the room. Russell was one of them. How could there be nothing to add to the case for the defence if the prisoner were not truly guilty? Russell supposed, with him being a man from away, there would be no one to vouch for his character.

And it was the prisoner's prerogative to not take the stand. Russell was certain, however, that his lawyers had strongly advised that he not testify. *What more could be said, and who would believe him anyway?*

Russell looked over at the prisoner, still sitting quietly, motionless, in the witness box. It was as if he had already given up and resigned himself to his future. He made no protest. He made no sound.

What else could be said, except to say "the defence rests"?

Justice Townshend banged his gavel, calling for a recess until two o'clock that afternoon.

Russell watched as many of the people in the courtroom stood, picking up umbrellas and hats from beneath their benches, and made their way to the streets in search of dinner. He contemplated going but realized he would probably lose his seat; and in this case, he could probably get closer to the front after all.

He dug around in his bag and found a half-eaten roll at the bottom, dusted it off, and moved to one of the seats at the front, alongside someone who looked like a reporter from a different newspaper. Russell tipped his imaginary hat in solidarity and ate his bun as he reviewed the morning's session in his mind.

53: These few brief observations

By the time court resumed, Russell had had a nap on the hard, wooden bench. The stampede of onlookers coming back in from the rain woke him. Despite his not going out himself, being crushed between damp people who had gave him the feeling he might as well have.

"Exciting isn't it?" a man said as he sat down next to Russell.

Russell looked up, raising his eyebrow. *Exciting* was not really the word he had in mind for when one man was murdered, and another's life was on the line. He supposed that, for a small town, this was the best free entertainment they had had in years.

Russell looked around in hopes that the woman would once again sit behind him, filling him in on the gossipy details of the townspeople. *No such luck.* At least things seemed to be wrapping up, and, judging by the time on his pocket watch, a lot faster than probably anyone had anticipated.

Sheriff O'Brien stood at the front of the room, and when the door opened, he motioned to those lucky enough to have found a seat to stand as Justice Townshend entered the room. The four lawyers took their seats at their tables, the jurors filed in, and the Justice called the afternoon proceedings to order.

O'Mullin stood, taking his final opportunity to address the jury. "Gentlemen of the jury," he began. "The prisoner sits before you, a stranger to this area. Therefore, it is incumbent upon you to ensure that this man receive a fair and impartial verdict. I am more than sure that you will do your duty in this manner."

O'Mullin took the time to make eye contact which each of the men, some of whom awkwardly lowered their heads. "Before we continue, I must warn you that you must be perfectly sure as to his guilt and that, if there is any doubt existing in your minds as to his guilt, he should have the benefit of this."

At this, O'Mullin gestured toward the prisoner box, where John looked up meekly, but quickly looked back down again. "Yes, an awful crime has been committed, but you need to decide whether the conduct of the prisoner prior to the alleged murder was that of a man about to commit a crime. During my cross examinations, I have tried to show you that there is not one jot or tittle of evidence to prove that Stanley had committed the crime, except what was circumstantial. The fact that Stanley stayed on the place and offered to sell the stock and contents was not the conduct of a man who had committed a crime."

O'Mullin placed his hands on the rail in front of the jurors, and rocked back and forth on his heels, wanting each of his statements to sink in. "There is the unfortunate fact that they were all drinking that weekend. And why would Stanley take the three Fishers into the house and leave them there with the dead body of Harvey? Was it a probable thing that he should have acted in this way?"

Russell looked up to see a few jurors nodding along with O'Mullin's address. If the Fishers fully understood the gravitas of the situation, it could give them nightmares for years to come. *I know it would me!*

"Now, let's contrast the behaviour of the prisoner when arrested with that of McCarthy on the witness stand. I need you to consider where McCarthy got the information that Harvey had his head off. The cellar door had not been opened when McCarthy told Fisher that Freeman Harvey was in the cellar with his head cut off."

Back to McCarthy, Russell thought. *Even if the man is not guilty, he's going to have a rough time recovering from these accusations.*

O'Mullin went over more of the evidence and the prisoner's demeanour. The delivery was strong, forceful and to the point.

"In conclusion, the Crown does not demand that because one man has been killed another should be sacrificed. I place the information before you and leave the fate of the unfortunate man in your hands."

O'Mullin let his final words linger in the air before he sat back down and was replaced by Attorney General Drysdale.

Drysdale gave a complete summary of all that had been presented.

"Now, gentlemen of the jury, I urge you not to pay any attention to any comments that have been made by the press or let any other consideration other than the evidence weigh with you in considering the verdict."

At mention of the press, both Russell and his seatmate from the *Hants Journal* looked up. What did he think they were publishing? He did not have time to take great offence as he had to race to capture every word of the closing statement.

"A horrible crime has been committed. Freeman Harvey was brutally murdered. You the jury do not need to establish that a murder has been committed. That has been proven beyond a doubt, and that the evidence points strongly toward Stanley's guilt."

Besides the unnecessary jab at the press, Russell thought Drysdale was not only convincing but logical, with every point being fully covered and given clearly to the jury to consider. He scanned the faces of the jury again, who too had been nodding in agreement along with Drysdale. He had no idea what the outcome would be.

Then, it was Justice Townshend's turn to address the jury. Russell knew, by the man's reputation, that this could be a long-winded speech, so he settled in to make the best of it.

"Gentlemen of the jury," Townshend began. He gathered the papers on his desk where he had been taking notes throughout the trial. He tapped them three times on the bench to straighten them.

"You are called upon to perform one of the highest and most solemn and responsible duties which falls to the lot of free men to perform. You are called upon to say whether or not the prisoner in the dock is guilty of the atrocious crime of murder with which he is charged. Do not fear to acquit the prisoner if the evidence fails to convince you of his guilt, and, on the other hand, do nor fear to render a verdict against him if the evidence satisfies you that he is guilty of the crime of murder. I hope therefore that you will not shrink from doing your duty as I shall not shrink from doing mine."

Russell sat back in his seat, trying to get comfortable, yet not miss a word of the address. His shorthand skills were being put to the test, and he knew the judge was just getting started.

Justice Townshend talked at length about how it is up to the accused to prove that malice was not intended when the death of another is involved. "In this case you will have no doubts on the question of malice as the circumstances are too clear that the crime was committed by a wicked, malicious and depraved person with the preconceived purpose of destroying the life of Freeman Harvey."

A few "Hear! Hear!" shouts rang from the back of the room.

"The man who did this deed undoubtedly did it with malice and therefore it is murder and nothing else. There is little or no contradiction in the evidence to establish the prisoner's guilt."

With a statement like that, Russell wondered, *what is the purpose of the jury today?*

"The evidence against the prisoner consists mainly of circumstances from which it will be your duty to draw inferences as to whether the prisoner is guilty or not. No one saw him do the deed, and this makes it

necessary for me to say a few words to you on the subject of circumstantial evidence."

Russell had heard that Townshend's lecture on circumstantial evidence was what he would like to read on nights he had trouble falling
asleep. He wondered if his fellow seatmates or the jury members felt the
same way.

Direct evidence versus circumstantial evidence. Which is stronger?
And while witnesses may testify to what is false, circumstance do not lie.
Russell's head was spinning trying to follow along. And just when he
thought it could not get any worse, Justice Townshend began reading
from a book about evidence.

From there, Justice Townshend spoke openly about witnesses who
falsely testified to what they had allegedly seen. Russell scratched his
head, wondering if he was so blatantly referring to the Fisher family.

"To find him guilty, the facts must lead to one conclusion and to no
other, to be justified in convicting the prisoner. The facts must be inconsistent throughout with his innocence and consistent with his guilt. And
in deciding innocence or guilt, you must remember that if there is a reasonable doubt, the prisoner is entitled to benefit from it."

Next came readings about reasonable doubt. Russell watched as a few
of the jury member heads nodded off with the tedium of the speech.

"With these few brief observations on the law let me now turn your
attention to the facts."

If that was brief, what is coming next?

"The prisoner appeared in the vicinity of Ellershouse last January. In
his conversations he first told them that his business was that of putting
in telephones and subsequently he gave it out that he had money in the
bank in England and that he was cabling for money, and that he had a sister who was coming to him from New York. I think it is clearly established that the prisoner had made Freeman Harvey's acquaintance and
that he had been to see him, making him believe that he was going to
purchase his farm."

Justice Townshend then reviewed the events of the weekend, going
over the timeline of the weekend in question. He asked the jury to consider why the prisoner would close up the door leading to the cellar.

"The next important fact is that on Monday he absconds when he
learns, as I should judge, although there is no direct evidence of that, that
suspicions had been aroused. He clears out and leaves behind him the
property that he said he had paid so much for, and he goes to the woods
and, as we learn from the evidence of different witnesses, attempts to

conceal himself from a possible search by constables and his arrest at the hands of justice.

"They are there all weekend with the body of Freeman Harvey, with the head cut off, lying in the cellar of his house. That is another thing that we only know from circumstances as we have no direct evidence from anyone who saw the body there until it was found there on Monday, but as reasonable men you cannot have any doubt that it was there all that time. The prisoner allowed no one to enter the cellar but himself, and, so far as we know, no one did."

Then, there was the matter of the prisoner going to get potatoes for dinner. "We can come to no other conclusion then on Sunday, he went into the cellar to get the potatoes. You will ask yourselves how he could have gone there on Sunday for potatoes without seeing the body of Free-man Harvey which was there partly covered by potatoes?"

Next was the blood. "I have said nothing about the blood on the side of the door or on the cellar stairs because it is immaterial here, as the murder is established beyond doubt, and we do not need to ascertain whether this was human blood or not."

For the next few minutes, Justice Townshend talked about the evidence against the prisoner from his lies about his telephone business and that he had money coming from England, and that he had been seen at the Harvey house on the Friday evening.

"You will remember that the prisoner came to the Fishers' house at something like eight o'clock in the morning, when he brought the keys and a bundle of papers and told them that he had bought the property and that these were the documents. Was that a lie or was it the truth? Has any deed been produced, or have we an atom of proof of that statement? Do we not know that it was false? Why should the prisoner have made that statement? But that was not all. He said that he had paid part of the purchase money and had received the deeds and that Freeman Harvey had gone to Halifax to complete the matter and that he was afterwards going to Windsor. Was that true? What would a reasonable man conclude from that taken in connection with any other circumstances?"

Then Townshend backtracked in his story to talk about the murder weapon. "I omitted to mention the fact of his obtaining the knife and sharpening it, and the evidence showing that the wounds which the poor old man had in his head were gashes as such a knife would make. We do not know of course, how Freeman Harvey came to his death, whether he was felled by a blow and thrown into the cellar, but that is immaterial. The man who did the one thing did all."

As the judge's speech became more interesting with the details, the gallery started coming back to life with whispered conversations and men making decisions as if they were on the jury.

"Now, something has been said respecting the evidence of Edgar McCarthy, and as to what he said about Harvey's headless body being in his cellar covered with potatoes before the door was opened and it was discovered there. If McCarthy did make any such statement, it must strike you, as it did me, as a very curious thing. Of course, the idea was to draw a red herring across the track. And at first sight that might throw suspicion on McCarthy. If he knew such a thing at that time, it certainly was very suspicious in regard to him."

Those who had been against McCarthy since the start booed and hissed their suspicions, again calling for his arrest.

"I have come to one of three conclusions. The first was that these witnesses who did not appear to be of high character might be lying in making that statement with the object of implicating McCarthy, though I think not. Then, there is the explanation that they are mixing up what was said afterwards with what was said before and putting on Sunday what was said on Monday, and I think that this is probably the explanation. It is possible also that the prisoner may have communicated with McCarthy but, taking it all together, that is not probable. The best explanation is that the witnesses got the thing mixed up. They appear to be ignorant and slow and they may not have said it deliberately, but have got it mixed up because everything is inconsistent with McCarthy having had anything to do with it."

Russell wondered if the Fishers realized what was being said about them.

"In relation to the question of motive—why this man should have murdered the deceased—it would seem to be a most silly act on his part to commit such a crime with apparently so little object, but a motive may be found in the money he thought was there. That may account for it. He could hardly expect to hold the property."

That is something Russell had wondered about as well. *How had Stanley thought he could manage the property? Had he ever really planned on living there?* The man refused to talk, so this might be an answer they would never have.

"Now gentlemen, I have only to say in conclusion that I hope you will give this case and all the facts presented to you your most serious, impartial consideration. A more horribly deliberate piece of work has rarely, if ever, been committed in this country, and if you are of the opinion that the circumstances detailed in the evidence irresistibly point to the prisoner as the author of the crime, do not shrink from finding him guilty. Do not allow any silly ideas of mere doubt to affect your minds. Act as men of common sense and as you would in your own affairs. Absolute certainty can never exist, but if the circumstances here are such as would convince reasonable men, you can have no difficulty in coming to a conclusion."

"Hang him now! Let him swing!"

"He's guilty as sin!"

"Let's get this Irish swine!"

The words rang through the courtroom as Russell wondered how impartial this address had actually been.

"If on the other hand you view the circumstances as falling short of proof that the prisoner is the man who committed this murder, it is your duty to acquit him."

With these last words, Justice Townshend abruptly stopped his summation. *His address was pretty convincing*, Russell thought, although it really left no doubt in the minds of anyone in that courtroom today whether Stanley was guilty.

Sheriff O'Brien motioned to the jury to stand and ushered them out through the door to begin their deliberations. Russell watched their expressions as they left. Some refused to look up, while others held their heads high with confidence. He did not envy them, but did wish he could be on the other side of the door to hear their discussion.

He looked around at the others seated next to him, wondering what to do. The jury could be out for hours, or they could be out for a few moments. There was no way to predict how long it would take, and he did not want to risk losing his seat.

Instead, Russell stood up and stretched, trying to compose headlines in his head for the story he would file later that evening. He knew it had to be catchy to sell papers.

> *"The Stanley Trial."*
> *"Harvey gets justice."*
> *"McCarthy is as evil as they say."*
> *"The great potato caper."*
> *"Stanley must pay!"*

As he daydreamed about headlines, there was a rap on the door at the front of the room that jolted Russell. He glanced down at his pocket watch. Only thirty minutes had passed. *Not even. Surely it could not be the jury coming back already.*

Sheriff O'Brien sauntered over the door and opened it a crack. Then he turned back to the half-empty room. "Ladies and gentlemen, the jury has a verdict. Please take your seats."

Like a children's game of whispers, the message spread through the room, while others shouted to those waiting in the hallway or under the eaves, sheltered from the rain on the front steps. The room quickly filled up again, with those entering casting their own judgments.

"He's going to be found guilty. I don't trust people who don't come from here. He's got a shifty look to him."

"He's going to get death by hanging, you mark my words."

"I'm still not convinced. That McCarthy knew too much and has always been trouble in these parts."

54: Fairly tried

William Stephens led the jury in, holding a document tightly in his hand. As they filed into their seats, an intense deathlike stillness shrouded the room, as if everyone was fearful of making a sound and missing the verdict.

When all was in order, the court clerk stood. "Gentlemen of the jury, have you found the prisoner, George Stanley, guilt or not guilty?"

Stephens pushed back in the chair to stand up, the sound of the wood scraping against the floor reverberating in the room. He took a big breath and swallowed loudly. "We the jury find him guilty."

Raucous shouting and hollering broke the silence. Justice Townshend banged his gavel continually, trying to regain order. Attorney General Drysdale and Prosecutor Christie shook hands, congratulating each other, while O'Mullin and Tremain at the defence table hung their heads.

Amidst it all, the prisoner remained silent, showing no emotion, as he had throughout the entire trial.

Once ordered was restored, the Justice turned to the prisoner. "Hearing the verdict, would you like to say anything before you have your sentence pronounced upon you?"

For the first time since the trial began, John Kavanagh stood. He moved so slowly and methodically within the prisoner's box that the crowd was transfixed. It was as if it were the first time people were fully aware of his actual presence in the courtroom.

John raised his head at the last moment. He slowly opened his eyes and looked at the room. He took a deep breath before addressing the court.

"Thank you, sir. I would like to begin by pointing out, your Honour, that I have not been given a fair trial these past few days. In fact, I would like to argue that my trial and subsequent condemnation already occurred last February by the *Halifax Herald*."

Russell scowled, thinking of the absurdity of the accusation. *There is no trial by the media. I am out to do what every other newspaper reporter intends to do—sell papers.*

"The press and all the people, including the officers of the law, were all prejudiced against me. Everybody who has come near me since I was confined in jail was against me from the start."

He took a step forward, as far as he could within the confines of the prisoner's box. "I am not guilty of this dreadful offence. I am not guilty!" As he spoke these words his voice kept rising until he was practically shouting at the room. "I am innocent of this awful crime with which I am charged. I am offered up as a terrible holocaust on the altar of prejudice and perjury."

A voice piped up from behind Russell in a loud stage whisper, "That was a well-delivered speech. Clearly, he's a schooled man and, for not being from here, he certainly knows English good."

After a few moments' pause, when Justice Townshend realized that the prisoner was finished, he said. "Mr. Stanley, you have indeed had a fair trial. You have no reason to complain of not being fairly tried, or of the treatment you have received. In all fairness, I regret to say that I just cannot believe your story. I have no doubt as to your guilt, Mr. Stanley. I consider the verdict of the jury to be a just one. Therefore, I will proceed to pass my sentence."

He turned once more toward the courtroom. "I declare that you, George Stanley, be taken from hence to the place of confinement in Windsor and thence taken to the place of execution on the first day of August 1906, and hanged between the hours of one o'clock in the morning and high noon, and may the Lord have mercy on your soul."

With another bang of the gavel, court was finished.

Cheering erupted throughout the courtroom. Many scrambled for the door, clambering over those still seated to be the first ones out to share the news with their friends and neighbours.

Sheriff O'Brien came forth, re-shackled the prisoner, and led him through the door to the cells below. Russell watched the man tread along behind, shuffling his feet, as if already marching to the gallows.

55: Full to the brim

July 9

John was finishing up the last letter in his final round of correspondence, when he looked up to see the pretty, young blonde woman standing in front of his locked cell.

When he caught her eye, she smiled cheerily, then stepped aside for her uncle the jailer to unlock the heavy metal door.

"Miss Smith," John, standing from his desk to shake her hand.

"Please, call me Winifred," she pretended to scold him. "We've been over this before."

"You got here as quick as a wink. I hope it's not raining cats and dogs out there."

Winifred clapped her white-gloved hands with glee. "You read it!"

"Aren't you as sharp as a tack." John patted a pile of books on the corner of his desk.

"I thought you would enjoy them. You needed to read something by Thomas Chandler Haliburton since you are"—she hesitated to find the right words— "are staying here in Windsor."

"Who knew that such a man from this small town could have come up with all these sayings? I'm going to see how many of these I can use. And please, let me take this from you."

John gently took the basket from Winifred and gestured for her to sit on the edge of the bed.

"And what have you brought with you today, Miss Smith?" He pulled back the tea towel to reveal a pint of raspberries, fresh biscuits, and more books.

"Just a few raspberries. I picked them myself. Not much, I'm afraid."

Winifred looked down at her shoes, knocking them together to brush off the dust from her walk through town, lest he see her reddening face. "I brought you *Dorian Gray*, by this man named Oscar Wilde—"

"Another Irish convict," John muttered.

"What's that?"

When he shook his head to indicate it was nothing, she continued, "And something about a time machine by Wells that my father enjoyed, and of course *Tom Sawyer* by Mark Twain to read next. I think you will find his misadventures amusing."

"Much like our own Daisy Bates, from back home in Roscrea. Now, she is quite the lady. She was born and raised right there on Main Street in the middle of town, near where this magnificent fountain stands in the middle of the street, by the market square. She was born to nothing, was left an orphan, worked as a monitor at a boarding school with all the snooty aristocracy girls, so she learned all their ways. She leaves Roscrea for Scotland and later Australia, where she tells everyone she is a lady from Ashbury House—the home of one of the rich families in town—and passes herself off as aristocracy. She has had three husbands, and now writes and fights for the rights of aborigines there in Australia. Can you imagine? Someone from my own hometown, and a lady, nonetheless— even if it was all her own fabrication."

As the two laughed over the tale, the jailer appeared again at the door with another visitor.

"Father Carroll!" John stood to embrace the priest's hand.

"No, please don't leave on my account," Carroll said, motioning to Winifred to sit back down as she made to leave.

"Mr. Stanley was just regaling me with one of his boyhood stories from Ireland."

"Pray, don't let me interrupt."

"Did I ever tell you the one about the barrel that was never empty? Father Carroll, you will appreciate this one. So, the Sacred Heart Sisters set up this convent in my home village of Roscrea and had this barrel by the door, and inside they kept packages of food for people who came in need of a morsel to eat. Well, during the great famine, what, 50 years ago or so, a steady stream of people kept coming, begging for food, and a good many days the sisters themselves went without food. One day, this woman came looking for food for her little ones, but all that was left was two loaves, and they had to feed the sisters in the convent. The Reverend Mother said to give the woman the bread, as God would provide. Shortly thereafter, another woman appeared at the door, and the Sister had to explain that nothing was left and told her as proof to look in the barrel. But, to her great surprise, when she lifted the lid, the barrel was full to the brim, and never was empty again!"

"Well that certainly sounds like God provided, much like the miracle of five loaves and two fish," Father Carroll said. "Speaking of which, should we get back to our Biblical studies?" He brought out a leather-bound Bible from an inside jacket pocket.

John turned to take his Bible, provided by the sheriff, from the stack of books on his desk. He gave the books he had finished back to Winifred with a wink.

"Now, the last time, we looked at Biblical passages that argue in favour of the death penalty. Remember, Genesis 9:6 says, 'Whoever sheds the blood of man, by man shall his blood be shed.' But today we are going to look at those scriptures that are against it."

John followed the priest's lead and turned to the book of Hebrews.

"The sacrifice of Jesus, the Lamb of God. His death made it unnecessary to execute murderers to maintain human dignity and value because the crucifixion forever established human value. And just how do you feel about your condition, Mr. Stanley?"

"Indeed, I am a poor unfortunate sinner whom drink has ruined. I am thanking the Lord Jesus for sending you to me to help save my poor soul."

"Bless you, indeed. We shall let the Lord lift your soul before the final hour."

At the mention of the death penalty, and the reminder of the date coming in less than a month, Winifred's eyes began to tear. She cleared her throat, put her gloves back on, picked up her basket and called for her uncle to come release her.

"I shall leave you to it, as I must return to help mother with a few things. I shall see you tomorrow, Mr. Stanley."

As they walked down the hall toward the main door, Smith turned to his niece and cautioned her. "I worry how much time you are spending with Mr. Stanley. I know you are doing your Christian duty, and God will reward you; however, I fear you are growing awfully fond of the man. I remind you that he is a convicted murderer and will go to the gallows on the first of August."

"Yes, Uncle. You needn't worry about me. I just hope to bring him a bit of joy in his final months."

"Although he has yet to confess, the man is very much guilty. Men of his class do not confess, on the whole, as they generally want the public to think of them as martyrs for the cause of justice."

"Yes, Uncle. I am aware. I do so enjoy his stories."

"Let me also remind you that he is very unreliable in his conversation. He told me just the other day how he was a prince of one of the Irish royal families."

Winifred started to laugh at the notion.

"I'm serious, Winifred. We have it on good authority that he has a tendency for insanity, as it runs in his family. His sister died in the Clonmel lunatic asylum back in Ireland."

"Don't you worry about me. I'm a grown woman now and can handle myself."

The jailer pursed his lips and said nothing more. He opened the door and let his young niece back onto the streets of Windsor.

56: You are not to be in here

July 30

"Do you think we will be ready for Wednesday's proceedings?" Christie shouted above the racket.

He and Chief McDonald stood in front of the Windsor courthouse as carpenters from Crowell and Singer fashioned the scaffolding for the gallows. The noise from the hammering and the banging of the lumber meant the two men had to yell to be heard.

"These gentlemen know what they are doing," the Chief said. "We had them erect the platform and crossbeam here on the same place where that other foreign fellow was hanged for that Tennycape murder. This one, when complete, will be fifteen feet high with an eleven-foot drop."

Christie rubbed his neck.

"Surrounding that," McDonald continued, "there will be the same high board wall fixed. We are trying to maintain the utmost of secrecy and decorum."

"You think Stanley is in there listening to every nail being driven into the scaffolding?"

"Really drives the matter home, doesn't it? There will be no escaping the hangman's noose."

"Speaking of the hangman, has Mr. Radclive arrived from Ottawa?"

"You must have missed the grand parade last night, then," McDonald said, rocking back on his heels. "It was quite the site. A crowd was there when he got off the train and followed him over to the hotel."

"Well, it's not every day that a real-live executioner comes to town. I'm sure they didn't quite know what to make of him."

"Indeed. Dressed as a gentleman, yet what kind of gentleman would take pleasure in a job in sending people to their death?"

"He is certainly a professional gentleman. Came to see me and wanted all the details of the case," McDonald said. "I think he was wanting to make sure the man was truly guilty, maybe to help ease his conscience."

"Did he make his way to the hotel's bar last night?" Christie said. "I've heard he's got quite the propensity for the drink. Maybe we should have sent him up to Ellershouse to have a round with our friends there."

"No, no trouble in town last night, or none that was reported to me, anyhow."

"Have you ever had a chance to ask him, I mean really ask him how he fell into this profession? How he got into the swing of it?" Christie laughed at his own joke, but quickly stopped himself, remembering the gravity of the topic.

"Apparently, when he was in the Royal Navy, he learned his dark art hanging pirates in the South China seas. Then he apprenticed under England's own executioner. When he came to Canada, he said that if there were going to be hangings, they'd better be done right. And he's been doing them right ever since. I reckon he's hanged close to 100 people by now."

"I'm not sure that's something I'd be proud of, or that it would let me sleep well at night."

"Well, we can sleep well knowing we've rid the world of one more murderous felon, I'd say."

"And we have all the final paperwork in place, I'd imagine," Christie said.

"Yes, his Excellency, the Governor General of Canada himself, sent the telegram stating he saw fit for the law to take its course. We are just to wire back indicating when the deed has been accomplished."

"And, as for the time? What have we been told regarding that?"

Chief McDonald scratched his head. "That has not changed from our last discussion. I hesitate to say it out loud, in case anyone hear us. As you know, we want to keep the exact hour a secret, lest the public show up for the show. Sheriff O'Brien is as adamant about that as he was four years ago. All we can say is: while the town sleeps."

Christie nodded. "Regardless, I'm sure there will be those who show up, hoping to catch a glimpse of the affair. Although, having said that, a great many of our finer citizens who have vacated town already. They just want to escape the ghastly sensations called up by the imagination over this terrible event."

"I don't blame them," McDonald said. "I, however, have yet to hear anyone who is proclaiming the man's innocence. I'd say there is not a shadow of doubt in the minds of the community as to Stanley's guilt."

"Yes, 'tis true. Those who stand by the belief in capital punishment definitely feel that his trial was fair, and his sentence was a just one. They just don't want to witness it or hear this infernal racket." Christie covered his ears and walked toward the street, with McDonald following.

When they were slightly more removed from the noise of construction, Christie asked, "Is Mr. Stanley prepared for Wednesday? Have there been any final-hour confessions?"

"Not a one. He has not uttered a word in relation to the crime at all. He's not showed an ounce of nervousness when preparing for the gallows, either. Father McManus is there now with him. He's the priest who came down this morning from Halifax. I believe he's administering one of his last communions."

"May God forgive him."

With all the building racket, Christie and McDonald had not heard a young man approach them from behind. Christie startled when an unfamiliar voice said, "I presume you are talking about Mr. Stanley."

McDonald looked the intruder up and down. "You are not to be in here. This area is for officials only. Don't we know you from somewhere?"

"Shaw. Russell Shaw, sir," he said, offering to shake their hands.

"You are that reporter from the *Herald*." Christie said. "We are going to have to ask you to leave. The events today are not open to the public, and most certainly not open to the media."

"I was hoping to have a chance to change your mind, gentlemen," Russell said. "I think it will be good for our public to know exactly what happens and to assure them that this mad murderer is indeed dead."

"No." McDonald left no room for discussion. "We will not be making this into a spectacle. We've had one too many hangings in the area that went awry because of the behaviour of crowds. We are not about to allow that to happen here under our watch. We ask you to kindly leave now, Mr. Shaw."

Russell was ushered back to the sidewalk, beyond the barricade. Not one to give up, he snuck around to the back of the building to see if he could find a gap between the fence boards through which he could see the gallows. He had been with the story of George Stanley from the beginning, and he would be with it at the very end. His career depended upon it, his readers expected it, and he was far too invested by this point.

Finding a decent spot, Russell spread out his coat and decided to take a nap until the main event began.

57: Barley sugar

August 1

Sheriff O'Brien rushed from room to room in the jailhouse, ensuring everything was in order. With so much adrenaline rushing through his body, he had no time to feel tired, despite the early hour of the morning.

He checked his pocket watch; it was already half-past two.

Just then, he heard a tapping at the door. Dr. Judson Black, the jail house's physician, appeared with a collection of twelve men who had been assigned to jury duty.

Dr. Black walked solemnly through the door; his head held high. Those present stepped back to make room, treating him with an air of royalty. This respect came from his having been the town's mayor for three years, only leaving the station to become a federal member of parliament. Despite his high office, Dr. Black continued to serve as the jailhouse doctor.

Tonight, however, he was here to lead the inquiry and pronounce the time of death of the prisoner.

The first to enter behind Dr. Black was Wesley Livingston, photographer at the crime scene as well as proprietor of Windsor's Kandy Kitchen. Following him were the rest of the jury: labourers, carpenters, masons, a few horsemen, merchants, and a church official.

Sheriff O'Brien ushered the group into the main office, where they crowded in to be sworn in and to learn their duties. Although these men would not witness the actual hanging, it was necessary they view the body afterwards to ensure George Stanley had indeed been hanged and was dead.

"You being good and lawful men of the county," Sheriff O'Brien began, "shall now be duly sworn in and charged to inquire for our said Lord the King, when, where, how, and by what means the said George Stanley, otherwise called George Stanley Kavanagh, otherwise called John Ryan, came to his death. You will be called upon to participate in an inquiry to these points as well as ascertain the identity of the body."

"What's it like to see a dead body?" juror Estey Cochran asked nervously. "I mean, I've seen a dead horse plenty of times, and even had to shoot a few, but a human?"

"You saw the body, didn't you, Livingston?" juror Ernest Jadis said. "I mean, you took the pictures and testified in court."

"Well, I suppose I did, but I tried to treat it as a subject in my photograph, only looking at it through the camera lens," Livingston said.

O'Brien checked his pocket watch again, knowing the spiritual advisors would soon be arriving. He swore in each gentleman and left them to wait in the office until the deed was complete.

He met Father Carroll in the hallway, bound for the condemned man's cell. O'Brien led the way, unlocking the cell for the final time.

John stood immediately to greet the two men and reached out to shake O'Brien's hand. "I just want to thank you, sir, for all your kindness you have shown me during these past few months. I would also greatly appreciate it if you would extend my word of thanks to the jailer, and in particular to Miss Smith. You have all made my time so much more bearable under these unfortunate conditions. People of this house have indeed been infinitely kind to me."

O'Brien bowed his head and pursed his lips. He was not prepared for such a display.

"Now, Sheriff." John turned to pick a stack of neatly addressed envelopes off the desk and handed them over. "I would ask one final kindness. Please ensure these letters are delivered accordingly."

O'Brien fanned through them. There must have been close to fifty letters in the stack. He merely nodded his head, then backed out of the room, leaving the condemned man with his spiritual advisor to prepare for death.

"Mr. Stanley," Father Carroll said, "we must now prepare you to meet your Maker. Have you any final thoughts or confessions you would like to make?"

John shook his head. For the first few weeks he had tried proclaiming his innocence, but lately had lost his energy and willpower. "Should we pray that God holds up my legs?" John had a twinkle in his eye when he said it, and the priest returned his look with a grimace.

"Let us pray together in these final moments."

~

O'Brien stood on the scaffolding, surveying the jail yard. Beside him Radclive was making his final preparations, calculating the length of the rope based on the measurements he had taken of the prisoner earlier that day.

In the distance, O'Brien heard some muffled noises and sticks breaking on the lawn behind the high board wall. He picked up the lantern beside him and used it to scan the perimeter. As expected, several people were standing in the shadows, peering between the cracks in the fence boards to catch a glimpse of what was happening.

With only moments before the hanging was to take place, he decided not to bother sending them away. They had probably camped out there all evening, waiting, as they were not told what time the event was to happen. They would only just go to another viewing position should he scold them.

He wondered if people's morbid curiosity would ever end.

"Alright then," Radclive said. "It is time."

~

"O God, our Father in heaven: Have mercy on us."

As Father Carroll prayed, John closed his eyes, letting the words wash over him. He drifted back to his days as a small child in Roscrea, the happiest and most secure he had ever felt.

"Do not remember, Lord, our offences or the offences of our forefathers: Spare us good Lord."

Sheriff O'Brien appeared at the door and guided John into the hallway. He placed handcuffs on him for the final march through the jail to the scaffolding outside.

John took a deep breath, breathing in the smell of the peat fire, and the brown bread and hot stew cooking over it.

"Spare your servant before you from all evil and harm, from the power of sin and the snares of the devil, from your wrath, and from everlasting damnation: Good Lord, deliver him."

With each firm step John imagined himself running up and down the streets of Ballyhall with his brother William, or playing tag around John's Tower and through St. Cronan's churchyard. He could hear his sister Maria's laugh.

"We sinners pray, hear us. That it may please you to uphold him with your free Spirit, to grant him true repentance, to forgive him all his sins."

At the top of the stairs, Radclive turned to face the man he was to see into the next world. "Come with me."

He took John from the sheriff and led him toward the centre of the platform where the rope lay in wait. No one else spoke a word, while the priest's solemn prayer continued to fill the air.

"O Lord God, our heavenly Father, you have no pleasure in the death of the wicked but that they turn from their ways and live. Regard this sick person with an eye of compassion."

Radclive bent to place leather straps around John's feet and legs, preventing him from kicking while hanging. He placed a black cap over his head, and adjusted the rope around his neck, placing the knot carefully behind the left ear.

"Do not let him be overwhelmed by any pains of body or any anguish of soul but grant to him in this world your pardon and peace."

In his mind, John saw himself in the sweet shop in Roscrea, the wide array of colours and flavours before him. He imagined himself taking a barley sugar from the big glass jar and popping it into his mouth. He jumbled it around his mouth with his tongue.

"May God have mercy on his soul," were the final words that fell from Father Carroll's lips.

As John felt his teeth crunch down on the barley sugar, there was a loud crack as the trap was sprung and he passed into eternity.

58: Secrets buried beneath

August 2

Medford Christie sat on the lawn of the Saint John the Evangelist cemetery. It was not quite eight o'clock in the morning, and yet he knew it was going to be hot. Above, the cardinals sang in the trees, not knowing what they had just witnessed below.

Father Carroll had done a stellar job conducting the funeral service for a man no one was saddened to send off. As the rosewood coffin was lowered into the ground, he said a prayer asking for forgiveness on Stanley's behalf. The grave would be left unmarked, in a site on the outskirts of the cemetery.

The place was quiet and empty, now that everyone had cleared out, gone back to work, gone back to their regular lives. Probably they would hardly spend another moment thinking about George Stanley, or whoever he might have been.

Who was this man?

All Christie knew was what they had pieced together from the police report in Ireland, along with the information the prisoner had offered himself. He was, however, an unreliable storyteller, so it was difficult to ascertain the truth.

Yes, he was from Ireland, where he had been well educated; and yes, of his forty years, he had spent twenty-five in prisons, although not consecutively, nor in the same prison.

Christie knew that, just over the hill men were already busy tearing down the scaffolding and high-board fence. By noon there would be no evidence that only a few hours ago a criminal had suffered the extreme penalty of the law.

He had decided not to attend the hanging, although he could have made a case to do so. They tried to keep the observers to a bare minimum, to ensure the hanging was under control.

Christie rested his head in his hands, to ease the spinning thoughts scrambling in his mind.

His office had been a revolving door this past week. He had lost count of the number of times townspeople had come in to give their opinion on the case. Capital punishment was against God's laws, or the death penalty was justified—"an eye for an eye".

Then, there were those who, after reading the full account of Stanley's past crimes in the *Hants Journal*, came trying to comprehend how a man with his criminal record was allowed into the country in the first place.

Stanley was supposed to have been under police supervision, yet he had slipped away to Canada, evading them all. If he had been kept under better wraps in the United Kingdom, perhaps Freeman Harvey would be alive today.

"Where looseness exists, it allows men of this character to land on our soil, and the officers appointed by government to inspect incoming immigrants are the men to stop such from landing, as it is done now in the United States where they make the steamship responsible for returning them and not allowing them to land."

He had heard many variants of this lecture since the end of the trial in May.

Christie could only respond with a sigh. He had met George Stanley and knew he could charm anyone and talk his way out of anything—save for a murder conviction and final execution.

He wondered why, after sentencing, Stanley had stopped talking. He stopped telling stories and trying to get himself out of trouble. Maybe he realized the truth had finally caught up to him. He was a dead man walking.

Christie reached into his breast pocket and pulled out the stack of letters that Stanley had passed over last night. They were combined with the others he had given in, and that the sheriff's office had never sent, as well as a few that had been returned as part of the evidence. He thumbed through them until he found one written to a John Lomas in Halifax. It was dated Tuesday, January 30, 1906, days before the murder. It was postmarked from the Ellershouse post office. He pulled it out to read it once more.

> *Dear Mr. Lomas,*
>
> *My uncle, having stayed with you on his visits to Halifax, has recommended me to write to you.*
>
> *I am a single man and I have had a farm left here for me, but I do not understand the business. I want you to please send me out a gentleman from Halifax that wants to buy cheap three heads of*

> *cattle, one splendid organ, a lot of hay, potatoes, apples, oats and so on. I am prepared to sell these things very cheap, so I will pay you a respectable commission on the transaction if you send me a purchaser.*
>
> *This is an out of the way place, and I can't go until I dispose of these things. If you want any of these items, please send a telegram to me at the Ellershouse Railway.*
>
> *George Stanley*

Christie rubbed his eyes. He had mulled this letter over and over in his head.

The letter was signed using the name George Stanley. The man had only started using that name when he arrived in Ellershouse, or so they believed. So, if Stanley is speaking about a real uncle and real events, how would Mr. Lomas know who the letter was from if it was indeed a recently acquired false name?

George Stanley arranged to sell the contents of Freeman Harvey's house on Tuesday, however he did not tell the Fishers until the following Saturday morning that he had purchased the property. Was the murder planned this far in advance?

Maybe George Stanley had really arranged with Freeman Harvey to purchase the farm. Was it a premeditated murder, or a coercion turned accident, with a fatal ending? And, if it was an accident, why mutilate the body? Perhaps disposing of the body became a bigger deed than he had originally thought. He could have been interrupted before he could finish.

There were more questions than answers.

In the end, Christie knew it did not really matter how the events had unfolded. The conclusion was the same. Freeman Harvey was dead, and George Stanley was guilty of it.

The answers to these questions were now secrets buried beneath, never to be found.

The noose used on August 1, 1906
West Hants Historical Society:
author's photo

Laura Churchill Duke

Afterword

I first heard the story of the murder of Freeman Harvey during the Windsor edition of Valley Ghost Walks (valleyghostwalks.com). It was such a peculiar story that I never forgot it.

After the success of my first novel, *Two Crows Sorrow*, about the murder of Theresa Balsor McAuley Robinson in Burlington, N.S. in 1904, I became interested in researching historical crimes in the Annapolis Valley. I was thinking about what I would like to investigate next when I recalled this story.

Luckily, I had already done extensive research in both the Acadia University and Halifax Provincial archives prior to the COVID-19 lockdown of 2020. Over the months of isolation, I wrote steadily, devoting the newfound time to the creation of this novel.

What I loved most about this process was the mystery element. It really became an episode of the genealogical program, "Who Do You Think You Are?"

When I started my research, I knew two things. Our convicted murderer came from Ireland, and he was a compulsive liar. It is very hard to research a man when you are not really sure what his actual name is, or if any of the details he provided to police were actually true.

In several places, John (or William or George) mentions having been from Roscrea in the County of Tipperary, in Ireland. I also knew a few of his aliases based on newspaper articles. One could have possibly been his real name.

On a whim, I sent the following email to the Roscrea Heritage Society.

> I am doing some research for a writing project, and I am trying to track down a family from Roscrea, Ireland.
>
> There was a man from there who spent 25 years in Maryborough Prison, and his sister was an inmate in, and died at, Clonmel Lunatic Asylum. In 1902, he was released from jail, went to England and later to Halifax. It is here that he murders a man and is

hanged for the murder in 1906 in Windsor, NS.

When he is arrested, he is going by George Stanley, but has also used the name John Ryan, but says his real name is William Kavanagh.

He says he was born in 1866 in Roscrea.

I am wondering if there are any town records or historical files I can search from afar to see if his family comes up, or even under any of those names.

Thus began a relationship with Pamela Aitken of the Roscrea Heritage Society, who worked with local historian Dick Conroy to delve into the mystery. Over the next few months, I received emails describing what they found, and slowly the whole picture began to come together.

First, they discovered his real name was John Kavanagh. We have his birth records, school records, and record of his conversion to Catholicism. We have his parents' wedding certificate, and his sister's death certificate at the Clonmel Asylum.

John's father's wedding certificate indicates he had been married before, although no records of the first marriage were found. Therefore, it is conceivable that there were an uncle and stepsister living in New York. Whether they were rich and planning on wiring money is highly unlikely.

John's father, Thomas, died young; however, we do not know why. His mother, Margaret, and his brother, William, both disappear from Irish records, so we have no idea what happened to either of them. All we know is that his sister does end up in the Clonmel Asylum and eventually dies there at age 28 from TB. In those days, poor residents could have been committed to the asylum along with those with mental health challenges. It is difficult to know for sure what Maria's situation was.

What we do know, and what I based the novel upon, were the court records, newspaper articles, and John Kavanagh's personal letters.

While writing this book, I have to admit, I became very sympathetic toward John Kavanagh. Although, I believe he was guilty of the crime, I wondered how much of his life circumstances had led him to that moment. I believe this was not a cold-blooded murder. How does one go from petty thievery to murder? This is not a usual route and there is no progression of crime or violence.

In John's prison records, the majority of his thievery happens in October, when he accused of stealing coats and boots. Is he doing this to keep warm? Was he unable to find employment? We will never know.

At first, I believed the murder was an accident. Perhaps Freeman Harvey fell down the stairs, after being coerced by John for money he thought was there. Then John acted quickly to avoid accusation.

After writing this book, however, I was listening to my favourite podcast, "Canadian True Crime" by Krisi Lee. In episode 38, she featured the murder of Daniel Levesque in 2011 in Victoria, B.C. Daniel was murdered by a conman. This conman realized that all his lies were about to be exposed, so he murdered Daniel to keep the truth from coming out. Upon listening to this, everything seemed to click into place. Perhaps John realized that his lies about buying Freeman Harvey's farm were about to be exposed, and he wanted to cover his trail and continue the story.

These are questions to which we will never know the answer.

At one point in his testimony, David Fisher tells the story that Stanley told him about how McCarthy killed Harvey. I believe this is probably what happened; however, it is what Stanley did, not McCarthy.

> *McCarthy ran out into the porch and took the rusty old axe and hit Harvey with it. He fell and tumbled him down into the cellar. Mr. Harvey was a strong, able, tough little man. Then, McCarthy took my jackknife which Stanley had borrowed, and cut his throat, the jugular vein and the windpipe. He cut the flesh all away, but the knife would not cut the bone. So, McCarthy took an old saw and cut off his head.*

One of the mysteries is why John's letters from prison were not sent. The archives hold dozens of letters that John Kavanagh wrote to officials across Canada, England and Ireland, trying to appeal his case and find someone to help him or write a character letter. None of these were sent. Were prisoners not allowed to send mail? Did the authorities think there was no point? In this way, I believe the system failed John Kavanagh in denying him this right. He is buried in an unmarked grave in St. John the Evangelist Catholic cemetery in Windsor, N.S.

In writing the prison scenes in Ireland, I relied heavily on the essays of Oscar Wilde, who was imprisoned around the same time, having been convicted of sodomy. My mother and I had intended to visit these jails, many of which are now museums; however, COVID-19 interrupted our plans. I shall make a journey there some day!

It was difficult to find information about many of the main characters in this novel, so many are described as I imagined them. The story timeline is accurate, but the conversations and details are created from my understanding of the events. Any errors, omissions and inaccuracies are fully mine.

Although the names of the people are accurate, I have taken great liberty to create their personalities. Sometimes I have been able to draw information from accounts, but for the most part, I have used artistic license. Their representation is not intended to cause offence to living family members.

I know very little about our victim, Freeman Harvey. I know he had three wives, and a daughter by one of them. I have never seen his picture, nor do I know much other than what was reported in my primary sources. Although this novel is primarily about the life of John Kavanagh, I do not want to lose sight of this victim, who had the unfortunate luck of having his path cross with the wrong person. Our sympathy goes to the descendants and extended relatives of the Harvey family. Freeman Harvey is buried in a marked grave in the community of Ellershouse.

Defence council Hadley Tremain was a young lawyer at the time of the murder. He was a member of the Windsor town council and went on to replace Dr. Black, the jailhouse doctor, as a Conservative member of the House of Commons for many years. During WWI, Tremain was a commanding officer of the 112th battalion and fought overseas. His family home, Kingscroft, still stands across from the Maplewood Cemetery in Windsor, where he is buried.

The year following the George Stanley trial, Attorney General Arthur Drysdale was appointed to the Supreme Court of Nova Scotia. In 1917, he was responsible for overseeing the inquiry into the Halifax Explosion, which devastated the city.

Dr. Black, the jailhouse doctor, was a member of the House of Commons for the district of Hants. His son, Bret, married Florence Shand. It was Florence's wedding dress that was saved in the vault of the first courthouse during the great Windsor fire of 1897. Interestingly, Dr. Black's father, Thomas, came from Armagh, Ireland, one of the places where John Kavanagh was in prison.

Thomas Chandler Haliburton is probably one of Windsor's most well-known residents. Not only was he a judge, but he was also a prolific writer. Through his character Sam Slick, Haliburton wrote his views on human nature. He also invented many expressions that we use today, some of which are featured in the novel. These include "raining cats and dogs," "drink like a fish", "quick as a wink," and "truth is stranger than fiction." Haliburton's house is now a museum, but at the time of this novel in 1906, it was the Sam Slick Hotel.

In the Haliburton House Museum is a display about the birth of hockey, said to have been invented on Long Pond, not far from where John Kavanagh is buried. The original game was hurley on ice, borrowed from the popular Irish game, also mentioned in the Irish section of this novel.

There seems to be some controversy over the career of Chief Nicholas Power in the Halifax Police Department. Some accounts hail him as the most illustrious police officer to serve on the Halifax force. Some historians believe that it was Power who compiled a 60-page scrapbook of international wanted posters, now held at the Nova Scotia Provincial archives and available online. Others have said that Power botched many cases, and was erroneous in his logic, although some have argued his methods were not that different from those of his contemporaries. In 1915, Power did receive the King's Police Medal, which some claim was self-nominated. Regardless, in the novel, I have Chief Power creating a scrapbook about his own accomplishments and kept him more on the side of bumbling fool, as it fit with the details of the present case and the lack of police action to arrest John.

The Fishers disappear from the record. We have no idea if they remained in the area, or if any descendants are around today.

The house in Ellershouse where the murder occurred has since burned down and a new one stands in its place. The train station is now a convenience store. Only the hall where the preliminary inquiry occurred, and the church where the funeral service was held, remain.

I have walked the back woods of Ellershouse, trying to find the roads where George Stanley was caught, using court testimonies as a descriptor, but it is hard to say exactly where, as roads have changed, and the logging camps of those days are long gone.

In Windsor, the courthouse where the trial took place was replaced by the current structure on the same location. The train station and tracks, too, are long gone.

If you travel through these communities today, there are few signs to indicate that such a gruesome murder, and the enthralling court case that drew hundreds of people, even happened.

Book club questions

1. The newspapers printed many stories about "John Ryan"—many of which turned out to be false and that the papers had to recant —in the quest to sell stories with sensational details. What damage would this have done to "John Ryan's" reputation? Did it cause damage?

2. What responsibility does the media have in ensuring accurate statements, versus wanting to get the story out right away? Does this still happen today in print media? Social media? What is our responsibility as subscribers or readers of breaking news?

3. What do you think happened at the scene of the crime? Did John mean to kill Freeman Harvey? Was it an accident? Or was it a means of covering up his lies?

4. The Fisher family were heavily involved with John Kavanagh. Do you think they were guilty and should have been charged, or were they merely pawns in John's plan?

5. Why do you think there was such a public fascination with crime during this era? Can the same be said today?

6. Do you think John received a fair trial and fair treatment in jail? Was it justified not to send his personal letters? Would sending them have helped his case?

7. When writing the novel, the author rearranged the order of events many times. The first rendition begins with John growing up in Ireland and leads into his jail time and coming to Canada, where he commits the murder. In the printed version, his personal life story falls in the middle of the novel. Would you

have liked to have known more about John before this point? Does having John's background at this point work in the story?

8. *Rooted in Deception* is not written from any one character's point of view. Do you think it would have been a different story told through the eyes of one person, or does this structure allow the reader to learn all sides of the story?

9. In the section of the book entitled "Treadmill", we hear of John's life in prisons in the United Kingdom. In Victorian times, there was an emphasis on punishment and hard labour so criminals would think about their actions and reform their ways. Did this view of crime and punishment work? What about our system today? Are we any better at rehabilitating those within the penal system? What reforms or attitudes need to change?

10. In the book there is a heavy emphasis on temperance—alcohol was banned to curtail crime and other vices. Was alcohol a contributing factor to this crime? Had alcohol been legal, would it have changed the outcome of this story?

11. Do methods like temperance work, or do they create a more hidden problem? Think about this in terms of countries like Canada, that legalize marijuana use, or countries like Portugal, that have decriminalized drug use and possession for personal use. What have the results been for individuals and for society as a whole?

12. The true story of John Kavanagh was discovered through extensive genealogical research completed in Roscrea, Ireland. Are there any hidden skeletons in your family's history? How would you find out?

Acknowledgements

I could not have written this novel without the help of so many people who provided research or answers to my numerous questions.

I did much of my research at the West Hants Historical Society in Windsor, where they have a wonderful display about George Stanley/ John Kavanagh, including a piece of the noose that was actually used in the hanging. Kel Hancock and Carole Ann Casey worked tirelessly, allowing me access and answering questions about the town's history.

I am forever grateful to Pamela Aitken from the Roscrea Heritage Society in Ireland, who enlisted the help of Dick Conroy. Together, they tracked down the historical documents and discovered our man's actual name. They spent endless hours hunting down birth and death certificates and school records, and even wrote many documents of their own about the case. Pamela sent me old photographs from the town, and even went around taking current pictures of places and sight lines to help me describe events in Roscrea. Pamela reviewed the sections that take place in Ireland for accuracy.

My brother-in-law, Paul Forrester, retired Chief Superintendent, Queen's Police Medal, of Merseyside in the United Kingdom, was so patient with me, answering all of my questions about the British legal system, and helped me wade through John Kavanagh's police report.

Thank you to Jeremy Novak of Valley Ghost Walks for originally sharing this story with me, and then his resources; to Phil Vogler, a fabulous local historian with an interest in a good murder story equal to my own; to my dear friend Juanita Rossiter, an archivist by trade and a genealogist by heart, who helped walk me through searching Library and Archives Canada to find the Supreme Court murder trial transcript for the Kavanagh case; to Gary Nelson and Gayla Reinhard for their Ellershouse history; to Stefanie Galliott-Conway, who passed away before this book was published, for tracking down old deeds to confirm where everyone lived; to Cheri Killam, Blake Brown and Kyle Williams for answering legal questions; to Brian Smit for explaining many farming terms and teaching me about lean-tos and hay mows and the proper way to pronounce them; and to train enthusiast Roger Prentice, who passed away before the publication of this book, for explaining much about the train and trolley systems.

Thank you to Ronan O'Driscoll, who spent hours poring over the manuscript to help me get southern-Irish terms and phrases correct. Ronan wrote the novel *Poor Farm*, also published by Moose House, and hails from the same area as John Kavanagh in Southern Ireland. As it turns out, Ronan has another connection to the story. While in prison, John Kavanagh wrote many letters of appeal for help. One of these letters was to the Charitable Irish Society in Halifax. This organization is still active today, and Ronan is a board member.

I owe so much to Tamar Marshall of Red Birch Media in Kentville, N.S. Once again, she has created an outstanding cover image for my novel, having designed the image for *Two Crows Sorrow* as well.

Because the story features potatoes, and because John Kavanagh is from Ireland, I knew immediately I wanted to use a photograph that my grandfather took. George Lewis was a potato inspector for the Federal Government in Prince Edward Island. He was also an amateur photographer.

Tamar took my grandfather's image and superimposed the actual silhouette of our murderer, John Kavanagh. Is the figure buried in the pile of potatoes? Is he looking down at his work buried beneath? You decide.

Tamar also came up with the book's title. 'Rooted' represents the potatoes, the basement/root cellar where he was found, and is the root of all the problems. It's perfect.

A big thank you to Brenda Thompson and Andrew Wetmore of Moose House Publications, who have once again taken me on! Their editing and support have made all the difference. It has been a pleasure to work with them again.

Thank you to Raina Noel for her incredible website design, and to Jennifer Williams Saklofske for her constant love and support.

A final huge thank you to my friends and family members who read early drafts of the manuscript, helping to edit, re-arrange and re-re-arrange sections. They include my husband, David Duke; my parents, John and Lana Churchill; my sister-in-law, Kathy Browne (who, being Irish, also helped to read the novel with "Irish eyes"); Elizabeth Jackson, Ann Greener and Christianne Rushton. It's a huge request, but they each willingly offered to help.

My heart is full.

LCD
August, 2022

About the author

Laura Churchill Duke is the author of the award-winning novel *Two Crows Sorrow*. When not writing novels, you can find Laura teaching communication in the School of Kinesiology at Acadia University working as a freelance journalist for newspapers in Atlantic Canada, or presenting community news on CBC Radio's Information Morning. She is also co-owns the home organization business, Your Last Resort.

Laura lives in Kentville, Nova Scotia with her husband and two sons. Find her at

LauraChurchillDuke.ca.

CPSIA information can be obtained
at www.ICGtesting.com
Printed in the USA
LVHW050339040323
740663LV00008B/407